DAWN OF DESTINY

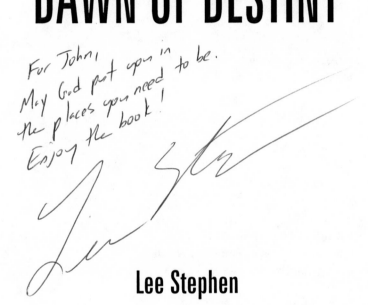

For John,
May God put you in
the places you need to be.
Enjoy the book!

Lee Stephen

stone aside
publishing

Stone Aside Publishing, L.L.C.

ISBN-10: 0-9788508-0-7
ISBN-13: 978-0-9788508-0-7

Editing by Arlene Prunkl
Cover Illustration by Francois Cannels
Book Design by Fiona Raven

First Printing January 2007
Printed in USA
v4

Published by
Stone Aside Publishing, L.L.C.

Dedicated to

GOD

0

IT WAS A TRAIN WRECK. A total train wreck. At least, that's what ran through the mind of Colonel Brent Lilan, commanding officer of Falcon Platoon. His unit was dispatched in Cleveland. It was a familiar scenario. The Bakma had attacked, and the Earth Defense Network—EDEN—had sent Falcon Platoon to defend the city. Only this time, it wasn't that simple. Buildings lay toppled across the street, shattered cars littered the roads and sidewalks, and fresh craters lined what was once Public Square. Even worse, Intelligence had been wrong about everything—the number of Bakma craft, the number of Bakma on the ground, everything. Even their maps were obsolete. The result was a Falcon Platoon bloodbath.

Lilan epitomized an EDEN veteran—a crew cut of steel gray hair, a body tattooed with scars, and a penetrating glare that reflected a pessimistic wisdom about the reality of the Alien War. Though unrecognized on the streets of the common man, the command staff at *Richmond* knew him well. If something needed to be done, Lilan could do it. He could do it better than most of them could.

Plasma bolts whizzed past Lilan's head as he retreated around the corner of an alleyway. He flung himself against the brick and muttered a string of obscenities. It was time to pull out. It was time to salvage whatever was left of Falcon Platoon and return to base. The fate of Cleveland would rest in the hands of whoever else *Richmond* could muster up on a whim.

Lilan loathed the Bakma. More than any other race. They fought dirty. They fought like cowards. Crimson leather skin, bulging black eyes, and a mouthful of hideous teeth. He loathed the sight of them almost as much as he loathed the stench of them.

He reloaded his E-35 assault rifle and barked into his helmet comm. "Tacker, check that bank on the corner of Ontario and Rockwell. They've got a sniper up there somewhere! Flush him from behind if you can, but don't force it!"

Confirmation came, and Lilan regripped his gun. There was no need to check on Tacker again. He'd do the job.

He rounded the corner and spotted a handful of operatives hunkered down across the street. It took a moment for Lilan to realize they were the only other operatives left. One thought surfaced in his mind—get them out of there. As they took cover behind an overturned van, he addressed his comm once more.

"Who's still alive over there?"

The comm channel crackled. "Me and Henrick, sir!"

"Who the hell is *me*?"

"Yalen, sir, sorry!"

Yalen and Henrick. It figured. At least Tacker was still alive.

As if on cue, Tacker's voice sliced through the comm. "Sniper down!"

"Excellent," Lilan answered. "Everyone on headset, listen! Base is going to have to send someone else in to clean up this mess! Fall back to the safe zone!" Yalen and Henrick withdrew from the fight. Lilan looked skyward. "*Seven*, where are you?"

"*Seven* in orbit, colonel."

"We're pulling an evac—grab us at the safe zone!"

"On my way, sir."

The Vulture transport broke its low orbit over the city and pointed its nose toward the north. Lilan's focus returned to the street. "John, do you have a clear way out?" For the first time that mission, he called Tacker by his first name. An accident.

Tacker's voice crackled again. "I don't know if I ha—" and that was it. There was a *pop*, and silence flooded the line. Tacker's voice was gone.

Lilan froze. "Tacker?...Tacker! *Seven*, what was the—" he stopped as he watched a plasma bolt tear through Yalen's back. A mist of red erupted from the soldier's chest; he collapsed to the ground. Lilan continued. "*Seven*, what was the last known position of Commander Tacker?"

"Last comm was approximately two hundred yards south of your location, sir."

"Thank you, *Seven*," Lilan said. Too far to foot it. He scanned for an alternative, and he soon found one parked right across the alley. A sedan. Perfect. He slammed the butt of his assault rifle against the driver's side window, and the glass shattered. It took just as much effort to hotwire it. The engine roared to life, and he floored the accelerator.

Though an occasional plasma bolt flashed across the hood, Lilan reached Tacker's position with minimal resistance. As soon as he spotted Tacker, he knew why the signal had been lost. The sniper's helmet was attached to his belt, charred beyond functionality.

"What happened?" Lilan asked as Tacker leapt inside.

Tacker buckled up. "They had *two* snipers." He ran a hand through his singed crew cut. "They just weren't very good."

Vulture-7 waited for them on its concrete perch. Only Henrick waited with it, a symbol of the mission's colossal failure. As Tacker abandoned the car and climbed aboard the blunt-nosed transport, Lilan offered the battle-torn streets of Cleveland one more gaze. A devastated city and a decimated unit—the price of underestimation.

It all fell on him.

PART I

1

THE DOOR to Room 419 slid open. Scott Remington stood in the doorway, staring inside. So this was it. This was home. This was where *they* had decided home was, anyway. His hazel eyes swept the room as he took it in. It was smaller than his room at the Academy. It was more cramped. There were metal bunks pushed up against the right wall. These were smaller, too.

He sighed and rubbed his hand behind his neck. This was all wrong. He wasn't supposed to be there. They had asked him if he had a geographic preference, and he'd told them. *Detroit Station.* He had gone to school at Michigan. That's where *she* was. That's where he was supposed to go. When they'd handed him his duty assignment and he saw that it was *Richmond*, he couldn't believe it. He scratched his head, fingertips disappearing under his tuft of short brown hair.

Scott was five feet and eleven inches tall, with a body as toned as one would expect from a soldier fresh out of *Philadelphia* Academy. He was a handsome young man, or at least she thought so. And her opinion was the only one that mattered.

He sighed again and took a step inside. It was done. He was officially there.

He slipped the duffle bag from his shoulder and plopped it on the floor. Turning around, he stepped back to the door and eased it shut with a quiet click. He scrutinized the room again.

A sink was built into the wall in the far corner, complemented by a small, cracked mirror. Moving to the faucet, he turned the knob and an instant rush of water and steam poured out. He slid his hands beneath the stream and massaged his face, then patted his sleeve against his forehead and eyes and turned the water off.

Returning to his duffle bag, Scott crouched down and tugged open the metal zipper. Inside was a collection of folded clothes, on top of which sat a black leather-backed Scripture, the name "Scott James Remington" inscribed in gold at the bottom right-hand corner. He passed his hand along the book's glossy surface. *God, what am I doing here?* He took hold of the book and rose to his feet, placing it atop the nightstand next to the bottom bunk.

The next item from the bag was a worn-out football, stained with grass and dirt from recent use. He gripped it for a moment before rolling it beneath the bed.

His gaze returned to the bag, where it lingered for a moment. *Her.* As much of her as there could be, anyway. It was the picture of a blue-eyed, beautiful brunette. Her smile caused two dimples to appear just beyond her lips, and her snow-white teeth sparkled from within the gold boundaries of the frame. His gaze trailed to the lower right corner, where the words *I love you!* were scripted in black marker. Beneath it was her name—Nicole. His focus returned to her face, and he breathed in softly. He hated *Richmond* even more. He rose and set the picture atop his nightstand, her face angled to the bed.

For the next half hour, he removed clothes and unpacked the essentials. There was no hurry in the task, only the lull that came after the bustle of a move. As soon as he had finished, he turned off the lights and dropped down on the bottom bunk, sliding his hands behind his head. For the first time that day, his eyes fell shut. There was nothing more to do. Within minutes, he was asleep.

The door swung open. A shaft of light cut in from the hall-way and Scott's eyes flickered awake. In the doorway stood the silhouette of a well-built man with a duffle bag similar to Scott's slung over his shoulder. His shoulders were broad, and though not massive, his stature made his power clear. Before Scott could gather his senses, the light flicked on and the stranger stepped inside. He blinked as he saw Scott in bed. "Sorry about that. Didn't expect anyone else to be here yet."

Scott flinched as the room lit up, and he propped up on his elbows. He mumbled incoherently as the stranger tossed his duffle bag onto the floor and extended a hand. "Hey. David Jurgen."

David's features came into detail as Scott gave the hand an absent shake. Black hair was combed back on his head, and his casual green eyes made direct contact. Faint streaks of gray filtered past his sideburns. He offered Scott a genuine smile. "I'm your roommate. Our convoy just got in from *Philadelphia*—guess yours must've come early. Sorry about waking you up."

Squinting at the clock on his nightstand, Scott said, "No, it's all right…what time is it?"

"Four past midnight."

"Oh wow."

David knelt next to his duffle bag and unzipped it. He smiled. "Yeah, the night's young." He reached into the bag, where he produced several pictures. He began to set them along the empty shelf space along the wall. "Guessing if you had stuff it'd be out by now. Mind?"

"No, not at all." Only one picture of Scott's mattered, and it was already in place.

"What was your name again?"

Scott blinked. "Hmm? Oh, I'm sorry, I'm still a little, you know…"

"Out of it, yeah. You look it."

"Scott Remington."

"Scott Remington, huh? Well, good to meet you."

Scott nodded as his gaze fell on the pictures. There were several family pictures, but the ones that stood out showed David in full police uniform. Other uniformed men stood around him. "You did police work?"

"Fourteen years, NYPD."

"Oh wow…how…?"

David continued to set the photos in place. "I'm forty. Joined the department at twenty-four, did it for fourte, then enrolled in *Philadelphia*. The math works."

Scott lingered on the pictures. "Didn't see you at the Academy."

"Well, it *is* pretty big…"

"That's true." And it was. In fact, the Academy wasn't just 'pretty big'. It was gargantuan. The only EDEN bases that rivaled it were behemoths like *Nagoya*, *Atlanta*, and to an extent *Novosibirsk*—the three largest facilities on Earth. "We still probably had some of the same instructors though."

"Oh, I'm sure. You ever had Captain Williams?"

Scott broke into a laugh. Captain Harold Williams. The man was a *Philadelphia* legend. A walking caricature of a drill sergeant. "I think *everybody* had Captain Williams. You had him for hand-to-hand training, right?"

"More like cadet beat-down training. You ever win?"

Scott shook his head. "Killed me. Every time."

"Yeah, same here." David finished with the pictures and knelt beside his duffle bag. "So what about you? Where'd you come from?"

Scott sat up, leaning against the lower bunk wall. "Lincoln, but I went to school at Michigan. I went to *Philadelphia* straight from there. Well…I didn't finish Michigan. Left in my second year."

"Lincoln…?"

"Nebraska."

"Why'd you leave school for this?"

Scott hated that question. The answer always sounded stupid. He hesitated for a moment before responding. "I guess I kind of felt led here. To EDEN, I mean."

"What, like a God thing?"

That was as good as he could have described it. "Yeah, I guess you could say that."

David nodded. "Okay. I respect that." Scott smiled faintly as David said, "I'm gonna take a walk around, learn the layout of the base some. Wanna come?"

Scott smiled. He was glad the conversation deviated from religion so quickly. It was an awkward topic to begin a partnership with. "It's past midnight on the first night of the most important career decision of my life. Might as well wander around."

He rose from his bunk. He wasn't tired now anyway, and the sooner he could get the base layout down, the better. There were few things more pathetic than the look of a lost rookie. The light to Room 419 flicked off and the two men stepped into the hallway.

Richmond was the smallest of the major EDEN facilities on Earth. It was the only one classified as a Class-1. There were five classes in all, and each one represented the number of enlisted operatives. Eleven of the facilities were considered major: EDEN Command, *Atlanta, Nagoya, Novosibirsk, Philadelphia, Richmond, Berlin, Dublin, London, Leningrad,* and *Cairo.* There were hundreds of smaller EDEN establishments across the planet, but they rated more as corner stations than military compounds. Despite its size, *Richmond* brandished a reputation for professionalism, and it was held in high regard by its counterparts across the planet.

As the two men trekked through *Richmond*'s corridors, they found sparse activity. There were occasional clusters of operatives in places such as the training center, but for the most part the base felt asleep. With the traditional morning hours of EDEN schedules, this was to be expected. The layout of the base was simple and effective, and within forty-five minutes they managed to venture through almost every allowable area. It was much smaller than *Philadelphia* Academy.

Conversation flowed as David unfolded his story to Scott. He was married to his wife of twelve years, Sharon. They had two boys, both in grade school in New York. David's stint with the NYPD was a proud one, and he left with honorable notice to enroll with EDEN. Sharon and the kids still lived in New York, though they were in the stages of a transplant to the city of Richmond to be closer to him.

In turn, Scott told him about Nicole.

The clocks peaked at 0100 when they finally returned to their wing of the living quarters. The hallways were vacant, and a stark silence reverberated from the walls. Because of this tomb-like state they were able to spot, with ease, the faint glow of a light down the hallway. It was the only sign of life they'd come across. As they drew nearer, they realized that it emanated from the room just beside theirs—Room 421. The closer they drew, the more apparent it became that a man stood in the doorway of the room, his shadow silhouetted across the linoleum floor. Once their footsteps were within earshot, the silhouetted man tilted his head in their direction.

He was slender, though height compensated for a lack of size. His arms were folded across his chest as he leaned against the doorway arch, and his shadowed gaze scrutinized them beneath a tuft of dusty brown hair.

"Who's that?"

"No idea." Scott shook his head.

"Hey there!"

Startled, the stranger shifted bodily to face them. Everything about the motion was uncomfortable, and his body language immediately withdrew. His gaze darted down to the floor, and he mumbled a response. "Howdy."

He had to be from Texas.

The insignia on his uniform identified him as an alpha private, and David extended his hand. "David Jurgen. I live next door."

Scott offered his hand immediately after. "Scott Remington, good to meet you. We're in 419." The stranger shook Scott's hand tentatively. His discomfort was impossible to ignore.

"...all right," the stranger said in a low voice. He looked young, barely in his twenties if at all. Averting his eyes, he again shied toward the doorway. "I'm Jayden. Timmons."

"Jayden Timmons?" David asked.

"Yessir."

David smiled warmly. "No...we just got here today, too. Away with the 'sir'."

Jayden's posture eased at the revelation. "Us too."

"Who's 'us'?" Scott asked.

A new voice emerged from 421. "Hey! Who's tha' yeh blatherin' with?" Scott and David exchanged a glance and then angled to the door. The accent was the first thing they heard.

"Our neighbors," Jayden answered the voice as he stepped to the side. Scott peered into the room.

At the edge of the lower bunk sat a young man with an impish grin. His viridian gaze surveyed Scott beneath a scattered tangle of brown hair. As he kicked to his feet, one word came to Scott's mind. Energy.

"Hi. Scott Remington. I live next door."

The newcomer slapped out a handshake. "Howyeh! Becan McCrae, likewise it's a pleasure! Yeh go by Remmy?"

Scott smiled. "Remmy works." Remmy actually worked well. A lot of his friends at Michigan called him that. It felt good to hear again.

"Class! Who yeh got with you?"

David leaned inside and offered his hand. "David Jurgen. Good to meet you."

Becan swatted David's palm. "Yis muckers, eh?"

"Uhh...we're roommates," Scott said uncertainly. He could only assume that a mucker was a roommate. Or a friend. Or something along those lines. Despite the fact that *Philadelphia* was a melting pot for nationalities—the only EDEN Academy on the planet—Scott had never met anyone from Ireland there. There were plenty of Americans, Britons, and Australians. The English speakers were undoubtedly the majority. Russia and Germany were also heavily represented, as were China and Japan. The rest of the global population, while still there, were far less common.

"Righ', righ', tha's wha' I meant."

David grinned. "Where are you from?"

"Broadford, Ireland. Yeh really have to ask, do yeh?"

"Are you guys just in from *Philadelphia*, too?"

"We are. Guessin' we're all alphas then, righ'?"

Scott nodded as Jayden slipped back into the room. As soon as Becan saw him, he said, "Tha's me boyo Jay, he's a bit o' a quiet one. He's one o' them cowboys."

Jayden made for his bunk bed and snagged a brown cowboy hat from the bed stand. He placed it firmly on his head.

"Jay's a sniper, he is," Becan said.

"You're a sniper?" Scott asked with an inspired stare. That was impressive. He knew a few snipers in *Philadelphia*, and their training was to be envied. There was no such thing as a sniper with a poor work ethic.

"Yeah…"

"Congratulations, man."

"Thanks…"

Meanwhile, Becan's gaze shifted to David, where it lingered for several moments. "How old are yeh?"

"Why?" David's eyes narrowed.

"Yeh look…older."

"I'm forty."

"*Tha's* why yeh look older…"

"How old are you?"

"A lot less old than *you* are."

Scott gave Becan a hard stare. A question was lingering in his head, and he had to ask. "Why did't you get stationed at *Dublin*?"

"Tha's a grand question. I've no bloody clue."

Scott laughed. *Richmond* didn't seem so far from home anymore. "And I thought being stationed outside of Michigan was bad. How does your family feel about this? They've got to be missing you like crazy."

"I've got no family," Becan said. "Me ma and me da died years ago. I've got no brothers or sisters."

Scott was oddly relieved by Becan's answer. Scott had lost his parents too, back when he was in high school. They died in a car accident. It was always comforting to find someone else who knew what it was like to lose parents at a young age. He felt an unspoken connection with them.

"Wha' abou' you now?" Becan asked. "Leave annyone back in the great state o' Michigan?"

"A fiancée and a brother," Scott answered. Mark. He hadn't seen Mark in months. Scott was like a brother and a father to him. Mark was still in his teens, but almost finished with high school. He planned to follow Scott's footsteps into EDEN, no matter how hard Scott tried to talk him out of it. "Mark lives in Nebraska, though."

"So wha' abou' this girl?"

"Her name is Nicole. We've been together for six years, she came to Michigan with me. We dated in high school, went to college together."

"So yeh been with this girl for six years an' you're not married yet?"

"We're engaged. Haven't really been able to set a date, though. I thought we'd be able to after the Academy, but I didn't think they'd send me here. Believe me, nobody wants it to happen sooner than me."

Becan nodded. "A lot o' people I knew in *Philadelphia* got married. Never understood tha', I didn't. Get married in the middle o' the Academy. Tha' place is hectic enough as it is."

"Yeah," Jayden said. "It's pretty crazy. I don't know how people had time to get hitched, classes kept me busy around the clock."

It was an odd mix, *Philadelphia*. On one hand, it was military training. On the other, it was no different from college. In the midst of workouts, drills, and weapons training, there were courses. Classroom courses with names that sounded as if they came straight out of a university booklet. Geography 101, Urban Tactics, Environmental Combat 300. You didn't only graduate from the Academy with a sense of accomplishment, you felt like you earned a college degree.

Scott folded his arms contemplatively. "Do you guys feel like *Philadelphia* prepared you for this?"

"I think it did," Becan answered. "I know a lot o' people find it weird with the classes an' everything, but everybody seems to come ou' all righ'."

"It's different." David stifled a yawn. "Was everyone here in the soldier program?" Jayden shook his head. "That's right—you're a sniper, sorry about that."

"S'all right."

"I know what they're trying to do. They're trying to create smarter operatives, and the best way to do that is through coursework combined with military training. It's a different system, yeah, but I think it works all right."

"I bloody *loved* Xenobiology," said Becan.

Scott concurred. Xenobiology alone made the Academy worth it. There were few things more fascinating than the in-depth study of extra-terrestrials. "I totally agree," he said.

"Grand stuff, tha' was. Flickin' amazin'."

"What was your favorite race?" Scott asked. There were three alien races in all that had made contact with Earth: the Bakma, Ceratopians, and Ithini. And of course, two animals in the canrassi and the necrilid. It was startling how little EDEN knew about each one, outside of general biology. Their cultures, their relationships, and most notably their motives for attacking remained a mystery.

"I'd like to say necrilids, but really tha' class jus' scared the hell out o' me. I liked learnin' abou' the Ceratopians, though."

Ceratopians. The brutes of the Alien War, like a page out of the prehistoric. Five-horned, bone-frilled warriors. Walking terrors. "Ceratopian class was good. You're right about the necrilids, though, they're pretty freaky. I think that's why people aren't as high on that class as you'd think, because as cool as they are, in the back in your mind you're thinking '*Veck*...I might have to *fight* that thing one day'."

"Yeah. Exactly. Those things are scary as all hell."

There was so much about the Alien War that didn't make sense. In fact, there was next to nothing about it that *made* sense. Three races appeared at almost the exact same time: the grotesque Bakma, the reptilian Ceratopians, and the quintessentially gray Ithini. The Bakma and the Ceratopians seemed to have nothing in common, except for one detail—they both worked with the Ithini. But oddly so. The Ithini were present with both races, except in seemingly mundane roles. It wasn't clear whether they were supervisors or servants. Or something else.

Then there were the canrassi and the necrilid, non-sentient alien animals. The canrassi—bearlike, spider-eyed beasts—were used by both the Bakma and the Ceratopians, either as mounted rides or animal labor. Necrilids were only seen with Ceratopians. That was just as well, as necrilids were generally regarded as the worst creatures imaginable. Black-skinned, sharp-clawed, long-fanged predators. Bugs with skin, with one horrible detail that stuck out from the rest. They were flesh-eaters.

Why were the Ithini and canrassi connected to the Bakma and Ceratopians? Why weren't the Bakma and Ceratopians connected with one another, and why did only the Ceratopians use the necrilid? They were all pertinent questions. But one question lingered above them. Why were they all after Earth? They appeared and attacked at the same time, within months of each other, without a clue as to their motives. Some media reporters nicknamed the Alien War "The Race for Earth," but nobody knew what was waiting at the finish line. Why were they here? It was a simple question without a single answer.

David pushed up from his chair. The other men turned to stare at him. "What's up?" Scott asked.

"Nothing," said David. "I think I'm just about to turn in, is all." He stifled a second yawn. "I'm feeling that move from *Philadelphia* now."

Becan smirked. "Old people just get tired early." David gave him a withering look, but the Irishman just laughed. "Fair enough, then. It was grand meetin' yeh."

"Same here," David answered amiably.

Scott sighed and lowered his head, then he too stood up from his prop against the wall. "That's probably a good idea. Tomorrow's going to come fast."

"Yeh goin' to bed too then?"

Scott nodded. "I don't want to be head-bobbing for whatever we have in the works tomorrow. I'm pretty sure that doesn't make a good first impression."

"Yeah. Righ', well I'm sure we'll see yis both tomorrow, then."

"There's a good chance we'll all be in the same unit," David said. "They usually group teammates close together in the living quarters, and we're in the very next room."

"Tha's true."

"I guess we'll find out tomorrow."

"Yeah." Becan plopped back down on his bunk and flung up a wave. "Night Remmy. Night Dave."

"Good night guys," Jayden said.

Scott and David bid their farewells, stepped into the hall, and closed the door to 421.

"Nice guys," Scott said. They seemed rather an odd couple, but he'd found them both friendly—in their own ways.

"Yeah," David agreed. "Unique little job of pairing EDEN did there."

"Yeah, really." The door to 419 opened and they stepped inside.

For the next several minutes, they prepared for the night. They took turns brushing their teeth at the sink, and then they slipped out of their jerseys and into nightwear. David climbed to the upper bunk as Scott flicked the light off from below.

"Do you really think there's a chance we'll all be in the same unit?" Scott asked as he laid back on the bottom bunk.

"I think there is."

"I hope so. That'd be fun." He closed his eyes.

Silence hung in the room for several moments before David spoke. "Right, because you know, EDEN stands for Earth's Daily Entertainment Network."

Scott made a face in the dark. "Ha ha. Whatever, good night." David chuckled, and Scott shook his head. "Earth's Daily Entertainment Network. I don't even know what that means."

"Maybe you will soon," said David. "Good night."

Scott pulled the covers to his chin and turned over on his side. The initial uneasiness he'd felt had simmered down in his system. At least he had other people to share it with now. He looked forward to seeing Becan and Jayden again. His mouth stretched open in a yawn, and he once again slid his eyes shut. Within minutes, he was asleep.

2

THE DOOR TO GENERAL James Hutchin's room slid open as Lilan stepped inside and paused at attention. Despite the fact that it was barely morning, Lilan's uniform and crew cut were models of perfection. He gave the impression of a man who had been awake for hours. The door closed behind him, and Hutchin removed his reading glasses from his face. "At ease, colonel." The general was a well-structured man, younger than Lilan, though his hair was streaked with dashes of gray.

Lilan's muscles relaxed. "Sir."

Hutchin motioned to the chair in front of his desk. "Have a seat, Brent." Lilan rested a hand on the back of the indicated chair and slid down into it. "I'm sorry to hear about your platoon. A lot of good men were lost."

Lilan nodded. "Yes sir, a lot of good men were."

"As you already know, this is war, and these things are unavoidable. That's why we don't make too many friends in this business."

"Yes sir."

"And I have no doubts that you will take your newly assigned crew and turn them into a platoon as functional as your last. Am I correct?"

Lilan's posture straightened. "Yes sir."

"I expect no less." Hutchin pushed back his chair and opened the topmost drawer of his desk. A single manila folder was produced, and he handed it across the desktop. "Here is your new crew, colonel."

Lilan accepted the folder, though his eyes remained on Hutchin. "Did you take my recommendation to promote John Tacker to major?"

"I did. John's had a good career with us, I think he'll fit the role well. He was a good recommendation."

"Thank you, sir." Lilan opened the manila folder and examined its contents. Hutchin's focus lingered on Lilan's expression as it shifted from businesslike to confused, and finally to disbelief. "Sir, this has to be a mistake…"

"There's no mistake, colonel," Hutchin answered. "That's your new roster."

Lilan's eyes flashed across the desk. "General, sir, this shows every single operative other than Tacker, Henrick, and myself as an alpha."

Hutchin's reply was blunt. "You are being assigned a rookie platoon."

"Sir, Alan Henrick was an exception," said Lilan, "but even he was a beta when he entered Falcon. These are *all* alphas."

"I understand, colonel, but there is no mistake. That is your new platoon."

"Permission to speak freely, sir?"

"Go ahead."

"Falcon Platoon has a reputation to protect. We worked hard to earn it. It does the entire platoon a great injustice to replace those polished veterans with rookies straight out of the Academy."

Hutchin leaned against the armrest of his chair. "First of all, the *we* you're referring to consists of three people. The old platoon is gone."

"Sir, I understand that, but—"

"Do you think rookies can benefit and learn from your example?"

"Sir, yes sir, but I—"

"Then I expect you to do your job as a colonel and lead this crew as you led the previous crew. I don't care about reputation. I care about results. I don't care if you were Klaus Faerber and this was Vector Squad, you'd still get a team full of rookies if that's all we had to choose from. We're undermanned. You know that. This is all we can afford to give you, and if we break up any other platoon further, we'll be jeopardizing their capabilities. That never has been acceptable, and it won't start being acceptable now."

"I understand that, sir—"

Hutchin cut him off again. "This is how it's going to be. When I make a decision, that decision is final. You know that. Now, you will take this team, and you will lead them as you led the Falcon Platoon of yesterday. Take the assignment that's been handed to you, and turn it into something to be proud of. Do what I've come to expect you to do. Make a bad situation good."

Lilan opened his mouth to reply, but no words came out. The decision had already been made, and the word *trainer* hovered in his mind. The room fell quiet, and he sighed surrender. "Yes sir."

"Is there anything else?"

Lilan bit his tongue. "No sir."

"Excellent. Your operatives have been notified and will meet in the hangar for your formal introduction at noon. I'm sure you'll have no trouble breaking them in."

"No sir." Lilan closed the manila folder and stood up. "If there's nothing else?"

"Nothing else. You're dismissed."

"Thank you, sir." Lilan nodded to the general, turned around, and left the room.

*   *   *

IT WASN'T UNTIL 0950 hours that Scott, David, Becan, and Jayden awoke from their slumber—a luxury they would not experience again for some time. It was a well-known fact that EDEN thrived on morning schedules. There was a saying that passed on from each graduating Academy class to the next: *Use your first day as an operative to sleep late—it may never happen again.* It was advice that few *Philadelphia* graduates neglected.

The four men went directly from their rooms to the cafeteria, where they discovered the vast difference between food services at the Academy and food services in the real EDEN. It was the difference between gourmet and cheap-as-possible. This was not a surprise—the Academy was designed to be reassuring on many levels. Once potential recruits became EDEN cadets, the pampering at the Academy began. Private rooms, fine cuisine, and a university atmosphere came together to form a grand scheme: convince them that EDEN was the right move, and when reality hit, they'll have gone too far to turn back. For a vast majority of those enlisted in *Philadelphia*, the plan worked—only eight percent dropped out before graduation.

When they returned to their rooms, they discovered that notes had been pushed under their doors. The notes bore simple instructions: *Report to the hangar at 1200 for unit assignment. On-time is late.* With little time to spare, they opted to dismiss further conversation and don their uniforms. By the time 1150 came around, all four were prepped and ready for the meeting. Together they ventured to the hangar.

Though the *Richmond* main hangar was spacious, it paled in comparison to the massive hangars found at larger bases. Nonetheless, the four soldiers found themselves transfixed on the ceiling—if for nothing more than to feel the awesome depth of the room. Vulture transports and Vindicator fighters covered the ground space in neat rows, and mammoth Grizzly APCs— Armored Personnel Carriers—sat parked in preparation for a mission. The mere sight of them broke goose bumps across their arms and sent forth a powerful, overwhelming sensation—the extra-terrestrials had picked the wrong planet to fight.

It was no challenge to locate the intended meeting area, as several perfect rows of steel chairs lined the center of the hangar. Scott guessed that there must have been at least forty of them. They were almost all full, occupied by various men and several women—all of whom chattered in hushed tones with one another as their gazes occasionally roamed the room. At the front of the rows stood an empty, olive-colored podium.

There was a cluster of empty chairs at the back of the seating area, and the four soldiers were quick to stake their claim. As they took their seats and listened, they could overhear parts of conversations taking place around them—introductions, comments on the size of the hangar and the taste of the cafeteria food, all small-talk. It was familiar conversation to the four, and Becan was the first to point out why. Everyone in the hangar was an alpha private.

At that point, a new sound presented itself—the sound of footsteps. The steps were no louder than any of the conversation in the hangar and no more unusual. They stood out because of their perfect synchronicity—three pairs of feet, one unified sound. A glance toward the hangar entrance explained why, as three men made their approach.

The man in the forefront was older, with cropped silver-gray hair. As he neared, there was no doubt as to his level of authority. He carried himself like a commanding officer. The second man was younger, taller, and steel-faced. His posture was perfectly erect, and he walked in total harmony with the older man in front of him. Of the three, he was the only one with a folder in hand. The last man was the shortest and sported a mop of short, curly brown hair. It was easy to identify the status of these men—they were all officers. Immediately, every operative in the seating area snapped up and rose their hands to their foreheads in attention. A cloud of anticipation could be sensed rising from the floor.

The older man continued his purposed march past the soldiers until he came to the podium in front of the seating area. When he placed his palms at its edges, it wobbled back and forth. He grimaced. "Get this piece of dung out of my sight."

The curly-haired officer nodded, took the podium aside, and returned.

The older man cleared his throat and settled his eyes on the throng of alpha privates. "At ease, everyone," he said. "I am Colonel Brent Lilan. To my right is Major John Tacker, and the other officer with us is Lieutenant Alan Henrick.

"The three of us make up the command staff of Falcon Platoon. If you haven't put it together yet, we are your new commanding officers. As you may have noticed already, you are all alpha privates. You're all fresh out of *Philadelphia*. That's not typical for a unit of this caliber." Scott exchanged a glance with David as Lilan spoke on. "In order to fully explain the special situation we're in, I must first briefly explain a bit of the history behind this platoon.

"Falcon Platoon is one of the oldest platoons at *Richmond*. It's been here since the base's establishment, and I have been her commanding officer for just as long. We have had a long and outstanding tradition of experience and leadership, and we're one of the most respected units at this base.

"Unfortunately, change has been forced upon us. Several days ago, the whole of Falcon was lost in Cleveland, Ohio. This loss was not due to failure on the part of Falcon, but due to a combination of events that could best be summed up as bad luck. As you'll learn, those things happen. Unfortunately, you can't hit rewind and change it. You can only hope to better prepare for the future.

"*Richmond* is the smallest EDEN facility on Earth. We don't receive nearly the number of new operatives as other stations do. In short…this facility is undermanned, and you are all we have to fill the shoes of those lost in battle."

The words were inspirational murder. The eager expressions on the alphas fell. The cloud of anticipation evaporated.

"That's why you're here now. That's not what you want to hear, it's not what I want to see. But that's how it is. Now, you can handle this in two ways. You can tuck your tails between your legs and prove my gut right, because my gut tells me that everything this unit's worked toward has just come crashing down. Or you can prove me wrong. I hope, for all of our sakes, that you prove me wrong. Because, if you don't…this is a sad day for the state of EDEN."

Tacker frowned as Lilan continued.

"This isn't a traditional war we've been faced with. This is a war unlike any we've ever seen. It's a war in which we can't choose the battlegrounds we fight on. It's a war in which we don't have the luxury of going on the offensive. An attack can happen anywhere on the planet, at any time. It's impossible to form coherent battle plans, since we never know what the battlefield will look like until we step off the transport. You can go from asleep in your beds to the middle of a firefight in minutes.

"Deaths are inevitable. My job as your commanding officer is to make sure your chance of dying by your own mistakes is diminished, and it's your job as my operatives to help me reach that goal by paying attention, following orders, and working as a team."

Scott laughed beneath his breath. Nice way to motivate a unit.

"I won't say what I look forward to," Lilan continued, "because it's not a very long list. I will say this, however. Five, six, maybe seven of you will impress me. I look forward to finding out who they are."

If a feather would have fallen, everyone in the hangar would have heard it. Silence hung in the air until Lilan's voice once again subdued it.

"I will now turn this over to Major Tacker."

All attention shifted to Tacker as he took Lilan's place. He offered the alphas a faint smile as he cleared his throat.

"Good afternoon, Falcons. As the colonel stated, my name is John Tacker and I am the executive officer of this platoon. I will be directly leading Charlie Squad, and Lieutenant Henrick right here behind me will be in charge of Delta Squad. Despite the fact that we're all one platoon, a majority of your work will be with your assigned squad. I have the squad rosters right here." He opened a manila folder.

"When I call your name, please stand and step to the far right. I'll meet you there shortly. This is for Charlie Squad." His eyes lowered to the folder. "Bell, Carter, Jurgen, Mathis, McCrae, Remington, Rhodes, Timmons, Valer, Zigler."

Scott grinned as he, David, Becan, and Jayden made their way to the side. So they had been right yesterday. They weren't only in the same platoon, they were in the same squad. Despite the severity of Lilan's opening welcome, Scott felt a sense of anticipation.

"The rest of you, the majority, have been assigned to Commander Henrick. He'll speak with you now." Tacker nodded to the curly-haired Henrick, who took his place in front of the seating area. As Henrick began to speak, Tacker stepped away from him and joined the operatives assigned to Charlie Squad.

"You all will be directly under my supervision so long as you're a part of Charlie," he said to them, capturing their full attention. "Charlie's always been a bit more specialized than Delta, which is why they have more than we do. You're rookies, but you won't be held to a rookie standard...though I'm sure the colonel's already made that clear." Tacker smiled. "I'm a bit more patient than the colonel. I was where you are—so was he, even though he'll never admit it. Contrary to popular belief, he actually *wasn't* born in an EDEN uniform."

Scott chuckled, as did several others around him.

"I do expect great things. I demand great things. There's a learning curve and I understand that, but the Bakma don't and the Ceratopians don't. Not even the Ithini. They don't care if you've been with the organization for twenty years or twenty minutes, they still won't hesitate to shoot you in the back of the head if they get the chance.

"It's vital to our survival as a squad that we communicate. Communication is the deciding factor in combat. A lot of that comes with familiarity. That said, I'd like to take a few minutes for each of us to introduce ourselves. We can do that since we're a relatively small group. Be brief, as brief as possible, but give us something to remember you by. But before we do that, does anyone have any questions?"

A lanky, blond-haired soldier raised his hand.

"Go ahead."

"Thank you, sir. I was just wondering why we were chosen for Charlie instead of Delta, sir?"

Scott wondered the same thing. It was a legitimate question.

Tacker smiled. "Your Academy records have all shown you to have more potential than most. That means a variety of different things, from physical skill, willingness to follow orders, examination scores...all those factor in. The goal is to have enough variety in a squad to cover all bases without letting one area slip. Academy scores mean nothing compared to true combat experience, but it gives us a sort of best guess. Hopefully, we evaluated correctly. If we were wrong in our evaluations, you will be removed. Any other questions?"

No hands were raised.

"Very good. As I mentioned before, I'd like each of us to give a brief introduction. Give us something to identify you with other than your name. I'll go ahead and go first—that's only fair. My full name is John Noah Tacker. I entered EDEN a sniper, and I've been one ever since. I'm a six-year veteran of the organization. I was a tertiary officer for Falcon Platoon before Cleveland, I was promoted to major today, actually. This is my first command assignment.

"That's all I want from you. Let's go ahead and start to the left and work our way right until everyone is done. Go ahead."

The first person to Tacker's left was a petite black woman. Her hair was tied back in a delicate bun, and she offered warm brown eyes and a smile to the group. "Hi everyone, my name is Sasha Rhodes and I'm a combat medic. I'm twenty-two, and…I'm *very* glad you're our commanding officer, sir." The group laughed. Scott couldn't help but grin. Compared to the bitter greeting of Colonel Lilan, Major Tacker's laid back persona was a relief to everyone.

Tacker smiled and shook his head. "Thank you, Ms. Rhodes. I'm sure you are."

The next operative down was the only other woman in the group. Her fiery red hair was pinned back in a bushy ponytail, and her striking green eyes glinted at Tacker. "My name is Natasha Valer, and I'm also a combat medic. I'm not sure if this is something to remember me by, but I was actually from Philadelphia. The city, I mean. I literally lived about a fifteen-minute drive from the Academy."

Tacker smiled. "So our two medics are Sasha and Natasha… that's wonderful." The group chuckled again. "As you can all see, we don't have any veteran medics in this squad. That's not a typical situation, but as you know, Falcon Platoon isn't in a typical situation. I expect a lot out of you two."

Scott restrained a frown and made a mental note not to get shot.

The next man down the row was tall and broad-shouldered. His height was rivaled only by David's and surpassed only by a giant black man farther down the line. He had piercing green eyes beneath a jet-black crew cut. "I'm Michael Carter, and I'm a soldier. I used to bounce in *Urban Rodeo*...I don't know if any-one's familiar with it, but it's a club in Oakland."

The black man farther down grinned. "Aw man, I been there once. Place is heavy."

Michael's face remained stoic. "You can't even imagine, man. I've had to bust out so many people, I'm talking on a nightly basis. Just stupid people, they can't behave."

"I believe it."

Silence prevailed, and Scott cleared his throat. "Scott Rem-ington, I'm twenty-three and a soldier. I used to QB for Michigan before I joined EDEN." David, who was next in line, raised his brow and stared at him. "Yeah, I was a Bobcat. I only had four starts. I was second-string most of my time there."

"How did you do?" David asked.

"I went two and two." And it should have been three and one. Poor receivers were the banes of decent quarterbacks. It was funny how Scott's mind could go back so easily. He remembered every drop back as if he just returned to the huddle.

David stepped forward. "David Jurgen, I spent fourteen years with the NYPD before this. Married man, wife and two great kids." He nodded toward Sasha and Natasha. "Sorry, ladies, I'm taken." Sasha laughed; Natasha offered him a coy smile.

Tacker canted his head and hesitated. "How old are you, Jurgen?"

Scott tried and failed to restrain his smile. Poor David. He was never going to get away from his age here.

"Forty, sir," David answered.

"Fourteen years in the NYPD and forty years old? Why didn't you come in as a gamma private?"

"Wasn't offered, sir."

"*Philadelphia* never opted you into that?"

"No sir. I asked about it. They said no. They told me that defend-ing a city and defending the planet were two different things alto-gether."

Tacker sighed and glanced across the squad. "Ladies and gen-tlemen, that is what happens when stupid people get to make deci-sions." He returned to David. "We'll get you where you belong as quickly as we can."

"Thank you, sir."

Becan was the next to step forward. His impish smile was still plastered across his face. Scott couldn't help but laugh silently. Becan reminded him of the kind of mischievous troublemaker that people actually *wanted* to be around. "Becan McCrae, from Broadford, Ireland! As class as it'd be for me to fancy up somethin' to remember me by, I think me accent'll do well enough! An' if tha' doesn't work for yeh, wait till yeh see me dance."

Scott closed his eyes and laughed along with the group. Becan was something else.

Jayden was the next man in line. Only after the group fell silent for several moments did he conjure up his words. "My name is Jayden Timmons and I'm twenty-two. I'm from Blue Creek, Texas, and I'm a sniper."

And that was it. Scott couldn't help but smile.

"Congratulations," Tacker said. "Snipers are the most important men on the battlefield." He cracked a smile. "And of course, I'm not biased at all."

Jayden allowed a shy grin. "Thank you, sir."

Only three more men remained: the lanky blond-haired man who had raised his hand earlier, the titan of a black man, and a smaller-framed individual with spiky black hair. The blond one cleared his throat.

"My name is Henry Mathis and I'm twenty-five. Before I joined EDEN, I spent four years as a talk-seller."

Scott's stomach twisted. A talk-seller. The most irritating kind of person on the planet. It didn't matter where you were, when you saw a talk-seller, you turned and walked the other way. Their name said it all—they talked until they sold. Or until whoever they talked to told them off and ran. But that posed the question…what on Earth was a talk-seller doing in EDEN?

No comments were made to Henry. After several moments of uncomfortable silence, the giant black man drew a breath. "I'm Donald Bell, I'm a demolitionist. Ain't nothin' else I can think to say. I'm the only big black man here…y'all probably gonna remember that fine."

It was true enough.

"I played football too, though," Donald said, glancing at Scott. "O-Line. I blocked for my cousin in high school."

Scott smiled. "You're my new best friend." Donald chuckled.

The last man, though small, was well-defined. His blue eyes iced over the rest of Charlie Squad. Scott recognized the expression right away. Superiority.

"David Zigler, I'm a soldier, and I've been involved in military training my entire life."

He said nothing else, despite the unfinished silence that lingered around him. Tacker finally spoke and re-established control.

"Good job, everyone, that's all I wanted from you. I can't stress how important it is that all of you bond, and quickly. If I didn't think it was important, I wouldn't have bothered with this. Friendship, as silly and clichéd as it might sound, could be the only thing that keeps you alive. It's amazing what you can do when you know someone's got your back.

"Now…I'm going to dismiss you, because I'm sure some of you still need to get acclimated to the base. This is a different world from the Academy, so take some time to get used to it."

A sporadic chorus of "yes sir" answered him. He continued.

"There's a box by the hangar door you came through. In that box, you'll find your personal comms. Find the one with your name on it. These are to follow you wherever you go. Sleep with it, eat with it, shower with it…do *everything* with it. When those comms go off, it's time to do your job.

"We have a five-minute rule in Falcon Platoon. When your comm goes off, you have five minutes to get from wherever you are, into uniform and in the hangar ready to go. The transport Charlie uses is *Vulture-7*—it's right over there." He motioned toward one of the transports in the hangar. The number seven was clearly visible on its dorsal fin.

"You were all fitted for personal combat armor in the Academy. That gear, along with your weaponry, will be housed in *Vulture-7*. There's a locker for each of you in it, you'll typically get suited up en route to your destination.

"Five minutes, people. Never longer. Understood?" They

acknowledged, and Tacker snapped a stern command of attention. After a moment of stillness, he nodded a final time. "You're dismissed."

As Tacker returned to Lilan's side, the operatives retrieved their comms and began to file out of the hangar. Henrick continued to speak with Delta as Lilan and Tacker observed in silence. Lilan shifted his attention to the operatives of Charlie Squad as they departed. "So what do you think of them?"

Tacker hesitated. "I hope they know what this is about. I don't know what I *can* think at this point."

Lilan half-frowned. "Did you open informally?"

"Yes sir."

"You know I hate that."

Tacker gave Lilan a sidelong glance. "I know...but it's so important that they bond quickly. That might be the only thing that saves them when the fighting starts. I mean, they sent us a *talk-seller*, for crying out loud." The last of the Charlie Squad operatives left the hangar.

"Who do you think has potential?" Lilan asked.

Tacker's gaze narrowed. "I think Jurgen will do well...he should have come in as a beta at lowest. Bell, Carter, Zigler maybe...I'm anxious to see what Timmons can do. There are a few that have potential, I think."

"Any foreseen problems?"

"Aside from the talk-seller—that's Mathis—I don't know. Nothing is glaring. It's just inexperience. I don't know about Rhodes and Valer, I'm not too fond of two alphas making up our medical crew."

Lilan's expression grew pointed. "I'm not fond of two *girls* making up your medical crew."

"I'm not either," Tacker answered, "but what can we do? We take what they send us. That's the trend right now. I'm glad Henrick has a medic with high marks, at least."

Lilan harrumphed and returned Tacker's assessment of Henrick. "The only thing he's missing is a clue." Tacker restrained a laugh, and Lilan continued. "You know what I want you to do. Right?"

Tacker met Lilan's eyes, and he nodded. His attention returned to Henrick. "Yes sir. I do."

"The chaff will show. Given time. And an opportunity."

Tacker only stared ahead.

They remained in the hangar for several more minutes as Henrick continued to address Delta Squad. Once Henrick had concluded and dismissed his operatives, Lilan offered a cordial nod of departure to Tacker. It was returned, and Lilan stepped away. Tacker remained behind only for a minute as Delta's soldiers retrieved their comms and made their own exits.

He left shortly after, and the hangar was abandoned.

3

THE CRACK OF POOL balls echoed over the banter of the *Black Cherry*, Richmond's premier nightclub. As soon as the orientation of Falcon Platoon had come to a close earlier in the afternoon, the men and women of Charlie Squad—minus Major Tacker—gathered together to plan their celebration. It was their first official day as active members of EDEN.

The *Black Cherry* wasn't the largest club in Richmond, nor the most elite. The reason for its popularity was simple: it felt good. When someone was at the *Black Cherry*, they were home. That was what prompted the members of Charlie Squad to enter its darkened doors and partake in its flavorful smells. Smells of liquor, smells of nachos and cheap finger foods. Smells of good times. It was the perfect way to kick off a new career path.

The group borrowed several excursion vehicles, intended for free operative use in public transit. Once they arrived, they claimed a pair of oval tables near the front door. Though conversation saturated the drive, it wasn't until they took seats together that words flowed with vigor. As could be expected, it centered on their new careers.

Henry was the first to bring the commanding officers into the discussion. "Can you guys believe that speech Colonel Lilan gave us? Was that supposed to be motivational or something?"

Sasha smiled as she sipped her beer. "Somehow I don't think motivation was very high on his list."

"I know! What kind of dung was that?"

Scott only half-smiled as he watched Sasha drink. Nightclubs weren't his thing, nor were alcoholic beverages. Apparently they were for most of the others. He, David, and Jayden were the only three who refrained. "It was honesty," he answered. "We're not what he expected, he just came out and said it."

"Don't you think a little encouragement would have been nice, though?"

Encouragement? This was war. "I guess it would've, but it's not necessary. It's not like he's obligated to make us feel good."

"He's righ'," Becan said. "I mean…I know yeh must remember all the talk in *Philly* abou' commandin' officers. We just got a rough one's all."

"But still!" Henry said. "All I'm saying is that he could have been nicer."

David sipped his soda. "He's not paid to be nice."

"Exactly," Scott said. "I mean, yeah, I guess as far as motivation for the unit goes, it probably wasn't the most uplifting speech in the world, but it still struck me as honest." Scott thought honesty was a good thing. It was always good to see it reflected in people.

Sasha smiled. "Well I'm just glad we got Major Tacker. He seems a bit more personal."

"Yeah," Henry said. "Lilan could have been more like Tacker, I think."

"*Anyway,*" Sasha said, "I bet the colonel is sweet. He just has to be serious about his job."

"Sweet?"

"Yeah. All old men are sweet."

Becan turned to David. "Yeh hear tha'? She thinks you're sweet." David's eyes narrowed.

"How old do you think the colonel is?" Scott asked. "He's got to be in his fifties or something."

Zigler set down his mug of beer and entered the discussion. "I think he's in his upper fifties."

Donald, the giant demolitionist, shook his head. "All's I know is he's for real. I don't wanna make him mad, man."

Henry scoffed. "Come on, you? I know that old lunkard doesn't scare you."

"I had coaches, man. Them old coaches is for real. Don't *ever* tell them they old."

Scott smiled. Donald was right. Tell a football coach he's old and you were liable to get a helmet thrown at you.

"Enough about Lilan," Sasha said. "What do you guys think of Tacker?" Natasha grinned at the mention of Tacker's name. "He said something about we're better than Delta Squad, or something, I don't remember exactly what it was, but what do you think we'll all be doing?"

"No idea," Henry answered. "Shoot stuff."

Zigler gave Henry a patronizing look and said to Sasha, "I'd imagine if there's a choice, we'd lead an assault over Delta. I don't think anyone expects much out of us as alphas. At least out of most of us, anyway."

"Of course," Becan said with a sage look, "I am the greatest warrior in the world, so he expects more out o' me."

Zigler mouthed the word "idiot" before he went on. "I don't think we'll be given anything serious until we prove ourselves. I wanted to say something about age, too. Don't forget that Klaus Faerber is forty-eight."

David snapped his fingers. "Thank you."

"Okay, yeah," Henry answered, "if we're going to talk about *Klaus Faerber.* And I didn't mean that age makes people useless, *thank you.* When I said that to Donald I meant that he could probably take the colonel if he wanted to."

"I ain't said nothin', man."

Zigler turned to Henry. "You were making a claim about age, and you were wrong. Faerber proves you wrong."

"Righ', hey man, lay off him," said Becan. "He wasn't makin' anny claim, he was ju—"

"Was I talking to you?" Zigler asked.

Becan's eyes widened. *"Excuse me?"*

"Fellas," Scott said.

Zigler glared at Becan as he pointed to Henry. "He was making an argument that wasn't worth of a pile of dung, and I shut him up."

"All righ'," Becan said. "Someone better shut down this bucket o' snots or he's goin' to get lamped out o' it."

"Guys, calm *down*." The last thing they needed was a unit full of anger to kick their careers off. "Nobody meant anything, just calm down. It's our first day, we're all a little anxious, let's get it off on the right foot, okay?"

Becan waved it off. "Righ', righ', whatever. Not worth it, let's be movin' on."

Henry frowned to Zigler. "I didn't mean to upset you, man. I wasn't trying to say anything."

"Whatever. Change it now, I don't care."

Sasha cut in before the argument could be revisited and turned to face Jayden and Michael. "You guys don't talk much, huh?"

"Just listening," Michael said. "I mean…nothing really to say. I do think it's cool that Captain Faerber is forty-eight and he's still the best leader in EDEN, but I mean…the conversation wasn't really going there."

"Well it's going there now, just for you," Sasha said with a smile. "Anyone here met Klaus Faerber?"

Scott was skeptical. *Met* Klaus Faerber? He didn't know anybody *could* meet Klaus Faerber. The man was a military legend, the commanding officer of Vector Squad—the most renowned and respected unit on the planet. They held as much weight as anyone in the High Command. "Does he even show up at the Academy?"

Zigler shook his head. "No. The only time he works outside of *Berlin* is when it's something serious. He wouldn't waste his time in *Philadelphia*."

"Isn't his son a cadet in *Philadelphia*?" Natasha asked.

"Strom Faerber, yeah. He'll probably be the most hyped soldier of the century. He's still got a ways to go, though."

Michael spoke up. "I saw Strom a couple times in the weight rooms. Looks just like his dad, blond hair and everything. Not quite as big, but still chiseled like nothing I've ever seen."

Zigler took a swig of beer. "If he takes his father's footsteps, he'll climb the chain of command like it's nothing. Klaus has been rocking the Alien War since it began."

The Alien War. Scott hoped the conversation would go to it in general. "Speaking of the war, anybody have any theories about it? Why we're even in it?"

Natasha wrinkled her forehead. "You know what's funny? They never once mentioned that in *Philadelphia*. Theories."

Zigler took another sip. "That's done on purpose. They don't want theories running rampant until they know something themselves."

"So when are they going to know something? I mean...how long has it been now? Ten years?"

"Nine. They came two years into the New Era."

"That's right," Henry said. "It was that January. It happened a week before the Second Annual World Peace Celebration."

David smiled sardonically. "Ironic, huh?"

Even though it was years ago, Scott remembered that day like it was yesterday. Everyone did. Friday, January 11th, 0002 NE. The world was anticipating the World Peace Celebration. The WPC. The day that honored mankind's transition from Old Era to New Era, an era of global harmony.

It was 3:14 in the afternoon when first contact was made. It was in Hong Kong. It was the Bakma. Four of their Noboats—alien attack ships with the ability to completely dematerialize from view—appeared over the city. There wasn't even time for humanity to hope for peaceful contact. The aliens engaged the moment they arrived. Thousands of citizens were killed before the Noboats vanished as mysteriously as they appeared, their ships dematerializing into the sky. In fact, it was their sudden dematerialization that gave birth to their names. When the ships disappeared, it prompted the commander of Hong Kong's defense force to ask his radar operator how many enemy 'boats' were still in the air. The radar operator's answer was obvious.

The world panicked, and EDEN was formed. The Earth Defense Network. Earth's unified attempt to defend itself from the very beings they sought to find for so long. For centuries, people wondered if they were alone in the galaxy. They finally had their answer.

By the time the Ceratopians and Ithini arrived, in late May of that same year, there were three fully-functional EDEN facilities on Earth: *Atlanta*, *Novosibirsk*, and *Berlin*. It was amazing how quickly EDEN was organized with a global community at the helm. It couldn't have been formed faster, as 0003 marked the year when the Alien War truly erupted. Incursions were no longer rare occurrences. They were commonplace. There were over one hundred and fifty alien attacks in 0003, as opposed to the five that took place in 0002. The increased attacks became the norm year after year. But they rarely consisted of more than a few spaceships. For some reason, the aliens never seemed to bring the full load. It was still a mystery why.

Natasha returned to Zigler. "So nine years later, and we still don't know anything. Doesn't that strike anybody as a little weird?"

Scott slid his hands into his pockets. Weird didn't begin to cover it.

"The news loves to talk about the Ithini Control Theory," said Zigler.

"Well, it makes the most sense," said Scott. "The grays are the only ones that have been seen with both the Bakma and the Ceratopians."

"Then why don't the Bakma and the Ceratopians work together?"

"I don't know. I never said it was the right theory."

"So what do you think is going on?" Natasha pursed her lips.

Zigler stared at her. "The Ithini Control Theory is a joke, that's all I know. If you had the Bakma and the Ceratopians at your fingertips, why wouldn't you send them in together? Why wouldn't you put them in your own ships instead of sending them in theirs? We've never even seen an Ithini vessel. Imagine a ship of Bakma and Ceratopians fighting side by side. How do you stop that?"

"Why don't we hear anything about interrogations?" asked Natasha. "I know they must happen."

"They do," Zigler answered. "It's just not something EDEN wants out in the public. That's all on a need-to-know basis and none of us need to know. Our job is just to shoot. We know the aliens are hostile—that's all that matters."

Henry turned to Zigler. "How do we know they're *all* hostile?"

"Maybe shooting people is their customary way of saying hello," said Natasha.

"Sorry. Forget it."

Natasha giggled. "I'm only pickin'."

Zigler sighed and prodded his glass. "The bottom line is we

don't know why they're here. It's just another aspect of the whole mystery. We may never know."

The room began to beep. Zigler blinked as the sound almost cut off his words, and the other operatives glanced about the room. The beeps were loud; they were sequenced. The operatives' focus shifted from the room down to their belts.

Their comms. It was a call to the hangar. Charlie Squad had a mission.

For a full second, the operatives dropped their jaws and stared. Then all hell broke loose. Every one of them leapt backward from the table, and drinks and chairs toppled to the floor in their wake. The other patrons of the bar started at the sudden chaos.

Charlie Squad bolted out of the door, and Scott flashed a glance to those behind him. "How much time did Tacker say we had?"

"Five minutes!" David answered. "We got five minutes!"

"We're in the middle o' the bloody city!" Becan said.

Scott threw himself into the driver's seat of one of the vehicles and engaged the ignition. "We can make it!"

The drag race back to *Richmond* was chaos. Amid the screech of tires and the blasts of horns, the EDEN vehicles tore through the city streets. The military highway that led to *Richmond* base was on the outskirts of the city, and traffic was dense. By the time they got there, it was 2317. They had received the call at 2309. *Richmond* loomed far in the distance, and the accelerators were slammed to the floorboards.

Scott radioed the EDEN checkpoints as they approached the airstrip, and clearance was given to them to bypass the gates and go directly to the field. It wasn't until the vehicles decelerated to an inertia-pained halt that Scott made another realization. Uniforms. None of the operatives were in their proper uniforms. The clock read 2325. They were eleven minutes late.

They reached the hangars twelve and a half minutes after the initial alert of the comms. As they gasped for breath, their eyes scanned the hangar for Falcon Platoon. They found only Major Tacker. He wasn't difficult to spot—he was the only man in the hangar. Not even the technicians were about. The Vulture transports were there, though none were prepped for flight.

As the pace of the operatives slowed, a wave of confusion washed over them. Something was not right. At that moment, Scott made the connection. He groaned, bent forward, and propped his hands against his knees.

It had been a test. It had been a trashing test.

From within the hangar, Tacker's wicked glare brooded. The operatives knew they were in trouble as soon as he spoke.

"I regret to inform the city of Cincinnati that, due to the inability of Charlie to reach its transport in time, a dozen citizens met untimely deaths while waiting for help to arrive." The operatives buckled over in exhaustion, and the major spoke into his comm. "Thank you, Command," he said. "It's over."

"Our pleasure, major," the comm crackled. The beeping stopped. The hangar fell silent.

Tacker's glare targeted Sasha. "Ms. Rhodes, how long did I tell you that you had to reach the hangar this morning?"

Sasha bowed her head to the ground. "Five minutes, sir."

Tacker shifted to Michael. "Mr. Carter, how long did I tell you that you had to reach the hangar this morning?"

"Five minutes, sir."

Becan was the next that Tacker scrutinized. "Private McCrae, can you vouch for that?"

Becan's gaze lowered. "Yes sir."

"Anyone want to take a guess at the time on my watch?" Tacker asked. None of the operatives spoke. "Oh, come on now, nobody wants to give it a guess?" Once again, no one replied. Tacker's glare narrowed further. "Thirteen minutes. Thirteen minutes. That, my fellow operatives…is not pathetic. It goes *far* beyond pathetic. This is absolutely pitiful. This is worthless." The operatives bent forward as they caught their breaths.

"Stand up straight!"

Charlie Squad snapped upright. Their hands shot to their sides.

"You have brought shame and humiliation to this squad, and

you haven't even been in it for a day! If this would have been a real call, people would have died because of you."

Scott's stomach twisted. Stupid. How could they have been so *stupid*?

"Since five minutes seems a little hard for you all, we're going to tweak that a little bit. In future calls, you have *three* minutes to get from wherever the *hell* you are to the hangar, or you'll find yourself looking for a new career faster than you can believe it."

Tacker drew a sharp breath. "I came prepared for this. I hoped it would have gone differently, but I came prepared anyway. Mr. Remington and Mr. Bell are familiar with suicide drills, I'm sure."

Scott almost groaned. Anyone who knew anything about sports was familiar with suicide drills. They were physical nightmares. They were the worst. His peripherals shifted to Donald. The large black man's frame sunk.

"Allow me to explain them to everyone else," Tacker said. "There are four officers waiting for you, right now, in the training field. They marked off ten yards for every minute you were late. One hundred and thirty yards."

One hundred and thirty yards? Scott had *never* run that before.

"Your instructions are simple. You have one hundred and thirty yards to run. You sprint ten, then you sprint back to the starting line. You sprint twenty, then you sprint back to the starting line. You sprint thirty, then you sprint back to the starting line, until you've returned from the one-hundred-thirty-yard mark. You *do not* stop running. You *do not* pause for a break. If you fall on your face because you can't stand, then you crawl. If anyone stops, everyone starts over. The four officers waiting for you will make sure of that.

"Furthermore, since you have collectively failed to protect humanity tonight, you will each have a chance to save humanity. In the corner of the hangar, you will find ten duffle bags. They have each been filled with the appropriate amount of sand to mimic the weight of your average citizen. During the course of this run, you will each have a 'citizen' strapped to you. The large bags are for the men to carry, and the small bags are for the women. They will be with you from the first step to the last step that you take."

Scott's mouth fell open. One hundred and thirty yards worth of suicide was enough. But carrying someone? That was insane.

Tacker's attention shifted to *Vulture-7*. "This, as I'm sure you remember, is our transport. I noticed tonight it's in need of a cleaning, and so that is exactly what you will do once your run is over. When the last runner finishes, not before, you will all come straight back to the hangar to clean and polish *Vulture-7*, inside and out. You'll find buckets and sponges in the mainte-nance closet. *Only* once this has been completed will the officers dismiss you to your quarters."

No one made a sound, and Tacker drew a remorseless breath.

"Let this show you the price of being careless. It will be worse if you fail a second time." The operatives' gazes sunk. "Now *get* to work."

There were no grumbles of disdain. There were no whispers of remorse. As the operatives shuffled across the hangar to claim their sandbag citizens, not a word was spoken. The bags were strapped on, and they filed toward the field, where they began the sprints.

Tacker watched them for several minutes as he stood in the doorway of the hangar, his hands in his pockets. It was a cool night—the operatives were fortunate for that. He stepped back from the doorway and filed back to the main building of *Rich-mond*. There was nothing more he wished to see.

4

SCOTT'S EYES CRACKED open, and he squinted through the darkness of his room. It was morning. His body ached, and an attempt to lift his head sent shockwaves through his shoulders and stomach. His muscles burned like fire.

He could barely remember the run. Aside from the pain, it felt like a dream. Several people had vomited, but he couldn't remember who. The one thing he knew was that no one had spoken. Not one word. They ran and they polished the Vulture, but not once had anyone opened their mouths.

He glanced at the clock and groaned. It was 1030. He had overslept for church. The congregations were already singing, and he was still in bed due to irresponsibility. Last night was stupid. He knew it was stupid then, but he had gone along with it anyway. Wisdom fell to peer pressure.

He slipped out of bed and stumbled to the sink, where he wet his face with a touch of cold water. He padded to the closet and glanced to the bunk. David was still asleep.

Nicole. He needed to call her. Two full days had passed since he'd heard her voice. He needed her words. Her oxygen. She was probably worried. His stupidity suddenly went beyond the scope of the *Black Cherry*. He'd been stupid for not calling her instead. He needed to call her.

But not now.

Scott tugged up the zipper of his jersey and gave a silent glance around the room. He crept to the door, opened it, and stepped into the hall.

While Scott had trained in *Philadelphia*, Nicole stayed at Michigan to finalize her medical degree. It would take her a little more than a month to finish now, at which point she would begin her residency with a local hospital. If everything panned out, she would then move to *Richmond*, they would get married and live happily ever after. That was the plan.

The hallways were empty, normal for typically lazy Sundays. Scott found a hall directory, where he searched for Tacker's office. He found it and began walking in that direction.

The problem came with the unknown. EDEN was a calling, he believed that with all of his heart. But was it a calling that left room for him and her? It was a question he asked himself often. He loved her, and she loved him. That was enough…wasn't it? Love could overcome anything, and love would win in the end. That was how it worked. That was how it was *supposed* to work. But was that how reality worked? What if she couldn't move to *Richmond*? What if it took her longer to finish school? What if one of them gave up? The answers were in the Hands of God. It still failed to bring him comfort.

It was only a matter of minutes until he stood before Tacker's office. The golden letters—Major John Tacker—glared imposingly at him from the woodwork of the door. What was he doing? This wasn't like football. An apology and a victory next week wouldn't erase a mistake. This was EDEN. This was Earth. An errant throw could be rectified. The loss of lives could not.

His fist reached for the door, where it hovered against the wood. What would he say? That he was sorry? That it wouldn't happen again? That it was a rookie mistake? It was only a drill, but it was a telling one. Had it been real, citizens would have died. Graves would have been dug. They would have failed.

His hand returned to his side. The hallway remained silent, as he continued to stare at the door. Finally, he pivoted his feet away from the door and walked slowly back down the hall. An apology would be useless. Tacker wouldn't want to hear it anyway.

David was still asleep when Scott returned to his room. It was easier to slide out of uniform than to climb in it, so Scott stripped to his boxers and hung his jersey with little disturbance. He brushed back the sheets of his bed and slipped under the covers. His eyes closed, and he fell asleep.

*   *   *

WHEN SCOTT OPENED his eyes again, the lights were still off. The upper bunk was still silent. The room was still idle. He glanced to the clock. Almost 1400.

He remembered finding Tacker's door only hours earlier. He remembered failing to knock on it. It was unlike him to hide from confrontation, even when it meant that he'd be the one issuing the apology. He was a leader—he was always a leader. He was a quarterback for the Michigan Bobcats. He was correct in his earlier judgment—EDEN wasn't like football. But leadership was the same across the board.

He wrenched himself out of bed, stretched, and looked into David's bunk, though David wasn't there. The room had been abandoned. With little else to do, Scott donned his jersey and stepped out into the hall.

He decided not to visit Tacker's door again. Not this time. He wanted to remember the guilt of not following through. He wanted to remember the guilt of not owning up when he knew he should have. He wanted to remember it, so that when the next opportunity to step up presented itself, there would be no hesitation.

For now, he would search for his roommate.

The search did not last long. The nearest point of interest was the soldiers' lounge, and it was there that Scott found David, along with Becan, Henry, and red-haired Natasha. There were about a dozen people in the room, and the four from Charlie Squad sat together at a table in the back corner. Scott weaved through the tables toward them.

David saw him first. "What's up, Scott?"

Scott stifled a yawn. He still felt tired, despite his second round of sleep. "Not much…what are you guys talking about?"

"Last night."

"Oh…where's Jay?"

"At the range," Becan answered. "Left there early this mornin'. Been there ever since, he has."

"He went by himself?"

"He did. Never said much o' nothin', just went."

"Did he take his hat?" asked Scott.

"He did, I'm bloody serious. He walked out o' the room with his hat on his head."

"Amazing." Scott glanced at Natasha. "How long you guys been here?"

"About an hour," she answered. "We've just been talking about other things. God, we must've talked about food for forty-five minutes." She laughed.

"Food?"

"Yeah, we ate together earlier. It was *bad*."

"What'd they have?"

"It's still up for debate."

"Wow," Scott said. "That's bad."

Henry blew out a breath, wincing as he did so. "You hurting as bad as we are?"

Scott nodded. "My legs are killing me. The fact that we screwed up feels just as bad, though."

Natasha smiled. "I don't know about that, this pain is *pretty* bad. I'm tired, too. I woke up completely out of it, I haven't felt this bad since the first month of *Philadelphia*."

Scott laughed.

"What?"

"I loved my first month in *Philadelphia*."

"Ugh. Not me. The early morning inspections killed me."

"We got up real early in the force," David said. "Real early. When I was new it was hard to get used to, but after the first week or so, I loved it. Even on my off days, I'd get up before sunrise. It's just better in the morning."

Natasha smiled. "I guess the Academy was a cakewalk for you then, right?"

"It wasn't a problem for me at all. I was used to it before I got there. As long as there's a pot of coffee ready to go in the morning, I'm wide awake."

Scott smiled. "I love coffee." There was nothing like the aroma of fresh brew to perk the nostrils. It alone could lure him out of bed on even the worst of mornings. "Speaking of which," he said as he stood up to fix himself a cup.

"I don't like it," Becan said. "Breakfast tea, now tha's grand."

"So what do you guys think about last night?" Scott asked.

"I agree with what you said before," David said. "Knowing it was our fault feels worse than being sore. It's especially bad because they preach to us from day one about responsibility. I for one feel like I should have said something. I think that's what was the worst for me, that I just went along with it. Frequenting bars and pubs isn't even my lifestyle."

Becan gave him a penetrating stare. "Yeah, but do yeh *really* think you'd have said somethin' even if yeh did realize it was wrong last night? I know for me, I wouldn't have. Everyone was havin' a grand time, an' it was our first nigh' together. I think it was bollocks tha' he gave a test at all. I mean…tha' was day-bloody-one. Let us live a little bit, righ'?"

"I have no problem with him doing it," David said. "We got careless, and we got what we deserved. What if it were real? If it were real, the people who died would've been on *us*."

"I think they should let people have the first nigh' to themselves," Becan answered. "Go out, get steamed, get it out o' your system."

"As an operative you can't do that, though. We're on call twenty-four, seve—"

"Righ', righ', I know tha'. I know yeh got a point, I know it was a mistake. I just…veck, I wish we wouldn't have fell for it. Tha's so clichéd, drillin' us on our first nigh'."

David looked across the table. "What do you think, Henry? You're quiet over there."

Henry's mouth fell open. "Uhh…I don't know. I just…for me… I guess it was kind of a reality check."

"What do you mean?"

"It's just when the comms started going off it hit me. When it was all over, I wasn't even worried about what Tacker was saying. That didn't matter to me much. It's just when the comms started going off, that's what I remember. I remember thinking, oh veck, I really have to do it now."

"You mean fight?"

"Well…yeah."

"And that got you scared?"

"Of course. I remember the first thing that popped in my head was I could die tonight."

Becan said kindly enough, "Henry, tha's a *baaad* way to go abou' lookin' at it. Yeh can't be thinkin' like tha'…I mean, yeh start thinkin' like tha' in the middle of a war, an'—"

"Yeah, I know that. That's what made me start to really think about this."

David shook his head. "Wait…you mean think about EDEN?"

"Yeah. I hope this was the right thing for me to do."

"Henry…bud, you shouldn't be thinking about that *now*. That's something you think about before you sign the paper to come on."

"I know, I know."

"Wha' made yeh decide to sign on then?" Becan asked.

Henry reflected. "It's like…I just wanted to do it. I don't want to just do nothing. Everyone has their thing, but nobody likes a talk-seller. So I think it was j—"

David's gaze bore into Henry's eyes. "Henry, did you do this to be liked?"

"No! I didn't do it to be liked. That's not it exactly, but I can see how you got there. I hated being a talk-seller. It's probably one of the worst jobs on the planet, because everybody hates you. Everywhere I'd go, for any job I applied for, I was always 'the talk-seller'. It's like a tag for life. The only place I could go where it didn't matter was here." He sighed. "Here nobody cares what you did. You're alive and you can shoot, that's all that matters. Here, I'm not a talk-seller. I'm a soldier defending Earth."

"But wha' if yeh die or get blown to bits? Is tha' better than talk-sellin'?"

"Yeah," Henry answered. "I thought it was, anyway. That's why I don't know now. It's like…that's how I came into it. I thought I wouldn't care. Then last night came and it was like *bam*, this is real."

David folded his arms. "Well, Henry, you've got to ask yourself now…do you think you're ready for EDEN?"

"I want to be," he answered. "I'm trying."

Silence fell over the table. David leaned back and broke it. "All right. I guess that's the best you can do. You got good marks at the Academy, anyway."

Becan glanced between them. "Well, *I* don't want to be blown to bits! Someone's got to keep the family genes alive!"

"And that's you?" Natasha asked, a touch provocatively.

"It is. It has to be, I'm the only son me ma had."

"Well you better find someone to help with that."

Scott and David exchanged a sidelong look.

"Yeh offerin'?"

She shrugged and smiled enigmatically.

Henry coughed. "Anyway, I think I can do good in EDEN. All I need is a chance to prove myself."

Henry was cut off as Natasha pushed up from her chair.

"You're leaving?" asked Scott.

"Yes…" she said as her gaze lingered on Becan. "I feel like going for a swim."

"Yeh want some company?" Becan asked.

Natasha curved up the corners of her lips. "Sure."

"Class." Becan rose from his chair and glanced at the other three men. "I'll talk to yis later." Before anyone could respond, the couple slipped through the tables and out of the room.

Scott watched as they disappeared out of view. "Is what just happened what I think just happened?"

"Amazing," laughed David.

"Just like that, huh?"

Henry shook his head. "Why can't I get women like that?"

"You don't want women like that," David said.

"So do you think they're…?"

"What, you really think they're *swimming*?"

"Man."

David shifted his gaze to Scott. "Speaking of people getting up and leaving, I've been meaning to ask you. Where'd you go this morning?"

Scott's eyes widened. "You heard me leave the room?"

"No, but I woke up and asked you what time it was, and you weren't there."

"Oh. I just went for a walk. It wasn't anything important."

"Where'd you go?"

Scott squirmed uncomfortably in his chair. "Just around, nowhere in particular. I needed to think."

"All right. I was just curious."

Silence fell over the table, and this time Henry eventually broke it. "I think I'm gonna head back to my room."

"You all right?" David asked.

"Yeah, I'm just tired."

"I think we're all pretty whipped up today," Scott said.

Henry stood up. "I'll talk to you guys later on."

"Later, bud."

"Take it easy, man."

The two men watched as Henry slipped out of the room. As soon as he was gone, David sighed. "I feel bad for him. He shouldn't be here."

Scott chuckled as he stared into his now-empty coffee cup. "You know who I feel bad for? Every person who leaves the table, because as soon as they're gone we start talking about them."

"Yeah. That's why I'm leaving with *you*. I'm afraid you'll talk about me once I'm gone."

"Right, 'cause you know, I love to have conversations with myself."

"Right," David answered.

"I know what you mean, though. I thought about death before I signed up—I think everyone does. That's when you've got to come to grips with reality, not after you've gone through *Philadelphia*."

"Yeah," David said. "Part of it's his fault, because if he jumped into this, it's on his shoulders…but at the same time, I know why he's doing it. I hate talk-sellers, too."

Scott frowned. "Me too."

"At least we're both jerks."

"Yeah, we can find comfort in that," Scott said as he rose from his chair. "I'm starving, man. I'm going to go grab a bite to eat if the cafeteria's still open."

"It might not be now. Go and check, I suppose."

"All right. I'll see you later."

"I'll be in the room."

The two men nodded to each other, stepped out of the soldiers' lounge, and went their separate ways.

The rest of the day was spent in routine. That evening, the members of Charlie Squad met and further discussed the day's events, from bad food to Tacker's discipline. When night came, they filed into their beds and slept.

This was the standard for the next few days, as group workouts and combat sessions took their place among morning activities. Operative life at *Richmond* took shape. Tacker never again mentioned the event that came to be known as the "Cincinnati Failure," nor were the operatives late for any unit meetings. That lesson was learned.

The Falcon was ready for flight.

5

THE COMMS SOUNDED at a quarter to two. Scott bolted upright in his bunk, his eyes squinting in the darkness. What in the world? *Beep! Beep! Beep!* In the upper bunk, David stirred beneath the covers. The rest of the room was silent. *Beep! Beep! Beep!* It repeated for several seconds, before Scott's eyes shot open wide. The comms. He leapt out of bed and scrambled toward the closet.

David blinked and propped up. His mouth hung open. "Wha—?"

"The comms! The comms are going off!"

David repeated dazedly, "The comms are going off!" He dove to the floor and lunged toward the closet. "We've got three minutes!"

Scott contorted his legs into his jersey. "Two and a half!" If that much. He ripped his hands through the sleeves, tugged up the zipper, and grabbed his comm. "Let's go!"

They collided into Becan and Jayden as soon as they left the room. "Time?" Becan hollered as they bolted down the hallway.

Scott flapped his watch into view. "Minute and a half!" Outside, Falcon Platoon's operatives flat-tracked toward the hangar.

Technicians hurried back and forth across the hangar space. *Vulture-7* glimmered in the night, the ground beneath it illuminated by the soft red and gold glow of running lights on its underbelly. Tacker waited next to it.

"Everyone in the transport!" he said. "Armor up!"

The operatives acknowledged with a unified *Yes sir!* and dashed up the Vulture's ramp. They opened their lockers, where their EDEN combat armor awaited. Lightweight, flexible, and technologically superior to anything else on the planet, it was the international symbol of the EDEN operative. Its blue and silver finish dulled everything around it. It personified pride.

The operatives fastened their helmets and lowered the sky-blue visors over their eyes and noses. Tacker ordered the pilot to lift. The pilot acknowledged, and *Vulture-7* ascended over the airstrip.

Tacker loaded his S-27 sniper rifle. "Listen up, everyone! This is a hot drop! Approximately one hour ago, two Bakma Carriers entered Earth's atmosphere over Chicago with a full fighter escort. They dropped in the middle of the city, and all citizens have been ordered underground. Expect *heavy* resistance!"

The operatives continued to gear themselves.

"Hawk, Condor, Cougar, and Gryphon units were initially dispatched, but they got hit hard. We've been called in to provide support. Medics, *be prepared* for extensive casualties."

Sasha and Natasha exchanged a glance.

"If you have *any* reason to suspect that Noboats are in the air, alert someone *immediately*! Just because you can't see them doesn't mean they aren't there. If any materialize, take cover and hunker down. Also, Chicago *is* out of power, so make sure your TCVs are on!"

The operatives acknowledged and activated the True-Color-Vision in their visors. The world took on an ethereal hue.

Tacker swung toward the cockpit. "ETA?"

"Five minutes, sir."

"Five minutes, people! Clear your minds, get focused, and get ready to land!"

HOPE FOR A SMOOTH descent vanished as soon as *Vulture-7* entered Chicago. Ground plasma fire blasted against its metal hull. Behind it, a small fleet of Vultures followed.

"Touchdown in thirty! We're landing behind a barricade on

South Michigan, so we should be able to exit without resistance. Stick together—I'm not chasing anyone down!"

The stomach-turning rush of descent kicked in, and the Vulture clumped to a landing. The rear door immediately burst open.

"Everyone out! Let's go!"

The remnants of a building lay strewn across South Michigan Avenue—the barricade. Gunfire erupted on the other side. Burnt asphalt polluted the air. Injured EDEN operatives littered the landing zone, and rows of soldiers fired from atop the rubble. Above, a squadron of Vindicator fighters streaked by.

Tacker shot a glare to Sasha and Natasha. "Get to the wounded!" he shouted. The women disappeared into the throng of injured. Tacker continued up the mound. "There's a company of Bakma en route to the barricade as we speak. Be prepared for heavy resistance."

Scott and Becan reached the summit of the barricade first, and their eyes immediately widened. Fire illuminated the cratered streets of South Michigan. Lightning-white plasma bolts streaked across the ground. Human shrieks mixed with the gunfire. It was a war zone. Bakma foot soldiers amassed in the streets. Even from a distance, their unmistakable crimson-purple skin identified them, and their nauseous black and brown body armor seemed to perfectly define their role.

Mingled with them were the brutish beasts themselves. The canrassis. The war-beasts of the Bakma. They tromped ahead like miniature fur-covered tyrannosaurs, as Bakma riders sat firm atop them and blasted the barricade with their mounted plasma cannons. The canrassis' soulless spider-eyes roamed the battle-field above their grotesquely excessive jaws.

Scott dropped to a knee and propped his assault rifle, but for a moment held fire. It was surreal. It couldn't be real. "Oh my God," he breathed.

Becan ducked to avoid plasma fire and then he, too, propped his assault rifle. "There's no way in hell we're goin' to hold this off!"

David and Henry hit the summit next. Donald, harnessed with a mini-gun, followed.

Beside them, Jayden glared through his sniper scope. *Pop!* He cracked the bolt-action. *Pop!*

David looked toward the Texan and then at Henry. "You okay over there?"

"Yeah! I'm good!" Henry yelled, stumbling to avoid plasma.

A white flash erupted several yards past Scott, and he felt the wave of impact wash over him. Someone had been hit. He whipped around to see Zigler tumble backward down the barricade. Zigler's faceplate smoldered and he hollered.

Scott said to Becan, "I'll be right back!" He shouldered his E-35 and rushed toward the fallen operative. "Hold still, I got you!"

Zigler struggled, and the scorched helmet was removed. A bloodied bruise bulged in the center of Zigler's forehead.

Scott stifled a gag. "You okay?"

"Yeah, watch out!" Zigler brushed past Scott, picked up his assault rifle, and charged up the hill again. Scott observed the soldier for a moment, then returned to Becan.

"He all righ'?"

"No."

Becan said nothing and continued to fire.

"Major!" Lilan said as he approached Tacker. "They've confirmed. There *are* reinforcements coming in from farther down the road. We've gotta keep holding them."

Tacker nodded.

"You got something else to worry about, though. There's a team from Cougar pinned down a couple blocks southwest of here near the Van Buren, South Wabash intersection. According to comm chatter, they're under direct assault from at least a dozen hostiles and they're too wounded to put up any real resistance."

Tacker crossed his arms. "And we're getting them out."

"Not you," Lilan said, "you're staying here. Henrick is going after them. He's got two guys from Delta ready to go, but I want you to give him a few more. Small team, just an in-and-out operation. They should be able to just follow the shuttle-rail."

Tacker drew a breath. "With all due respect sir, I wouldn't trust Henrick to walk my dog, let alone lead a rescue party."

"That's why I want some of your guys with him," Lilan answered. "I would send you, but I want you here. I don't want to risk you getting dropped on some random errand and leaving me with a platoon full of rookies. If I lose you, they're not gonna give me another major."

"Understood, sir." Tacker examined his operatives and made quick decisions. "Remington, McCrae, Jurgen, Timmons, get over here now!"

"Four's too many, send three."

Tacker nodded as Lilan stepped away.

"Correction," Tacker said. "Jurgen, you stay put, the rest of you come!" Scott, Becan, and Jayden arrived a moment later, as did Henrick and his operatives, two privates named Donner and Wilkins. Tacker dropped to a knee.

"Here's the deal, gentlemen. We've got some guys from Cougar Platoon pinned down several blocks southwest. Some are wounded. The streets you're looking for are Van Buren and South Wabash. There should be a shuttle-rail along that route. Track their comm signals and get them some help. Search and rescue, not rocket science. Who's the medic here?"

The operatives exchanged looks, though none spoke. Tacker's eyes widened, and he glared at Henrick.

"Did Lilan explain this to you before?"

"Yes sir, I—"

"And you didn't take a trashing *medic*? Veck!" He cut off Henrick's reply. "Rhodes, get over here." Sasha arrived a moment later, and Tacker explained the situation again.

"If anything happens to Lieutenant Henrick, Remington will assume command. Understand, private?"

Scott was momentarily taken aback. "Yes sir." He was the executive officer? As much as it didn't make sense, Scott knew it was Tacker's only option. Everyone in Falcon was an alpha private. One of them *had* to do it.

"Good. Go."

THE SMALL BAND of operatives moved immediately. Henrick led them to the far right of the mound, where he signaled them to lower themselves to a knee. "We're using the alleys to get to South Wabash," he said, "but we have to cross the barricade to get to the first one. From there, we'll start tracking them. We'll all cross at once so we don't give the Bakma a sequence to shoot at. What are your names?"

After each had responded, Henrick continued, "All right, count will be on three, then we run. One…two…three!"

Henrick launched over the barricade and skidded into the nearest alleyway. The others did the same. No plasma bolts followed them, and they soon found themselves alone and out of sight.

At the far end of the alley stood a brick partition with a rusty ladder. Henrick trotted toward it. "According to Intelligence, a building collapsed earlier about a hundred yards that way." He pointed toward the brick partition. "We'll have to find a way around it once we get to it." He gripped the ladder. "Wilkins, come up after me! Then Donner, uhh…you," he pointed to Becan. "Then you two!" Jayden and Sasha. "Remington goes last!"

As Henrick and Wilkins climbed, Jayden leaned toward Becan. "Should he be shoutin' like that?"

"Probably not."

Each pair that followed Henrick and Wilkins maintained distance between the pair in front and behind them, and eventually, all had crossed over the brick partition. They found themselves bunched together on the other side of the alley. It was perfectly symmetrical with the alley from which they had come, though it exited out into South Wabash—the main avenue they were seeking. Henrick and Wilkins strode toward the mouth of the alley as the cluster of other operatives followed close behind.

Rubble walled off South Wabash, as it did South Michigan.

Unlike South Michigan, however, this wall was impassable. A segment of the shuttle-rail was down as well.

Henrick emerged from the alley first. "This is South Wabash— Van Buren should be a little south of here! We've got to find a way to cross this mound! Come on!" he bellowed.

Becan crept beside Scott and leaned close to him. "Does this nuggerknocker know wha' a comm is?"

Scott hesitated. His thoughts were the same. This guy was announcing their presence as if they just stepped into a party. "Maybe there's no Bakma here."

"If there *are* anny, they sure as bloody hell know where *we* are."

Jayden caught up with them. "This guy's a moron."

Moron or not, he was in charge. "Just follow his orders," Scott said.

Henrick stood in the center of the street and propped his hands on his hips. "We're going to have to get *over* this rubble!"

Becan grunted. "Righ', wha' are we goin' to do, climb?"

"Yes! What looks like the easiest route up?"

"I was bein' sarcastic!"

"Sir," Scott said, "may I suggest an alternative route?" There was a building across the street that looked accessible. They could probably move through it and come out on the other side of the rubble.

Henrick's eyes narrowed. "Do you *see* an alternative route anywhere, private?"

Scott blinked. Was this guy serious? "Well, uhh…yes…"

"We are *climbing*, Remington! If you're scared of heights, get over it quick!"

HUMAN AND BAKMA bodies littered South Michigan as Charlie Squad continued to engage. Several additional platoons joined alongside them, and the two opposing forces stalemated.
Above the battle, a dogfight between Vindicators and Couriers— Bakma fighter planes—broke loose.

BACK ON SOUTH WABASH, the search for a path up the rubble continued. Each attempt to climb met failure, and the atmosphere of impatience grew palpable.

"Sir," Scott said to Henrick as he stepped beside Wilkins, "I *strongly* suggest an alternative route."

In that instant, two sounds simultaneously erupted. The first was Henrick as he whipped around and shouted, "*Remington!*"

The second was plasma fire. Flashes of white streaked toward them, and Henrick, Scott, and Donner were jolted violently. A bolt struck Wilkins in the chest, and he was thrown against the rubble, where three more blasts punctured his torso. Scott ducked back as blood splattered across his armor, and he bolted to the far alley behind Henrick and Donner. The gig was up. The other operatives parted in the opposite direction.

Henrick screamed as a plasma bolt ripped through his leg, and he stumbled several yards from cover. Donner grabbed him and dragged him into the alley.

From across South Wabash, Becan howled in anger. "I'm up to ninety!"

Henrick moaned as Donner secured him against a wall. Scott skidded into the alley. "Can anyone over there see where that came from?" he asked through the comm.

Becan surveyed the corner of his alley, and a volley of plasma blasted his way. He ducked back. "Best I could see they're on your side, abou' thirty or so meters down! They're in the next alley down—it's on your end!"

"How many?"

"No clue!"

Scott looked over at Henrick. The lieutenant's armor had been penetrated, and his leg was torn open. He was out of the fight. Scott was in command.

Only days before, the guilt of not knocking on Tacker's door had consumed him. It had consumed him enough to make him swear to himself that he would never hesitate again. He wanted to remember the guilt for that reason. And now, he was the one.

There was no hesitation.

"Everyone," he said, "here's what I want you to do. Sasha, inform Major Tacker of our status, and tell him I've assumed command."

"Yes sir!"

"Becan, engage them from right where you are. Donner, you'll do the same from over here. Distract them!"

Scott continued calling out orders—with assurance, considering the circumstances.

"Jay, while they're doing that, I want you to break into that building right in front of you and get as high as you can on the other side. Find a window and get in a comfortable sniping position! Comm me when you've done that."

"Got it!" Jayden answered.

Enough playing around. "I'm going to mirror you on this end through this building! When we're both in position on the other side, we'll hit them at the same time from opposite directions."

"Gotcha!"

Scott drew a deep breath. "Let's go!"

Becan and Donner engaged the Bakma as Scott and Jayden traversed their respective buildings, Jayden up a fire escape and Scott through a steel emergency door. Once Scott had crossed through the building, he found a similar steel door. The Bakma shouted to one another and reloaded their plasma rifles beyond it. Scott pressed against the door and waited.

Jayden's voice broke through the comm. "In position," he said in a low voice. "I'm layin' down on the roof, I can see 'em good. There're four of 'em."

"Can they see you?" Scott whispered.

"Not right now."

"How many can you take?"

Jayden paused. "I think I can get two before they realize I'm here."

Two. Good enough. "Okay…take out as many as you can and tell me when they find you out. Go."

"Goin'."

Jayden squinted through the scope of his sniper rifle as the Bakma exchanged fire with Becan and Donner. He eased the crosshairs over the nearest Bakma's forehead. His finger flexed, and the gun barrel exploded with a flash of orange. Blood sprayed from behind the Bakma's head.

"One down."

He cracked the bolt-action and slid the crosshairs over a second target. His finger flexed.

"Two down. They're onto me." The Texan rolled back.

Scott closed his eyes, took a breath, and slammed his body against the steel door. The door gave way, and momentum carried him into the alley, where the two battle-scarred Bakma whipped around to face him. His finger took control, and he yanked the trigger. The two Bakma toppled backward before they could fire a shot.

For several seconds, Scott stood paralyzed. Gun exhaust filtered the air. The Bakma lay crumpled, face-up on the concrete. He stared at their corpses. Assault rifle shouldered, he drew nearer to them.

He had never seen Bakma at such close range before. Their cheekbones bulged from the crimson-purple leather of their skin. Their eyes—black eyes without visible pupils—stared lifelessly skyward. Alien insignias covered their breastplates in a grotesque gold, and their plasma rifles lay strewn beside their talonless claws. Beneath them oozed a puddle of dark red blood. Scott propped his hands against his knees and gazed at them. It was still surreal. Finally, he breathed into his comm. "Targets down."

TACKER DUCKED TO AVOID plasma fire as he stumbled toward David. "Jurgen!"

David held his fire. "Yes sir?"

"We have reinforcements coming right now," Tacker said. "They'll be here in about ten minutes! Once they arrive, we're going to press over the mound and into the avenue. Be ready!" Tacker glanced at Henry. "How is he doing?" he whispered.

David hesitated. "Very good, sir."

"You take care of him." Tacker half-frowned.

David eyed Henry, who continued to open fire. He replied to Tacker. "Yes sir."

Tacker nodded and continued across the barricade.

SHOULDERING HIS ASSAULT rifle, Scott approached the now-clustered team. "Attention, everybody. Henrick is incapacitated, therefore I am assuming command. If something should happen to me, leadership falls to Becan." The Irishman looked impassive. "Get Wilkins' body and put it in the alley for now. If anyone is low on ammunition, take his. He won't be needing it," he added needlessly.

Becan raised a brow. "An' Henrick?"

Scott appraised the lieutenant. "Sir, can you still walk?"

Henrick stifled a groan. "I don't think so."

He turned to Donner. "Get him to his feet and help him along. We can't bog down here."

Scott inspected the building alongside the far alley, where he noticed for the first time that it was the same building that caused the rubble. Though the top half of it had been blown across the street, the lower half remained intact. It must have been a strafe attack on the two streets, but the bottom of this building still looked passable. "Come on," he said, "we're crossing through here."

Becan eyed Henrick. "We should've been doin' tha' all along," he said brashly.

Henrick tried to defend himself. "For all I knew, the foundation was damaged!"

Scott didn't bother with a response. He slung his assault rifle over his shoulder, jerked open a side door, and stepped inside.

Dust hung in the building, but it was passable. The group exercised caution as they trekked from office to empty office until they emerged clean on the other side. South Wabash came into full view. Gunfire echoed ahead, and Scott crept up the alley to the edge of the street. The scene was clear now. The pinned operatives from Cougar Platoon took cover behind two wartorn cars at the edge of a squat structure. Farther down the street, plasma bolts shot in their direction.

Scott's eyes narrowed. "We're not going to get them in the open—that plasma fire is too heavy. We're taking the inside route again. We'll keep moving through buildings until we get to them." He turned to Sasha. "Take Henrick. I want Donner free."

The plan was set into motion, and the team traversed from one building to the next. When they reached the alley along the squat structure's edge, Scott searched for a door. He found one, but it was locked. He launched two solid kicks against the doorway, and it burst open.

"Find a room in here that can act as a temporary hospital," he said to Sasha as he slipped inside. "We have to assume they have heavily wounded—they wouldn't still be here if they didn't. Jay," he said, "get as high as you can again, find a window, and work on those Bakma. You're on your own, just go do your thing."

Jayden acknowledged and weaved up a stairwell. Scott led the rest of the team ahead. The structure was undamaged, though projectile and plasma fire erupted from beyond the walls. Muffled shouts echoed outside. They were close. When Scott stepped into the large room that formed the building's corner, it became clear why the operatives were still outside.

One window. Only one window offered access to the inside. The corner lacked anything else. Scott pressed against the edge of the window and peered outside. He could see the pinned soldiers. Three wounded were among them, sprawled behind the cover vehicles. There was no way they'd last there. Plasma flashed toward the window, and Scott ducked back inside.

Three wounded. One window. The vehicles were on the verge of destruction. Scott knelt as the other operatives watched him. His mind raced. The vehicles. If only the vehicles were closer to the window. Then they'd have enough cover to ferry the wounded inside.

He blinked hard. It hit him.

Scott leapt to a stand and returned to the window. "Guys," he shouted to the pinned unit, "sit tight for one minute! We're on our way!"

Scott swiveled to face his team. "Who can hotwire a car?"

Donner raised his hand.

"Becan, go with Donner outside and see if you can't find another vehicle. The bigger the better."

Becan rubbed his neck. "I saw a big ol' van across the street on the way here."

A van. Perfect. "That'll work. Go get it. Give Donner as much cover as you can. You're going to park that van right in front of the window. We're extending the wall of cars."

"Righ'," Becan said as he and Donner retreated back through the building.

"Hurry!" Scott urged. "We don't have much time!"

Jayden knelt down beside a fifth-floor window and leaned against the wall. He was right above the pinned operatives—perfect position. He snaked his hand toward the window, unlocked it, and slid it upward just enough to leave a slit for his sniper rifle. Maneuvering the rifle into position and slipping the barrel outside, he squinted through the scope. The Bakma suppressors were, as before, clustered in an alley.

"I think there's 'bout five or six," he said through the comm. He eased the crosshairs over the corner of the alley and waited for one of the suppressors to lean around. It happened right away. There was a puff of red, and Jayden worked the bolt-action. "One down."

Becan and Donner bolted across the street. "Keep at 'em, Jay," Becan said. "We need time to hotwire."

"I'm on 'em." The bolt-action cracked through the comm. "Two down."

The Bakma suppressors halted their assault as a third fell. Becan and Donner skidded to the van. Unlocked. Becan slid into the passenger seat as Donner set to hotwire. Several twisted wires later, the van roared to life.

Becan jerked his door closed. "Go, go!"

Donner slammed the van into reverse and manhandled the wheel toward the wall of cars. Only seconds later, it screeched to a stop in front of the window. Becan leapt from the passenger door as Donner climbed over the center console. The wall of cars was extended. The window was covered.

Time to move. "Let's go!" Scott said. He scampered out of the window, rolled to the ground behind the van, and dashed to the pinned operatives behind the wall of cars.

A goateed man awaited him. His armor was charred with scorch marks. "Delta Trooper Grammar of Cougar Platoon, sir! We have three wounded, two good to go. Everyone else is dead."

Scott's ears perked. "What's the condition of the wounded?"

"They're pretty bad off."

"Can they be moved through the window?"

Grammar glanced to the window. "Better than keeping them here, sir."

Scott pivoted around. "Becan, give us a hand!"

As Scott, Becan, and Grammar transferred the wounded through the window, Donner, Jayden, and another unidentified man behind the cars held off the Bakma attack. After several minutes of suppression fire and struggle, the transfer was accomplished. Sasha wasted no time in attending to the wounded as soon as they were secure. Becan, Donner, and Jayden continued to engage the Bakma as Scott, Grammar, and the unidentified man slipped inside.

Grammar caught his breath and turned to Scott. "Our team, sir." He motioned toward a stocky individual—the only other uninjured man. "Gamma Private Vause, our techie, and the three wounded are Commander José Diaz, Lieutenant Bowen, and Gamma Private Parsons. Commander Diaz took command when our captain fell. We're all that's left of a team of twenty, sir."

Scott lifted a brow. *Sir?* He shifted his peripherals down to his armor, where dried blood—Wilkins' blood—crusted over his name badge. His insignia was completely hidden. Grammar didn't know he was an alpha. A moment of decision ticked in Scott's mind, and he answered. "Scott Remington. What were you doing here?"

Becan's voice interrupted from outside. "We could use a bloody hand ou' here!"

Scott hurried to the window and motioned for Grammar to follow. "How many down?"

Becan laughed. "None!"

"What about you, Jay?"

The Texan's voice crackled through the comm. "I been workin' on the ones farther up the road, I killed one and hit another, but there're still more. I think there's two or three still here but they know I'm here now. S'about five or six more down the road."

"Are the only Bakma *here* the ones in the alley?"

"Yep."

Scott climbed out the window and ducked behind the van. He glanced to Grammar. "I guess if you had any grenades left you'd be using them?"

"Yes sir. We used them earlier, you should've seen how many Bakma there were before—way more than we thought there'd be. We think they must've used up all of theirs, too."

Scott unfastened a grenade from his belt and placed his finger on the activation button. "Give me three seconds of cover! Fire everything!"

Becan, Donner, and Grammar opened fire. Above, Jayden did the same.

Scott pressed the button, whipped up from behind the van, and flung the small orb toward the alley. The operatives ducked down as soon as he released it. The grenade ricocheted off the wall of the alley and bounced out of view. An explosion boomed.

Scott leapt over the hood of the van. "Charge the alley! Come on!"

Jayden's voice sounded through the comm. "I got 'em pinned down the street—go, go, go!"

They reached the alley several seconds later. The smell of open flesh hung in the air as they penetrated the smoke, assault rifles poised to fire on any survivors. Remains were scattered across the ground, and entrails dripped from the brick walls. The ground beneath them turned moist.

"They're movin'!" yelled Jayden through the comm. "The Bakma down the street are movin'!" His sniper rifle exploded through the line.

They were trying to escape. Scott charged into the street. There were three Bakma in full retreat. "Stop them!" As soon as he, Becan, Donner, and Grammar were in the open, they knelt, propped their assault rifles, and attacked the triggers. The Bakma toppled over. Scott leapt to his feet and bolted toward the alley where they'd come from. The other three men followed close behind. They charged around the corner and trained their assault rifles, but without need. There were no Bakma left. Their mission was accomplished.

As reinforcements arrived from *Richmond*, the battle on South Michigan turned in EDEN's favor. Several colonels—Lilan included—led a full assault against the Bakma foot soldiers. They charged into the Bakma stronghold, where an intense melee began.

David and Henry were in the onslaught and adopted a back-to-back protection system. With David's on-the-spot tactical commands, the two men formed an effective duo.

Nonetheless, the battle was far from over.

Once the Bakma corpses were collected, Scott and his team returned to the squat structure. Jayden remained on his fifth-floor perch, where he kept watch over South Wabash.

As soon as Scott re-entered the makeshift hospital, he stepped over to Sasha. "How are they?"

"Diaz is stable," she answered. "Parsons should be shortly. Bowen will be okay, too. They should all be okay, provided they aren't here much longer. They *will* need more medical treatment, though. More than I can give them."

Scott turned to Grammar. "Why were you out here?"

Grammar saddled his hands on his hips. "We were initially sent to disable the southernmost Carrier," he motioned down the avenue, "but we met far heavier resistance than Command expected. We had a cover unit, but they got ambushed before we were even set up to go. The five of us are the last alive out of a strike force of twenty."

Scott's brow furrowed. "You were sent to disable one of the Bakma Carriers?"

"Yes sir. Command wanted salvage, and that was the best way to get it. It also sends a strong message to the Bakma when their ships don't come back home."

A thought materialized in Scott's mind. "How far is the Carrier from here?"

"Not that far. Stay down Wabash, take a right on Harrison,

then take a left down Clark. The Carrier's in the Clark, Polk inter-section. That was the plan."

Scott looked away for a moment, still thinking. Five men. That's what he had. Was that crazy? His gaze returned to Grammar. "Is it still possible to disable it?"

Grammar's jaw sagged, and he cleared his throat. "Uhh...yes sir, we still have Vause, he was the assigned technician for this thing..." Becan eyed Scott from the corner of the room.

Scott turned and stepped out of the room, where he adjusted the frequency of his comm. "Major?"

There was a moment of static before Tacker's voice emerged on the other side. "Tacker here. You get them out yet?"

"Yes sir, area cleared."

"Great."

Here it went. "Sir, with Command's permission, I'd like to complete Cougar Platoon's objective. They were ordered to dis-able the southern Bakma Carrier."

Silence hung over the line before Tacker replied. "Are you joking?"

"No sir, I think we have a chance. The Bakma here have been isolated and things are quiet. I think we might be able to get close enough in to make a real run at this thing."

"How many of you are there?"

"Five able to go."

"You want to assault a Bakma Carrier with *five* operatives?"

Was it crazy? No...it couldn't be crazy. "Yes sir. It's the last thing they'd expect."

"You got *that* right," Tacker said. "Give me a minute to talk to the colonel."

LILAN WAS IN THE midst of the offensive when Tacker's voice burst through his headset.

"Colonel, I have Remington on the line. He wants to make a run at the southern Carrier. You know anything about that?"

Lilan ducked behind a barricade. Around him, the orange flashes of assault rifles blazed as gunfire saturated the air. "Yes," Lilan answered, "Command wanted salvage, that's what Cougar was doing befo—...Remington wants to do *what?*"

"He wants to assault the Carrier."

"Did he get shot in the head?"

"I have no idea, sir."

Lilan reloaded his assault rifle and opened fire into the Bakma foot soldiers. "How many men does he have?"

"He says five. I shouldn't even be asking you this."

"What the hell? He wants to assault the Carrier with *five* men?"

"That's what he says, s—"

"I'm talking to him." The channel closed, and Lilan adjusted to message Scott. "This is Lilan. Are you requesting permission to *assault* the Carrier?"

There was a moment of silence before Scott answered. "Yes sir. Things are calm on this end, I think we can catch them off guard."

"Do you have *any* idea what you're asking?"

"Yes sir. I wouldn't ask if I didn't think we could do it."

Lilan grew quiet. The request was suicide, but there was something unexpected in Scott's tone. It was confidence. Even in addressing the colonel, it was total confidence. It was the tone of a veteran.

EDEN loved salvage. They grew giddy at the mention of it. Five men would never survive a Carrier assault, but they didn't have to. None of them had to. If a technician survived long enough to reach the engine room and shut it down, the mission was accomplished. Their survival was unnecessary. But was a captured Carrier worth the lives of five men? Could five men even *reach* the engine room?

"Do you really think you can do this?"

"Positive, sir."

Lilan barely hesitated. "Do it."

"Thank you, sir!"

"Just get to the engine room. Make that your priority, then do what you can."

"Yes sir."

"Good luck," Lilan said before he closed the channel. He stared down at the assault rifle in his hands. He had just given five men permission to kill themselves.

Scott returned to the hospital. "Listen up, everyone! The original objective for this mission was to disable the southern Carrier." Becan stood from his perch in the corner. "We are going to take it upon ourselves to complete this objective."

Vause's jaw hung loose. He was speechless.

"Becan, Donner, Grammar, Vause, and myself are going to infiltrate the Carrier and deactivate its main drive. Henrick's going to assist Sasha with the wounded. Jay, stay where you are and protect the hospital. Just do your thing."

"Yessir!" Jayden said.

Scott slammed a fresh clip into his assault rifle. "Let's have some fun."

6

SOUTH WABASH OFFERED no resistance. Scott led the five-man team right on Harrison, as Grammar had instructed, and they worked their way toward Clark Street. One turn separated them from the Bakma Carrier. Combat echoed far away in the direction of Grant Park, though it was too distant to affect them.

They stopped next to a brick-red facility at the corner of Harrison and Clark. Scott pulled a spot mirror from his belt and slipped it past the corner. "Vause, do you know the way to the engine room?" Scott tilted his head to angle Clark Street into the reflection.

"Yes sir."

The Carrier took up the entire Clark/Polk intersection. Its mammoth bay doors were wide open, and a metal ramp led into it. The Bakma defenders came into view.

"All right," Scott said, "I count at least a dozen Bakma, possibly more. Here's what we're going to do." He turned and spoke to Donner. "I want you to go back and get that van we used earlier, drive it here to the corner and stop. Go, now. Run." Donner left, and Scott addressed Vause next. "Bring up the Carrier's schematics."

Vause handed Scott a small device with an embedded monitor. Scott's brow furrowed as he examined the display.

The bay was square and deep. It ended against a wall with a single central corridor. It was almost laughably simple. "Does this hall lead to the engine room?"

"Yes sir, that's where we were going to go. It's *the* big main corridor—it leads to everything."

"How wide is it?"

"About two meters…"

Two meters. That was wide enough. "We get in the van, and Donner drives us up the ramp. Even if they shoot the van, we should be okay. It's a lot safer than storming it by foot."

Grammar's eyes widened. "Are you telling me he's *driving* us to the corridor? *Into* the Carrier, *to* the corridor?"

"Right," Scott answered. "We don't have to drive *down* the corridor—all he has to do is get us to it."

"Righ', I see a problem," said Becan. "How are we goin' to get from the van to the corridor withou' gettin' reefed?"

"Because Donner's going to drive the van *backward*," said Scott confidently.

"And *we* stay in the back of the van! He'll drive it righ' to the corridor, against it even, an' all we do is open the back door an' there we are!"

"Exactly," Scott said. "It'll happen so fast, they won't have time to think."

Grammar laughed and shook his head. "That's genius."

"Get on the comm and explain the plan to Donner," Scott said. "Make sure he understands *exactly* what he has to do."

Grammar nodded and knelt to relay the plan.

THE OFFENSIVE ON South Michigan continued, as the arrival of EDEN reinforcements shifted momentum in their favor. The Bakma that remained, now outnumbered, were in full retreat.

David and Henry, out of ammunition, had since returned to the landing zone. Wounded were spread across the ground, as the available medical crews hustled between those in critical condition and those more stable.

David stepped through them to reach *Vulture-7*, where the rest of Charlie Squad, also ammo-depleted, waited. "How's the rescue team?"

Donald, unharnessed from the mini-gun, glanced to him. "They assaultin' a Carrier."

"*What*?"

"Scott found out about the other team. They was supposed to take out one of the Bakma Carriers. Scott got permission to continue the mission."

Henry stooped to a kneel. "Wait, *Scott*'s assaulting a Carrier? What happened to Henrick?"

"He's out," Donald answered. "I guess he got taken down, I don't know if he's dead or *what*."

David looked at Henry and then turned back to Donald. "How many people does he have with him?"

Donald laughed under his breath and nodded to the rest of Charlie Squad. "Count who ain't here. That's how many."

David gripped the back of his neck. "Can they survive that?"

Donald didn't reply. He only feigned a smile and lowered his gaze to the street.

As soon as Donner pulled up, Scott swung the back doors of the van open. "Everybody check your ammo count, and make sure you're fully loaded!" He slammed the door as soon as everyone was in, and he turned to Donner. "Do you get the plan?"

"Yes sir, understood!"

"Can you do it?"

"Yes sir, I can!"

Scott returned his attention to the others. It was time. "All right everyone, let's do it right!" His gaze swiveled back to Donner. "Go!"

Donner slammed down the accelerator, and the van rocketed backward into Clark Street. The operatives grabbed the van's support rails. Donner whipped the wheel around, and the van swerved around the corner. His gaze narrowed in the rearview.

"Ku'nessa te`mach naas," the slender Bakma mumbled as he leaned against the wall of the Carrier's deployment bay.

The smaller Bakma next to him grunted. "Kanaas. U`tekn no'las`tun."

The conversation drew to an abrupt close. The two Bakma and their dozen counterparts turned to face the street. In the center of the road, a worn-out van rocketed at them—in reverse. The deployment bay fell silent.

The slender warrior started, leapt up, and trained his plasma rifle. "'Uman! 'Uman!" The Bakma surrounding him scurried for their weapons.

PLASMA SOARED TOWARD the van. The vehicle wavered back and forth as several bolts ripped through its metal frame, though the operatives went untouched.

Donner white-knuckled the wheel as the metal ramp loomed nearer. "Hold on!"

Impact. The van slammed into the ramp, and the back end buckled off the ground and crashed against the metal floor in an explosion of sparks. Bakma defenders dove out of the way. Donner regained his focus and checked the rearview. The corridor was in sight. He whipped his head around and focused through the back window as plasma bolts rocked the van. They were on target. It was time to brake.

Donner readied his foot. "Open the doors!" Scott and Becan swung them open, and Donner slammed the brakes. A screech pierced the deployment.

The crash came like a train wreck. The van crunched against the metal frame of the corridor, and the operatives were jolted through the air. They slammed against the center of the corridor itself. It took a moment for them to regain their senses before they leapt to their feet and spun around. The van was in place. They were inside.

Donner slammed the parking brake and locked the doors. As plasma bolts crashed through the front window, he leapt over the console and scrambled to join the others. Inside the Carrier, a siren wailed.

The corridor was lit by a row of light down the center of the ceiling. Doors lined the corridor to its end, which came in the form of a two-way split.

Resistance hit them immediately. The door nearest them slid open, and a single Bakma rushed into the hall. Grammar raised his assault rifle and pulled the trigger.

Scott waved his arm forward. "Vause, take the lead! We've

got to move!" Vause took the point position. As they ran, doors opened behind them.

Grammar skidded around and dropped to a knee. "Keep going! I'll cover behind you!" His finger pressed against the trigger as he held position.

Scott turned to Vause as they reached the two-way split. "Which way?"

"Left! Then right, then there's a door!"

"What's after that?"

"Nothing! That's it!" Vause said, reaching back to fumble with his tools.

Scott stifled a laugh. Fair enough.

Vause darted around the left corner as they reached the split. "Someone should stay here! And one person come with me!"

Scott slapped Becan's chest. "Go with him." Becan disappeared with Vause. Scott and Donner fortified the split as Grammar rejoined them. "What's the news?" Scott asked.

"I should be dead," Grammar said as he caught his breath and reloaded.

"Did you get hit?"

"No, but I don't know how! There's a *ton* of them! When they storm this hall, there's no way we're getting out."

Scott turned to Donner. "Go with Vause. Grammar and I have this covered. We'll be there soon."

Becan and Vause were outside the engine room door when Donner caught up with them. Gunfire erupted from the main corridor. Becan wheeled around. "Where's Remmy?" he asked.

Donner pointed to the turn. "They're back at the split."

"How many Bakma are there?"

"A *lot* more than us."

The door to the engine room *whooshed* into the ceiling. Becan and Donner jumped and aimed their assault rifles. But the engine room was empty.

Becan glared at Vause. "The hell was tha'? Yeh mind tellin' us before you open important doors?"

"Sorry," Vause said, shuffling through the doorway.

The engine room was circular with a metal platform at its center. Various controls flickered on it, where Vause inputted his instruments. "Sir," he said through the comm, "we're in the engine room and it's secure. It's probably safer for you here. I'm working on the drive now."

Scott's voice emerged. "We're on our way!"

Scott ducked as plasma bolt soared over his head. Grammar was on his heels. "Come on!" Scott said as they rounded the corner to the engine room. "Vause, can you seal the engine room door?"

Vause's voice was interrupted by static through the comm. "Yes, I can seal it and lock it from inside. I've almost got the drive deactivated."

"We're coming to you! Get ready to seal the door!"

Becan waved the two men on. "Hurry up!"

"Drive disabled!" Vause said, thrusting his hands into the air.

Scott skidded into the engine room. "Door!" Grammar entered a moment later. Behind them, a team of Bakma rounded the corner.

Plasma bolts whizzed into the engine room as Vause dashed to the door. Scott, Becan, Grammar, and Donner returned fire.

"Door, door, door!" yelled Becan.

Vause's breathing intensified. His fingers tore at the controls. It wasn't until the Bakma were within meters of the entrance that the door slammed down. "Sealed and locked!"

"How long until they figure out how to open it again?" Scott asked Vause.

"Uhh…"

"Okay," Scott said, "I'll take that as an urgent request for backup." As the other operatives remained in defensive positions, Scott knelt and adjusted his comm.

LILAN BARKED COMMANDS as the throng of EDEN operatives charged the remnants of the Bakma attack force. The Bakma Carrier nearest them was airborne, and Lilan was ready to finish off whatever forces remained on the ground.

In the midst of the final charge, a static-filled voice cut through the frantic comm chatter. Though distorted, Lilan recognized it immediately. Remington.

"—activated the drive!"

Lilan dropped to a knee and placed his hand over his earpiece. "Please repeat, over!"

"This is Remington! We have deactivated the drive!"

Lilan paused as the battle continued to rage around him. His mouth hung open, but for a moment, he didn't know what to say. "Private," he answered, "am I correct in understanding that you have *deactivated* the Carrier?"

"Yes sir! Wings are clipped!"

Lilan laughed. "How in the hell did...what's your situa—?"

Scott's reply cut off the question. "We need immediate assistance, sir! We're trapped inside the engine room!"

"How many wounded?"

"None!"

Lilan didn't hesitate. "All right—I'll dispatch a unit to get you out of there right now. Sit tight for a while longer."

"Yes sir!"

Lilan cracked a rare smile. "Hey Remington..."

"Yes sir?"

"Nice work."

"Thank you, sir." The comm channel closed.

Lilan snatched a nearby officer. "Hey! You—whoever you are!"

The officer faced Lilan. "Sir?"

"You still got a unit?"

"Yes sir, we're sti—"

"Shut up. We have a strike team inside the southern Carrier. They're pinned inside the engine room. Take your unit, find a second unit, and go get them out. Fast. Got that?"

The officer nodded. "Yes sir."

"Good," Lilan said, "now go."

DAVID PACED IN front of *Vulture-7*. Henry, Michael, and Donald stood alongside him, all silent as they waited for an update.

"They did it!"

They all jumped at the sound of the jubilant voice. It was Tacker.

"They did it!" Tacker said as he trotted toward them. "They grounded the transport!"

"Are they okay?" asked David.

Tacker stopped beside him. "They're all fine! We've got two units en route to assist them now!"

David thrust a fist into the air. "Hell *yes*!" The other men grinned.

"With five men, they disabled a transport! That's unheard of!" Tacker eyed the barricade. "I've got other messages to deliver, but go find the others. Let them know everyone's okay."

"Yes sir."

Donald shook his head and smiled. "They's all right. I knew they's all right."

SCOTT, GRAMMAR, VAUSE, Becan, and Donner knelt along the walls. Their assault rifles were propped against their shoulders, trained on the door. On the other side, the Bakma shouted at one another in their alien tongue.

Five minutes passed before anything changed. Footsteps were heard, and the Bakma broke into a mad holler. Gunshots—both plasma and projectile—erupted. The battle was short-lived, as a familiar word spilled from the Bakma defenders. *Grrashna! Grrashna!* The Bakma word for self-surrender.

Footsteps grew quiet as weapons clunked together and human voices emerged. Several minutes passed before someone knocked on the door.

"Everyone okay in there?"

Scott signaled, and Vause opened the door. There were no Bakma on the other side—only the relieved expressions of EDEN soldiers.

Scott let out a breath of relief.

The soldier who knocked smiled. "You're actually in here... wow. There's two jeeps out front waiting to take you back to the landing zone. How'd you guys *do* this?"

Scott laughed. He wasn't sure how else to respond. More operatives filed into the engine room, and the five men stepped out.

As far as they could see, no Bakma remained in the Carrier. Several sweeper teams from EDEN were in the hallways, as were various other operatives, but no one else. As soon as they stepped outside, the reason became clear. Alongside Clark Street stood several rows of Bakma warriors, their purple, wrinkled hands clasped together as armed EDEN soldiers presided over them. Scott knew the aliens' destination. Confinement. Each base had one, and *Richmond* was no exception. There, they would be prodded and probably tortured for whatever information they could provide. At the moment, Scott didn't much care.

As promised, a pair of jeeps awaited the five men. The ride back to the safe zone revealed the battle's aftermath. Bloodied soldiers walked the streets, and Bakma survivors were herded together. The skirmish was over.

When they arrived back at the barricade, Lilan and two other colonels were there to meet them. The jeeps stopped, and all five of the operatives leapt from them and snapped off salutes.

Lilan was first to speak through the wide smile plastered across his face. "Fellas, this is Colonel Young of Hawk Platoon and Colonel Ledet of Gryphon." The two colonels shot off salutes.

Young immediately surveyed the five. "Remington?"

Scott lifted his chin. "Here, sir."

Young curved his mouth into a smile and extended his hand. Scott shook it. "Excellent job, soldier," Young said.

"Thank you, sir."

Young took a step back, turned to Lilan, and patted him on the shoulder. "Keep provin' 'em wrong."

Lilan chuckled, "That's the idea."

Young and Ledet nodded to the five again and turned from the group. Lilan watched them leave before he refocused on his operatives. His smile surfaced once more. "You turned some heads tonight." The operatives regarded him in silence. "Remington, McCrae, and Donner...catch a ride back with Hawk. The rest of Falcon's already left for base."

The three men nodded, exchanged handshakes with Grammar and Vause, and hurried behind Colonel Young.

Grammar waited for them to disappear before he cleared his throat. "Permission to speak freely, sir?"

Lilan glanced to him. "Go ahead."

"You have the best commander in all of *Richmond*, sir."

Lilan raised a brow. "What?"

"Commander Remington, sir."

Lilan stared. Commander? "Wait...you mean *him*?" He turned around to indicate the barricade, behind which Scott had just disappeared.

"Yes sir," said Grammar. "He is a Falcon...right sir?"

"*Commander* Remington?"

Grammar was silent.

Lilan shifted to face Grammar fully. "Wait a minute...you thought he was a commander?"

Still Grammar said nothing. Lilan broke into laughter.

"Sir," Grammar said, "I don't understand..."

"I just realized that, that's why I'm laughing." Lilan grinned. "Congratulations, fellas. You just got duped by a rookie." Grammar and Vause looked puzzled. "Remington is an alpha," said Lilan.

Lilan stepped away as Grammar and Vause dropped their jaws. Once more, he found himself laughing. Remington snuck into command. He pretended to be a commander, and he snuck into command. The crazy part was, the men under him had bought it. It had worked.

It was exactly what good behavior wasn't. It was reckless, dishonest, and completely out of line for an EDEN operative.

Lilan loved every part of it.

*   *   *

WHEN SCOTT, BECAN, and Donner stepped into the Richmond hangar, the rest of Falcon Platoon awaited.

David slammed into Scott as soon as Scott emerged from the transport. Backslaps pounded against the young soldier. "That's how you do it!"

Scott laughed as he fought to maintain balance. "I guess it is!"

"Do you have any idea what you guys just did?"

"Just what the other team couldn't, it's no big deal."

"It hasn't dawned on you yet…has it?"

Scott gave him a quizzical stare.

Becan's eyes searched for someone else, though she found him first. It was Natasha. She approached him from the side and captured him in a full-bodied embrace.

Becan's hands wrapped around her as he stumbled. "Grand to see yeh too!"

Natasha beamed. "Becan, you're a hero!"

"I am in me wick."

She leaned back as a serious expression washed over her face. "Becan, everyone is talking about this. That's all the comm chatter was about during the ride home. None of the commanding officers can believe you pulled this off."

"Really?"

She widened her smile. "Really."

Tacker cut through the crowd toward Scott. "Remington!"

Scott spun away from David to face the voice. He immediately snapped to attention. "Sir."

Tacker laughed and shook his head. "Remington, that was unbelievable. How in God's name you pulled that off is beyond me."

"Thank you, sir!"

"I've got to get the colonel up to par with our side of the fight, but I had to tell you that. Pull some more stuff like that and you'll have my job."

"Thank you, sir." Salutes were exchanged, and Tacker filed away.

Becan was there a moment later. "Can yeh bloody believe this?"

Scott barely stifled a grin. "I guess we did something right."

"We're goin' to be on the telly national news!"

Scott's jaw flapped. "You're joking!"

"I'm not! Remmy, do yeh realize tha' the battle tonigh' was the third-largest land battle fought on American soil since the Alien War began?"

"How do you—"

"Natasha. She told me a *lot* just now, mostly wha' they heard from the COs on their way back to base. The battle is goin' to be aired all over the world...I know tha's nothin' unusual, most fights are, but they might mention us!"

"Us as in *us*?" Scott's eyes widened.

"They're goin' to talk about how a five-man team took ou' an entire Bakma Carrier withou' takin' a hit!"

Scott blinked. "...wow."

Becan laughed. "Yeah, wow. Wow."

The two men stared at each other for a moment before they turned their attention to the hangar. Activity bustled in every direction, as the full capacity of Vultures returned to base.

The next hour was spent in recollection as Scott, Becan, and Donner retold the story of the Carrier to officer after officer. As time passed, excitement gave way to exhaustion, and exhaustion reminded them that before Chicago, they had been asleep in their beds. They took advantage of their first opportunity to slip away and return to the living quarters, where they showered and retired to their rooms.

It didn't take any Falcon Platoon operatives long to fall asleep. The clock neared seven in the morning when the last operative turned in, and rest became a well-deserved ally.

Their comms never beeped.

7

IT WAS 1300 HOURS when Lilan knocked on General Hutchin's door. The weather outside was a meteorological nightmare—the whole of the Virginias were in the midst of a liquid bombardment. Humid smells festered in the base. It was more than apparent in Hutchin's office, despite the portable fan that whirred in the corner.

"Sir," Lilan said as he stepped inside. Hutchin was poring over a stack of memos.

"Hi Brent, have a seat. Sleep all right?"

"Didn't sleep. Would've been pointless to try."

Hutchin's eyes left the papers as he leaned back in his chair. Rain pounded on the roof above. "I read over the reports from last night, yours several times. Very interesting stuff. There are a few things that caught my eye though, mostly your requests...you want to make Remington a delta?"

"I'd like it to be considered, sir."

"You realize that that's a three-rank promotion? That's borderline absurd."

Lilan heaved his chest, saying, "Sir, with all due respect, the line of absurdity was crossed when I was given a platoon full of rookies."

The room fell quiet. The fan continued to whir. "Is that why this recommends McCrae and Jurgen for gamma, and Timmons, Bell, Rhodes, and Donner for beta?"

"I believe that's reasonable."

Hutchin exhaled and propped on his elbows. "Brent...you've been a colonel since EDEN began. You know these requests are ridiculous."

"I don't do anything without a reason, you know that," Lilan said, clearing his throat. "I'd never promote someone unless I knew they could handle it. Do you have any idea what Remington did? Any idea what he accomplished?" Hutchin was silent. "Do you know how many Bakma were on that ship, sir?"

"No…"

"Forty-four. Eighteen were killed, twenty-six were captured. Do you understand the odds five men have against forty-four Bakma?"

"I'll admit, that *is* fairly impressive."

Lilan shifted uncomfortably in his chair. "That's not all to take into consideration, sir. You're right, it's impressive. It's impressive for *anyone* to take a forty-four-man Carrier. These men weren't anyone. Three of them were rookies. Not *only* rookies, but rookies on their first mission. Remington was on his first mission. The last combat he saw was in a *Philadelphia* simulator.

"Consider that for a moment, general. A rookie *led* a team that *shut down* a Bakma Carrier with a crew of forty-four. And to make it that much better, they did it without a single casualty. This was originally assigned to a crew of *twenty* from Cougar Platoon."

Hutchin folded his arms across his chest in contemplation.

"When I first heard that, I was astounded," continued Lilan. "I knew that there were three possibilities. The Bakma could have been completely incompetent. They've never been that before.

"Or it could have been that this was a fluke of astronomical proportions. They happen. Flukes are inevitable.

"The *third* possibility, though…is that Remington out-led the original task force. Completely. I thought about it when I got back. Remington's decision was voluntary. Nobody told him to do it. I listened over his audio transmissions, and he was adamant about it. *Five* times he asked permission to proceed, to both me and Major Tacker. We weren't reassuring when we spoke to him. Remington *knew* what he was asking. He knew the odds, and he repeatedly asked for it. He knew he could do it."

"Or he thought he knew," Hutchin said.

"Which would make it a fluke," Lilan answered. He pulled a small disk from his jersey and tossed it on the desk.

Hutchin reached for it. "What's this?"

"That's his audio log. I listened to it from start to finish. He doesn't act like a rookie. Not once did his voice waver. When Henrick fell, he didn't wait for someone to tell him to take over. He took over immediately. He *wanted* it.

"His command style is better than some captains I've worked with. He's decisive, and his decisions *work*. If I were listening to this for the first time without knowing who it was, I'd swear this was a commanding officer."

Hutchin turned the disk over in his palm. "According to your report, some operatives did."

"Nobody questioned his authority. When a delta confuses an alpha with a bona fide CO, you know something's going on. He had charisma. They *wanted* to follow him. That's not something you can teach."

Hutchin chuckled. "I did enjoy the part about the van. That's as original an idea as I've ever heard. All right Brent, I'll admit, you've got some valid arguments for this kid."

"There's one more request I have for him."

Hutchin raised a brow.

"I'd like to nominate him for a Golden Lion."

The room quieted. Hutchin stared at Lilan and then lowered his gaze again to the disk. "You realize that the Lion medals are meant for commanding officers?"

"He was the commanding officer, sir. The fact that he was an alpha is irrelevant. The Golden Lion calls for courage, wisdom, and fortitude in a position of leadership against overwhelming odds. Everything it asks for, he gave. His actions define what the Golden Lion is about, maybe better than anyone who's ever earned it."

"You realize that no rookie has ever received a Golden Lion? Or any Lion medal. Hell, Faerber didn't get one until he was an epsilon, and his first was a bronze."

"I'm aware of that, sir."

"That would make Remington the first man in EDEN history to earn a Golden Lion on his first mission. Nobody else has even come close."

"Nobody else could have led that operation."

Hutchin sighed. "I'm not going to let you bump him to delta

trooper. Not this fast. I'll let you bump him to gamma, but that's it for right now. I want to make *sure* this kid is what you say he is before he starts scaling the chain of command. I realize, though, that if you're right...holding him back will only hurt us. Good leaders are hard to come by."

Lilan nodded. "I want to lead him personally in our next assignment, to see how he behaves first-hand. I want to see if he can follow orders as well as he gives them."

"That sounds acceptable."

"And the others?"

"Why Jurgen? He wasn't on the rescue team."

"The other operatives already look up to him. He served with the NYPD for fourteen years, I think he could serve well as a role model."

"I'll let you move McCrae, Timmons, Donner, and Rhodes to beta. As for Jurgen...not yet. I realize his experience is valuable... but I still want to wait a bit longer. That's my final decision."

"And the Golden Lion?"

Hutchin leaned back. "I'll think about it. I want to make sure I'm not putting someone in the history books without a good reason. I'll give this disk a listen and talk it over with EDEN Command. I would say...that he has a fairly good chance. I'll make his case as you did."

"Understood, sir."

"Is that all you have for me?"

"Yes sir."

"All right then, you're free to go, thank you for the report."

Lilan rose, thanked the general, and stepped out of the room.

*   *   *

THE PHONE RANG at 1330. It took several seconds for the repetitive reverberation to register in Scott's mind, at which point his eyes shot open in a dazed frenzy. He bolted upright as David started in the bunk above.

What's going on? Scott's mind panicked. *Jerseys! Three minutes! Find Tacker!* Then it clicked. The phone. It was only the phone.

"What the hell?" David asked from above as his legs swung over the side of the bunk.

"The phone," Scott answered. "It's only the flicking phone." David flopped back down as Scott chuckled. His heart settled, and he fumbled for the receiver. "Hello?" His morning-deep voice rumbled from his stomach.

"Scott! Oh, thank God!" said Nicole.

He grunted in realization and sat upright. He glanced at the clock. It was past one-thirty. "Hey, baby. What's going on?" One-thirty. Unbelievable. He must have been out like a corpse.

She fluttered a breath. "What's going *on*? I got back from class, turned on the television, and saw that *Richmond* got called into Chicago! They said the city was a war zone! Then I checked and saw that you never called…"

He winced. Of course. "No…baby, I'm fine."

Her voice faltered. "…were you *sleeping*?"

"Yeah." He laughed under his breath—he couldn't help it. "I'm sorry, I should have called last night. I was caught up in everything."

"Caught up in everything?"

"Yeah. The fight." God, how was he going to explain this?

He heard her inhale sharply.

"No, no," he said. "I'm fine, everything was fine."

"That Nicole?" David croaked from the top bunk.

Scott covered the receiver. "Yeah man, hold on."

David rolled over and chuckled. "Have fun with *this* one."

"Scott?"

"I'm here, sorry."

"You were there last night?"

Was he there? He was more there than anyone else in the city. "Yes, I was there." He ran a hand back through his hair. "Don't worry though, I'm fine. I didn't get hurt, I didn't get shot or anything." *I just led a random strike team into a Carrier.*

She released another audible breath. "Thank God." Scott leaned back against the wall of the bed. "So you were there? How bad was it?"

Here it came. "It was…pretty bad. I mean, not like…*really* bad, but…" He didn't even know how to begin. "We got called in as backup. The first wave from EDEN got hammered."

"Were there a lot of Bakma?"

"Yeah...there was a pretty fair amount." That was an understatement. There were more Bakma than clips to drop them. But that wasn't what she needed to hear. What was inevitable, however, was much more complicated. "Baby...there's something I have to tell you."

Total quiet. In the second that followed, Scott's mind played over the typical words that followed that statement. *I'm calling from prison. I gambled all our money. I'm having an affair.* "Don't worry, I'm not having an affair or anything."

He could almost hear her shrink back. *"What?"*

"Huh?"

"An affair?"

Stupid. That was stupid. "No no, baby, I'm *not* having an affair."

"Scott, why did you say that?"

Because I'm a moron. "I just said it, I'm sorry, I was just thinking of...you know, when people say they have something to tell someone, and like..." David lost it on the upper bunk. "Baby. I just woke up. My mind's not even *here* yet. There's no affair, that's not what I have to tell you."

She stayed quiet.

"Did you hear anything about...a Carrier?"

"What?"

"On the news. Did they say anything about a Bakma Carrier? Getting captured?"

There was a silence on the line. "Yes," she answered. "I think I remember that..."

It was time. There were no more bushes to beat around. Drop back. "I was part of the team that captured it."

She stifled a gasp. "You were *inside* an alien spaceship? Scott, how many of you were there?"

Pass. "...five."

"Five! Scott, what were you doing?"

Touchdown. "I led it." There were only two ways she could respond. The first was with total awe. He was her hero, a champion of the world. A knight. He bravely took up his sword and charged into the dragon's lair, to come out the victor on the other side.

"*Scott!*"

That was the second way. "Baby, baby, calm down…"

"Scott! You expect me to *calm down* when I find out you're assaulting alien spaceships? Oh my God, Scott!"

"Baby…"

"I can't believe that! It's your first mission, what were they *thinking*? Who in their right mind orders a soldier to lead an assault on his *first mission*? Are they really that *crazy*?"

"Baby…"

"Who ordered you to do it? Scott, I want to know who this lunatic is."

There was no way this would be good. The hammer had already fallen. The nail was in the coffin. "I volunteered."

In the upper bunk, David mimicked a bomb drop.

"*What!*"

"Wow, I actually heard that," said David.

"Baby, please," Scott said.

"*What!*"

"Baby—"

"Have you lost your *mind*? Have you—*Scott*! Oh my God, I can't believe I'm hearing this!"

Scott sat up. "Nikki, listen, just give me a second to t—"

"Scott, do you have any idea how I *feel* right now? Do you know how many nights I'm wide awake in bed praying for you to be *safe*? And now you're telling me…oh my God, I can't believe this!"

It was about as bad as he figured it could get, if everything that could possibly go wrong went wrong in the worst possible way. "Baby, I was fine…"

Tears poured out as she sobbed at the other end of the line. "I'm supposed to be *okay* with this? Are you *joking*?"

"Baby, no…I mean…"

"Scott, do you know how I've felt since the first day you told me you were joining EDEN? Every day since, I've been holding in the back of my mind, what if you die? What if I wake up and find out that you're dead?" His stomach knotted. "And now, you're *volunteering* to die? *Why*? *Why* are you doing this?"

He rubbed his neck. "Nikki, you know why I'm doing thi—"

"No! Please don't tell me you thought it was God's will, because that's the *same* thing you said about us!" She choked out her words. "Nothing about this has worked in *any* way that is good for us! You leave school out of *nowhere* when everything is going for you, you tell me you'll be stationed in Detroit, now you're in *Virginia*, and now you expect me to hear that you're just throwing your life around, and I'm supposed to be *okay* with that?"

Scott bent forward and rubbed his forehead. "Nikki…"

"Scott, it *can't* be both ways. It says that in Scripture, we both know it! God's will does not contradict itself! How can He want us together but ask you to do everything that pulls us apart?"

Scott covered his face and lowered his head. He never could explain how he felt. He just knew that EDEN was right. Yet in this argument, he was defeated. "Nikki, I can't answer that. I can't explain why I feel the way I do. I just feel like I need to be here."

"What about us? I don't think I can last like this!"

His heart broke. "Nikki…I *love* you. I want to *marry* you. You know I've felt since the beginning that God had something special for us, I still feel that. Don't you?"

The line was silent. She whimpered. "Yes…I've loved you for so long, I don't remember how it feels *not* to love you. I don't want to remember."

"But…don't you feel like God has something special for us?"

"Yes." A burden lifted in Scott's chest. "I have always felt that, and I still do. I just don't feel what you're doing. I don't feel it, not at *all*. I feel like you're running off on your own somewhere, and I don't understand why." Sobs cascaded from her voice.

He dropped his hand from his face. "The same way I feel like there's something special for us, I feel like there's something special for me here. I don't understand it either. I wish I could just let you feel this like I do."

Her voice broke again. "Scott, please…*please*, I'm begging you… don't leave me alone. I love you so much. I don't want you to die…"

"I love you too. I won't die…"

"All I want is you." He could hear her shivering. "You're it. I don't want to wake up alone anymore. I don't want to wonder if you're okay."

Scott leaned back against the wall. He hated this. He hated it so bad. "Nikki, we're going to be together. This is a rough spot right now, but I am not putting this ahead of us. This will come to an end."

"Soon?"

"I don't know. God, I hope so."

"It *has* to be soon."

"I can't promise that."

David cleared his throat from above. "Scott, I really do hate to say this, right now, but…it's past one-thirty, and the cafeteria stops serving at two…"

"Hang on, baby." Scott covered the receiver with his hand.

David continued. "And you don't want to unload how you feel right now. You just woke up, you're emotional, she's emotional… trust me, Scott. Hang up right now, and give both yourself and her time to think."

Scott angled the receiver away from his mouth. "It's fine," he said to David, "everything's—"

"Scott, believe me. I was where you are a long time ago. It will amaze you how fast a conversation like this can shift in an ugly way. A lot of bad things are said when emotions run high. Let it go for now, give yourselves time. She'll be okay for a few more hours."

Scott was silent as David finished. David had been with the NYPD for fourteen years, he and Sharon must have gone through the same thing. Probably many times. Maybe he was right. With two kids…if anyone knew how to handle the situation, he did.

Scott uncapped the receiver. "Nikki?"

"Scott? Is everything all right?"

"Yeah," he breathed. "I actually have to be somewhere pretty soon, I forgot about it…" It was true. He forgot about eating. "Will you be home tonight?"

She fell silent. "I didn't have anything planned…are you going to call?"

"Yeah. I can't tell you what time, but it won't be too late. But we're going to talk about this, okay?"

She hesitated. "Okay."

"Nikki…" He hated hanging up. He didn't want to.

"Just hang up, Scott," David said. "End it as fast as you can."

"I love you, girl."

She smiled. He could tell. "I love you, Scott."

"I'll call you tonight."

"Okay."

"I love you."

"I love you."

"Bye."

And that was it. The phone was down, and the room fell quiet.

The upper bunk creaked as David sat upright. "You did good. Believe me, in a few hours, you'll understand why you did that. It'll go fine tonight."

Scott sighed. It was incredible how quickly things changed. Barely eight hours ago, he was a hero. Now, he was a misguided fool. It had to go fine tonight. If it didn't…he didn't even want to think about it. "I hope so…"

David smiled and dropped to his feet on the floor. "It will, I know. Not because I'm smart, or wise, or any of those things. I've just been where you are before. Women who marry us are the toughest women on the planet. We put them through hell every time we leave home."

"Yeah."

"Few women can rival a soldier's wife. They're a lot stronger than we are," David said as Scott slid out of bed. "She'll be fine tonight. She'll cry a few times between now and then, she'll mull it over in her head, and she'll make the decision to love you. The decision is just as important as the emotion. That's real love."

Scott went to the closet and pulled out his jersey. "What a way to start the day."

"Don't think about it."

"I shouldn't have hung up."

"Scott, you did right. She will appreciate the time to calm down and clear her mind."

"Do you think Sharon's going to call?"

"Nope," David answered. "She knows I'll call as soon as I can. And I will, after we eat."

Scott pushed his arms through his sleeves and pulled up the zipper. "You ready to go?"

"You're in the lead."

Scott grabbed his wallet, and they filed out of the room.

*   *   *

THE REST OF THE afternoon passed in routine. Lunch was conversational, as could be expected on the day after a massive operation. As the two men finished their meals and returned to Room 419, they were greeted with information—courtesy of a note under their door—concerning a unit-wide meeting. It was scheduled for 1900 hours, and its location was once again the *Richmond* hangar. With time to spare until that point, they sought the company of Becan and Jayden. For the rest of the open evening, the four neighbors engaged in spirited storytelling, mostly from the aftermath of Chicago.

David excused himself from the conversation to call Sharon, a call that lasted well over an hour. A solemn, yet reassured David returned to them. Jayden spoke of a call he placed earlier to his parents and brother, all of whom met the news with skepticism and then pride. The Texan was in contented spirits. Becan had no one to call, though he listened to the others with quiet satisfaction. For the first time that day, Scott found himself in the midst of smiles and laughter. For the moment, the tension-filled conversation with Nicole disappeared from his head. When 1900 finally arrived, the four men abandoned their room and made their way to the hangar.

The chairs were situated exactly as they had been on the first day that Lilan spoke, though the conversations around them were now much lighter in tone. Lilan and Tacker were there when they arrived, and as soon as everyone's watches struck 1900, the colonel cleared his throat. The operatives poised themselves at attention, and Lilan smiled. "At ease," he said. It was a warmer tone. It was a safer tone. "Don't worry, I'm not here to scare you today. That day has come and gone...and this day is much better." Scott smiled as he observed the colonel. So Lilan did have a heart. Perhaps today he would find favor with the rest of Charlie Squad.

As the unit listened, Lilan nodded his head toward several

empty chairs in the room. For a moment, his pleasant countenance fell. "You may have noticed that some of the chairs among you are empty. The men and women who once sat in them lost their lives yesterday in Chicago. These things happen—but that doesn't make them any easier." Scott's minded drifted to Wilkins as he focused on one of the chairs. He could see the soldier's face clear in his mind. He could recall the expression on his face when he died. The Bakma hadn't killed Wilkins. Henrick's carelessness had.

"They gave their lives for something they believed in, and I'd like us all to remember them for that for a few moments." Lilan fell silent, and the hangar hushed. Scott had been standing right next to Wilkins when he died. It could just as easily have been him.

Lilan cleared his throat a second time, and the room's collective attention was diverted from the empty chairs back to him. "But remorse is not why I asked you here. I asked you here for something much more appropriate. I asked you here for celebration." Scott and Becan exchanged subtle smiles. "I'm sure you've all heard by now about the incredible rescue made by some of our fellow comrades, as well as the capture of a Bakma Carrier, a feat that may very well go down in the annals of EDEN history as one of the most daring captures ever." All of Charlie Squad broke into open grins.

"It is my pleasure," Lilan continued, "to recognize those individuals with the first promotions of the new Falcon Platoon." Scott's smile widened. Promotions. On their first mission. It wasn't unheard of, but it was still quite an accomplishment.

"Promotions are meant to recognize skill, bravery, and leadership, and these men and women have shown that to the fullest degree. Those operatives are John Donner, Becan McCrae, Sasha Rhodes, and Jayden Timmons. Congratulations to you all… you are now beta privates. You will receive your patches tomorrow morning, and your armors' insignias will be adjusted accordingly." Despite the round of applause that erupted at the sound of their names, the four recognized operatives exchanged perplexed expressions. As they stood to be recognized, they looked at Scott.

Scott's expression was contented, and he too clapped his hands in celebration. He knew better, even though a part of him hated the fact that he knew better. There was something for him. There had to be. Was that arrogance? No…a team would not receive promotion and the leader of that team nothing. It wasn't arrogance. It was inevitable. The applause simmered down, and the four new betas lowered.

Lilan smiled. "There's somebody missing, isn't there?" The expressions on Becan, Jayden, Sasha, and John's faces widened. An array of smiles stretched across Charlie Squad, and Scott leaned forward on his knees. He wasn't forgotten. He couldn't have been.

"Every now and then, somebody does something so impressive that you can't help but take notice. Last night, one of our fellow comrades did just that, and a *lot* of people noticed. Taking the burden of leadership on his shoulders, he led one of the most impressive capture operations that EDEN has ever seen."

Was it really that impressive? Scott had done what anyone else would have done. Wouldn't they? Was the success of the capture really…all about him?

"Allow me to put what he did into perspective. A strike team of twenty specialists from Cougar Platoon was assigned the task of capturing a fully functional Bakma Carrier. These ranked officers were decimated in the attempt, and forced to abandon the mission. When Scott Remington arrived on the scene, only two of them were still in fighting condition." Several of Scott's teammates slapped him on the back. "Remington rounded them up, and of his own accord, requested permission to continue the operation. He, with only *four* other men, assaulted and captured the Carrier. They did it without a single casualty. Thanks to his actions, EDEN has captured not only a Carrier, but over twenty-five live Bakma."

The colonel smiled as he looked at Scott. "It is my honor…to promote Scott Remington to gamma private."

Even Scott was surprised. It was more than just special recognition. It was a two-rank jump. That, he had not expected. As he rose, applause broke out throughout the platoon. Gamma private. One rank beneath delta trooper, and two ranks beneath epsilon—officer training. He tried and failed to restrain an all-out grin, and after several nods of acknowledgment turned to sink back into his chair. Lilan cut him off before he could.

"Don't sit yet, private." Scott halted his descent and stared at the colonel, puzzled. There was more? How could there be more? They had received beta, and he gamma. What else could there be?

"I put in a special request to General Hutchin earlier today, and he promptly forwarded it to EDEN Command. It took only one hour for Command to get back to us." From Lilan's right, Tacker smiled broadly and handed the colonel a small wooden box. Lilan continued. "EDEN has a series of awards specifically designed for leaders who have gone above and beyond the call of duty. It's not an award that is handed down very often. It's an award that specifically calls for heroism, wisdom, and fortitude against overwhelming odds." Several hushed gasps crossed the room.

Scott shivered. Only one medal stood for that. A Lion medal. No…there was no way…not for him. A Lion medal was more than just a medal. It was a symbol laced heavily with status. Colonels received Lion medals. And even that was a rarity.

Lilan drew a breath, eased open a smile, and puffed his chest. "Remington, congratulations on being the youngest operative in EDEN history…to earn a Golden Lion."

An almost audible silence swept through the hangar.

No. That was not possible. He heard wrong. He *had* to have heard wrong. The silence continued. Before anyone could utter a reaction, Lilan resumed.

"You are the first operative to ever receive a Lion on his first mission, and the first operative to earn one as an alpha private. Congratulations, Remington. You have just made history." Lilan extended the wooden box.

The applause that exploded was deafening. Amid the hoots and whistles, Scott found himself stepping, almost floating, to the front of the room. A Golden Lion. It was the most prestigious—and beautiful—medal of honor EDEN could offer. The medallion's surface sparkled gold, and the proud pose of a lion's head sat confident in its center, prepared with dauntless ambition for anything that might challenge it. A Golden Lion. EDEN's designation of a hero. As Scott took the medallion in his hands, his pupils dilated. After several seconds of admiration, he snapped to awareness and saluted both Lilan and Tacker. Both men returned the salute and extended their hands.

"Do you realize what you've done?" Lilan asked over the roar of the audience.

He didn't know how to answer. "It's amazing…"

Lilan chuckled. "If you think *that's* amazing…wait till you see your armor."

Scott shook their hands, closed the wooden box, and returned to his seat. *Wait till you see your armor.* What did that mean? Was he to get new armor? No…that would be too much. It wasn't until Scott sat down that Lilan cleared his throat a final time.

"You all did it," he said. "This unit had something to prove, and you have proved it beyond even my expectations. I have *no* doubts now that whenever *Richmond* needs something done, we will no longer be considered a backup option." He paused for effect. "You have the rest of today, and all of tomorrow, off. You deserve it. You're dismissed."

Though the call of dismissal was given, the hangar hovered with activity. Congratulations were given to all those who were promoted, and jovial celebration hung in the air. Lilan and Tacker made their silent departures, as the rest of the unit was permitted to revel in its success.

For Scott, the success was beyond his own comprehension. With a Golden Lion, he was more than an ordinary soldier. He was…well…a Golden Lion.

He engaged in celebration with the others for a short while, though as time filtered past, something familiar resurfaced in his head. The business of EDEN was finished for that day, but he still had one thing left to do. He had promised her a call. It was a promise he intended to keep.

He left the hangar with renewed optimism. She was going to be okay. They were going to be okay. David was right—everything was going to be fine. For the first time that day, he actually believed it.

Scott slipped into his room, locked the door, and patched through to a familiar voice.

The conversation went wonderfully.

8

THE NEXT MORNING

THOUGH SLEEP WAS well-deserved, it was not uninterrupted. Scott was in the middle of an abstract dream when a knock at the door informed him that his rest that morning was not assured. In fact, he was assured quite the opposite. The media, upon learning of the dare-devil Carrier assault, was requesting an immediate press conference. EDEN jumped at the chance for good publicity. That was where Scott came into play. Who better to address the media than the strike team's leader—the youngest soldier to ever earn a Golden Lion. And now…here he was, hastened awake, dressed in standard EDEN attire, and waiting outside *Richmond*'s media room.

"You ready to go?" The words came from the officer who escorted him to the conference. It took several moments for the question to register, at which point Scott regarded the man with an absent stare. "They're about to introduce you."

It had all happened so fast. He had just been asleep in his bunk, and now he was one set of double doors away from a room full of cameras and reporters. His only protection would be a wooden podium and a microphone. "Yes sir."

The officer nodded and slapped Scott on the shoulder. "Good luck out there. You'll do fine."

He had barely had time to slip in a call to Nicole and one to his brother before he left his room. Nicole was excited for him, more so than he was excited for himself. It was a stark contrast to the frightened girl he had spoken to the day before. As for Mark, he offered Scott the typical advice of a younger brother: *tell them you got all your ideas straight from God, then flip out and start making all kinds of predictions!* Nicole's advice served him better. *Just be you, and they'll fall in love.*

As he approached the double doors, he looked down at the Golden Lion that hung around his neck. That was why they were there. Because he'd been given that medallion. The shock still hadn't worn off.

The doors opened, and Scott heard his name as it was introduced to the media. An officer stood behind the wooden podium that would soon be Scott's and motioned for the young soldier to come forward. In the back of his mind, Scott felt the pressure build. This was international. This was the world. Only one thought came to mind. Humor. Break the nervousness with humor. If you don't start with some kind of laugh, you're going to fall to pieces for all the Earth to see.

As he took the podium, he shifted his attention to the reporters. He was met with a barrage of plastic smiles. Not a single one of them looked sincere, merely the artificial expressions required of their roles. Beneath the masks were sharks. A room full of sharks, and he was fresh chum. Humor. Break it with humor. Sweat covered his palms. The room fell silent. He edged toward the mic.

"If this is my day off, I'd hate to see overtime."

God. That was *bad*. He could see Nicole wincing from her couch. He could hear Mark laughing his head off. Nonetheless, a wave of sporadic chuckles flitted across the room. That was all he needed. He felt himself find center.

"Good morning everyone. For record purposes, my name is Scott James Remington, and I am a gamma private in Charlie Squad of Falcon Platoon." He paused and inhaled. "I was asked to answer a few questions, so we can go ahead and begin that whenever you'd like."

Every hand in the room shot toward the ceiling. Scott picked one in the front row. It belonged to a short, stocky man. "You, sir."

The man rose. "Thank you. Grant Boone of the *Virginia Reporter*. Could you give us a brief summary of the mission, and then how you came to take command of the unit as an alpha private?"

He had known that would be the first question. "Certainly. Falcon Platoon was called into Chicago at approximately 1:40 a.m. on Wednesday, April the 6th. Operatives from Charlie and Delta Squads were selected to partake in a rescue operation for a suppressed unit, in which I was instructed to assume command if our team leader was taken down. Being that Falcon Platoon had been restocked with only alpha privates from the Academy, there were no veteran officers available to assume a backup leadership role. That, to the best of my knowledge, is why I as an alpha private was given secondary command."

The reporters in the room scribbled furiously as Scott paused briefly then continued.

"While en route to the suppression area, our team was ambushed by Bakma forces, and our team leader was incapacitated. As instructed, I assumed command. The threats were neutralized, and we located and secured the suppression zone.

"From that point, we learned that the original mission of the suppressed team was to capture one of the two Bakma Carriers. We took it upon ourselves to finish that obligation, and myself, along with four others from both my unit and the suppressed unit, set out to do so. Without getting into too many specifics, we were able to infiltrate the transport by use of a van, at which point we fought our way into the engine room and disabled the drive. We locked ourselves in and waited for backup to arrive and get us out."

The reporter followed up. "Can you tell us about the van?"

Scott laughed under his breath. "The van was an ad lib. I realized that the five of us would have never gotten close enough to the transport to make a difference, so we needed a quicker way to get there. We took advantage of a van that we had used for cover earlier, and drove it backward down the street, up the ramp of the transport, and right up to the central corridor, which opens directly into the transport's troop bay." Scott observed the reporter for a moment, and then his gaze once again roamed the room. "Some other questions?"

Hands shot up. Scott locked onto a slender woman in the back and offered her a nod.

"Michelle Kinler, *Direct One*," she said as she rose. "How does it feel to be the youngest soldier to earn a Golden Lion?"

It was a question he knew was inevitable the moment he found out about the conference. He had rehearsed his answer several times in his head. "It's an honor. But I realize that without the efforts of the men and women I presided over at the time, the mission would have been a failure. This medal is a testament to their effort and ability." Before the reporter could offer a follow-up, Scott moved his gaze to another eager-handed reporter. "Go ahead, sir."

The gentleman cleared his throat. "Robert Doan, *Suburban Times*. In what way did you prepare for this mission?"

Prepare? There was so little time to prepare…it was a mad rush from his room to the hangars and from the hangars to Chicago. "Do you mean Chicago as a whole, or the rescue operation?"

"Either one."

Scott nodded as he gave his answer. "With prayer. In this occupation, you don't have the luxury of an advanced warning, so for me, personally, I prayed before our transport even landed in Chicago. As a man of faith, I believe in the power of prayer. I'd like to think that the success of our mission had a lot to do with that."

It had everything to do with it. He was convinced of that. His attention shifted to another reporter in the middle of the room. The reporter stood as Scott acknowledged him. "Thank you, Jeremy White from the *East Coast Chronicle*. Following up on your answer concerning faith…at any time did you doubt that the assault on the transport would succeed?"

"No," Scott answered. "Not at all. There wasn't a doubt in my mind that we would take the transport. Personal faith aside, I don't think doubt is something you can allow into your mind in a combat situation. You have to be confident—that's not a choice." The reporters scribbled furiously as he continued. "There's no room for second guessing in battle. Once a decision is made, you have to stay committed to that decision. Once we were given the mission of assaulting the transport, at no time did I think we would fail."

After several seconds of quiet, the hands in the room once again reached skyward. "Go ahead," he said to a younger man on the front row.

The reporter rose to his feet. "Lee Charrier from the *Richmond Journalist*. Are you the next Klaus Faerber?"

Scott gaped. Klaus Faerber? How could he even be compared with Klaus Faerber? Faerber was a living legend. Scott was...well, aside from a single good operation, nobody. What an ignorant thing to ask. "How can you possibly compare me to Captain Faerber, who's been a part of this organization since day one? Next question."

Before another question could be raised, the young reporter spoke again. "But is it safe to say that you're off to a better start than he is?"

No. He wasn't even going to entertain that line of questioning. "Next." He nodded to another reporter.

"Hello Mr. Remington," the man said. "Brandon Cooper from *The Metropolitan*. There were fifty-five civilian lives lost in Chicago. How would you assess the success of EDEN relative to those lost lives?"

Scott hesitated. The room grew quiet as he shifted on his feet, cleared his throat, and swallowed. "I realize that as good as our efforts may have been, nothing can replace the loss of civilian life. Or military life. It's unfortunate that lives were lost, and I wish we could fight under different circumstances."

"Is there anything you'd like to say to those families?"

"Yes, I would. I'm deeply sorry for the loss of their loved ones. All of our thoughts and prayers are with them today." That was all he could say. This was war, and lives were destined to be lost. All they could do was try their best to curb it. His gaze slid to a woman on the third row. "Go ahead, ma'am."

"April Cox, *Focus News*. Have you ever met Captain Faerber?"

What was their problem? Did they not understand that he wasn't going there? "No I have not. Next question."

A well-dressed lady in the back of the room stood. "Good morning, Mr. Remington, Jessica Smith of *ORS News*. After such a successful inaugural mission and after becoming the Golden Lion, would you consider yourself to be one of the rising stars in EDEN?"

The Golden Lion? Others had earned the award before him. Not many, granted, but still he wasn't alone—the award wasn't designed for him. He wondered if they even knew what a Golden Lion was. "I don't think I can speculate on that after one mission. I was fortunate to have a good crew of men and women behind me, so I attribute a lot of credit to them. How much of the mission's success was a direct reflection on me, I can't say. I don't know if anybody can say."

"But at no point did you feel overwhelmed or flustered?"

Scott shook his head. "It's like I said before, there's no room for that in this line of work. All that matters is that the job gets done. You've got to be able to turn feeling off. But no, to answer your question."

Before Scott could offer correction on *the* Golden Lion, the officer who had initially escorted him into the media room stepped up to the podium. Scott backed away from the mic, while the officer smiled and faced the reporters. "Thank you all for your questions. That's all for now, the vice-general will be here shortly to give you an update on mainland security."

Scott was promptly escorted out of the media room and into the green room, where the double doors once again sealed him away from the spotlight. The chatter of reporters rose as each subsequent station awaited the vice-general. Who was the vice-general? Scott didn't even know.

The officer grinned. "You did good, Faerber."

Scott laughed. He might as well have been Captain Faerber. That was apparently who the media wanted to talk to. "Thanks, sir. Those weren't exactly my favorite questions."

The officer chuckled. "They'll pull those on you every now and then. You handled it well. Next time tell them to drag off."

"I was thinking about it, sir."

"Fine work in Chicago, by the way."

Scott nodded as he read the officer's name badge. Meyer. "Thank you, sir."

"Tell Lilan he's done a great job with Falcon."

"Yes sir."

Meyer sighed and turned to leave. "You know how to get out of here, right?"

"Yes sir, same way I came in, I'm guessing."

The man mm-hmm-ed. "That'll do it." They exchanged salutes, and Meyer disappeared.

Scott slid his hands into his pockets and stood alone in the green room. The distanced chatter of the reporters still filtered through the double doors. Waiting for their vice-general. Whoever he was. He slid his hand from its pocket and curled his fingers around the Golden Lion. *The* Golden Lion. The beast's gaze stared back at him. It was just a piece of fancy metal. That was all. It didn't have superpowers; it wasn't worth a fortune. It was just fancy metal. How could just fancy metal create such an ordeal? He honestly didn't know.

He made his way to the exit. This morning had already been more than he'd bargained for, and a bed awaited him in 419. This was supposed to be his day off.

The next few days returned Charlie Squad to the pace of routine. The day of rest was used, appropriately, for unit-wide rest. When the first day of regularly scheduled business came, they were right back to work with daily combat drills, workout sessions, and discussions of hypothetical mission scenarios.

The media frenzy over Scott was short-lived. Soon enough, more substantial news of the world reclaimed the public spotlight. While the *Battle of Chicago*, as it came to be called, remained in prime coverage, the operatives of the five-man strike team fell back into quiet anonymity.

Their initiation was over. They were tried soldiers of EDEN.

9

SCOTT AND DAVID raced into the hangar. Their comms had beeped only minutes before, which prompted them to don their uniforms quickly and report to *Vulture-7*. No explanation was given prior to their arrival. No other operatives were in the hallways. Nonetheless, *Vulture-7* sat perched in its concrete cage, as the hue of the reddened evening sky cast a reflective glow over its nose.

Lilan stood at the ramp of the Vulture, joined by Henry and Michael. Before Scott and David reached them, the footsteps of another emerged from behind. Zigler.

"All the soldiers," David said.

Scott hmm-ed. "Where's Becan?"

Lilan cleared his throat. "All right guys, over here." His voice was calm. Patient. Nothing about this felt at all urgent. It was a total contrast to Chicago.

"Where's McCrae?" he asked. Scott and David glanced at each other, though remained silent. Before Lilan could speak again, hastened footsteps emerged from across the room. Becan tore into the hangar and drew to a stop in front of Lilan.

"Sorry sir," Becan huffed.

Lilan nodded dismissively. "It's okay. The seven of us have an unusual assignment tonight. It's not the first time this has happened, but it's still pretty rare. I'll explain once we get airborne and geared up. Let's go."

The men climbed aboard the aircraft and held onto the support bars as they awaited liftoff to somewhere. What a difference, Scott thought. Prior to Chicago, the hangar had been flooded with activity. Rushing footsteps, competitive shouting, and the roar of engines. Now, it was just them.

The Vulture taxied onto the runway, and after several moments, lifted off the ground. Once the course steadied and the Vulture assumed its forward glide, the soldiers stood to open their lockers and don their armor. The recently promoted operatives were quick to notice the new chrome badges attached to their breastplates. For Scott, there was a bit more.

He had been tipped about the armor of the Golden Lion, and now he understood what was meant. Everything about his armor looked the same, except for one strikingly distinct feature—a polished golden collar molded around the neck of his breastplate. It was boldly simple. It was fitting for the most prestigious honor in the organization. As he fit into it, several of his comrades offered him comments of praise.

Nonetheless, a cloud of tension hovered in the troop bay. The truth was, none of them knew where they were going, or why they were even in the transport. As soon as Lilan saw that everyone was geared up, the elaboration began.

"Gentlemen...this evening you will be participating in your first bug-hunt." Scott and David exchanged troubled expressions. A bug-hunt. Necrilid. "Three necrilids were spotted approximately thirty minutes ago on the outskirts of Danville, Arkansas." The hair on Scott's arms tingled. Lilan went on.

"There were no alien spacecraft in the vicinity, so we're pretty sure this wasn't a drop-off. Eight days ago, a Ceratopian Cruiser was shot down over the Ouachita Mountains. Our best assumption is that these three necrilids were on board the craft, and they somehow escaped from the scene unnoticed. They probably worked their way west through the mountains until they showed up in Danville. This is rare, but it has happened before. As for why we're dealing with this instead of *Atlanta* dealing with it, I don't know. This is a junk job, and they may not have felt like working it.

"The necrilids were first spotted approaching a high school, and then seen crawling inside the school through a hole in the roof—probably one they made. It's a rural area, and everyone has been ordered to remain in their homes.

"Fortunately, school ended a few hours ago. There were a few people in the parking lot who saw the necrilids, but they've since left the scene. The local police are there now with some sharp-shooters keeping an eye on the building in case the critters leave, though we doubt they're going to do that. When necrilids settle down somewhere, it's usually for a while. The school is dark, it's got a lot of corridors, and it's probably going to be pretty warm. If any of them are female, they're probably looking for a place to breed." Scott's skin pricked a second time. Somewhere, in some dark corner of that vacant school, alien predators were perhaps breeding. It felt surreal to imagine.

"Necrilid eggs can hatch in a matter of days, and it's very easy to miss an egg or two when you're sweeping an area. It only takes hours for a female to conceive and lay, so infestation is a very real threat. Our orders are simple. Hunt them down. Once they're cleared, a sweeper team will come in to look for any eggs that may have been laid. We don't have a floor plan of the school on hand, so we're on our own once we get there."

Lilan hesitated. All eyes were trained on him. Finally, he launched into his closing statement. "I know none of you have seen a necrilid in combat before. I don't know what they taught you in the Academy, but I'm willing to bet it wasn't very pleasant. Let me reassure you...it's much worse. There's a reason nobody wants these missions.

"You're about to fight something that's going to scare the living hell out of you. The last things a lot of operatives see on bug-hunts are fangs and claws. I'm going to brief you as best I can in the short time that we have before we land.

"The average necrilid stands about four, four and a half feet tall when it's hunched over. If it rises up, some can hit about six feet. Usually the females. This doesn't mean they're easy to see. They're designed for the dark, and in an unlit room with a lot of clutter, they *will* find you before you find them. You won't sneak up on one. The one thing you *can* look for are the eyes. They glow yellow like a cat's if they hit any kind of reflection. But that's about it.

"They're quick, and they can move very quietly. The claws on their hands and feet can retract completely, so don't think you'll be able to hear skittering. If you hear claws, they're trying to lure you. Use caution. Necrilids can climb walls and ceilings as easy as they can walk on the floor, so don't just look ahead. Look everywhere.

"They do make a wide range of noise. They breathe, they hiss, they bark, they shriek. They communicate. They coordinate. They have an odor like a wet dog, but if you're close enough to smell it and you still haven't found it, that's not a good thing.

"If you find a necrilid, don't try to outperform it. Distract it. Go at it from two sides, throw a shoe, do something. Outthink it. Always remember…it is hunting you.

"Any questions?"

Quiet hung in the transport bay. The operatives exchanged silent, somber looks, though none dared to make a sound. It was Zigler who finally broke the stillness, as he lifted a hand toward the ceiling.

"Yes?" Lilan asked.

"Sir…why don't we have any medics?"

Lilan stared at Zigler for several seconds, before a faint smile curved from his lips. A hollow chuckle broke through the air. "Because if you get caught by a necrilid, you won't need one."

WHEN THE VULTURE's landing lights hit the school, it was already dark. The aircraft set down just in front of the main doors on a small patch of grass amid a triangle of large trees. Lilan stood and nodded at the pilot, who promptly shut off the Vulture's exterior lights.

"We're going to break up into two teams," Lilan said. "Jurgen, you're heading Team-1, consisting of yourself, McCrae, Mathis, and Zigler."

David nodded. "Yes sir."

"I'll lead Remington and Carter with Team-2. Jurgen, Zigler, and Carter, take a shotgun. The rest of you take your E-35s. Stay on the comm at all times, and move quietly. Follow my lead for now." Lilan motioned toward the rear door. The pilot proceeded to lower it, and after several seconds of mechanical whining, the ramp thumped against the fresh ground.

There was a heavy smell in the air, one that was impossible to pin down. It was thick. It was brooding. It was fear. Scott felt the sweat emanating from his fingertips, as his hands clasped firm against his assault rifle. This was totally different from Chicago. In Chicago, the enemy was right there in front of him. It fired at him with rifles and grenades. Scott could fight it fearlessly. Here, the enemy lurked in the shadows. And it wanted to eat him.

The operatives crept from the Vulture toward the large double doors at the school's entrance. Behind them, *Vulture-7*'s ramp whirred as it raised to a close. The pilot had the best seat in the house. Safety.

"An off-campus security system should have unlocked the doors," Lilan said. He took hold of one of the door handles and gave it a gentle pull. It eased open without a sound. A ray of moonlight cut through the darkness beyond the doors. Everything else inside was pitch black. "Keep your guns up at all times. Be aware."

Scott swallowed as Lilan took his first step inside. Into darkness. Scott's heart felt as if it would burst in his chest. His palms sweated more fluidly. He took a step forward. The instinct to turn and run was strong. Everything in him told him to go the other way. Flight over fight. What about the others? He looked over at David. The former police officer appeared stoic. Hardened. Zigler? Zigler was afraid. He looked afraid. Becan…Becan wiped damp hands on his jersey. Everyone was afraid. Everyone but Lilan and David…no…David was afraid, too—he just didn't show it.

Scott closed his eyes and hesitated. He had trained for this. He knew fear wasn't real, it was burrowed in his mind. He had trained for this. He couldn't make it on his own, but that's why there were six others with him. He had trained for this. He was a Golden Lion.

Scott's eyes opened. He centered his focus. He wasn't going to die. He stepped forward again, right behind Lilan, and entered the school.

It felt like a tomb. Aside from the faint sounds of the operatives' breathing, there was complete silence. An unusual warmth hung in the air. A thick warmth; a musty warmth. It felt stagnant. As the last of the operatives filed in, the double doors eased shut. They were in total darkness. Scott reached up to his visor and switched on his TCV.

The immediate area was spacious—a commons area. Benches and lockers lined the walls, as did several offices. There were two pairs of hallways: one pair on the right and one pair on the left. At the far end of the commons sat a pair of double doors and an open cafeteria. There was no sound. No spark of electronics, no skitter of necrilids. Total silence.

"Word from Command is that they checked with the local power distributor," Lilan said. "The school's dead. There's no reason to turn off your visor at all. Don't use your helmet light unless you have no choice. Necrilids can already find you easily enough without them." Lilan knelt on the floor. He stared ahead at the commons.

"It looks to me like there are two wings here…left and right. Pay attention, we're about to label everything."

Scott looked back at the others. David and Michael had knelt to the ground. Becan, Henry, and Zigler remained standing. Scott's attention shifted to Lilan, as the colonel pointed to the nearest hallway on the right.

"This is Alpha. Next one down," he pointed to the hallway farthest on the same side, "is Bravo." He turned in the other direction. "Near hall on the left is Echo, farther hall on the left is Foxtrot." Everyone nodded in silence.

"Jurgen, move your team down Alpha. Hopefully it connects to Bravo farther down. If they connect, work down Alpha, switch over to Bravo, and then work you way back *out* of Bravo and into the commons. If they don't connect, double back up Alpha to the commons, then hit Bravo. We'll check out the cafeteria and whatever those double doors are way down there. The double doors are Golf for now. After that, we'll hit Echo and Foxtrot ourselves."

"Yes sir," David whispered.

"If you come across anything, comm us immediately."

"Yes sir."

Lilan nodded. "One more thing. Don't use grenades unless absolutely necessary. The last thing we need is the press saying we're blowing up schools." The operatives exchanged hesitant looks, and Lilan drew a deep breath. "Now split up, and stay alert."

DAVID GATHERED HIS crew together and crept toward Alpha's entrance. He cleared his throat and whispered to Team-1 through the comm. "Henry, stay with me. Becan, Zig, keep an eye on the rear. We're going to move slow." The other men whispered affirmation.

Two parallel corridors intersected Alpha farther down. The vibrant hues of the TCVs lit them in frightening fashion. David paused. "We have two intersecting corridors up ahead, one right after the other. They may both connect to Bravo." The group slowed to a halt as they approached the first of the two intersections.

David and Henry's weapons trained ahead as Becan and Zigler sidestepped from behind. As Becan stopped behind David, he peered back into the commons. Everything was silent and still. He stared at the false colors of the TCVs for several seconds before drifting his hand to his visor. His finger floated over the TCV switch, and he clicked it off. All color faded. The world was thrust into blackness. He lowered his stare to the ground. Not even his feet were visible. Becan swallowed and reached back up to flick on his visor. A massive spotlight burst from his helmet and rayed into the commons.

"Veck!"

Everyone in Team-1 jumped and slammed against the wall. Their gazes darted to Becan, who frantically groped his helmet. The spotlight went out, and the halls were once again dark.

"What the hell was *that*?" Zigler spat out.

Becan's heart pounded. "I hit the wrong flickin' switch."

"You hit the wrong *switch*?"

"I'm bloody nervous, alrigh'?"

Scott's voice broke through the comm. "Everything okay? We saw a light."

David shut his eyes and caught his breath. "Yeah, Becan hit the wrong switch."

"What?"

"He…" David shot a dark look at Becan, "what were you doing?"

Becan bent forward and tried to steady his breathing. "I turned off me TCV just to see the darkness, then I went to turn it back on an' I hit the wrong button, I'm a bloody eejit. It won't happen again."

Zigler snarled, "Why do you wait till a draggin' *necrilid* mission to test your trashin' visor?"

"Enough. We're moving on." David turned back to the first intersection in Alpha hallway. "Everyone stay to the left side of the hall. I'm going to look around the corner of the first intersection and see if this connects to Bravo." He hesitated. "I guess we'd better label this, too. We'll call the first intersecting corridor Romeo and the second intersecting corridor Juliet." He pressed against the left wall and inched toward Romeo. There was once again an absence of sound.

He pressed against the corner of Alpha and kept a constant eye on the right side of Romeo. Through his TCV, he could see that various doors lined Romeo as far as vision allowed. There were no signs of life. He drew another breath and pressed against the wall again. He inched his head toward the corner just enough to allow his peripheral vision to angle around it. He poked his head around, and the hallway came into view. Romeo was long, and it did appear to connect to Bravo. It ran past Bravo, where it ended in a right-hand turn. A U-turn around into Juliet. He looked quickly behind him, where he saw the same pattern. The two ends of Romeo mirrored each other.

"Okay," David said, "it looks like Romeo does run all the way down to Bravo. I see a turn at both ends…it must loop around to Juliet on both sides." His gaze lingered on the Bravo intersection.

"We have to check out this end before we move toward Bravo. Henry and Zig, you guys are going to come with me to do that. Becan, I want you to stay right here in this intersection while we do so."

"Like hell!" Becan said.

"Becan…we need to check all the rooms, but we can't let anything slip by. You'll be in constant view at all times."

"Bloody grand. So yeh can see me get eaten alive first-hand, class."

"We're only meters away. If you see anything, just let us know, we're right there."

"Yeh think?" Becan scoffed. "Don't be long."

BACK IN THE school's center, Lilan surveyed the cafeteria while Scott and Michael focused on the commons. Only their footsteps had broken the silence. "Commons still clear, sir," Scott whispered. It almost began to feel safe where they were. Even though the necrilid predators were somewhere in the school, Scott couldn't envision them bounding across the room. It seemed too frightening a possibility to be real.

"Let's move to the kitchen, make sure there's nothing back there," Lilan said. "Then we'll hit the double doors. Carter, stay with us but keep an eye on the commons." Michael nodded.

They weaved through the tables and chairs until they reached the only metal door—a swing door—along the back wall of the cafeteria. Lilan pressed against it, assault rifle firmly in grasp, and pushed his way through it. The door groaned, though the noise was short-lived. The kitchen came into view. It was a small two-lane galley. He motioned for Scott to enter and scan the galley. Scott did so while Lilan held the door open. Michael's focus remained outside, on the commons.

Scott's inspection of the galley was short but thorough. As soon as he was certain of its abandonment, he offered Lilan a thumbs up.

Lilan nodded and beckoned Scott out of the kitchen. The metal door swung shut behind them, and the colonel pointed to the set of double doors opposite the cafeteria. Point Golf. Scott and Michael nodded, and the three men worked their way back through the tables and chairs.

BECAN'S HEART POUNDED as he crouched in the middle of the intersection. Though his vision was shared by all directions, an unidentifiable force lured him toward one. The far end of Romeo, past the Bravo intersection. Something drew him there—something unnatural. Every moment his eyes left it felt like a mistake. Something about it was not right.

It took several minutes for David, Henry, and Zigler to finish the inspection of the near side of Romeo. It indeed U-turned into Juliet, as it appeared to do on both ends. The soldiers peered through classroom windows as they inspected; though there were no signs of necrilid presence anywhere. Midway through the near side of Juliet, David spoke quietly to Becan again. "Becan, we're coming back to you down Juliet...move yourself to the second intersection so we can see you."

Silence hung on the line. Becan's voice murmured through. "Righ', I'd like to stay here. Yeh guys can see down tha' hall fine, but I want to keep an eye ou' on tha' corner way up ahead."

David paused. "The other end of Romeo?"

Silence fell again. As David awaited Becan's response, Henry and Zigler drew to his side and watched him. "Yeah," Becan answered. "I think somethin' is down there."

The three men froze. They exchanged widened expressions, and David focused on the comm. "Did you see something?"

Becan hesitated. "I didn't..."

No further elaboration came. "What makes you think something's down there?" David asked.

"It's..." Becan's words trailed off. His attention was completely fixated on the far end of Romeo. The hairs on his neck and on his arms tingled, and he engaged the zoom on his visor. "...it's just a feelin'."

David raised a brow. "A *feeling*?" He turned to Henry and Zigler. "Okay. Becan...stay there, then. We're going to finish here, then meet up with you again."

Becan's response was quick. "All righ'. Hurry. I'm brickin' it over here."

David reaffirmed his grip on the shotgun. "Let's get this wing finished. I'll take the doors on the left, you two take the doors on the right. Look through the glass, make sure nothing is there, then move on to the next one." Henry and Zigler nodded, and they continued the search.

LILAN, SCOTT, AND Michael stood outside the double doors of Golf. "I'll go first," Lilan said. "You two follow right behind. Same as before." The colonel squared his E-35 against his shoulder and pressed against the door. It opened without noise.

It was an auditorium. There were three seating sections, all of which angled downward to a stage. The colonel gave a brief look up at the ceiling and grimaced. It was a labyrinth of lights, cables, and helicopter wire. "Okay," he said, "let's move in here. I'll take the center aisle, Remington take right, Carter take left. Sweep the floor and meet on the stage."

Scott and Michael affirmed, and they stepped ahead.

DAVID PAUSED TO speak to Becan as he, Henry, and Zigler reappeared in the Alpha/Juliet intersection. "Still feel like there's some—"

"I do," Becan said.

David scrutinized the Irishman. His gaze was fixated down Romeo in a trancelike state. His attention never once wavered to look at David or the others.

David refocused down Juliet. "These corridors run parallel. We'll move in pairs. Henry, stay with me—we'll move down Juliet. Becan and Zig, you two move down Romeo. Step careful."

The air hung with an intangible weight. With every step they took, it grew heavier. The temperature was still warm and alive, and sweat drops formed on their foreheads. There was still no sound. The two pairs were almost at the adjacent intersections of Bravo when Henry suddenly stopped.

David halted to face him. Henry's expression was locked in a dead stare. "Everyone hold up for a bit," David said.

Becan and Zigler froze in Romeo.

David followed Henry's gaze toward the corner of Juliet, though nothing seemed out of place. His attention returned to Henry. "What is it?"

"Do you smell that?" Henry asked.

David shifted his gaze back down Juliet. He drew in a breath through his nostrils. The air was musty, as it had been since they first set foot in the school. He cocked his head slightly. "I don't smell anything new...either of you smell anything over there?"

Becan and Zigler eyed one another; they hardly dared to breathe. "We don't," Becan answered. "Nothin' here."

Henry was quick to defend himself. "I smell something. I have a good sense of smell."

"Does it smell like a wet dog?" asked Becan, his senses pricking again.

Henry shook his head from the other hallway. "No...it's..." His expression contorted. "I don't know. I've never smelled anything like this. It's almost...sweet? But not good at all, it's different. It's strong."

David hesitated, then offered a slow half-nod. "All right...let's keep walking. Stop if you smell *anything*." The foursome resumed their steady track in the direction of Bravo hallway. Moments later, all four abruptly stopped.

Zigler's voice emerged first. "I smell it."

"I do too," Becan said.

David inhaled deeply, and the odor came to him. It was not pleasant at all. It was the exact opposite. It was like rancid nectar. It was like nothing else. He recognized it immediately.

"It's flesh."

Everyone froze. The hair on their arms and necks screamed for the walls. "Are yeh kiddin' me?" Becan asked in a hushed whisper.

David stepped forward, and the odor intensified. His expression hardened. "Yes," he said as he chapped his mouth. "That's human flesh."

Henry's voice wavered for the first time. "I thought nobody was supposed to be in here."

Becan swallowed hard but did not utter a word.

TEAM-2 WAS HALFWAY through the auditorium when David's voice emerged through the comm. "Colonel?"

Lilan raised an open hand. Scott and Michael halted. "What is it?" Lilan asked.

Silence spanned several seconds. "Sir, someone in the school died over here. We can smell it."

Goose bumps erupted across Scott's skin. Someone *died*? Wasn't the school supposed to be empty? If someone died, something killed them. That was an obvious truth. He almost wished he didn't know what that something was.

Lilan's voice remained steady. "Do you see anything?"

"No sir," David answered. "We can only smell it."

Lilan nodded and resumed his slow pace across the auditorium. "Proceed to it. Be careful. Something's probably close."

Something's probably close. *It* is probably close. Scott closed his eyes and thought a prayer.

David acknowledged, and the comm channel was closed.

DAVID REGRIPPED HIS shotgun. "You heard him," he said. "Continue forward, and stay alert."

After several more steps, all four men were in view of one another again in the two intersections of Bravo. The commons area was visible in the far distance, though their attention focused on the ends of Romeo and Juliet. The odor grew worse.

Only moments after he passed the intersections, Zigler drew to a halt. Becan froze and stared at him. "Wha'?"

Zigler released one hand from his combat shotgun and pointed forward. "Left wall. Look."

Becan followed Zigler's finger, until he too came across it. His eyes locked on it for several seconds, and a span of silence lingered before he uttered into the comm.

"There's blood on the wall."

David inched closer to the corner of Juliet. "How much?"

Becan zoomed in his visor. The dark red smears streaked across the wall in long dashes, then dropped to the floor, where they trailed around the corner. "A lot," he answered. "Yeh migh' see some where yeh are. It looks like somethin' was dragged."

Henry's breathing grew heavier.

David inspected the wall ahead. As he concentrated his vision, he identified speckled crimson against the wall and floor. It would have been impossible to see had he not known to look for it. "I see it now," he said.

Becan and Zigler remained fixated on the stains. The Irishman could make out a bloodied handprint along the bottom of the right-hand wall. It smeared along the pale white paint until it disappeared completely around the corner. "...I'm movin' to it," he said.

"Careful, everyone," David said. Though their noses were almost fully adjusted to the odor, new inhalations occasionally freshened it.

Becan took his final step to the corner. Silence lingered in all directions. The smell was as intense as ever. With every second that passed, his stomach grew more and more nauseated. He closed his eyes. He regripped his assault rifle. He counted to three. As soon as he opened his eyes and rounded the edge, he gagged over the comm.

David tore around the other corner. His eyes captured Becan, who had doubled back and covered his mouth. David's attention shifted down to the floor, where he saw the cause of the Irishman's disgust. The remains were not even identifiable.

Becan swallowed as his gaze rose to David. "Is tha'...?"

"Yeah," David answered.

"God..."

"What is it?" Henry asked.

David and Becan pivoted their heads upward. Directly above the remains, a hole was torn through the ceiling panels. Claw marks were visible from where it was slashed open.

"What is it?" Henry asked again.

Becan closed his eyes and whispered as David spoke through the comm. "Colonel, we've got something."

Lilan's voice emerged a second later. "What do you have?"

"Human remains and a hole in the ceiling."

"Can you reach it?"

David and Becan eyed each other. "Possibly, sir," David answered.

"Find a way up," Lilan said. "Chances are, it leads to the nest. Whoever goes first, be *extremely* careful. Don't start searching until at least two people are up."

"Yes sir," David answered, and he closed the comm channel. He stared up at the hole, then he lowered his gaze to Becan. "You're lighter than me."

Becan's mouth dropped. "Big bloody deal!"

"Shh!" Zigler warned.

David sighed. "I can probably lift you up enough for you to climb through."

"Well tha's just grand, isn't it?"

"Okay?" David asked.

"Why do I have to go through the bloody hole first?"

"Because there's no way you can lift me up."

"Put Henry in the hole first."

"Hell no," Henry answered.

David's expression narrowed. "Becan, you're going up first. Someone will be right behind you."

"Who?"

"Zig. He's small, too."

Zigler muttered under his breath.

Becan shot David a look of disapproval, and shook his head acceptingly. "If I go up there an' somethin' bites me head off, I hope to flickin' God my body falls on yeh."

David lowered himself to the ground and entwined his fingers together. Becan hesitated, then set his foot into place. He slung his rifle over his shoulder and peered up as he braced for David's lift.

David's muscles tightened, and he raised Becan just enough for him to grab the edge of the hole. He waited until Becan had a firm grip on it and began to pull himself up before he stepped away and took up his shotgun again. Ceiling timbers crinkled in the previously undisturbed silence as flecks of construction material drifted down to the floor.

Becan scanned every direction as he pulled himself into place on a rafter. The ceiling space could be easily traversed via a cat-walk of supports. It was unnaturally warm, and beads of sweat dripped from his brow. He glanced up. The roof of the building was twenty feet above him. Everything else was a series of pipes, rafters, and units. He slipped his assault rifle from his shoulder and gripped it in his hands. Without a look down, he gave David a thumbs up.

Zigler watched the climb from beyond the corner. He had yet to see the remains on the floor, and he fought the urge to duck around the corner and look. The sound of Becan situating himself was disturbing enough.

At that very moment, a sensation tingled across Zigler's arms.

Every hair on the back of his neck stood on end. He held his breath as he froze. Silence prevailed all around him. Only the odor of flesh hung in the air. Yet still, his senses screamed. His breath released. His eyes bulged.

Something was behind him.

He spun around and propped his shotgun against his shoulder pointing at the intersection of Romeo and Bravo.

It was empty.

Zigler whispered into the comm, "I think something was just here."

Becan froze on the ceiling rafter.

"What do you mean?" asked David.

"I think something was just in the intersection."

"You guys smell that?" Henry asked.

David backed against the wall. "Are you saying you *saw* something?"

"I think something saw me. I didn't see it, but I sure as hell felt it."

"Something stinks over here…"

"Guys," Becan said, "Henry says somethin' stinks."

David looked up at Becan, then returned his focus to Zigler. "It was by the intersection?" Zigler nodded. Silence fell around them, and David stepped back in Henry's direction. "Okay… Henry, work your w—"

He was cut off. From just beyond the intersection, in the visually blocked space between Romeo and Juliet, something shrieked. It lasted a mere second, then it stopped. Team-1 went rigid. The school fell silent.

For almost ten seconds, no one spoke. Their stances froze as they neared the intersection. Above, Becan cupped his hands over his mouth. The next sound they heard was Lilan's voice through the comm.

"Anyone over there hear that?"

David swallowed hard for the first time. "Yes sir."

"Find it and kill it. Remember what I said. Distract."

David wiped his hand across his face and then wiped it on his armor. It streaked across the silver metal. He offered Lilan an instinctive nod, then whispered to his team through the comm.

"It's right there. In the hallway between the intersections." Henry began to shake. "Henry...I want you to work your way slowly toward it. Zig and I are going to mirror you on this end."

Henry didn't reply. He only trembled in the corridor.

"Henry? You read me?"

"Yes sir..."

"All right," David said. He took a deep breath and exhaled through his mouth. "Move."

Henry was the closest to the corner, meters away from where the creature had shrieked. The odor was exactly as Lilan claimed—like a wet dog. His fingers curled around his E-35, and he crept closer.

A rasping breath sputtered from around the corner, followed by a flapping grunt. The creature was making noise. Henry inched forward, his body pressed close against the far wall, his head goose-necked just enough to give him an angled view of the intersection between Romeo and Juliet.

He froze.

On the floor, thrusting out from the corner just enough to be visible, were two of the necrilid's toes. Its claws tapped twice on the linoleum, then slid back out of view. Henry drew a short, sharp breath, swallowed, and stuttered a whisper into the comm. "I'm...I'm in position."

David inched ahead. "We're almost there...hold for a few more seconds..."

Becan's voice cut through the comm. "Throw a flickin' shoe."

David drifted up a foot and began to fiddle with his bootstraps.

Becan breathed again. "Throw a flickin' shoe."

"I'm throwing a flicking shoe! They're not slip-ons—give me a second."

Becan listened to the transmissions from his crouched position on the rafter at the edge of the hole, his assault rifle firm in his grip. For the first time, he was thankful to have been the one to go through the ceiling.

David's voice came again. "Boot's untied. Few more seconds."

A few more seconds. Every second seemed an eternity. Becan waited for the sound of gunfire, for some alien scream to pierce the silent tomb. He waited for any sound at all.

Thud.

He started. It was a sound, but not the one he expected to hear. More alarmingly, it was not the sound he expected to feel. It jolted beneath his feet, as if a loaded sack had dropped from the rafters behind him. His first inclination was to pivot around and look, but he froze before the impulse took over. He already knew what it was.

It was *it*.

The next two seconds were a blur. He whirled around. Something strong slammed into his chest. He pulled the trigger of his assault rifle. Something screamed. The next sensation to come over him was gravity, as he fell from the ceiling. Everything faded to black.

Zigler leapt against the wall and spun around. He registered David behind him, also against the wall. Then Becan, sprawled out on the floor. Then the sound of contortions in the ceiling. In the split second it took to realize what happened, it was too late. He whipped his head back around to the intersection of Romeo and Bravo, but the necrilid was already in mid-leap. The last thing Zigler felt were claws in his throat.

David turned toward Zigler. As Zigler crumpled to the ground, the necrilid bounded straight from his body toward David. David was struck in the chest, and his shotgun flew from his grip. He landed flat on his back. The creature was atop him.

The necrilid was as horrible as Lilan had described. Its dark gray body was grotesquely defined, and its flattened head formed a sinister frame for the rows of razor-trimmed teeth that glistened within its oversized mouth. Its yellow eyes gleamed in the true-color vision, and it let loose a soulless wail.

David closed his eyes and braced for death.

Rat-tat-tat-tat-tat-tat!

David opened his eyes. It was Henry. He stood in the intersection of Bravo and Romeo as the barrel of his assault rifle flashed repeatedly. The necrilid atop David stuttered, leapt off him, and bounded from wall to wall toward Henry. Henry peddled backward and continued to fire. David scrambled back to his feet.

It took a moment for Becan to realize he wasn't dead. Everything was black, and he shot up a hand to his visor. His TCV was broken. He reached to the floor. His assault rifle was gone. Above, the ceiling tiles thumped as the necrilid reoriented itself.

Panic struck Becan as he leapt to his feet. He bolted to the nearest classroom door and felt in the darkness until he found the handle. He swung the door open. The necrilid landed on the floor behind him. Becan dove, jerked around, and kicked the door shut. He fiddled with his helmet until he found his helmet light, and clicked it on. It still worked. Through the glass of the door, the necrilid's yellow eyes gleamed at him.

David flinched as Henry's shots ricocheted around him. "Henry!" David screamed as he propped up and reclaimed his shotgun. The necrilid was bounding after Henry, growing closer with every leap. "Get down!"

LILAN, SCOTT, AND Michael had finished their sweep of the auditorium and were halfway down Echo hall when gunfire erupted across the school. Before they could react, another sound emerged from their end. Another shriek, just like the one near Team-1. Lilan turned to face it. "You two go assist Team-1," he said, "I've got this one."

Scott blinked. *He's* got this one? What did that mean? He was going after it alone? That was the one thing he had told everyone else not to do. "Sir…"

Lilan exploded. "Are you *questioning me*?"

Michael gave Scott an ominous look.

No, he wasn't questioning. He was just watching out for his colonel. But if he said to go…then he had to go. Lilan knew what he was doing. "No sir," Scott answered. Without hesitation, he and Michael fell back in the direction of the commons.

"Get down!" David shouted again as he dropped to a knee and raised his shotgun. "Henry, get *down*!"

Henry stumbled backward as the necrilid bounced from wall to wall in an effort to get closer to him. He no longer fired his assault rifle.

David gritted his teeth and pulled the trigger. *Boom!* The necrilid screamed. David pumped the shotgun and pulled again. *Boom!* Henry toppled backward. A third pump, and another flash of orange. *Boom!* The necrilid's back exploded, and it collapsed forward. It scraped desperately toward the now-fallen Henry.

Becan deadlocked his gape with the glare of the necrilid in the window. Its fangs curved with saliva, and for the first time, the Irishman looked straight into its eyes. His body shuddered.

The creature's head snapped around. It rumbled a low growl, and in the next instant, it was gone. Panic overtook Becan.

It was going after David.

Becan flung the door open and bolted into the hallway. His helmet light illuminated the back of the creature as it tore toward David from behind. "Dave!" Becan said as he reached for his sidearm, "Mind your house!"

David whirled around. The necrilid behind him was in mid-lurch. David dove into Bravo hallway. The necrilid swiped at his shoulder in mid-flight, and David's shotgun was knocked from his hands a second time. The creature skidded past him down the intersection and spun around to face him again. David stutter-stepped backward, ripped the handgun out from his belt, and raised it to try and aim. Before he could fire a shot, the necrilid started to leap from wall to wall toward him. He realized in that instant why Henry no longer attempted to fire. The necrilid were too fast.

From around the intersection, Henry let loose a blood-curdling scream.

Lilan strode to the bend as the echo of gunfire sounded through the hallways behind him. There was no stealth or urgency in his steps, and his boots clopped solidly against the linoleum floor. In a single fluid motion, he slung his assault rifle down from his shoulder, engaged the safety, and underhanded it toward the bend. He reached down, unholstered his sidearm, and aimed it forward.

The assault rifle racketed past the corner, and the necrilid pounced from around the corner after it. As soon as the creature landed, it skidded to a halt and jerked its head at Lilan. It released an angry scream, but it was too late. Lilan pulled the trigger, and a procession of bullets flew straight into the necrilid's head. A gurgle of blood spat from the creature's mouth, and it toppled onto the floor. Lilan stepped beyond it, bent down, and retrieved his assault rifle.

BECAN STORMED FULL-SPEED down the hallway to the intersection. He could make out his necrilid as it chased David around the corner, though the tortured scream of Henry arrested his mission momentarily. He could see the other necrilid squatted above Henry, where its claws rose and fell with murderous abandon. Becan steadied his handgun, aimed it directly at the creature, and unloaded several shots into its back. The necrilid screamed and then collapsed to the side.

"Man down!" Becan said.

David stumbled backward as the second necrilid pounced after him. Every attempt to aim was futile, and before David's mind could register his failure, the creature leapt onto his chest. David was flung onto his back.

For a second time, a necrilid was poised atop him with its claws in the air, and for a second time, gunfire saved his life. Bullets tore through the necrilid's body, and it whirled its head around.

It was Becan.

The necrilid howled. David ripped out his sidearm, placed it straight at the necrilid's head, and pulled the trigger. The creature's head erupted, and it cocked up and backward, where it toppled to the floor. David squirmed away and skittered back along the ground. He gasped to catch his breath, then looked up to find

Becan. The Irishman was nowhere to be seen. David immediately knew why.

Henry.

By the time David arrived on the scene, Becan was already there. The Irishman was almost delusional. "Yeh goin' to be all righ'," he stuttered. "Just sit tigh' for a minute!"

Henry was a wreck. The lower portion of his body was mauled beyond recognition. His chest heaved up and down as he struggled for breath, and his eyes bore straight to the ceiling with frozen terror. His teeth rattled together.

Scott and Michael arrived a second later. The instant Scott saw Henry, he whirled around, and a wave of vomit spewed from his throat. Michael gagged, but bit back an eruption.

David fell to Henry's side. Henry's glazed eyes found him, and David took hold of the soldier's bloodied hand.

Becan continued to stutter. "Yeh goin' to be all righ'!"

David knew better. He understood now what Lilan had said before the mission. There was no need for a medic. As he held fast to Henry's hand, Henry continued to flicker a hollow stare at him. The fallen soldier couldn't speak—the only sounds that came from him were gurgled gasps—but he could look. David's eyes moistened as Henry's blurred gaze locked against his, and he felt the soldier squeeze his hand.

Then it was over.

The hand went limp, and the muscles behind Henry's clenched expression grew soft. He was dead.

David's eyes slid shut as he clutched the lifeless fist. There had not even been any final words. The last sound Henry ever made was a scream of torment. David didn't know what to say.

"Good work, men."

The operatives swung their heads around to where Lilan stood shrouded in the intersection. His voice was completely neutral.

"McCrae, Remington—take Zigler and Mathis back to the ship. Jurgen, Carter—help me round up the necrilids' corpses. Nothing stays behind."

The four men stared as Lilan turned to walk away, though he paused a moment later as he glanced down at Zigler's body.

"If you want to take a minute over there," he said, "that's fine. Just be sure you take one here, too."

Lilan never said another word. There were no eulogies or tears of regret; he simply walked away.

The four soldiers gave Henry and Zigler their moments of silence, then did as told. They rounded up the corpses of the dead necrilids and placed the bodies of their fellow-soldiers into the Vulture. It took twenty minutes to secure everything for travel. They wasted no further time as the Vulture lifted off the ground, swung its nose east, and soared back home to *Richmond*.

Not one of them spoke on the ride home.

10

A FOG FELL over Charlie Squad. Upon their return to *Richmond*, Scott, David, Becan, and Michael reported the news of the fallen to the rest of the unit. Lilan did not accompany them; he retired to his quarters after the bodies were attended.

The squad received the news as well as expected. Sasha and Natasha reacted with tears, while others offered quiet condolences. All were in mourning.

In the first hours of the next morning, Charlie Squad was summoned to be debriefed. The mission was reviewed, and the operatives were advised how to better execute an operation of similar parameters next time. Nonetheless, Lilan considered the mission a success.

David and Michael were informed of their immediate promotion to beta private, after which the meeting was adjourned. The operatives left, as Lilan and Tacker went about their respective duties. The remainder of the afternoon was spent in somber silence.

*　　*　　*

IT WAS 2100 HOURS when General Hutchin's door opened and Colonel Lilan stepped inside. Hutchin was hunched over a letter when Lilan entered. "Have a seat, colonel. Thank you for coming in on such short notice. I know you're not used to late-night calls."

Lilan sat. "Sir."

"Good job last night. The deaths were unfortunate, but that's to be expected."

"Yes sir, thank you."

Hutchin exhaled. "No use beating around the bush. I didn't call you in here for a debriefing. I have something else for you." Lilan remained silent. "You know as well as I do that good soldiers are hard to come by these days. I will admit, I had my doubts as to whether or not you could adequately break in these operatives, and I must confess that you've done a superb job. Better than most would've."

Lilan's expression narrowed. The muscles in his arms tensed.

"We as a base are fortunate to have received such promising talent, I'm sure you've recognized this already. But not all of our international cousins have been so lucky..."

"No," Lilan growled, "you are *not* about to tell me—"

"We got a request from *Novosibirsk* for operatives yesterday."

"If you do this to me again, so help me *God*—"

"We're transferring one of your sections. The one with Jurgen, McCrae, Remington, and Timmons."

Lilan's face flushed red.

"Quite frankly, you've done such a good job breaking in the new operatives that we're going to make that your new role, at least for the time being. You'll still run missions, but they'll be mostly training missions for new arrivals on base, until we have a chance to place them in more experienced units. *Richmond* may actually be the new hub for rookies fresh out of *Philadelphia*."

"I trashing *knew* it."

"Tone, colonel, watch your tone. It's hard to come by officers who have not only experience, but patience like yours. You'll be training the future of EDEN."

Lilan inched forward in his chair. "It was all a lie to keep me motivated, *wasn't* it? All that talk of restoring Falcon and all that dung."

"Brent, you know that's not true."

"Shut up! I've seen this happen before! You use us until you get enough new blood to put us on the bench. I *knew* this was coming when you gave me a unit full of rookies!"

"Brent..."

"What about *Tacker*? You want to move him, too? I'm just holding him back, *right*?"

Hutchin's tone rose. "Colonel…"

"In fact, why not transfer me to *Philadelphia*? Put me in front of a classroom giving lectures on the history of EDEN!"

Hutchin pounded his fist on the desktop. "Silence! One more word, *colonel*, and you'll find yourself looking for another career! If you were any other man, you'd have been relieved a *long* time ago!"

Lilan opened his mouth, but Hutchin interrupted.

"You are temporarily relieved from command until further notice. I will *not* tolerate disrespect, not from you, nor anybody else. You are to inform Major Tacker of the situation, and have *him* relay the message to the unit. He will have command of Falcon Platoon until I see fit to put you back in charge. Is that understood?"

Lilan broke eye contact. "Dregg."

Silence descended upon the room. Hutchin's eyes broke wide. "*What* did you just say?"

Lilan glared across the table. The room was quiet. "I said nothing. Sir."

Hutchin's face remained red. "That is what I *thought* you said."

"Thoor is going to ruin those four men."

"You're dismissed."

Lilan snapped to a salute. Hutchin saluted back, and Lilan swung around to walk out the room. He didn't bother to close the door behind him.

*   *   *

"So much for bein' the first to go," said Becan. He, Scott, and Jayden sat across from one another in Room 421. They had been there for almost thirty minutes, as it neared 10 p.m.

Scott was stoic. "I still can't believe how fast it happened. Two days ago everything was great. One mission, and bang. Blink of an eye."

"It should've been me. If I had paid atten—"

"Don't even think like that."

"I'm bloody serious. I should have been payin' attention."

Jayden glanced to Becan. "It happens, man."

"Won't happen again, I cross m'heart."

Scott sighed and turned to Jayden. "Be glad you weren't there."

"I wish I was."

"Yeh don't," Becan said. "Not in tha' hellhole."

"It was like living a nightmare," Scott said. "I didn't even see anything first-hand, and it was still the most terrifying experience of my life."

Jayden sighed. "I still wish I'da been there."

Scott's eyes trailed to the floor. Truth be told...it would have been better had Jayden been there. The comfort of a sniper at your back was hard to replace. "I wish so, too, actually." Jayden smiled at Scott. "Nothing can be done about that now, though."

"How's Dave holdin' up?" Becan asked.

Scott nodded his head. "He's doing all right. He took it hard because of Henry...he liked Henry." He pitied Henry. That was the truth of the matter. David had seen him for what he was...a man with no business being enlisted in EDEN.

"I think we all liked him," Becan said. "Had a bloody miserable job, we'll give him tha', but he was tryin' to do his part. Tryin' to not be ordinary."

Scott smiled half-heartedly. "I think that was his problem. He was here for the wrong reason." Nobody could make themselves a hero. It was something that just happened naturally—instinctively.

The room fell silent. Jayden slid down against the floor. Becan's legs fidgeted. "How do yeh think they went?"

Scott raised his head. "What do you mean?"

"I mean...do yeh think they were...yeh know, met by someone? Or did it all just fade to black? Their conscious mind just shut off, an' now it's just over?"

Jayden glanced to the Irishman. "You mean how did they die?"

"Righ'."

Scott gazed down. How does one meet death? The question that was destined to haunt man for as long as he lived. What is death? Scott himself knew his fate. An afterlife was there, for him, in Paradise. God was there. But what about Henry and Zigler? Were they met by an angel...or something worse? Zigler...Zigler always carried an attitude. Angry, coercive, bitter. Who waited for him on the other side? It couldn't have been God. There was no reflection of God in his life. God fueled goodness.

He shook his head. No. What was he thinking? How could he even speculate that, on the day of Zigler's death? *Fool, Scott. You're a fool for that. You deserve to die for that.* For a moment, he hated himself.

"...Remmy?"

Scott looked across to Becan. "Huh?"

"Yeh got this blank look on your face."

"Oh," Scott said. "Sorry, just...thought of something, that's all."

Becan fell quiet. "So how do yeh think they died?"

Forgive me, Father. Please forgive me for that. Scott's gaze fell. "I hope in peace. It's no one's right to say. We can only hope that they found peace."

"Yeh believe in Heaven, righ'?"

"Yes."

"Do yeh think they made it?"

It didn't matter what he thought. It only mattered what they thought, Henry and Zigler. It only mattered what they believed. "I don't know."

Becan gazed at his feet. "...I hope I make it."

Scott stared at him. It had nothing to do with hope. It had to do with faith. Belief in God, divine mercy. Didn't Becan know that? No...if he knew that, he wouldn't have said what he said. Before he could say anything further, there was a knock at the door.

"Probably Dave," Becan said.

Scott nodded as Jayden rose to answer it. David, Scott thought. The unit needed someone like him, especially in times like this. David knew about death, he knew about the loss of comrades. Henry's death had hit him hard, that much Scott knew...but he also knew that David would pull through. It was funny how much faith he had in him. A month ago, the name David Jurgen had meant nothing to Scott. Now, it was synonymous with wisdom.

Jayden snapped to attention. Scott and Becan canted their heads to the door. It wasn't David. It was Major Tacker. They leapt to their feet and saluted crisply.

"At ease," Tacker said. He stepped past Jayden into the room and sat down in an unclaimed chair.

Scott's posture relaxed, though not completely. It was impossible to be completely at ease around superiors, even those as amiable as Tacker. But why was Tacker's countenance so...informal wasn't the word. Blank. He just walked in and sat down. And said nothing.

Something was wrong.

Tacker stared at the floor and rubbed his neck. Silence hung in the air. Becan and Jayden stood side by side as Scott watched from the far wall. Before any of them could open their mouths to inquire, Tacker took a deep breath and spoke. "You're all being transferred. So is Jurgen."

Scott's jaw dropped as Tacker resumed.

"Don't ask me why, and don't ask me what I think about it. You leave for *Novosibirsk* tomorrow morning at 0700, in *Vulture-15*. It's already late, so I don't have to tell you how soon that is. Get in your goodbyes, get your things packed, and get as much rest as you can. Morning comes quick."

Tacker pushed to his feet. "That's all." Scott's brow furrowed as the major left through the door and disappeared into the hallway. His footsteps echoed away seconds later.

The room stood in silence. There was no conversation. There was no argument. There wasn't enough time for it.

THE NIGHT WAS a blur. Becan and Jayden said their goodbyes, while Scott sought out David. Together, they called Nicole and Sharon. The calls were almost too brief to be fully registered. Several emotions—shock, panic, and disbelief—emanated from the two women. Even from the two men. But there was no time for that now. There was no time to try to understand. As soon as they hung up, they packed what few belongings they had into their duffle bags. Soon, Room 419 was as barren as the day they had arrived.

Scott and David spent the rest of the night in the hangar. Despite Tacker's recommendation, sleep was impossible. They stored their bags in their assigned transport—*Vulture-15*—then made their way to *Vulture-7*. The Vulture they knew. They leaned against its hull as conversation ensued.

Neither knew specifics about *Novosibirsk*, though both knew *of* it. It was one of the worst environments for EDEN operatives on the planet. It was larger than *Richmond*, classified as a Class-4 facility, and it was one of the oldest in the organization.

Novosibirsk was home to the Nightmen—a defunct sect of the Russian military. It had been disbanded and outlawed for its brutality when the New Era began, though *Novosibirsk* became the landing spot for many of its former officers. The general of *Novosibirsk*—Ignatius van Thoor—was a former Nightman captain. When Thoor inherited command of *Novosibirsk*, every ex-Nightmen who had served under him flocked there to reunite. Though Thoor was unknown outside of EDEN, he was regarded within the organization as one of the most brutally effective leaders in the world. His men were proud to serve under him and terrified to stand against him.

It was five in the morning when Jayden arrived; his brown cowboy hat gave him away immediately. He joined Scott and David in conversation as soon as his belongings were stored.

Jayden was more talkative than usual, as he explained how the news of the move made him miss his hometown of Blue Creek. When he'd called his parents to tell them, they hadn't believed him.

As they leaned against *Vulture-7*'s hull, the reddish hue of sunrise peaked over the distant treetops. In the time the sun took to rise completely, the conversation died. Their eyes remained on the horizon, as their noses remained on the scent of a Virginian morning.

Becan didn't arrive until 0640—twenty minutes before departure. His uniform and hair were unkempt as usual, and his wrinkled duffle bag slung sloppily over one shoulder. He tossed it into the transport and joined his comrades. He spoke next to nothing in the short time they propped themselves against *Vulture-7* together. Even under the circumstances, it was an odd quiet from the Irishman. No reason was given as to why, nor was one requested. Silence was not to be argued.

Nobody was there to send them off when they climbed into the transport. No colonel, no major, no teammates—only the technicians and pilots as they walked about the hangar doing their routine checks. The operatives strapped themselves into the transport's matted chairs and gazed out of the cold portholes of its hull. The running lights were lit, and *Vulture-15* taxied onto the runway. As it rolled forward, Scott peered out of the window—a last look for anyone there to see them away. There was no one.

Clearance was given for takeoff, and the craft ascended. Scott hadn't slept since Tacker's visit, and fatigue finally set in. As they rocketed forward, he closed his eyes. He fell asleep right away, and David and Jayden were soon to follow.

Only Becan remained awake for the first half of the journey. He gazed out the window as the clouds glided past, his eyes lingering absently on the sky. He never once turned his head to see if the others were asleep. He only stared at the horizon, eyes distant and thoughtful, as he watched and waited for *Novosibirsk*.

PART II

11

EDEN COMMAND

CARL PAULING, PRESIDENT of EDEN, nodded to the slender man across from him. "Proceed with your report, Judge Kentwood," he said as he motioned for the man to rise. The other eleven judges watched Kentwood closely as he stood.

Kentwood covered his mouth with his fist and cleared his throat. "My fellow judges…we have a problem."

A murmur spread through the High Command. Pauling's gaze spanned the large, black, circular table, and the twelve men who sat around it—the twelve judges of EDEN. There were no others present in the conference room. There were no others allowed. Behind Pauling, a wall-sized display screen showed a gently rotating Earth.

Kentwood continued. "We're all aware of the increased Bakma activity in North Asia, particularly in Siberia and Northern China. Our outpost at the North Pole has been assaulted several times in recent weeks, and though none of the attacks have been heavy, there has been significant damage to the facility's structure, at least enough to force us to allocate our resources there more heavily." Kentwood was eloquent in his presentation. He had always been that way. "It was feared for some time that the Bakma have been targeting the North Pole to clear it completely from EDEN influence in order to possibly establish an outpost of their own there. An outpost on Earth would be valuable, and the two poles represent prime locations for such."

He regarded the other judges thoughtfully. "We were half right."

He reached beneath the table to retrieve a manila folder. He opened its pale cover and produced a thin stack of papers, which he then handed to the judge on his left. "What I am passing out to you now is a satellite image of Northern Siberia." The stack of papers began to circulate.

"You'll note the red dot just above the Arctic Circle. Its approximate coordinates are 125 degrees, 14 minutes east longitude, and 67 degrees, 25 minutes north latitude. Seven hours ago, *Novosibirsk* radar picked up the signal out of nowhere, marked by that dot. It was a stationary signal, extra-terrestrial in origin. A team was sent to investigate, and they discovered a crashed Bakma Noboat. There was no indication of a fight between it and another vessel, and they came to the conclusion that it must have crashed there accidentally, materializing in the process. No crew members were found alive."

The last paper reached the judge to his right. "When the dispatchers investigated further, they discovered that the Noboat was not filled with soldiers. Rather, it was stocked with supplies... food, water, platforms, mountable sensors. We think...we think that they already have a base established." The silence was broken with a wave of whispers. The room grew quiet again. "We believe they're using Noboats for cargo ships. By doing that, they would be able to construct an outpost right under our noses, provided they built it underground where it wouldn't be easily detected. We're fortunate that this particular one crashed or we'd still be completely in the dark about this."

Judge Jason Rath, a smaller, darker man, shifted in his chair. "Siberia would be an ideal location for a colony as well."

"Exactly," Kentwood said. "It's remote, and EDEN has no reason to go there on its own accord. It's not heavily populated, so there's really no one there for us to protect."

"How sure is Intelligence that there is indeed a Bakma colony there?"

"Fairly confident," Kentwood answered. "It fits in place with the recent assaults on the North Pole. We thought they were trying to clear a way for a potential base, but it's clear now that they were more likely trying to destroy the facility with the greatest chance of detecting them."

"What about *Novosibirsk*?"

"*Novosibirsk* would have probably been their second target, or possibly *Nagoya*. *Novosibirsk*'s closer, but *Nagoya* is huge, definitely a larger threat."

"That's debatable," another judge murmured.

"How do we locate this facility?" Rath asked. "If it's underground then it won't exactly be a flashing beacon."

"We're going to have to start scouting, and heavily," Kentwood answered. "I would like to start an active reconnaissance campaign in that area, in all of Siberia. The primary work would come from units stationed at *Novosibirsk* and *Nagoya*, but we also have *Leningrad* and *Berlin*, they're not much farther away. Obviously, this is something that we're going to want to consider a priority. The last thing we need is a fully functional alien facility on Earth."

"Agreed," Pauling said. "But let's hypothesize for a moment... let's say we do find a fully functional alien facility...who handles it? Do we make this a global coordination?"

Kentwood turned to regard the president. "That all depends on the size of it, sir. It may be no bigger than one of the polar outposts. If that's the case, then it may only take several units to isolate it. If it rivals one of our major facilities, which is highly unlikely since we think it's relatively new, then it will take a much larger effort."

"We're aware of this facility," said Pauling quietly. "That's been a stroke of good luck. But how do we know this is the only one? If it's this easy for them to set up a base undetected, then who's to say they don't have facilities all across the planet?"

Kentwood nodded. "That's why coming up with a detection system for their chameleon technology is so important. We hope this is the only base they have, but there could very well be more. There could be a Bakma armada surrounding Earth right now that we just don't see."

The president glanced down to his paper for several moments, then placed it face up in front of him. "Have R&D here allocate more resources to that very thing. Stress the importance of this. It's an issue we can ignore no longer. Send a message to Thoor, let him know that *Novosibirsk* may very well be fronting this little campaign. Get in touch with Faerber, too, and inform him that Vector Squad may be needed in the near future."

"Yes sir," Kentwood answered.

"We have a planet to protect, gentlemen," Pauling said, surveying the judges. "We can't very well protect it if we're fighting an invisible enemy."

Silence lingered in the conference room for several moments, before the president concluded. "Everyone is dismissed. Thank you, Darryl."

Kentwood nodded, then turned to leave the room, as the other judges rose to make their exits as well. Quiet murmurs accompanied them as they filed out. Within a minute the room was cleared, and Carl Pauling was alone. He absorbed the quiet for several seconds before he swiveled around in his chair and slowed to a stop only when the large display screen was in front of him. Earth continued its ethereal rotation, and Pauling's eyes fell on the city of Novosibirsk. The city of The Machine.

"Thoor…"

*   *   *

TUESDAY, APRIL 12ᵀᴴ, 0011 NE
2323 HOURS

NOVOSIBIRSK, RUSSIA

SCOTT'S EYES JOLTED open as the Vulture rocked to a landing. Thunder rumbled outside, though the pounding of rain drowned it out as it drummed against the transport's hull. He sat up straight. What was going on? Were they there already? He didn't remember waking up at all during the flight. Aside from the haunting glow of red ceiling lights, the troop bay was dark. He squinted as he returned from the lost depths of sleep.

The pilot emerged from the cockpit. "We're down."

Soft groans came from all around as Scott sat up to see David, Jayden, and Becan stir in their seats—their eyes squinted and glazed as silent yawns escaped their lips. Scott's focus drifted to the rain. It was incessant, murderous. It was a far cry from the warm sunrise of *Richmond*.

David stood first, as he pressed his hands against the wall of the Vulture and arched his back and neck with a series of heavy pops. The others followed suit, and the rear door of the craft lowered with a mechanical whine. They were hit with a blast of icy mist.

"Everyone out!" the pilot said. "This bird's gotta fly!" The clunk of nozzle against metal could be heard from outside as the transport was recharged.

Becan dragged up his bag of clothes and hoisted it over his shoulder. "Wha' time is it?"

The pilot smiled. "Thirty minutes to tomorrow! Welcome to the other side of the world!"

Vulture-15 was perched on an open stretch of airstrip, in the midst of a storm so deep that it shrouded the very blackness of night itself. The only lights were those of the gargantuan hangar that menaced before them, and even they were only barely visible through the downpour. With no cover between the men and the hangar, they had no choice but to dash from the sanctuary of the transport, through the rain and on to the structure.

Two silhouettes were poised outside of the hangar, assault rifles aimed to the thunder as they stood motionless under the liquid bombardment. Scott, drenched to the skin, scrutinized them as he and his comrades neared. Their forms came into view moments later.

Neither of them were dressed in standard EDEN armor. Their armor was solid black metal, and it covered them from head to toe. It made them look huge—like walking tanks. They were obviously guards of some kind, but nothing about them was familiar. Their faces were hidden behind black helmets, and opaque lenses covered their eyes. Their zombified gazes bore ahead with no indication as to where or what they observed. Uneasiness birthed in the pits of Scott's stomach.

The guards thrust out their palms, and the four transfers drew to a halt. Behind the guards, a larger form came into view. He was dressed in a flat-black uniform, and a black visor hat sat atop his head. His frame was enormous. No patches or insignia were distinguishable on his jersey, but there was no doubt in Scott's mind that he was an officer. He walked like he was *more* than an officer. Behind him, a dark cloak flowed over the ground, as if it followed some wicked emperor on his inaugural march.

The officer seemed unconcerned with the downpour, as the rain tattered hard against his garments. His gloved hands were clasped behind his back as he patiently strode forward, his eyes shrouded beneath the shadow of the visor.

Jayden removed his cowboy hat from his head and shrank involuntarily as the coldness of the rain hit his face for the first time.

As the officer drew near, Scott could make out the first indication of an insignia on his visor hat. It was a red, upside-down triangle divided by a vertical black line. He had never seen the symbol before.

David tilted his head toward Scott and whispered, "These are Nightmen."

The two guards snapped to attention. Scott and his comrades did the same. The Nightman officer slammed to a halt in front of them.

For the first time, Scott could discern the officer's features. His face bore diminutive scars, none distinguishable enough to stand out on their own, though together they formed an invincible countenance. Traces of brown hair arched above his ears, though the rest remained concealed beneath the visor hat. His massive frame left no mystery as to the purpose of his role. Power.

His eyes were cold. They bore a kind of hateful arrogance that Scott had never seen before, as they shifted from one operative to the other, and then to the next, and then to the next, as if each stare summed up the men's worth with an unimpressed glance. The voice they heard next was not Russian, but it was unmistakably dominant. Each syllable was enunciated to perfect authority.

"I am Thoor."

Scott's body was captivated by a coldness that had nothing to do with the rain. Thoor. Ignatius van Thoor, former captain of the Nightmen. The general of *Novosibirsk*. It couldn't be. No. It couldn't be him. Before any of them could utter a syllable, the man's autocratic drone resumed.

"And you are David Jurgen, Becan McCrae, Scott Remington, and Jayden Timmons."

It was really him. It was General Thoor—the most feared man in all of EDEN. Standing right there in front of them.

"Yes, I know you," Thoor said. "I know you well. I know every man and every woman who sets foot on this concrete. I am the first voice you hear when you arrive, and I will be the last voice you hear when you leave, if I find you insufficient enough to bear the privilege of being stationed at my facility."

Scott dared not glance at his comrades. His eyes remained frozen ahead in perfect attention.

"I know that Private Timmons scored in the upper eighth percentile as a graduating sniper, and that Private McCrae was heralded as one of the more competent fighters in his division. I know that Private Jurgen was a member of the New York Police Department, and after a mediocre run at law enforcement took his lack of talents to the Academy."

Scott blinked. *Mediocre* run? David's eyes flicked downward.

"I know that Private Remington is the youngest soldier to earn a Golden Lion…a young man who has a 'natural talent for leadership', as his former colonel so eloquently put it." Thoor's glare narrowed. "I know everything that each of you has ever done, and I will know everything you ever do, so long as you reside inside the walls of this Machine known as *Novosibirsk*.

"We are not nice here. You will not be catered to, and your opinions will not be tolerated. You are here for one reason—to pull the trigger without mercy. You are here to kill. You are soldiers, not thinkers. The moment you deceive yourself into believing that you have a free will, you will receive an awakening like none you have experienced.

"Those of you who are destined to remain followers will follow without question. You will obey each and every order to maximum capacity, putting your lives as secondary to completing your objectives. Those of you who are destined to become leaders will learn to lead without sympathy. You will learn to sacrifice your own lives as well as the lives of those around you for the sake of the task at hand, without allowing the pitiful shadows of mercy to hinder your judgment. We are not here to protect humanity. We are here to destroy all those who oppose it.

"Whatever leniency you were given before vanishes now. You are here because you are above average for your rank, and you will be expected to execute as if you are above average for your rank. Failure to do so, at any time, for any reason, will result in immediate termination."

Immediate termination. Scott's stomach knotted as he wondered what that meant.

"I will not ask you if there are any questions. If you are asking questions, then you are thinking. If you are thinking, then you are not focusing on the task at hand. If you are not focusing on the task at hand, then you are useless to me and will be extinguished. Your task at hand is and always will be subordination. There is nothing else you need to consider."

Thoor paused, and his haughty gaze narrowed for a final time. It swept from one operative to the next until it was satisfied, at which point he hammered a conclusive statement.

"That is all."

He swung around, and his saturated cloak sloshed behind him. Without another word, he strode back to *Novosibirsk*.

None of them spoke. The rain continued to pelt down, and the thunder continued to rumble. Not one of them uttered a word. For almost thirty entire seconds, the only disturbance of nature were the vapors of their breaths as they huffed in frozen silence. Becan finally broke with a wet sputter.

"God—"

One of the guards cut him off. "Report to the billeting office at once." His tone—mechanized behind the veil of his zombified helmet—left no room for argument. They made their way past the hangar to the main building, with no more outside remarks.

As they entered, they found themselves standing in the mouth of a dimly lit corridor. The floor was not furnished tile as it was at

Richmond, but instead flat gray pavement. The walls were a pale green, and they were marred with cracks and chips. The air was bland and stale.

Becan shivered as he closed the outer door. "So where's the bloody billeting office?"

Scott shook his head as water drops ran down his cheeks. "I have no idea." They weren't given anything to go by. They were just turned loose. So much for not thinking on their own. Next to him, Jayden shook his rain-soaked hat.

Scott inspected the corridor. Several hallways were attached to it, along with various wooden doors. Surely the billeting office was somewhere nearby. He searched his comrades' faces, where his gaze lingered on David, who hadn't said a thing since Thoor's speech. Since Thoor called his tenure with the NYPD a 'mediocre run'. Was it true? Scott frowned but said nothing. He turned back to Becan. "There's got to be a directory here. Let's find it."

It took them only a few minutes to locate a directory down one of the hallways, and only a minute more to locate the billeting office. It was locked, apparently for the night. Aside from themselves, Thoor, and the two guards, they had yet to come across any other signs of life. It was as if the hallways were completely abandoned.

Scott scanned the hall near the billeting office, where he found a terminal embedded in the wall. The EDEN logo blinked in an algae-green display monitor. Scott stepped to the terminal and tapped a finger against it. The logo disappeared, and a list of languages replaced it. Scott selected English, and a screen of user options emerged.

"Here's hoping they're up to date," Scott mumbled as he accessed the personnel directory. An alphabetical list appeared, out of which he selected R. Once there, it took him only a moment to scroll down and find his last name. They were already in the system. He tapped on his roster entry, and a green screen appeared with his full name, rank, and position. Beneath it, the display indicated that he resided in structure B-1, Room 14.

"Simple enough," Scott said. He returned to the roster and found Jurgen on the alphabetical list. David was in Room 14 as well.

Becan observed from Scott's side. "Roommates again."

Scott nodded. "Wonder if you guys are next door again." Scott navigated the roster until he came to M, where he found McCrae. As soon as Becan's information arose, both Scott and Becan raised their eyebrows.

"Mm…"

Jayden stepped over to them. "Where are we?"

"Room 14…" said Becan.

Jayden's expression widened as he craned to the monitor. "What?" David stared at the screen in silence.

"I'm in Room 14," Becan said.

Jayden fidgeted. "What about me?"

"Hang on," Scott said as he backtracked out of Becan's file found Jayden's.

Room 14.

Jayden's mouth hung open. "We're all in the same room?"

"What are they, quads?" David asked as he squinted at the monitor.

"Must be," Scott said as he inspected the terminal for a moment, then backed out of the personnel files to access the base map. After a brief search, he found B-1. "It's a few buildings behind this one." After a few more taps, he found Room 14. It was on the ground level of a building that had a sublevel beneath it.

"That looks like one hell of a big room," said David with some surprise.

Scott laughed under his breath. "Only one way to find out." He took a step away from the terminal and faced his comrades. The four men exchanged looks.

The trek to B-1 was cold and wet, and they were once again forced to dash through the downpour to reach the building. By the time they arrived, they were as wet as they had been on the airstrip. B-1 was a large building, like the one from which they had come, though its hallways were stark gray. As was the case with the main building, there were no signs of life anywhere. The men shivered as they traversed the ground level for Room 14.

The building was a catacomb. Narrow corridors branched off

of wider corridors both left and right, and the sheer size of the structure hit them. *Novosibirsk* was more massive than *Richmond* in every way.

The numerical layout was simple, and they were able to find the door to Room 14 without a directory. It was in the exact center of the ground level. Only the number "14" graced its pale gray finish.

Becan crossed his arms. "How are we supposed to be gettin' in? We've no bloody key."

Scott gripped the knob, where it turned effortlessly in his hand. The door cracked open, and Scott gave Becan a smug smile. The Irishman said nothing.

A ray of hallway light cut through the darkness of the room. As it widened, the four men poked their heads into their new home. It took several seconds for their eyes to adjust, but soon the features of the room came into view. It was not the view they expected, or wanted, to see. Bunks. Rows and rows of bunks. Slumbered breaths reverberated through the room, and Jayden summed up the scene. "Barracks," he whispered. "B-1…barracks number one."

A groggy voice mumbled in the blackness. Scott eased the door shut, then turned to stare at his comrades.

"Aw, man," Jayden said.

Scott almost laughed. If not for the fact that he was cold, wet, and miserable, he might have laughed out loud. "We're going to have to sneak in and *find* empty bunks. We might end up on the floor tonight."

Becan snorted. "If I were mad, I would!"

"Would you rather sleep out here in the hall?"

Becan's gaze narrowed. "Righ', well how abou' this? I'm knackered an' wrecked as all bloody hell, an' I don't exactly consider barrelin' around in me underrods with a bunch o' torn off Russian hardchaws suckin' ion."

"First of all," Scott answered, "I have no idea what you just said. Second of all, whatever it was, I don't think there's anything we can do about it."

Becan opened his mouth to reply, but Jayden cut him off. "We're all tired, man. We're all freezin', we're all soakin' wet, but the thing said we're in Room 14, and Room 14 is right here. Personally, I don't care if I get those people mad or not. I'm draggin' tired, and they didn't just fly across the world after packin' up everything they own at the drop of a hat. If they have a problem they can talk to their supervisor, but it ain't my problem. Let's just find some hot showers, get warmed up, and find beds. All right?"

Becan eyed Jayden for a moment and remained silent for just as long, before he drew in a breath and gave a single nod. "Yeah. All righ'."

Jayden nodded, and David cleared his throat. "Let's find some showers, then," he said. "Do we all have dry clothes?" The other three men motioned to their duffle bags. "Okay. Let's get warmed up before we catch hypothermia."

They ventured as a group throughout the maze of hallways, though soon realized that there was no shower room to be found. They explored every inch of the building, on both the ground level and sublevel, but came across only sporadically placed restrooms. After twenty minutes in search, they settled on a dark corner of their floor, where they removed their wet clothes and changed into multiple layers of dryer, warmer outfits. Through the entire ordeal, the corridors stayed secluded and silent. Once they were in dry clothes, they returned to Room 14.

Upon entrance to the room, they discovered that, though not spacious, there was sufficient space between the bunks to allow reasonable movement. A brief count by Scott revealed twelve bunks, in four rows of three, half of which were occupied. The quest for a place to shower came to a conclusion as well, as they discovered three open stalls along the far side of the room, all of which drained through holes in the floor. Only beige curtains sheltered the stalls from the rest of the room.

After a brief search, they found two empty bunks on the far side of the room, one next to the other. They set their bags on the floor, claimed their mattresses, then nestled warmly under their covers. Jet lag was not an issue that night, as they all fell asleep in a matter of minutes.

12

BECAN HAD NEVER felt so tired. He had never felt so out of it. As his eyes squinted and opened, a cold head-rush washed across his brain. What time was it? He had no idea. He knew it must have been early still—the windowless room was still dim. His head rang. He could hear the constant tone assault his ears. Russia? Why the hell were they in Russia? It felt like a dream, and for a moment he wondered if it might have been. No. It was real. Yesterday really did happen, and today he was halfway across the globe.

He muttered under his breath as he pressed a palm against his forehead. He knew he was out of it. He could feel it in his equilibrium. It felt as if he just awoken from a merry-go-round. He continued to squint between partially opened eyes. It was painful. God. He felt like a miserable dog. He felt cold. None of them had been given the chance to warm themselves before they snuck into bed, and now it showed. *No bloody showers*, Becan thought. *Don't want to wake up the bloody Russians, do we?* His palm pressed harder into his forehead as he clenched his teeth. *Bollocks. I'm takin' me bloody shower. Drag 'em to hell.*

Still groggy-eyed and disoriented, Becan twisted over to the side of the bed and set his feet on the floor. It was frigid. It was absolutely frigid. He drew in a breath and pushed up. He could hear the constant tone in his head still; it was as if this were a hangover that had nothing to do with alcohol. It was a sleepover. He grumbled at the thought of the word as he stumbled forward and to the showers.

Trashin' Russians, he thought. *Trashin' Russians and their stupid trashin' barracks.* One foot in front of the other. One heavy thump forward after the next. His vision was blurry. The tone in his ears still rung. *Trashin' Russians.* He reached forward with reckless abandon and whisked open the curtain.

She whipped her wet head around as soon as the curtains exposed her. Her eyes shot open as the downpour of water plastered her golden locks to the sides of her face. Becan gasped. She screamed.

"Ahh!" Becan back-peddled and stumbled onto the floor in an explosion of thumps and bangs.

Scott jolted up from his bed as the shower curtain was yanked shut. "What in the world?" Several others had leapt up around him, and he focused his attention to the floor, where Becan was a tangled mess.

"I decided to take a bloody shower," Becan grumbled.

Scott gaped across at the showers in time to see a green towel jerk down from behind the shower stall.

Russian words were mumbled out loud from farther back in the room. The woman behind the curtain yelled something back as the showerhead twisted off.

What time was it? Everything felt like a blur. Seconds ago, Scott had been off in some distant dream, none of which he could remember now. And now, crashing, yelling, people suddenly rousing all over…it was too early for this. Was it too early for this?

"God," Becan said as he staggered to a stand. "Top o' the mornin' to yis."

Scott blinked as a woman dressed only in undergarments stormed out from behind the shower. A towel whisked through her wet hair as she glared at Becan, and Russian fury poured from her mouth.

Before she could finish her spiel, a male voice farther back in the room cut her off. "Zatknis, Sveta." More Russian ensued.

"English!" someone hollered. "Speak English, you Commies!"

The Russian voice groaned. "I said it's almost time to get up anyway."

The *Richmond* transfers cringed as an overhead light flicked on, and various men and women slid out of their bunks. They made their way toward a long closet that ran along the wall opposite the showers. Scott droned in his morning-deep voice, "What's going on?"

David rubbed his eyes as he sat up. "I think…we just woke up."

Scott pushed a hand through his unkempt hair and regarded David. "Were we *supposed* to wake up?"

"I want to sleep," mumbled Jayden from beneath his covers.

Scott's attention returned to Becan. "What in the world were you doing?"

"Nothin'!" Becan said. "Don't get your knickers in a twist."

"How do you do, gentlemen?"

The new voice came from directly behind them. It was a voice laden with a distinct British dialect. Scott, David, and Becan turned to face it, where they found a brown-haired man dressed in an officer's uniform. After a brief moment of scrutiny, Scott saw that he was a captain. The captain offered a courteous smile as he trained his eyes on Jayden's bunk, where the Texan was still completely beneath the covers.

"Aah," Becan said as he jerked the covers from atop Jayden. "Get up."

Jayden mumbled something inaudible, then raised his head. When he saw the captain, he briskly sat upright.

"Sorry," the captain said. "It looks like you've all had a rough night. You needn't beetle around the room getting organized, but do get showered and get into uniform as soon as you're able. When you've finished, please join us through *that* door." He pointed to a door along the back wall, where several Russian operatives were already passing through. The four transfers nodded as the captain excused himself and made his own way through the indicated doorway.

By the time they had woken up, taken showers, and donned their uniforms, they were the only four left in the bunk room. Everyone else had passed through the indicated door. As soon as Scott stepped through it, he realized what it was.

It was a small lounge, complete with a culinary counter and several tables, all of which had a full complement of occupied chairs. The mingled smell of tea and coffee floated through the air as conversation in both English and Russian bustled, accompanied by an occasional burst of laughter. Scott noticed right away that there were no other doors in the room—it must have been specifically designed for this unit. He wondered if every unit had its own lounge.

They stood in the doorway for several moments before the captain noticed them. He regarded them with a proper smile. "I see you've finally got up and about then? Welcome to the lounge. While you're in here, there's no need for formalities. We wouldn't survive without a casual atmosphere once in a while." Scott nodded, and he and his comrades assumed more at-ease postures. Scott allowed his eyes to scan the operatives clustered around the tables.

Smiles were few and far between. Most of their expressions were blank, with the captain a rare exception. The only other familiar face belonged to the blond-haired woman from the shower, whose pointed glare narrowed at Becan.

The captain continued. "I'm sorry, you four must be zonked out...I'll go ahead and explain to you why you're here. Just to be certain...you *are* David Jurgen, Becan McCrae, Scott Remington, and Jayden Timmons, correct?"

They nodded.

"Brilliant," the captain said. "As you may or may not be aware, *Novosibirsk* Command are in the process of restocking our base. A few units, ourselves included, have received entirely new sections in addition to the personnel already in place. You're ours. I apologize that your transfer seems to have come in quite the inconvenient manner for you, but you're here, and that's all that matters now."

He motioned his head to the nearest table of operatives. "I suppose introductions are in order." Introductions. A whole new unit. Scott had just become comfortable with everyone back in Charlie Squad. "At my right is Gamma Private Fox Powers, our only resident sniper until now." Scott glanced toward Fox. He was a tanned, black-haired individual. His expression was stoic, yet not uninviting. He fit as a sniper.

"Technician and Delta Trooper Matthew Axen, otherwise known as Max..." Scott's attention swung to Max. He was a taller

American with short dirty blond hair, complemented by a thick brush of five o'clock shadow. There was something else that stood out about him, though. His eyes. They locked onto Scott with a pointed stare. More than a stare. Almost angered. Before Scott could scrutinize it further, Clarke went on.

"Delta Trooper Travis Navarro, our pilot."

Travis. There was an amiable look to Travis. It was an ordinary look. Brown hair, brown eyes, not overly handsome or repulsive. Ordinary. The pilot smiled and tipped his head.

"And Beta Private Kevin Carpenter."

Another average looking, somewhat smaller man.

"At the next table is Commander Ivan Baranov, our second in command…"

There came the change. Baranov was massive. Larger than General Thoor. His dark crew cut was trimmed to perfection; it was completely militant. There was another distinct feature about him. His uniform…it was different. It was dark, almost free of emblems. Except for a red triangle. A Nightman. Baranov nodded as Clarke continued.

"Lieutenant Yuri Dostoevsky."

Smaller. But just as militant as Baranov. Maybe more so. His eyes stood out. They were blue, yet they pierced toward the transfers with bridled fury. Not…not toward the *transfers*. Toward Scott. Dostoevsky too was a Nightman.

"Lieutenant Anatoly Novikov, our head technician." Less stout than the previous two Russian officers. Blond-haired, blue eyed. Handsome. Another Nightman. The three officers beneath the captain, all Nightmen. Scott looked around at the other tables. Everyone else was standard EDEN.

"Beta Private Konstantin Makarovich, otherwise known as Kostya." Scott watched Kostya. He was young. Younger than… was he younger than Jayden? Kostya smiled as he waved.

"And Beta Private Boris Evteev, our final technician." There were three technicians in the unit. That was different from Charlie. This unit was more versatile, perhaps all-purpose. Boris tipped his mop of curly black hair to them as the captain directed to the final table.

"And at our very last table are the three women you *don't* want to see, because if you do, that means something's gone gammy." He nodded to the first woman. It was the blond-haired woman from before. The one from the shower. "We have Delta Trooper Svetlana Voronova, our chief medic…"

She was beautiful. Despite the daggers in her eyes. Her body was gracefully athletic, and her cascade of golden-blond hair fell damply to her shoulders. As soon as she was mentioned, Dostoevsky murmured in her direction. The men around him chuckled.

"Zatknis," she spat back.

The captain went on. "And her medical staff. Gamma Private Galina Lebesheva." Galina seemed the oldest of the three women. She might have been as old as David. Her hair was shorter, almost butch. Definitely butch. But her body was toned. She smiled cordially, but was otherwise uninspirational.

"And Beta Private Varvara Yudina." Varvara had blond hair as well, though slightly longer and slightly darker than Svetlana's. And unlike Svetlana's shoulder-length bob, Varvara's hair was curly. As she smiled, two miniscule dimples emerged from her cheeks. Scott tilted his head and grinned. She really smiled. No daggers, no cordiality. Genuine. He liked her already.

The captain stood abrupt. "And I am Captain Nathan Clarke, your commanding officer. We make up the Fourteenth. When we asked for additional operatives, I must admit I was slightly concerned when I heard they were sending us men not even a month out of the Academy, but when I looked at your records and what you did in Chicago, I was most impressed." Clarke's focus shifted to Scott. "Congratulations on your promotion to gamma private, and for the Golden Lion. I know that's only a medal, but, well, it's never been earned like this before. We're going to expect a lot out of you, out of *all* of you. You've all earned excellent marks from your superiors at *Richmond*. Now…I know Remington from the news…who else is who?"

David, Becan, and Jayden briefly introduced themselves. They were met with continued apathy from the tables. Aside from a handful—Clarke, Travis, Varvara—perhaps one or two others, it was a relatively cold reception.

"Welcome to the Fourteenth," Clarke said. "There are a few things I still need to discuss with you, so I'll go ahead and tend to that right now. The rest of you may go about your business," he said to the other operatives. "We won't hold a session this morning."

A sporadic round of affirmations murmured forth as the operatives rose and filed out of the room. Several of them nodded in departure to the four transfers. Most just walked by without acknowledging them. After several moments, the lounge was clear.

Clarke waited several seconds before he stepped to the door, closed it, and sighed. "That was a giggle." He smiled half-heartedly and meandered to one of the tables.

"Have a seat, please." They joined him as he sat down.

"I'm sorry. I wish I could say that your arrival here will be a fantastic opportunity for you, but I'm not sure that'd be entirely honest. Any rumors you've heard about *Novosibirsk* are probably true. This place is a hellhole, and a tense one at that."

Scott was puzzled—*this* was different. The atmosphere shifted from the confines of the military to the casual sensation of a fireside chat.

"I'm sure you were given a proper greeting when you first arrived."

A proper greeting? He had to be talking about the general meeting them on the airstrip. How did he know about that? "Do you mean General Thoor, sir?"

"Yes, General Thoor. He personally meets every individual who sets foot on this base. He and his Nightmen."

David spoke up for the first time. "I thought the Nightmen were disbanded years ago. Why are they working with EDEN?"

"The Nightmen aren't working for EDEN," Clarke answered. "They never have and they never will. They officially don't even exist, but they're still here. When *Novosibirsk* opened her doors, a lot of Nightmen flocked here to sign up. Thoor was already well known in the Nightman circuit, so when he got the role of general, it was added incentive to join. Make no mistake…this base may be owned by EDEN, but it's run by the Nightmen."

"Why doesn't EDEN stop it?" David asked. "Why don't they enforce their own regulations?"

"Because Thoor is too effective to risk losing," Clarke answered.

"And they know he wouldn't readily give up *Novosibirsk* without a fight."

Without a fight? Was Thoor an EDEN general or a madman? "You mean to tell me he'd *fight* EDEN?"

"Abso-bloody-lutely. But that will never happen. He stays within EDEN guidelines just enough to keep Command out of his business. They're not going to risk losing *Novosibirsk* over which uniform he and his men decide to wear."

Scott shot a look in the direction of the lounge door, still closed. He couldn't help but wonder if all new arrivals got this conversation.

"How many Nightmen are there, sir?" Becan asked.

Clarke shifted in his chair. "This facility has slightly over ten thousand operatives...I'd say about three thousand of those are former Nightmen."

"That's only a third."

"That third is in command," Clarke answered. "That's how this place is run, with key Nightmen in key positions. Just look at this unit. Ivan, Yuri, and Anatoly—the other three officers. They're loyal to my command, but they're dead loyal to Thoor's. They're great men though, especially Ivan. I couldn't ask for a better executive officer. Nonetheless...they are Nightmen."

As far as Scott knew, most Nightmen were Russian. But not Thoor. His voice had been something different. If Clarke was in the mood to dish out answers, Scott was going to ask questions. "Thoor's not Russian, is he?"

"No, he's not," Clarke answered. "And if you're thinking that most Nightmen are Russian, you're correct. I would estimate that over ninety-five percent of them are. Thoor is Dutch. He was known as the 'Terror of Amsterdam' before he came to *Novosibirsk*. As far as how he became a leader in the Nightman sect...if you knew him well enough, you'd understand. He's a formidable leader. He's heartless, treacherous, merciless, but formidable. He's got the mentality for it. All of the Nightmen are that way, that's why they're so effective. The Nightmen are trained like no one else I've seen, and it shows."

Clarke smiled. "As much as I enjoy being interrogated, I did want to go over a few things with you. Morning call is at six o'clock, and we usually start in here. Tea and coffee are always here if you need them. By seven, we're out of the door for our morning routine. We usually run several kilometers in the training center as a unit, though sometimes we swim laps…whatever I decide at the time, really. At 1700 on Mondays, Wednesdays, and Fridays, we meet in the gymnasium for a group workout, in the form of weight lifting, free sparring, or something of the sort. You're free to use the gymnasium as often as you'd like on your own time, and though I don't demand it, I highly encourage it. There's a strict curfew at 2100, everyone is to be in his or her room by then, preferably sleeping, though the back room is always open for coffee or a late-night chinwag if sleep is evasive.

"And as I'm sure you've discovered," he grinned and glanced to Becan, "we've got three showers in the main room."

Becan folded his arms across his chest and looked down.

"You probably aren't accustomed to showering right next to everyone as they sleep," Clarke said, "but you'll adjust. There's no set time for showering."

No one spoke, and Clarke pushed back his chair and stood.

"That's all I wanted to talk about. You gentlemen are free to go about your business until 1700. I'm going to make my way to the cafeteria for some breakfast—you're more than welcomed to come if you'd like. You should have privacy here for another half hour or so, when people start filing back in from breakfast."

Scott rose after Clarke with the others, and he watched as the captain meandered to the door. This was the strangest military introduction he had ever been a part of. It was completely casual, and completely uncalled for. It was enough to commit him to one last question. "Sir?"

Clarke stopped and turned back to the table.

"Why did you tell us all of this?"

David, Becan, and Jayden all looked at Scott, then turned to Clarke. That very same question lingered on all their expressions.

Clarke scrutinized Scott for a moment, before he offered a half-hearted smile. "It's because you're new here. You haven't been tainted yet. And I suppose…I want to influence you as much as possible before they do."

Again silence pervaded the room. They? The Nightmen? Before Scott could think further, Clarke said, "Now if you'll excuse me, I've got to tuck into some breakfast. Cheerio."

Scott watched him leave the room. No more explanations were offered. The lounge door eased shut behind Clarke, and they were alone for the first time since they had arrived on the transport from *Richmond*.

They remained in the lounge for another minute, though said little. They then filed out of the room, retrieved their duffle bags, and set up their bunks for permanent residence.

*   *   *

THEY FINISHED THEIR acclimation to Room 14 by 0730, at which point they ventured out together in search of the cafeteria. The sun had risen two hours earlier, though no sunlight shone on the ground. The sky was blanketed in funereal gray. The earth was saturated with wetness from the previous night's storm. The air was frigid. There were few trees on the outskirts of the base, and it seemed to Scott that *Novosibirsk* was in the middle of an epic expanse of nothing—only snow-covered hills and fields.

The cafeteria was bustling when they arrived. Men and sporadic women lined up to receive their meals, colorless pale trays in their hands as they anticipated cold servings from uninspired attendants. Nobody looked familiar. During the time from when Scott took his tray to when he received his meal, he saw no one from the Fourteenth in the cafeteria. Smiles were sparse, though they were there. All of the conversation he took in was in Russian, or at least some language other than English.

As they weaved through the cafeteria in search of a place to sit, one table in particular caught Scott's eye. It stood out for a reason he hadn't expected. At it sat a black man. He was the only black man in the entire cafeteria. Directly across from him sat a giant of a soldier. There were no others with them. Their postures were casual, relaxed. As they talked, their gestures swayed in familiar patterns. From his distance, Scott couldn't make out what they were saying. He didn't need to.

"Americans."

"Mm?"

Scott glanced to Becan. "Americans, over there. They've got to be."

"How can yeh tell?"

Scott offered no explanation. He didn't need to. He altered his direction for their table, and the other three followed. The black man and the giant turned to face them as soon as they neared.

"Mind if we sit down?" Scott asked.

The larger man looked surprised, and a broad smile painted itself across the black man's face. "USA?"

Scott grinned. He knew it. "USA and looking for more."

"Well, you got two more right here," the black man said as he gestured for them to sit. "Joe Janson. My friend here's William Harbinger."

As Scott sat down, he sized up William. The guy was huge. His hands were like boxing gloves, and his frame was as wide as a door. Harbinger was an appropriate moniker. Scott introduced himself, and David, Becan, and Jayden followed suit.

William flashed a broad grin. "So y'all new here?"

David chuckled. "It's that easy to tell?"

"Nobody else is that friendly. Where y'all from?"

"*Richmond.* Got here last night."

William nodded. "We been here 'bout a month. We were both stationed in *Atlanta* for about three days before they shipped us out here. Had one mission in *Atlanta* on our second day, they got rid of us the day after."

Joe chuckled. "Had enough of us, I guess. What are you guys, soldiers?"

Scott nodded. "Soldiers and a sniper." He motioned to Jayden, who waved. "What about you?"

"Soldier," Joe answered.

"Scout," said William.

A scout? Scott wondered skeptically. The pride of the Academy, known for their acrobatics and their ability to crawl through small spaces? William the harbinger? Scott's eyes narrowed with scrutiny.

"Yeah, he's a scout," Joe said. "He's a scout like I'm an Ithini."

"Demolitionist," William confessed with a smirk.

Scott smiled. "That's more like it." He liked them already. Easygoing, conversational, and not equipped with the cold shoulder that seemed standard on Russian personnel. "So what's it like here? You've been here a month—any action?"

"We went out once," William answered, "about two weeks ago, I guess. Bakma Cruiser got shot down about a hundred miles south of here, so they sent our team in after it. That's what got us up to beta. Haven't seen any Ceratopians...not here or in *Atlanta*."

"We haven't either," David said. "We did go on a little bug-hunt, though."

Joe's expression widened. "Are you serious?"

"Yeah. One of the worst experiences of my life."

William swallowed a bite of food. "That what got you all to beta?"

"No," David answered. "That was Chicago. For most of us, anyway."

William's attention perked immediately. "Oh man, you were there for Chicago? That made the news everywhere!"

Before anyone else could comment, Joe's eyes shot wide. He stared at Scott and perked upright. "Oh veck!" Scott sighed. William stared at Joe. Everyone else remained silent. "Oh veck!"

"What?" William asked, looking perplexedly around the group.

"I knew I knew you!" Joe said.

Scott knew what Joe was talking about immediately. Fame had followed him to Russia.

"Come on, Will, you know!"

William's eyes widened. "Oh veck!"

"This is the Golden Lion guy!"

"Yeah," William said, "the Golden Lion!"

Scott feigned a smile as he acknowledged with a nod. There it was again. *The* Golden Lion. Was that what he was now? No—he was a soldier, not some movie star or action hero. And certainly not a walking medal. He was a soldier who had done the right thing at the right time, around the right people in the right positions. Nicole didn't think he was a hero. She thought he was an idiot. "God was watching over me. I had nothing to do with it." He cringed inwardly. What an automatic answer. Did he mean it?

Joe smiled and shook his head. "Man, if you and God are *that* close, I want me and you to be good friends." The others laughed.

"Seriously," Scott said, "it was nothing special. Anyone could have done it." Yes, God had been watching over him. But nobody else could have pulled that off like he did. Anyone could have done it? That was a lie. He had known what he was doing. He had known it would work.

Yet it didn't save Henry and Zigler.

"What unit are you guys in?" Scott asked.

"The Eighth," William answered. "One of the bigger units here. I mean in physical size, not…size…I mean we, in the unit, are bigger people than those in other units."

Joe laughed. "Will's a little slow."

"Shut up."

"He's right, though. We're a pretty big group. Got five demos… no mystery what we were made to do."

William gleamed. "Blow junk up."

"How many are in the Eighth?" David asked.

"Eighteen," Joe answered. "Most of 'em ate already. I'd introduce you to some if they were around."

William pointed across the room. "There's Cole right there."

Scott followed William's gesture across the room, where an average-sized man with jet-black hair strode toward their table. He looked scruffy. A patch of black hair under his chin formed an off-centered goatee. Barely off, but definitely off. To the left. God. That was going to drive Scott crazy.

Joe smiled as the man approached. "That's Derrick Cole, another one of our soldiers. He's American. As southern country as you can get."

David grinned at William. "I don't know—you sound pretty southern."

William shook his head. "No, see…I'm southern. Cole is a hick."

Cole smiled as he lowered himself into a chair next to Joe. "Hey y'all, how y'all doin'?"

Scott smiled. Will was right. Cole had the longest drawl he had ever heard. His voice was deep. Like a bass. But that goatee...God, how did that happen? Didn't the Eighth have a mirror somewhere?"

"Cole-C-Cole-Cole-Cooole!" William sang.

Cole shot him a look. "Shut up, Harbringer."

William's expression dropped. "Hey man, come on, don't do that."

Joe laughed. "They misspelled Big Will's name on his graduate paper from the Academy, put Harbringer instead of Harbinger. Even his name badge is misspelled."

William stopped eating. "It's not funny."

Cole laughed, then lowered his head in silence. Again, Scott smiled. Prayer before eating. Good. Suddenly, Scott's smile faded. He had forgotten to pray for his own meal.

Becan glanced at Cole's tray. It was piled with what appeared to be the *Novosibirsk* equivalent of chili and beans. Or something of the gaseous persuasion. "Hell of a bloody breakfast, eh?"

"Derrick likes anything that makes him fart," smirked William.

"Yer *momma* likes anything that makes her fart."

Joe nodded at Scott and his comrades. "They just came in from *Richmond*."

Cole swallowed a bite and smiled. "This is definitely a step down from there. What unit y'all in?"

"Fourteenth," David answered.

"Oh, that's what his face's..."

Joe nodded. "Clarke."

"Yeah, Clarke."

William took a sip of water. "That's one of the general's favorite units. They get a lot of good calls, I dunno if that has anything to do with Clarke. Sometimes they get to go on missions that others don't."

"It's because of the Nightmen in it," Joe said.

Cole nodded. "Y'all got a good commander."

William smiled. "Yeah. Ivan's a tank, but he's a good guy, too. Can't say that about many Nightmen."

"What makes the Nightmen so bad?" Scott asked. Brutal, he knew they were that. But every military organization had some level of brutality.

William began his explanation with a question. "Do you know what you have to do to become a Nightman?"

"No," Scott answered as he looked around the table. The others too wore uninformed expressions.

William shot a quick look to Joe and Cole.

"You got to tell 'em, now," Joe said. His voice was different now. It was hushed.

William leaned in close to Scott. "You have to kill somebody."

Kill somebody? "Soldiers kill all the time…"

William shook his head. "No, not aliens or anything like that. You have to kill someone here."

"Yeh have to *murder* someone?" Becan asked.

"Shh!" William flagged his hand. "We're not supposed to know that. Although everybody knows it, it's just that nobody talks about it."

"Yeh been here a month an' yeh know it already?" asked Becan. "Tha's not tha' good of a secret…"

"We only know it 'cause someone in our unit told us. Romanian guy."

"Was he a Nightman?" David asked.

"Hell no. You ask a Nightman about that and you're likely to get killed yourself."

Scott shook his head slowly. Did he understand this right? "Let me get this straight…you have to *murder* someone to become a Nightman?"

William nodded. "It's like one of their rights of passage, or something. They call it the Murder Rule. The last step."

"But *why*?"

"To sell your soul, I guess. If you'll kill someone in cold blood for them, you'll probably do anything for them. That's what they want."

"What about the ones who won't do it?"

"I don't know. I don't think I *want* to know."

David leaned forward. "Wait a second…how the hell can they do that? EDEN's *got* to know about this."

"That's *Novosibirsk*, the exception to the rules. EDEN just looks the other way."

"This place is Thoor's little empire," Joe said. "EDEN doesn't care what he does, long as he does it good."

Cole fidgeted in his chair. "Guys, let's change the subject."

Joe nodded. "Yeah. Best not to talk about it here. We don't know much more anyhow."

Scott didn't want to change the subject, and by the looks of everyone else, neither did they. Even Jayden, silent on the far end, looked engrossed.

William slid his glass of water to the side. "You guys are going to free-spar today."

Whether he liked it or not, the subject was changing. Scott said nothing, though he had a dozen questions on his mind.

"Are we now?" Becan asked.

"Yeah," William answered. "It's Wednesday, and the Fourteenth always spars on Wednesday."

"How d'yeh know this?"

"Because of Ivan. The guy is a tank. Everyone goes there to watch him."

"Actually they go to watch whoever he ends up beatin' to death," said Cole sardonically.

"It's rarely a good fight," William said with a grin. "Except when that other Russian guy in your unit fights him. I don't know his name. Then it's good."

He had to be talking about one of the lieutenants. Unless he was talking about Boris the technician. Somehow, Scott doubted that.

"Yeah," Cole said, "that one guy gives him a hell of a fight."

Joe laughed. "You guys are in for it if you have to fight Ivan. You ever fight a guy back in the Academy by the name of—"

"Captain Williams?" Scott asked with a knowing smile.

Both Joe and William laughed out loud. "Yeah! You fought Captain Williams, too?"

David grinned. "I think everyone fought Captain Williams."

"Well," Joe said, "if you couldn't handle Williams, there's no way you're gonna handle Ivan."

"Could you handle Williams?" David asked.

Joe shook his head. "None of us could handle Williams."

Scott sized up William. He was almost twice Captain Williams' size, and Captain Williams was no small man. "Not even you?"

William shook his head. "Nope. He got me just like he got everyone else."

Joe smiled. "Just like Ivan gets everybody in the Fourteenth."

William leaned back and grinned. "Speaking of that again… you got some babes in your unit, man."

Scott laughed. That comment seemed appropriate from someone like William.

Jayden spoke for the first time. It was almost odd to hear his voice. "Man, you are right." Scott cracked a surprise grin at the Texan. That was the last thing he expected to hear from him. "Every woman in EDEN is hot."

"It's their bodies, man," Joe said. "It's not that they got pretty faces…they just got some fine bodies. All that exercise."

"Becan can tell you all about their bodies," said David slyly.

Scott laughed. "Or at least Svetlana's."

Becan leaned back with a grin spread across his face. "Yeh just jealous. All o' yeh."

William looked around, puzzled.

"It's nothin'," Becan said. "Inside joke."

"Hey guys," Cole interrupted, "what time is it?"

Joe and William looked at their watches. Joe jumped up. "Oh veck, we got to go."

"What is it?" Scott asked.

"We got a meeting at 8:30. It's 8:15."

Scott watched as Joe, William, and Cole pushed back from their chairs and picked up their trays.

"It was great talking to you guys," Joe said. "Not a whole lot of Americans here if you haven't noticed already."

"Yeah," William said. "We're the only Americans in the Eighth and we're a pretty Americanized unit. I think the Fourteenth is, too…how many you got in yours again?"

Scott had to think about that one. Jayden answered immediately. "Eight, counting us." Scott was surprised. That was quick…

he couldn't even remember half of their new comrades' names. Leave it to a sniper.

"Oh wow," Joe said. "That's a lot...that might be more than in any other unit here. I mean...we got a lot, and we only got three."

"If you count Clarke, that's nine English people," Jayden said.

"Wow."

Silence spanned the table for a second, and waves and handshakes were exchanged.

"Great meeting you guys," William said.

Scott smiled. "Same here. We'll see you around, right?"

"I'm sure of it."

It wasn't until the three men of the Eighth turned to leave that Scott fully took in William's size. He towered above Joe and Cole as if they were children. He may not have beaten Captain Williams back at the Academy, but Scott was sure it must've been one beautiful fight.

Scott, David, Becan, and Jayden remained in the cafeteria together for a good while, as they talked about the conversation with their new-found friends. The Murder Rule was the primary topic. They found it astounding that such a rule existed, and more astounding that EDEN did nothing about it. The entire atmosphere of *Novosibirsk* took on a darker, evil persona. No part of it felt more evil than General Thoor.

The hours that followed were spent in personal endeavors, as they took valuable time to explore the base. If William was correct, they were destined for a fight later that evening. They weren't sure whether to look forward to that or not.

13

WHEN THEY RENDEZVOUSED with the Fourteenth in the gym at 1700 hours, they discovered that William had been right. The unit was gathered around an open area on the floor—a sparring circle. It was a fight night. As they approached, Scott tried to associate faces with names. Clarke. He knew Clarke easily. Ivan Baranov was the one William and Joe had spoken of earlier—the tank. He would be hard to forget now. As they neared the sparring circle, Clarke addressed them.

"How goes it, gentlemen? Glad to see you've found us. Today we're going to partake in some hand-to-hand combat training."

Scott's gaze deviated from Clarke slightly. Svetlana stood out, equally for her beauty and the memory of her exposure to Becan in the shower. If not for Nicole, Scott would have been jealous. Maybe he still was, just a little bit. No—that wasn't allowed. Then there was Travis Navarro. The pilot. He was the most average-looking individual, yet his identity stuck in Scott's mind. Perhaps because he seemed friendly. Clarke continued.

"We dedicate each and every Wednesday to that very thing, as I'm sure you'll grow accustomed. I'm sure you've all had your share of free sparring in the Academy, and *Richmond* as well. The same rules apply here. No ropes, no ring, no mat…just the floor and some space."

For the life of him, he couldn't remember the two lieutenants beneath Clarke and Baranov. One of their names started with a D. D…something. He remembered Varvara Yudina well, the youngest medic. She flashed a cute smile at them. It was very engaging.

"You won't have a mat beneath you when you find yourself face to face with a Ceratopian," Clarke said, "so you haven't got one here either, sorry. All right ladies and gentlemen...please prepare yourselves."

As Scott geared up with the rest of the unit, his mind continued to compare the Fourteenth's faces with his memory. He couldn't remember the medic with the butch haircut. He remembered Boris Evteev, the technician with the black beard. He remembered Fox Powers, the sniper. And Max. Something about Max had embedded itself in his mind. It was the way Max had looked him over when he was introduced to the unit. Was it anger? How could it be? He didn't even know Scott. Before he realized it, he was fully equipped in proper sparring attire, and so was everyone else. He joined them in preparatory stretches.

Scott surveyed the room, when William Harbinger caught his eye. The giant demolitionist stood in the distance, where a crowd gathered to observe. God, William was huge. He stood out like a titan.

As soon as everyone was finished, Clarke began. "We might as well hold a proper initiation since we've got newcomers to the unit. Typically, we all just partner up on our own and spar as we wish, though occasionally I like to do specific bouts, as we'll do today. Here's how we'll run things this evening. I'll have each of our new arrivals, McCrae, Remington, Jurgen, and Timmons match up against three operatives. They shall act as a tag team, while you," he motioned to the operatives, "remain in the ring alone. They are free to tag as often as they'd like."

Three-on-one? That was worse than mean. It was disgustingly awkward. They hadn't even met everyone yet, they hadn't had a single conversation with anyone other than Clarke. Now they were going to fight them three-on-one? Scott didn't like that idea at all. Maybe it would bond them. Somehow, he doubted it.

"I'll just observe today," Clarke said. "I'd like to see how the four of you handle yourselves. Any questions?"

Tension prevailed.

"Very well then. Anyone care to offer themselves out first?"

Scott stared at David, Becan, and Jayden. They all stared back at him, then at each other. None of them said a word. Scott almost laughed. He didn't know who the first fool to volunteer himself would be, but it sure wasn't going to be him.

"Well then, let's observe Remington first, if he'll please. I'm curious to see how the Golden Lion composes himself."

Scott's eyes rolled shut. Typical. Four transfers. Three-to-one odds of *not* being the one singled out. It figured.

"Lieutenant Dostoevsky, please give the good gamma private a run, will you?"

Dostoevsky. *That* was the D-name. Yuri Dostoevsky. Like the old Russian writer.

Dostoevsky nodded as he stood. "Yes sir." He scanned the rest of the unit. "Does anyone want to fight Remington?"

There was no hesitation, as Max leapt to his feet. "I do."

Max stepped into the circle. What was it with him? That response was a little too immediate to be general submission.

Dostoevsky smirked in Max's direction. "Anyone else?" No response came, and he motioned to Varvara. "Varya, come."

The cute one with the compelling smile. Scott didn't want to have to fight her.

"Da, lieutenant," Varvara answered as she stood and stepped to the circle.

Scott flinched as David and Becan slapped his back. The support was a good touch, but he knew what they were thinking. They were glad it wasn't them.

Scott stepped to the center of the circle. Dostoevsky spoke again. "Max will go first, I will follow, then Varya. Ready?"

Scott nodded. "Yes sir." He was as ready as he'd ever be. All EDEN cadets went through sparring drills in *Philadelphia*. This couldn't be much different. Max was tall, athletic. Experienced. He'd be a good fight. Max approached the center of the circle, where his eyes locked onto Scott's. That familiar gleam was there again. Scott recognized it. It wasn't anger. It was hatred.

"Ready," Max said.

Dostoevsky nodded. "Go. Tag if you need to, Max."

Scott bounced as soon as Dostoevsky spoke. His eyes focused on Max, who lightened on his feet as well. From beyond the circle, Scott heard Becan's chant.

"Come on, Remmy, take him down…"

Attack first. Take the initiative. Scott danced forward to jab in Max's direction. Experimental jabs. Testing Max's speed. Max was sure to do the same.

Or not. As soon as Scott's first half-speeded jab reached out, Max slammed it out of the way and cracked his fist against Scott's face. Before Scott could register a reaction, he was hammered with a dead-solid hook. His feet buckled. He fell backward to the floor.

From the edge of the circle, Becan, David, and Jayden cringed.

Scott finally found his focus and stared at Max. That wasn't an attack. That was a passion. His gaze narrowed as he pushed to his feet. That was a bad start. A rushed start. Now he'd be more tactical. He cocked his arm and prepared for another jab. Another half-speeded pop. A decoy. As soon as Max stepped forward to intercept, as he had before, Scott withdrew the jab, bent to the side, and slammed his other fist into the side of Max's headgear.

Becan pumped his fist at the edge of the circle.

Before Max could regain his footing, Scott sent a left hook straight into his face. Max stumbled and fell onto the floor.

They exchanged glares, and Max slammed himself to a stand. He leered and gritted his teeth. "All right…" As soon as he was up, Max started forward and stomped on the ground. Scott flinched. Max attacked. The next thing Scott knew, Max was upon him. His fists struck ahead as Scott tried to counter them. Scott blocked a jab. Max popped him in the cheek. Scott parried an uppercut. Max pounded him in the ribs. For every attack that Scott blocked, Max landed another. Scott never had a second to retaliate.

What was going on? This wasn't an exercise. This was a brawl. No one in training attacked like this. Scott was pushed to the edge of the ring as his defenses faltered. The next thing he knew, Max grabbed him around the waist and hurled him back toward the center of the circle.

Scott skidded to the ground and spun his head around. Then

it happened. Something slammed into his face. His lips erupted. His vision blacked. He flopped flat on his back.

It didn't take long for his senses to reemerge, and for him to realize what happened. Max had kicked him in the face. Max had kicked him in the face while he was on the ground. Everything about practice etiquette just flew out the window.

Get up. You have to get up.

Scott staggered to his feet, but Max was on him. He grabbed Scott's head with both hands and slung him around and away. Scott's feet tripped up, and he fell at the edge of the ring. Before Max could attack again, Dostoevsky's voice broke the fight.

"Tag."

Max glared at Dostoevsky, then leaned his mouth next to Scott's ear. "Nice work, Golden Lion," he spat under his breath. He shoved at Scott's head, then strolled to the edge of the circle.

"Get ready, Remington," Dostoevsky said.

Scott couldn't even think straight, despite his slow rise from the floor. What just happened? He got his tail torn off, that's what happened. God, his jaw hurt. No time for that. Only time for Dostoevsky.

Dostoevsky.

As soon as Scott moved to face the lieutenant, the attack was there. A jab stung him in the face. Scott flew back, and the assault followed. Face. Chest. Ribs. Strike after strike, Dostoevsky pushed Scott to the edge of the ring again. The lieutenant was fast. Faster than Max. More painful than Max.

He had to do something. *Defend yourself!* Even an effort was better than a total beating. He mustered his pride and surged forward with a fist. Dostoevsky snatched it in mid-flight. His fingers curled around it, and he twisted it. A simple, effortless twist. The pain was electric. It sparked through Scott's body like ten thousand volts, and he found himself completely paralyzed, arm outstretched and pathetic like a captive, helpless fool. Dostoevsky's grip tightened, then he swept Scott's feet out from under him.

A groan emerged from the crowd of spectators.

Scott clutched his wrist and pushed to his feet. This was bad. This was total shame. *Defend yourself, you idiot! Fight back!* He struck out again, though his wrist was grabbed again in mid-flight. Dostoevsky flicked it, and Scott flipped flat on his back with a loud thud.

His spine throbbed, but there was no time to register the pain. Dostoevsky kicked him in the face, just as Max had, then stomped on his chest and stomach with vehement force. Nightman force.

Scott's head rolled backward and he rasped, his breathing uneven. He couldn't move. Everything hurt. Everything felt battered. He knew he was bleeding, he could feel blood oozing from his lips and his eyebrow. His body was bruised. It was over.

Dostoevsky murmured something to Varvara, then he stepped past Clarke. "This is a joke."

Clarke half-frowned.

The next touch Scott felt wasn't a kick to the face, or a foot to the stomach. It was a hand as it slid gently beneath his head and neck. Varvara. He hadn't wanted to fight her, and now he didn't have to. What happened? How could this have happened? This all had to be a dream.

She slipped Scott's headgear off him and rolled it to the side. As Scott opened his eyes for the first time since he last fell, she smiled at him. It wasn't quite the cute smile she had given him before. Now it was a smile of apology. The Fourteenth watched in silence as she aided him upright, then to a stand.

A joke. That's what he was now, so said his new lieutenant. He was a joke in front of everybody…his friends, his new unit, even William and everyone who had observed this disgrace of a fight. Scott wanted to disappear. To be dug down in a hole would have been to dwell in paradise. Sheer determination allowed him to carry himself out the circle, though Varvara remained at his side the entire way. He lowered himself to a seat, and she took one beside him. The apologetic smile remained as she slid a cloth to his lips and dabbed away the blood. Scott's gaze remained downcast to the floor.

Clarke finally spoke up. "I'm very sorry…that was one of the most heartfelt initiations I've seen in my life.…" Silent tension hung in the air. Nobody said a word, until Clarke resumed. "Anyone care to go next, please?"

Becan hopped to his feet, slid on his headgear, and trotted into the ring. "I do."

Scott blinked as he watched Becan. That eagerness…why?

Clarke opened his mouth, but thought the better of it and stifled his words. He cleared his throat and turned to Lieutenant Novikov. "Very well then. Anatoly, will you please entertain the good beta?"

Lieutenant Novikov—the third Nightman—nodded. "Yes, captain." He rose and motioned to Travis, the pilot, and Boris Evteev, the technician. "Come. Either of you want to go first?"

Becan cleared his throat before they could answer. "All."

Novikov shot a look to him. "What?"

"All three. Same time."

Scott couldn't believe it. Becan wanted to fight all three of them at the same time? Was he insane?

Clarke laughed. "I'm sorry, but you can't be serious."

"Am are, sir," Becan answered.

Clarke and Novikov eyed one another; everyone else stared at Becan in astonishment. Farther away with the rest of the spectators, William Harbinger looked impassive.

Clarke half-smiled. "Well, if he desires a three-on-one punch up, by all means give him one."

Scott watched Becan as he made his way into the circle on the floor. Travis and Boris weren't Nightmen, but Novikov was. Becan was up to something. He had to be up to something. If he wasn't, then he had lost his mind.

Novikov, Travis, and Boris grouped themselves into a semicircle in front of Becan, who tilted his head to flex his neck muscles. Otherwise, he seemed unprepared. No other stretches, no loosening up. Nothing.

"Are you ready?" Novikov asked.

"Yes sir," Becan answered as he assumed a loose stance. His eyes darted to the edge of the ring, where they found Svetlana. He winked at her.

"Go."

Before Travis or Boris could acknowledge with a yes sir, Becan leapt at Lieutenant Novikov and flung his foot through the air. It collided with Novikov's face. Novikov spun in a circle and dropped to the floor.

Svetlana gasped.

Next, Becan lunged at Boris, grabbed him by his headgear, and punched him square in the face. A mist of red exploded from Boris's lips as he stumbled out of the arena.

Jayden's jaw dropped. "Holy *God*."

As Novikov stammered and attempted to stand, Travis thrust a fist at Becan from behind. Becan swirled around, snatched it in mid-flight, and balanced against it as he popped three kicks at the pilot's cheek. Travis teetered as a final kick slammed into his chest. He toppled to the ground.

Novikov had staggered to his feet, but before he could gather his bearings, Becan dashed at him, spun around, and smashed an elbow into the center of his forehead. Novikov's head cocked backward and he collapsed. Still. He was out cold, and both of the other men were sprawled on the ground.

The fight was over.

There was no sound. If a pin had fallen, it would have echoed throughout the gym. Scott's swollen lips parted as he watched in a dead stare. Three men against one. The one had won. How could that be? Novikov was a Nightman. Becan was a beta. Scott had barely scored a hit on anyone. Becan never missed. This was all wrong. None of this was supposed to be, and yet there the Irishman was, standing in the center of a ring like a prize-winning boxer among children. A point had been made with thundering authority.

Becan's devilish smile curled up at Max, and he mouthed the word, "you." Max made no response.

Clarke could hardly speak. Finally, he managed, "That...was the most impressive thing I've ever seen in my life..."

"Thank yeh, sir," Becan answered as he filtered through the audience back to his seat.

Jayden stared at him wide-eyed. "Why the hell didn't you tell me you could do that?"

"Yeh never asked."

The lull of the gym lingered on Becan for a moment, before Clarke regained his poise. "Next please?"

The rest of the fights were lackluster. Scott observed as David and Jayden held their own in their matches, though neither could replicate Becan's three-on-one feat. As for Novikov, he was tended to personally by Svetlana. When that tender aid involved a kiss, Scott knew that she and the lieutenant were more than comrades.

Clarke's small talk concluded the evening, and they dismissed for Room 14. Showers came next, and food in the cafeteria after. As before, Scott and his companions found acceptance with William and Joe, though now they were joined by two Fourteenth defectors—Travis and Fox Powers. Travis, despite his beating, enthusiastically praised Becan for his fighting prowess. Fox exchanged sniper-talk with Jayden.

William was more interested in ribbing Scott for his downfall than in joining any meaningful conversation, but Scott only laughed it off and changed the subject. By the time conversation died down, it was almost 2100. Almost curfew, and time for the Fourteenth to retire to its room. Day one was over.

Night number two was just beginning.

*　　*　　*

SCOTT LAY WIDE awake. He peered to the bunk bed above, where David slept out of view. It was past midnight, and the Fourteenth was asleep—all except for Scott. He wasn't sure whether to blame it on jet lag or the day's events, but nonetheless he laid in sleeplessness, hands behind his head as he listened to the steady breathing of those around him. The soreness had begun to set in. The embarrassment had set in much earlier, despite his efforts at bravado.

For the first time since the whirlwind of the transfer, Scott missed his comrades from Charlie Squad—Colonel Lilan and Major Tacker, Michael Carter and Donald, and of course the two girls. He missed Henry and Zigler. He missed immortality.

But more than anything, he missed Nicole.

He had called her earlier that day, but the conversation was almost painfully short. She didn't have time to talk. She had other things to do. For the first time, he noticed something different about her voice. Something gone that had always been there in the past. Hope. He hadn't seen her in four months. He knew it would be much longer before he'd see her again.

The thought of *Richmond* being too far away seemed laughable now. He would have gladly stayed there had he known Russia was the alternative. But now, what did it matter? He was there. There was nothing he could do to change it.

He recalled every detail about the day he had proposed. Every little thing. It had been a gorgeous Sunday afternoon. The sun shone splendidly. She wore a yellow shirt and blue jeans, and her hair was tied back in a ponytail. They were on a picnic. She always loved them, he always got dragged along. But this time it was his idea. She was delighted with his initiative.

He knew if he tried to pull off anything cute it would come off sounding clichéd, so he just told her. *You were put in my life to be my love. If I tried to tell you what you mean to me, we'd be here all night. I love you. I intend to love you forever, and there's no other girl who can change that. You are my girl. I want to be your man. Nikki...will you marry me?*

He remembered her eyes as they glistened, and her smile lit up. *Scott...you're already my man. I can't wait to marry you.* He could still taste the passion in her kiss.

Sleep was futile. It was pointless to even try. He reached down to the floor and felt around with his fingers for the cover of his Scripture. His hand curled around it, he propped himself up, and slid out of bed. He was well adjusted to the darkness by that point, and he quietly padded to the lounge.

It wasn't until he was only steps away that he noticed an orange glow beneath its door. There could only be one explanation—someone was there. He hadn't heard anyone leave their beds all night. Either he *had* fallen asleep, or someone had never left the lounge in the first place.

He gripped the knob, turned it, and gave the door a gentle push. He saw her the moment he stepped inside. Svetlana. She sat at a corner table, her hands clasped together as golden strands of her hair shone down the sides of her face. Her posture tensed as she turned to acknowledge him. Scott froze in the doorway. The atmosphere became awkward.

Scott wasn't sure how he was supposed to greet her. Was it appropriate to say something? Was he supposed to put on a fake smile and pretend she was a friend, despite the fact that he had never spoken to her? He knew two things about Svetlana. She was beautiful, and she was sour. At least, that's how she struck him. He wasn't sure if that was his fault or hers.

His body went rigid as the orange flicker of the countertop lamp bled through the lounge door. Svetlana and him. Two strangers with nothing in common except shower stalls and forced camaraderie. Nothing in common. And nothing to talk about.

He sensed the bunk room behind him. Someone would wake up any second, and once again Scott would find himself in the midst of anger. The Golden Lion—pathetic fighter and disturber of a good night's sleep. Him.

"You Americans have strange customs," Svetlana said.

Scott's mind snapped back to the present. His eyes flickered at her. "What?"

"You open the door, stare at me, and say nothing," she answered. "That is indeed strange custom."

It took him a moment to realize what she meant. She was being sarcastic. It wasn't something he expected. "I'm sorry," he said. "I didn't know if coming in would bother you."

She sat back in her chair. "Come in if you wish. But whatever you do, please close the door, or you will learn new *Russian* custom. Knock down the man who wakes everyone up."

He chuckled. A single breath of amusement. That was indeed a custom he wanted nothing to do with. He had taken his fair share of beating already. He had a busted lip and a bruised jaw to prove it.

He nodded, stepped inside, and eased the door shut. It still felt awkward, but not quite as much as before. The burden of first words was over. She had taken the initiative. Sarcasm wasn't the best way to start a relationship, but he could work with it. A relationship. How in the world could he relate to anything in Svetlana's world?

"So what is so troubling that it keeps the Golden Lion awake at night?" she asked.

He stared at her. It sounded so venomous the way she said it. The *Golden Lion*. It was as if the title itself was created for mockery. It hadn't been that way at *Richmond*.

Svetlana lowered her head. "I'm sorry...does it offend you when I call you that?"

It didn't offend him. It disappointed him. He wasn't a medal. He was Scott James Remington, a soldier doing the best he could to help the war. He had never asked for anything else. But he'd accepted it when it was given to him. Did that make him bad? It didn't offend him. It hurt him. It hurt him because, in his heart of hearts, he wasn't *just* a soldier. He was a human being trying to make a difference. Not just in the war. In the lives of the people around him. He was a nice guy with a gun.

Why am I here, God? Why have You brought me here? I thought You wanted this...but was I wrong?

Nicole said it herself. *God's will doesn't contradict itself.* If God wanted him to be with Nicole, why had He sent him to Russia? It hit him as soon as the question entered his mind. God hadn't sent him to Russia.

He'd sent himself there.

"Remington?"

For a second time, Svetlana's voice freed him from his thoughts. His focus snapped back to her, and once again he beheld her form. But something was different. Her narrowed gaze was missing. Her pointed expression had melted away. She was no longer the woman who'd invited him in with venomous sarcasm. Her dark blond brows were arched. Her lips were thinly parted. She was a girl who realized he was hurting.

"Remington?" she asked again.

Scott shook his head. "I'm sorry." He hated this. He felt

emotional, and he knew he looked emotional. That was why he had come to the lounge in the first place. To be alone. He hadn't expected anyone else to be there.

"It is okay," she said. Her voice was different too. It was concerned. She motioned to the chair beside her. "Come and sit, please."

"I really don't want to disturb you," he answered. "I didn't think anyone would be here."

She shook her head. "No, please. You are not disturbing me. Come and sit and we will talk, okay?"

Before he moved to the table and slid into the chair, he allowed himself a moment of composure. He hated sympathy. He hated it more than he hated the spite in the words *Golden Lion* when Max and Svetlana said them.

As he sat, she offered her apology. "I am sorry about what I said when you came in. It was stupid of me."

He waved it off. "It's all right."

"No it is not. I am sorry."

Scott took his seat in silence. The room still felt awkward, but not because she was his enemy. It was awkward because he was vulnerable.

"So let me do it again, better this time," Svetlana said, smiling. Insincerely, he thought. "I am glad for the company tonight. What is it that keeps you awake?"

He knew she wasn't glad. But at least she was trying, even if only for the sake of courtesy. "I don't know," he answered. "Not sure if it's jet lag, or just thinking."

Her eyes narrowed, and the forced smile remained. "I think we both know that it is something you are thinking."

He laughed. It was obvious. "Okay. You win there."

She tucked a strand of hair behind her ear. "So what is it then?"

What was he supposed to tell her? He was dealing with all sorts of things. Loneliness. Anxiety. Doubt. She wanted the truth? He wasn't sure he was ready for that. "Just some personal things I'm dealing with."

"Mr. Remington," she said as she shied her smile away. "A doctor hears all kinds of personal things. You may tell me if you wish…"

"Are you really asking me for medical reasons?" Scott asked skeptically.

The lounge fell quiet. The lamp flickered on the countertop. As Svetlana leaned back to mirror him, she played her fingers on the table. "No. It is not. But now you have me curious." She paused. "So I want to know what you are thinking."

"Why are you curious?"

She pursed her lips. "Can not a girl be curious of the Golden Lion?"

"Why does everyone keep calling me that?"

"Is that not what you are?"

It wasn't what he was. Why couldn't anyone understand? "No. It's not. My name is Scott, not Golden Lion."

She laughed lightly. "Mr. Remington, surely—"

"My name is Scott."

"Very well. Scott, surely you do not expect me to ignore the fact you are the holder of most famous award in EDEN."

"I honestly wish you would," he said. "I don't want to be treated differently because I got some stupid piece of metal."

She crossed one arm beneath her breasts and lifted the other contemplatively to her chin. She leaned closer. "You think it is stupid?"

The medal wasn't stupid. The inflated symbolism that came with it was. "It hasn't brought me anything good," he answered. "Everywhere I go, it's all everyone talks about…how I'm a hero, or a celebrity, or some kind of knight. I'm not. I'm just a normal person going through something I never asked for." He wasn't a hero to Nicole. "Do you know what my fiancée said when they gave it to me?"

Svetlana edged back. "No…"

"She went crazy. She was terrified, she was furious. She thought I was a fool for risking my life when we've got a future together. Everyone thinks I've been riding on some high horse since Chicago, but I haven't." Chicago was the easiest thing he had done. Everything after that went downhill.

"…you do not want Golden Lion?" she asked slowly.

"They gave it to me," he said. "I didn't pick it out for myself.

Everyone thinks I wanted *all* of this, but that's not the truth. If I had known what I know now, I'd have never accepted it."

Her gaze was fixated on him. "I am sorry to be so curious… it is only that I did not expect you to say these things. I never thought that you might not like what you are."

"Look where I am, Svetlana. I'm in the middle of Russia. My fiancée's in Michigan. People in my unit hate me, when all I ever wanted to be was a teammate." He didn't understand any of it. "What do I have to do to get rid of this?"

The lounge fell silent. Svetlana's lips parted, though she said nothing.

It was all true. The more he thought about it, the more Scott wished he had never assaulted the Carrier. But he couldn't blame himself for it. He had felt—he had known he could do it. He had done what any good soldier would have done. He'd finished the job.

His attention returned to her. The expression on her face was a mixture of confusion and intrigue. As she brushed loose strands of hair from her cheek, she said, "I did not know you felt this way. I thought…" Her words trailed off.

"What?"

She sighed. "I do not know what I thought of you."

Scott knew. She thought he was a walking ego. She thought he would walk into the unit with guns ablaze as his attitude pulled the trigger. She thought he would act like a Golden Lion.

"I hear you now," she said, "and you are different from what I expected. You see…when the captain heard that you were coming, that is all that he talked about. We will be getting Golden Lion, over and over. And not only that, but…you have been here for so little, and you are already gamma private. It took me two years to become delta, as it did for Max. But you did all of these things in one mission." Her eyes sunk and her lips parted down. "And now to hear you say these things…I do not know what to say. I am…how do you say it? Amazed?"

"Amazed that I don't want all this?"

She looked up. "Amazed that you hate it."

What she said was true. He did hate it. Every time someone talked about it or made a comment to him, he wished everything he had done would go away. Or at least not be common knowl-edge. "I never asked to be a gamma. I never asked for a Golden Lion. I never asked to be transferred here." He had never asked for anything. "It all just happened. I did the best I could, and this is where it got me. I don't know why I was chosen for any of this, and I know it's not fair. But what am I supposed to do? All I can do is to do best that I can."

She stared at him for several seconds before a smile escaped her lips. "I think that if everyone could hear what I am hearing...I do not know. You have caught me off guard." She almost laughed. "I think this is the first time that I have heard your voice. You do not sound like I expected. You do not sound like a man who loves to be special soldier."

"I don't love to be one," he said. "I never did. How do I tell every-one that?"

She shook her head. "I do not know. Maybe wait until they are alone in the lounge...then stand in the door until they invite you in." She chuckled. "I really do not know. I really cannot explain how everyone feels, and how you make me feel now. It is good to hear these things from you."

"How do you feel now?"

"Not the same," she answered. "There is something about you. It is good, I think. It is different. I think...that you are not like I expected Golden Lion to be. You do not talk about yourself in that way."

"I understand how you thought I might be," he said. He really did. "But I'm not like that. I just want to be a soldier. I want to be a soldier and a good teammate."

"I am afraid I must apologize. I am now feeling very guilty about the things I thought of you."

Scott sighed. "You don't need to apologize..."

"No, no...I do. I thought *bad* things..."

"How bad are we talking about?"

"I do not think I want to say."

"You have to tell me now."

She peered at him, examining his countenance carefully. "If I tell you, you will hold them against me forever."

Good God. Were they *that* bad? "If you *don't tell* me, I'll hold it against you forever."

She offered an embarrassed smile. "Are you sure?"

"Yes."

"Then, if I must..." She shied away from him, her gaze falling to the tabletop. "I thought bad things when you fought with Max..."

The fight with Max. That was the one thing he wished everyone would forget.

"Must I continue?" she asked.

Scott caught himself in a snort. "You certainly can't stop *there*."

She stifled a nervous laugh. "...very well...I thought you looked better with busted lip...and..."

"And...?"

The rest tumbled out. "And maybe if he hit you hard enough we could send you back to America on rolling bed."

"You actually thought that?"

Her expression grew defensive. "That was before this! I did not know! Now I feel terrible!"

"You *should* feel terrible!"

"Do you feel better now?"

"What else did you think?"

She rolled her eyes. "Do I have to tell you everything? I thought many things, but that was the worst."

Scott nodded. "That was pretty bad."

"That is why I must apologize," she said. "I am afraid I will go to Hell now if I do not."

She had a sense of humor. It was nice. "You still might. That was pretty wrong of you."

"I am redeemed through my apology. What more must I do?"

"Nothing else. You warned me beforehand. I asked anyway."

"No," she answered. "What more must I do to make you feel better?"

She was a woman admitting fault. That rarely happened. He thought about taking advantage of it. He didn't have to think for long. "Do I get to name anything?"

She hesitated. "Maybe. We will see."

"That's not much of a promise."

"I said we will see."

"Obviously, you aren't *too* worried about Hell. Can you cook?"

Her eyes shot open. "Can I *cook*?"

"Yeah. Can you cook?"

She laughed heartily. "What do you call cooking?"

"What can you do?"

"I can put sugar in tea." She giggled. "I can put butter on toast."

Well. That answered that. "So, since neither of those are actually cooking, I'll take that as a 'not at all'."

She leaned against the table and smirked. "Very well. I will cook for you. Is it breakfast that you want?"

He matched her smirk with one of his own. "As wonderful as tea and toast sounds, I don't think that qualifies as a cooked meal."

"I will cook for you," she answered. "It will be a surprise one day. But you must not tell Tolya."

"Tolya?"

"Yes, Lieutenant Novikov. Tolya is short for his first name. Anatoly."

That's right. She had kissed him after his fight with Becan. If it could even be called a fight. "Fair enough," he said.

Svetlana smiled, and her eyes lingered on him. After a moment, she breathed deeply and looked away. "I think I like you now. Maybe not before, but...I think at first I saw someone else when I saw you. Someone dangerous to the unit." She locked her stare with his. For the first time, Scott noticed she had blue eyes. Blue like the ocean. She smiled. "You are not dangerous."

He wasn't. He had never wanted to be.

She sighed. "You act like...how Golden Lion should be."

Scott realized a different woman than he'd imagined was seated across the table from him. She wasn't sour. She wasn't laced with venom. He had misread her, just as she had misread him. Now, she was just beautiful. "Svetlana..."

"You may call me Sveta."

He smiled. "Sveta...thank you for tonight. Thank you for taking the time to hear me out, and to laugh with me. You're one of the few people who's actually done that." David, Becan, and Jayden had. And now her. For a moment, he didn't miss Nicole.

Her smile was broad and warm. "Thank you for coming in. It would have been sad if you turned away."

Scott glanced down at the table. "I think so too."

"Other people do not think like I do now," she said, "but if they speak to me of you…I will tell them how I feel. I will tell them that you are good." Her eyes lifted to meet him. "If you will be there for me, I will be there for you. I promise."

Friendship. That was all he had ever wanted. He wanted someone to look out for who would also look out for him. Of all the friends he'd made in EDEN, she felt the best. And that was because he won her over. He had earned her respect. "I'll be there for you," he answered. "I promise."

As a smile broke from Scott's lips, Svetlana matched it. "You are cute when you smile. It is good to see you do it." She paused thoughtfully. "You should watch yourself around us Russian women. One of us may steal you away."

Scott chuckled. "Nicole would love to hear you say that, I'm sure."

"Is that your love's name?"

He nodded.

She grinned. "That is a nice name. I would like to know how you met her."

"Next time we get together, I'll tell you," he answered.

"Yes," she said. "You must. And I will tell you how I swept Tolya off of his feet."

Scott winked at her playfully. "Was it your beauty or your charm?"

Svetlana burst out with a laugh, then caught herself. "I am sure it must have been my charm. But I will tell you about that another day." She winked back. "What you need to do now is sleep. This is order from your new doctor. Sleep would be good for you, and you will feel better about things in the morning."

She was right. It always worked that way. He had been through every negative emotion that night…fear, depression, anger, doubt… he needed to end while he was still on a good note. "That's probably a good idea."

Her blond locks once again fell across the side of her face. "Have you heard Ivan snore yet?"

"Not yet."

"Now *that* will cause many sleepless nights. But you will adjust."

Scott glanced at her for a moment more, and once again their gazes held together. Ocean blue eyes. The bluest he had ever seen.

As Scott pushed back from his chair, she said, "Sleep good."

"I'll try," he answered.

"Do not forget your book."

His black, leather-bound Scripture lay on the tabletop, almost forgotten. Her words repeated in his head, but differently. *Do not forget your God.* He could never forget his God. His God had gotten him through the night. His God had given him her—a new friend. In spite of himself.

Scott took the Scripture in hand and made his way to the lounge door. As he turned the knob to pull it open, he looked back to Svetlana and mouthed a good night. She whispered it in return, as a final smile was cast his way.

He stepped out.

Room 14 was still silent, aside from the breathing of those who slept. As Scott gently closed the door, his eyes began to readjust to the darkness. When the door padded shut, he once again weaved his way through the bunks, back to his own. He was quiet as he slid under the covers and placed his Scripture under the bed. He laid still for a moment, before exhaling and closing his eyes.

Thank you for tonight, God. Thank you for Svetlana. I'm sorry that I doubted.

He *was* supposed to be there. He didn't know why, and he didn't know for how long, but he knew he was supposed to be there. In the morning, everything would feel better. In the morning, he would be all right.

He never heard Svetlana leave the lounge that night. He was asleep before the lamp in the lounge went off.

14

THE OPERATIVES OF the Fourteenth awoke to the presence of Captain Clarke. It was the presence of a man who had himself been awake for some time. Without a spoken word, his aura of controlled urgency enveloped the room. This morning was different. This morning, something would happen.

For Scott, it was a morning of clarity. The conversation with Svetlana was still fresh in his mind, and things were indeed as she claimed. He felt refreshed. He felt energized. He felt ready for whatever Clarke had to convey to them.

Within minutes, the operatives donned their uniforms and collected in the lounge. Each table was filled to maximum capacity, as the captain presided over them at the front of the room. There was no coffee or tea in brew. There was no casual conversation. There was only the stern countenance of a man whose quiet authority ended with a single sentence.

"Today we face a formidable challenge."

That was it. No small talk. No morning ice breaker. Only, *today we face a formidable challenge.* Every operative stared undividedly.

"Approximately three hours ago," Clarke said, "a squadron from *Nagoya* intercepted a Bakma vessel, Cargo class. A scouting unit detected it shortly after it entered Earth's airspace. It was far enough along to allow a calculation of its trajectory. An investigation of that trajectory followed. What it revealed…was a fully functional Bakma facility on the planet Earth." An audible silence overtook the lounge. "It will be our responsibility, with the aid of two supplementary units, to isolate and incapacitate this facility."

A base assault. On Earth. That was unprecedented.

"It gets worse," Clarke said. "The Bakma constructed this facility between Cherskogo and Verkhoyanskiy, in Northern Siberia." The Russian officers closed their eyes and inhaled. Clarke measured his words. "The coldest place on Earth."

Scott unconsciously rubbed the back of his neck. The coldest place on Earth? How had they gotten there? How had they built it without being noticed?

Clarke continued. "This place holds the record for the all-time lowest temperature in the northern hemisphere. Expect temperatures anywhere from thirty below freezing on down—it will be harsh.

"We've got daylight, so visibility should be good. Though the facility itself lies underground, what Intelligence hopes to be an above-ground entrance has been sighted on the surface. EDEN Command estimate that the facility is still relatively new and probably small in size, though as always, we won't know until we arrive." He hesitated. "General Thoor will be overseeing this operation personally."

All eyes shot open. Thoor? Personally overseeing the mission? What did that mean? Still, no one spoke. Finally, Dostoevsky broke the silence and whispered something to Baranov.

"As always," Clarke continued, "I shall settle for nothing less than your maximum potential."

"Gear up, please. Then we move to the hangar."

Scott exchanged a look with his *Richmond* comrades. Their expressions echoed the same sentiment. Was Clarke to be taken literally? Was the general of *Novosibirsk* actually going with them?

There was no time to speculate. The operatives returned to the bunk room to gather their armor and weapons, geared themselves, and left.

During this trek, Scott saw the Russian officers in their Nightman armor for the first time. The armor was black, much like the armor of the guards who had met them when they first arrived. But it was different. It was leaner. It was more purposeful. Dark curves outlined their frames; only the crimson symbols of the Nightmen struck out in bold proclamation. On two of the Nightmen—Commander Baranov and Lieutenant Dostoevsky—the armor came with spiked back half-collars, like horns on hell-spawned knights. The contrast between them and EDEN was astounding.

No comments were made about Scott's golden collar. The prestige of the Golden Lion paled next to the dark intimidation of the Nightmen.

The walk itself was silent. *General Thoor will be overseeing this operation personally.* What did that mean? Surely the general of *Novosibirsk* would know better than to risk his life on a ground mission. Or would he? As soon as Scott stepped into the hangar, he knew the answer. Thoor stood along the far wall. His stature was unmistakable.

"Yeh got to be pullin' me wire…" Becan said.

In a matter of minutes, all three units—the Fourteenth, the Twelfth, and the Third—were lined up in front of the general. The silence was unholy. It was as if the whole of the hangar stood before an evil deity that would strike them down if they dared to open their mouths on their own accord. From across the hangar, he began his approach. The same visor hat shrouded his eyes, and the same black cloak swirled behind him. The only difference was that now, beneath it all, he wore a full suit of Nightman battle armor.

Thoor stopped in front of the operatives, where his nightmarish glare assaulted them. It was a glare of uncontrollable animosity. It was the glare of a killer. Almost thirty seconds passed before he uttered a single statement.

"You know my expectations."

The room snapped into a salute, as a unified *Yes, general!* erupted throughout the hangar. Thoor spun around, nodded to his guards, and strode toward the pack of Vultures that waited on the runway.

Scott and Becan exchanged looks of uncertainty. Clarke cleared his throat.

"There shall be one team from each of the three units going

out on first strike at the facility. Their orders will be more clearly defined once we arrive at the target area.

"Those representing our unit on the primary assault are as follows: Commander Baranov, Lieutenant Novikov, Max, Powers, Galina, Private Remington, Private Jurgen, Kevin, and Kostya.

"As ordained by Thoor beforehand, I shall remain behind in the transport with the rest of the unit until our presence is deemed necessary. Those not named will remain with me. Are there any questions?"

There were none.

"Very well, then. Please board, and prepare for ascent."

The operatives of the Fourteenth boarded their Vulture. It was the first time that Scott had laid eyes on it. It was an older craft with a vast array of scars and dents along its hull. Painted across its dorsal fin in black letters were two words: The *Pariah*. Scrawled in paint above the name was head of a feral dog, its gray fur blotted with disease.

The ships were boarded, and they soon ascended. Only when the ride smoothed out did conversation filter among the crew. "Wha' do yeh think abou' this whole business with Thoor?" Becan asked.

Scott looked steadily at the Irishman. David and Jayden were at his side. "I don't know," Scott answered. "I don't understand why he's coming."

"Think we're onto somethin' big here?"

"I don't know."

Jayden indicated the Russian officers; all three of whom huddled in whispered discussion. "There's something going on with those guys. I wonder what Clarke thinks."

"He doesn't," David said. "It's not his job to."

The four fell silent. Scott turned his attention to Svetlana. She, Galina, and Varvara were in quiet conversation across the troop bay. She'd know what was going on. Better than any of them could speculate, anyway. His eyes lingered on her for a moment until she made contact. She nodded at him, then returned to her conversation.

"Wha's all tha' abou'?" asked Becan suspiciously.

"Just getting her attention," Scott answered.

"Righ'…didn't know yis was all buddy-buddy."

"I talked to her for a bit last night. She's not as bad as you think."

Svetlana left the two medics and knelt beside them. "What is it?"

"Sveta, what's the deal with Thoor?" Scott asked.

She canted her head. "How do you mean, 'what's the deal with Thoor'?"

"Is he actually *fighting* with us?"

Her eyes flitted between Scott and the other three, all of whom were listening intently. "Maybe. I don't know. It is how he is. He does this every now and then—goes on a mission with his soldiers. He is the only general I know of who does such a thing."

"What if he gets killed?" David asked.

She stared at him in silence. "He will never get killed."

Scott blinked. *Never?* How could she say never? Who *was* Ignatius van Thoor?

Becan cleared his throat. "I have a question."

Svetlana turned to Becan. Her eyes narrowed. "Yes?"

"If you were my pilot, would yeh take me for a ride?"

Scott closed his eyes and slammed the back of his head against the wall. David stifled a chortle.

Svetlana's face sunk into a full-fledged glare. "Not in your best of dreams."

"Then how would I go on anny *missions*?"

She rose to her feet, turned away, and stalked back to the other medics.

"Nice work," Scott said. "That was brilliant, thank you."

Becan smirked. "She's charmin', really."

David continued to chuckle.

As the Vultures neared Verkhoyanskiy, the operatives prepared their gear. They replaced the standard blue and silver armor plates with shades of white and light gray, a more appropriate combination for the terrain of Northern Siberia.

"ETA fifteen!" Travis's voice cracked over the speaker system.

Clarke rose to his feet. "We should be receiving more specific orders at any moment! Make sure your internal heaters are on!"

"Hey Fox," Becan said, "why do they call this one the *Pariah*?"

"Do you really want to know?"

Becan nodded.

"Are you sure?"

The *Richmond* transfers exchanged glances. Why was Fox so unwilling to share the information? "Is there a reason you're askin'?" Becan asked.

Fox chuckled and leaned back in his seat. "When it got called out on its first mission, it wouldn't start. It was with the Sixth then. They sent it back to *Atlanta* to get repaired. When *Atlanta* turned it on, it fired up with no problem. They sent it back. Second mission, wouldn't start again. Sent it to *Atlanta* again, it worked, and again they sent it back. Couldn't find a problem with it.

"Third mission, starts up fine. Ceratopian mission. The Sixth cleans out a small Cruiser, packs up some salvage and a couple corpses to bring back to base. About halfway home, *Novosibirsk* loses contact with it. It's still on radar, it's still coming home... there's just no communication. Comes in for a landing, touches down right on the strip where it's supposed to. Still no contact with the crew.

"They opened her up, and it was a mess. Blood everywhere, mangled bodies everywhere. Not a person alive, not even the pilot. In the middle of the bay, in the middle of the bodies, was the corpse of a necrilid. It killed them mid-flight before it died. They had thought it was dead before they loaded it."

The operatives stared, momentarily speechless. The cabin suddenly felt colder to Scott.

"But...how did it...?" Becan stuttered.

"Autopilot," Fox answered. "Thing flew itself home with a dead crew."

The hair on Scott's arms tingled. All four of the *Richmond* transfers shivered with unanticipated dread.

"So they started calling it that," Fox said. "The *Pariah*. The ship nobody wanted. Thing went through two more units. Both swore it was cursed, and it just got passed right on down the line. Now it's with us."

Nobody said a word. Their gazes drifted off Fox and around the inner hull of the craft.

Fox smiled humorlessly and resumed his gear-up. "Welcome aboard."

Clarke called out from the front of the troop bay. "We've got our orders." He stepped over to a display on the wall, where a digital map of Verkhoyanskiy appeared. "The hypothesized entrance to the facility rests directly between two small ridges. It's in a valley of sorts. We will land approximately five hundred meters west of the structure. The Twelfth will land five hundred meters east, and the Third will land north…essentially a triangle formation. The Twelfth and ourselves will be positioned behind the ridges, as the Third move down the valley." Several arrows appeared on the map.

"This part of the world is above the tree line, so we won't have the luxury of good cover. Once we start over the ridges, there's going to be nothing but snow between us and the entrance. The Twelfth and ourselves will clear the area and storm the entrance. Once we've secured it, we shall enter the complex as the Third move in from the north."

The Russian officers whispered among themselves.

"Commander Baranov will work in conjunction with Captain Keldysh and his team from the Twelfth. The captain will evaluate the situation once the entrance is breached, and he will determine the next course of action. General Thoor will supervise the situation from his position with the Third, inside *Vulture-3*. Are there any questions?"

No hands raised.

"Very well then. Ivan, please gather your team and prepare for first action."

The large Russian nodded, and the teams gathered together.

It was only a matter of minutes until the *Pariah* descended upon the snow-covered ground.

"We're down," Travis said.

Baranov stood and clamped on his helmet. His tone intensified behind its zombified stare. "All of my operatives, remember to put your heaters on. As soon as we get the signal from Thoor, we shall move."

Becan watched David and Scott as the two men prepared to disembark. "Good luck then, eh?"

"Yeah, you guys be careful," Jayden said.

David offered them a half-smile. "Just like Chicago."

Scott smiled. It was nothing like Chicago. In Chicago they had been on the defense. This was the opposite. Scott's eyes swept across the troop bay until they rested on Svetlana, whose hands encircled Lieutenant Novikov's waist.

She leaned her forehead to rest against his shoulder. She whispered something, likely in Russian, and her eyes closed.

Novikov slid his hands around the small of her back as he held her against his body.

"Don't have to speak Russian to know what that's about," David whispered.

"No joke," Scott answered.

David held out a fist. "To women who want us home."

Scott hit it. "To women who want us home."

Baranov hoisted his assault rifle to the ceiling. "My team! Get ready to move! The doors will open soon!"

Travis peered into the troop bay. "Back door's comin' down! Put on your mittens!"

The cold blew in like an arctic hurricane. As soon as the first crack appeared at the top of the rear door, the temperature in the *Pariah* plummeted. The operatives shrank back as their skin froze, despite their armor. Icy air whipped through the bay.

"Good *God* that's cold!" Jayden said, his teeth chattering.

"*Great,*" Fox said.

Travis announced over the speaker, "No mercy from Weather Mike today, huh?"

"Why can't they build a base in Bermuda?" Fox grumbled.

As the initial blast of ice died away, Scott bit back his groan and stared out the bay door. Whiteness. It stretched out ahead as far he could see. Pure, smooth, pristine whiteness. Not a single tree anywhere. Only the occasional gray rock jetted up from the ground. If not for the reality of why they were there, it might have been beautiful. Far ahead, the incline of the western ridge loomed.

"Reminds me of how I used to walk to school," David said.

Scott remained silent, his thoughts in prayer. *Father, I don't know why we're here or what You have planned, but protect us. Protect us from whatever is out here to harm us. Give us the strength to…harm it instead…* Choose us over them. But was that right? What if the Bakma, the Ceratopians, and the Ithini were all on a Holy War granted by God? Who was to say that the conquering of Earth wasn't for the greater good of the universe? Could that be…right? *I know that I don't understand, Father. Just give me the wisdom and clarity to see Your will, and the strength and courage to follow It. I will not be afraid, for Your Hand protects me. So be it.*

"Gotta quench the imagination, huh?"

Startled out of his reverie, Scott turned to the unexpected voice. Max.

"No god's gonna save you out here, Goldilocks," Max said.

Scott was silent. His attention returned to the terrain. "Whatever."

Max laughed disdainfully and stepped away.

Baranov stalked down the ramp. "We move now. Rows are me and Tolya, then Max and Fox, then Remington, Galya, and Kostya, then Kevin and Jurgen in the rear."

The teams acknowledged him and took their place in row. The air was fresh, and as the operatives' heaters came alive, they assumed more comfortable postures. Aside from them, there were no signs of animal or plant life. Together, the strike teams trudged ahead.

The top of the ridge rounded off into a ledge that plunged into the valley where the Bakma facility was located. The teams moved at a snail's pace as each step seemed a step into nowhere, but gradually the ridge grew closer. Only Galina was hindered by the snow, though she managed to keep up enough to not get left behind.

"We are close," Baranov said through the comm. "Almost there."

Within minutes, the ridge's depth became tangible. Baranov knelt and raised an open palm.

"Inch forward to look down. Nobody cross to other side." Their sight lines declined with every step until the bottom of the valley came into view.

The Bakma structure was no larger than a shed, and it was covered in snow. If not for prior knowledge of its whereabouts, it could have been mistaken for a shaft of rock. No Bakma were in sight.

"When we go down, we will proceed in two rows," Baranov said. "Front row is myself, Tolya, Remington, Fox, and Jurgen. Back line is Max, Galya, Kevin, and Kostya. We wait for confirmation before we move."

BECAN AND JAYDEN listened from the transport, where the operatives were clustered around the wall speaker.

"Twelfth in position."

Baranov's voice emerged a moment later. "Fourteenth in position."

"Third in position."

Grim looks were exchanged throughout the *Pariah*. Svetlana fidgeted.

"Proceed."

"WE MOVE," BARANOV said. "Go!" He charged down the hill, assault rifle in hand. The other operatives sprung to life behind him. The snow loosened as the hill declined, and the charge shifted into a tactical slide. Far across the valley, the Twelfth began their rush.

The first signs of resistance appeared. Four Bakma emerged from the structure. The front row of Baranov's team dropped to their knees and opened fire. The Bakma unleashed several blasts of their own, though they were felled before they could mount a defensive.

Baranov reached the bottom of the valley a moment later. "Fourteenth clear, four Bakma down."

"THEY'RE STILL OKAY," Becan said to Svetlana. Her gaze remained riveted on the speaker.

VINDICATOR FIGHTERS BUZZED into a low orbit over the structure. Scott and David paired together at its outer entrance—a metal doorway. The remainder of the Fourteenth and Twelfth assumed defensive positions. The snow beneath them was tainted with the red sprays of Bakma blood.

A slim, pale-skinned officer slipped past Scott and David toward Baranov. "Commander Baranov?"

Baranov nodded.

"I am Captain Keldysh. Our orders are to storm this compound and isolate it. We take as many hostages as possible and we keep the facility intact. If we cannot do this, our orders will be to destroy the facility by demolitions. Our technicians have high explosives. They will set the charge and explode the facility remotely if need be. Is this understood?"

"Yes, captain."

"Your technicians will now open the door to the facility, and we will send a six-man strike team down the shaft into the complex's core to set up a stronghold. The rest of our operatives will follow as needed. Our technicians will go down second, followed by your operatives if need be. Is this understood?"

"Yes, captain."

"Very well," Keldysh said. "Open the door."

Baranov turned around. "Max!"

Max moved quickly to the metal door, where he removed a round suction device from his belt. He placed it against the door and depressed a small button. The device clicked and whirred. The door slid halfway open. A small circular lift was inside.

"That's as good as it gets," Max said. "It's not compatible enough to open all the way."

"That is all we need," Keldysh said. Six soldiers from the Twelfth slid through the metal doorway. Keldysh turned to Baranov. "We will need your technician to operate the lift."

"Go with them," Baranov said to Max.

"Naturally, sir," Max answered. He slid through the door into the lift. "Goin' down, fellas?" He used the same suction device, and the metal door slid shut. Behind it, the lift rumbled. Max's voice emerged through the comm. "We're on our way down."

Kevin slung his assault rifle over his shoulder and said to Scott and David, "Now what?"

"Now we wait," Scott said.

Baranov fidgeted as he placed a hand to his helmet mic. "Progress?"

"Still going down," Max answered. "Hell of a deep hole. It's been a straight drop, totally vertical. Best guess is about fifty meters so far, but we've got to be getting clo—all right, sir, we're slowing."

"Okay. We're down…opening the door…"

Metal clunked through the comm, then the channel went silent. Baranov placed his hand against the door. The silence broke. Gunfire erupted. Shouts flooded the comm. The noise lasted for almost ten seconds before it faded, and a Russian voice emerged.

"Area secure, bringing the lift back up. One casualty on his way."

"Max?" Baranov actually sounded frightened.

"It's not me," Max answered.

Baranov closed his eyes and exhaled.

"Thank you," Keldysh said. "Bring him up and we will send down our technicians."

Keldysh signaled to his team of techs, who positioned themselves beside the structure's door. Within a minute, the lift reached ground level and the door slid open. Max was the first to emerge, followed by the wounded man. His shoulder was gored straight through the armor, and his teeth clenched firm. Scott stifled a gag as he deliberately looked in the opposite direction. The wounded man was ferried past, where Galina began to examine him.

The same Russian voice from before spoke through the comm. "We are going to need more help down here, there are many more hostiles." The sound of sporadic gunfire rattled in the background.

Keldysh whirled around to face Max. "How many can fit in the lift?"

"I wouldn't send anymore than what we just had, about seven. Maybe eight," Max said.

Keldysh shifted his attention to Baranov. "Send three of yours."

Baranov paused, before turning to Lieutenant Novikov. "Tolya," he said, "take Jurgen and Kevin."

Novikov nodded, "Yes, commander." He glanced to the two indicated soldiers. "Jurgen, Carpenter—come! You too, Max!"

"Should be fun," David said to Scott as he and Kevin slid through the door.

"Be careful!" Scott said.

As Novikov and Max followed behind them, David laughed out loud. "Come on man, it's me!"

"That's what I'm worried about!"

IN THE *PARIAH*, the remainder of the Fourteenth listened as Novikov, David, Max, and Kevin were lowered into the compound. Svetlana clutched her wrist, pressing her hand against the hull. She stared hard at the floor.

KELDYSH KNELT BESIDE Galina and the injured operative. "How is he?"

"He cannot stay here, captain," Galina answered. "We must get him to a transport."

Keldysh motioned to two soldiers from the Twelfth. "Ebeling! Zamanian! Escort these two to the transport!" The soldiers acknowledged him and rushed to Galina's side.

At that moment, the Third became visible as they approached from the north valley. Keldysh and Baranov gazed in their direction as the sound of gunfire again erupted through the comm.

Keldysh rushed back to the structure. "Status?"

The Russian voice crackled through the comm. "We are under heavy fire, captain!"

"There is a team dispatched," Keldysh answered. "They should arrive soon."

AS THE LIFT lowered Novikov's team to the sublevel, the crackle of gunfire intensified. "Assume defensive positions," Novikov said. "Get ready to exit." David, Max, and Kevin pressed themselves against the walls of the lift. The technicians huddled out of the way.

Max gripped the lift controls. "Get ready." The lift slowed, then clunked to a halt. They were down. "Open in three...two...one!" yelled Max.

The door slid up. Plasma bolts streamed into the lift. All four members of the Fourteenth stayed pressed against the lift walls, out of the line of fire.

Novikov leaned around the lift door and unleashed a blind volley. "Out of the elevator!" He dashed free amid the plasma fire. Projectile retaliation ensued. David affirmed his grip on his assault rifle and followed in step. As soon as he stepped out, he knew they were in trouble.

The circular lift had dropped into a circular room not much larger than the lift itself. A corridor led straight forward, and a quick glance to the left and right indicated two more on each side of the lift. They were surrounded by options.

Bakma were fortified at the end of the front corridor. Plasma fire rained at the lift.

"Take position!" Novikov said as the rest of the team poured from the elevator. "Where the hell is isolation team?"

"Over here, lieutenant!"

The voice came from the corridor farthest left. Novikov spun to face it. "Technicians, go! Max, come on!" David and Kevin took positions around the corner of the front corridor, where they exchanged fire with the Bakma. "Kevin and Jurgen! Hold the lift!"

"Yes sir!" David answered as he angled around the corner and fired a volley. As he flung himself back out of danger, his gaze stopped on Kevin's leg. A fresh char mark stretched across the soldier's armor. Open flesh sizzled beneath. David held his fire. "You all right?"

"Yeah," Kevin answered as he knelt around the corner and popped off a shot. He rolled back out of fire. "Got skimmed is all!"

Novikov followed the voice down the far left corridor until he came across a trio of soldiers fortified at a T-junction. As two soldiers exchanged fire with Bakma defenders on their end, one pivoted to face the lieutenant.

"What happened?" Novikov asked.

The soldier reloaded his assault rifle. "Lieutenant, we did not have the position we expected when we came out of the lift. There was no cover, we had to move or we would have been killed!"

"And now?"

"Now we are holding okay. If we can get more men down here soon, we can take this facility!"

Max emerged from behind Novikov. "If it's an outpost as we expect, there won't be very many more Bakma. We've got the entrance covered. That's the most important part."

Novikov adjusted his comm. "Captain, we are holding the lift area as of now. I suspect we will need perhaps ten or fifteen more soldiers to begin a tactical sweep. We can take this outpost."

The channel hissed with static. "Understood, Novikov. We will assemble a strike team once the Third arrives. Hold your area until then."

"Understood, captain."

ON THE SURFACE, Keldysh tromped toward Baranov. "Commander Baranov, you will lead a team of two down the lift to assist in isolation. When Captain Gavich arrives with the Third, a larger team of his men will join you."

"Understood, captain," Baranov said, turning. "Remington, Kostya! You two, come with me! We assist the isolation team!"

Scott and Konstantin moved to Baranov's side. Konstantin. Scott didn't know him well. He didn't know if he was reliable.

"Tolya," Baranov said through the comm, "myself, Kostya, and Remington are on our way down. Send Max up with the li—"

He was cut off mid-sentence as the sky erupted with a tremendous explosion. The operatives threw back their heads to witness the display. Behind the Third, the fiery remnants of a Vindicator fighter plummeted to the earth.

THE COMMS EXPLODED with pilot chatter.

"Noboats! We have Noboats! Two mat—three materializing!"

The squadron of Vindicators streaked past and three Bakma Noboats appeared behind them. Within seconds, a second Vindicator was set ablaze with plasma fire.

ON THE GROUND below, Keldysh swung toward the operatives as two of the Noboats rotated for a descent. "Behind the structure! Take cover behind the structure!"

Novikov's voice broke through the comm noise. "What is going on up there?"

"Three Noboats have just materialized!" Baranov answered. "Two are coming in for landing!"

"So what are *we* supposed to do?"

THE SCATTERED VINDICATOR fighters reoriented over the structure. Their pilots' voices flooded the airwaves.

"Pull back and close in. We have two descenders, one strafer."

"Copy that, wing commander."

"Red Flight, are you in position for a run?"

"Negative, Green Flight, we're split two-one."

"Red, run the gauntlet on the ground, we'll take the strafer."

"Affirmative, Green Flight, regrouping."

"TRAVIS," CLARKE SAID from the bay of the *Pariah*, "please take us to the ridge!"

Travis acknowledged him, and the transport dragged itself off the ground.

Clarke faced the operatives with him. "Ladies and gentlemen, ready yourselves for a ground assault! We'll attack the Bakma from behind the ridge and give them something else to shoot at!"

Jayden grinned and cocked his sniper rifle. "'Bout time I get to do somethin'."

"Hell yeah," Becan said.

INSIDE THE STRUCTURE, David roared as a plasma bolt struck his left arm and knocked him backward. "What did they just say?" he asked, jumping back into position by the corridor.

Kevin reloaded his assault rifle and resumed fire. "Three Noboats just materialized!"

David inspected his shoulder. His armor was sizzled, and charred flesh reeked underneath. He gritted his teeth. "We're not going to hold them here forever!"

"Just gotta keep firing!" Kevin yelled back.

"Any orders?" asked Novikov through the comm as the underground fight continued. "Is anyone up there?"

The comm channel cracked with quiet. A solitary voice resonated over the airwaves. "This is Thoor. Prepare the facility for detonation."

For several seconds, Novikov looked dazed. He glanced at Max before returning his attention to the comm. "Yes, general!" Next, he addressed the technicians. "Can you set the explosives from this position?"

"Da, lieutenant," the chief technician answered. "We have a chamber freed up down the hallway. We can set it up there and they will probably never find it."

"Do it."

ON THE SURFACE, the Third was in pursuit of the structure when the two Noboats landed behind them. Snow churned from the ground as the vessels depressed. As their metal ramps lowered, the airborne Noboat made its attack run. Bodies flew through the air, white bolts colliding in their midst.

Farther away, the Vindicators finished their loops.

"We cannot stay here!" Baranov said as Bakma emerged from the Noboats on the ground.

Keldysh spoke through the comm a moment later. "This is Captain Keldysh requesting an evacuation!"

Thoor's voice responded. "Request granted. All Vultures, rendezvous with the ground team for evacuation."

AS THE *PARIAH* descended on the ridge, Clarke rushed into the cockpit to join Travis. "Let us off here then loop back around to the structure! Please pick us up on your way out! Boris, stay with him! You too, Varvara! Svetlana, come with us! I want a medic with each team!"

The operatives acknowledged the instructions, and Clarke's drop-off team was released, leaving Travis, Boris, and Varvara alone in the ship. The *Pariah* revolved to face the structure.

WHILE THE REMNANTS of the underground strike team battled the Bakma, the technicians secured the explosives. Novikov's attention was a constant shift between the techs and the Bakma. "How long until it's in place?"

"Almost set, lieutenant!"

Max growled as he reloaded his assault rifle. "Tolya, we're *not* going to be able to hold here much longer!"

Novikov glared at the technicians. "*Faster with the explosive! Time is what we do not have!*"

OUTSIDE AND ABOVE, two flights of Vindicators began their attack runs. Two more Noboats materialized north of the valley. Pilot chatter erupted again.

"God!"

"What is that, five?"

"We have two more Noboats inbound, I repeat, *we have two more Noboats inbound!*"

"Red Flight, we're breaking off of the ground assault and engaging the twins!"

"Copy that, Green, we've engaged the strafer."

"Watch for more distortions."

"Ground team, we can't help you down there, you're on your own with the evac!"

BEHIND THE STRUCTURE, Fox yelped as a plasma bolt skimmed his shoulder armor. He fumbled his gun and it dropped to the snow. "C'mon, where's the trashing Vulture?"

"It's coming," Baranov answered. "They're coming around!"

The survivors from the Third joined the Fourteenth and Twelfth as they covered behind the structure.

"We have to stay by the lift," Baranov said. "We must cover the underground team as the lift rises!"

BELOW THE SURFACE, the chief technician spun around to Novikov. "Explosives set, lieutenant! We can detonate from out-side—all we need to do now is get out of here!"

Novikov was on the comm immediately. "Structure ready for detonation!"

"About time we can get the hell out of here!" Max said.

Thoor's voice resonated through the comm. "What is your overall situation?"

"Explosives are set, general," Novikov answered. "We have a clear path to the lift, and we are good to leave!"

"Very good. You will remain with the explosives to ensure their detonation. The rest of your team may leave."

CLARKE'S TEAM FROZE on the ridge. Svetlana gasped and covered her mouth.

UNDERGROUND BY THE lift, David and Kevin stopped dead in their tracks.

Max's trigger finger went rigid, and he spun to face Novikov. Silence struck amid the gunfire. The comm channel went quiet.

At the corner of the T-junction, Novikov's mouth sunk open, and he droned into his headset. "I am sorry general, could you repeat your last order?"

"You are to remain with the explosives to ensure their detonation. The rest of your team may leave."

SCOTT'S JAW DROPPED as the surface battle raged. The rest of the team may leave? No...that couldn't have been what he said. Could it?

Over the private comm of the Fourteenth, Travis's voice crackled. "What the hell? Did we just hear that right?"

BECAN AND JAYDEN swiveled around as Svetlana dropped to her knees on the ridge. Her hand shot to her chest. "Nyet..." she breathed as her eyes widened with moisture. "Nyet!" Panic struck as she clutched her helmet mic. "Tolya, *ne slushay! Ne slushay!*"

"DO YOU UNDERSTAND your orders, Lieutenant Novikov?"

Below, Novikov fell silent as both voices—Thoor's and Svetlana's—cut through the comm channels.

Max faced him head on. "Tolya, don't tell me you're actually thinking about doing this…"

Thoor spoke again. "I will ask only once more…do you understand your orders?" Silence brooded over the channel. "You know the price of disobedience…"

Novikov's face froze. His eyes trailed to the floor, and he swallowed nervously. Before Max could say another word, Thoor got his answer.

"Yes, general," Novikov said. "I understand."

"Nyet!" Svetlana collapsed to the ground. Her hands smashed into the snow. "Tolya, *nyet!*" Tears poured down her face.

Max erupted. "Like hell you understand those orders!"

Novikov closed his eyes and murmured through the comm. "Sveta, *ya dolzhen.*" He turned to Max. "I have to. I have orders and I must follow them. It is not my decision."

"Anatoly!" David yelled through the comm, "you've got to be *kidding* me!"

Svetlana screamed. "Nyet, Tolya! *Nyet!*"

"If I do not stay, the mission could fail," Novikov answered. "The explosives must go off!"

"Can you hold this hall by yourself?" David asked Kevin by the lift.

"Yeah," Kevin answered. "Where are you going?"

David backed toward the left hallway. "To insert common sense!"

"How in the *hell* are Bakma going to disarm human explosives?" Max said, slamming his fist against the wall.

Novikov shot back, "The same way humans can unlock Bakma doors!"

"If the bombs don't go off, *so what*? We come back and attack the base again! It's not like this is the battle for the end of the universe!"

CLARKE KNELT BESIDE Svetlana as she continued to wail. "Tolya, nyet!"

"This is bloody insane!" said Becan as he spun around to Jayden and threw his hands up.

Dostoevsky watched Svetlana from the edge of the ridge.

BENEATH THE STRUCTURE, David rounded the corner nearest to Novikov and Max. He shouted as soon as he saw the lieutenant. "How can you hear that voice pleading with you and still stay?"

"If I do not stay…!" Novikov began. He cut himself off. His glare first fixated on David, then it blazed at Max. "*You* know," he said off-comm. "You know what will happen."

Max opened his mouth to reply, then bit back the words. The three men fell in silence.

"*What?*" David said. "What in *God's name* is going on here?"

"This is not like the rest of EDEN," Novikov answered. "Orders must be followed. This is not my decision…"

"*Why* does this order have to be followed?" said David in frustration. "What the hell could be worse? They'll kill you when you get back to base? Well *great*, add an extra hour to your life, but give it a trashing *chance*!"

"Tolya, *nyet!*"

"…there is much worse," Novikov said gravely.

David stared at Novikov. The blank look lasted for several seconds, as gunfire rallied around them. Then David's expression changed as realization dawned on him. His eyes widened, and he took a sharp breath. "No…you have got to be kidding me…"

Novikov pointed to Max. "Ask him. Ask him what will happen."

"You have got to be *kidding* me!"

Max turned to David and said solemnly, "If Tolya doesn't listen, he's not the one who'll get killed…she will."

David lost it. "*How? How can that happen?* How c—"

"This is how it has to be!" Novikov cried. "I do not do this for me! I do this for her! You know this now! I have no choice!"

"It has to be this way," Max said.

David tore off his helmet. "No! How can he get away with that?"

"It's the truth!" Max answered. "You don't like it, it doesn't matter! This isn't EDEN you're dealing with! You might have thought that when you got here, but you were wrong!"

Novikov said to David, "You hear? There is not even time to think about it."

"It's the truth," Max said again.

Before David could respond, Novikov said to Max, "Can you lock me in the chamber with the explosive?"

"Yeah…" Max muttered. He retrieved the suction device from his belt and moved to the detonation chamber. "You can close the door from inside. It'll lock when you do."

Novikov nodded and lowered his assault rifle to the ground. His eyes began to glisten. "Max…I have to ask you to…"

"I'll watch her. I promise."

"Thank you, Max. You were always my favorite capitalist pig." Novikov feigned a smile.

Max offered a failed smirk. "Whatever, communist."

David listened in silence as the lieutenant said, "Now get out of here. Before we *all* die."

Max adjusted his comm. "All underground operatives, congregate and hold the lift area. We're going back up."

BARANOV WAS SILENT on the surface as Max's evacuation order broke through the airwaves. None of his team had spoken a word since Thoor's order. Before they could, an explosion shook the ground in front of the structure. The Bakma were on the attack.

"No time to think about it!" Baranov said. "Get ready to get them out of the lift!"

SVETLANA LAY CRUMPLED on the ground at the ridge, her pleas reduced to quiet whimpers. Dostoevsky knelt beside her, his hand falling against her back.

Becan's face reddened. "I can't bloody *believe* this!"

Clarke interrupted before a discussion could begin. For the first time, his voice quivered. "Come on. We've got to engage. We've got to."

He, Becan, and Jayden took position at the edge of the ridge, as Dostoevsky whispered into Svetlana's ear. The medic nodded, rose to her feet, and joined the others.

SCOTT DUCKED BEHIND the structure as a plasma bolt seared past his head. The Bakma were closer, and with every shot he fired, the intensity of their oppression grew heavier. Not only was EDEN outnumbered, they were out-positioned. This was not going to last.

He shrank behind the structure to avoid fire, when a scream rang out. Konstantin. Scott surveyed the immediate area, where he caught sight of the soldier. His thigh had been struck dead on by a plasma bolt.

"Hold on!" Scott said as he darted from the structure, through the mass of soldiers toward Konstantin. He wasn't a doctor, but he knew as soon as he saw the wound that it was serious.

Konstantin winced and clutched his leg. The once-white snow beneath him was stained with red.

Scott scanned for Galina, but she was overtaken with other wounded. The medical staff was overwhelmed. He grabbed the injured soldier's armpits. "Hang on—I'll get you to cover!"

Max's voice emerged from the comm. "We're coming up and we've got wounded!"

Scott growled under his breath. Everything was happening too fast. The Noboats. Novikov and Svetlana. Konstantin. The lift. He didn't know what to do. As soon as Konstantin was behind the structure, Scott scanned the area to find his teammates. Fox was on his own on the other side of the fight, where he continued to fire his sniper rifle. Baranov was nowhere to be seen.

Max's voice emerged again. "We're coming to the top! We'd *better* have cover!"

Scott abandoned Konstantin for the front of the structure, where the lift exited. Konstantin was safe where he was...now they had to secure Max's team. The doors were going to open in a dead stare with the oncoming Bakma. When Scott arrived on the scene, Baranov and several others were already in midbattle. The mechanical clunks of the lift resonated in the background.

"Assist the wounded first!" Baranov said. "Draw the fire away!"

Before Scott could fire a shot, the door to the structure slid open. Soldiers crammed the lift.

The wounded were ferried from the lift first as EDEN defenders held off the Bakma. "How many are in there?" Baranov asked.

"Everyone!" Max answered.

"I thought only eight could go down at a time?"

"Necessity is the mother of compromise!"

ATOP THE RIDGE, Clarke and his team rained fire upon the Bakma, though their efforts were dwarfed by the timed strafes of the Vindicators.

Dostoevsky once again whispered to Svetlana as they took their positions on the ridge. She shook as she drew her sidearm.

SCOTT WAS IN the middle of the transfer of wounded when a scorching blast slammed into his left shoulder. His feet left the ground and he landed flat on his back. For a moment, his vision flashed white. There was silence. Pain. The reek of burnt skin. He had been shot. As suddenly as it disappeared, his vision returned. The overcast sky loomed above. He was alive, but he could hear his armor sizzling. His teeth clenched as he attempted to peer at his shoulder. His armor was torn almost completely open. It burned like fire.

Before he could muster the endurance to stand, a pair of hands grabbed him and jerked him to his feet. They were David's.

"Scott, you all right?"

Scott winced as he regained his balance. His assault rifle lay sprawled in the snow. "Yeah." He lied. "Veck!"

David hurried him to the side of the structure. "If it makes you feel any better, the rest of us are shot to hell, too."

It took a few moments for Scott to register David's presence. David was okay. Shot, but okay. But what about...? "Where's Lieutenant Novikov?"

David's expression shifted. "I'll tell you about it later. There's nothing we can do."

Before Scott could reply, Travis's voice cut through the comm chatter. "We're landing—get everyone in quick! This place is getting ugly fast!"

Scott and David turned their faces skyward, where the trio of Vultures began their descents. The *Pariah* led the pack.

The rush to the transports was frenzied chaos. Where the wounded were not escorted, soldiers waved for their comrades to fall back. Konstantin was the first of the Fourteenth to be assisted into the *Pariah*, followed by Fox and Kevin. Varvara was quick to give them attention.

Baranov and Max were the last two in, as the commander carried Max against his shoulder. Max's armor smoldered and there were dots of blood on his face. Fox stared at them. "What happened?"

"He got shot—what does it look like happened?" Baranov snarled.

Max gave the okay sign. "I'm all right, I'm not dying. I was almost behind the structure when some lucky dregg hopper caught me at the last second."

"Where is everyone else?" asked Baranov.

"We dropped them off on the ridge," said Boris as Travis readied the *Pariah* for ascent. "They're giving us cover."

"Where is Galya?"

"I am too busy!" she answered through the comm. "You go! I will catch ride with Keldysh!"

Plasma bolts slammed into the *Pariah*'s hull as the operatives strapped themselves in. "Is anyone back there critical?" Travis asked.

"No, let's *go*!" Max clenched his teeth.

"I'm keeping the back door open till we pick everyone up at the ridge!" Travis said. "Don't fall out!"

Baranov glared. "Do not *make* us fall out!"

CLARKE ROLLED TO his knees behind the ridge as the *Pariah* took flight. "Everyone! I'm sorry, sink back! Travis will be here shortly!"

A round of acknowledgments followed as Dostoevsky, Becan, and Jayden abandoned the ridge's edge. The battle between the

Noboats and Vindicators was still fierce, as occasional explosions rocked the sky.

Becan slung his assault rifle over his shoulder and knelt in the snow. "Abou' time we can get out o' here."

"Be grateful you weren't down there, gentlemen," said Clarke. "We got the better end of the deal." The men nodded in agreement.

At that moment, the captain frowned, and he turned to face the men. He passed a fleeting glance over each one—Dostoevsky, Becan, and Jayden. Dostoevsky. Becan. And Jayden. A second after, his eyes shot wide.

Svetlana was gone.

TRAVIS'S FOCUS NARROWED on the ridge as he centered the *Pariah*'s nose. They were midway between Clarke's team and the outpost.

In the troop bay, the operatives peered down at the battle-weary earth. Bodies were strewn across the ground, none of which were recovered before the mass retreat. They would return for bodies later—after the Bakma had left.

Fox was the first to catch sight of the straggler. Despite the many figures that trekked through the snow—almost all Bakma—this one stood out. It wasn't a Bakma at all. It was a lone EDEN operative, sprinting across the battlefield. "There's someone down there," he said, standing.

The others followed Fox's stare. David raised a brow. "Where do they think they're going? They're running straight for the out-post…"

Before another comment could be made, Fox's jaw dropped. "Oh my God!"

Clarke's tone gave away the revelation. "Does anybody up there see Svetlana? She's gone!"

Scott leapt to his feet. Svetlana! What was she doing? No...he knew what she was doing. She was doing exactly what he'd be doing.

Max propped himself up. "Oh my God. She's going back for Tolya."

Varvara gasped; Baranov sprinted to the back of the *Pariah*. "We just passed over her! She's running back to the outpost! She's running straight for the Bakma!"

Plasma bolts flew in Svetlana's direction. *She'll never make it*, thought Scott. "She's not gonna make it…" She couldn't die. Not her. Anyone but her. He had just gotten to know her.

Cupping his hands over his mouth, Baranov shouted from the doorway. "Sveta!" Just as he called her name, a plasma bolt clipped her in the leg. She toppled forward into the snow. Baranov tore off his helmet and rushed his hand through his hair. "She's going to be gunned down!"

"I told Tolya I'd watch her!" Max said, panicking.

Scott's heart pounded as he lurched toward the doorway. She would die any second. "She's not gonna make it!" His legs tensed. His eyes judged the ground.

As soon as Scott had bent his knees, David cried, "Scott, don't even thi—"

It was too late. Scott leapt from the open door of the *Pariah* and fell to the snow.

Max froze as Scott disappeared.

David sprinted to the door. "What are you *doing*?" Before he could say another word, Baranov's hand intercepted his chest and held him in place.

"Wait," Baranov said. "Let him go…"

Far below, Scott hit the snow and tumbled into a ball.

AIRBORNE IN *VULTURE-3*, distant but not oblivious, General Thoor's eyes narrowed on the newly snowbound operative. The soldier's golden collar shone atop the snow.

THE STING THAT surged through Scott's arm as he landed hard reminded him that he was wounded. He bit back the pain and scrambled to his feet. It wasn't hard to find Svetlana—she was the only other human on the ground. The nearest Bakma trained his weapon on her. Scott lifted his assault rifle and fired first. He missed.

"Sveta, stay down!"

The Bakma shifted his aim to Scott, as did several others. Diving into the snow as they opened fire, Scott propped himself to a knee and pulled the trigger. One Bakma fell.

He was outnumbered. He knew it. He counted five Bakma close enough to Svetlana and himself to actively engage, and he was too far away to make a difference. He would never make it to her in time.

Suddenly, one of the Bakma jolted back and dropped. Before Scott could react, a second Bakma did the same. Jayden's unmistakable Texas drawl slurred over the comm.

"Git 'er, man. I got you covered."

There was no more hesitation. Scott leapt to his feet and chased full speed after Svetlana. With Jayden's suppression, he caught up to her unmolested.

"Sveta, stay down!" He grabbed her from behind and tackled her into the snow. She was very much awake, though her armor was charred deep. Her eyes were half-crazed. "Are you hurt bad?"

She shoved him back and spat a torrent of Russian his way, then twisted to escape his grip.

He grabbed her a second time. The pain in his arm surged again. *"Stay down!"*

Before he could utter another word, an explosion of gunfire erupted behind him. He looked back. It was the *Pariah*. Its nose-mounted chain gun blazed orange as it unleashed a flurry of rounds into the Bakma below.

Svetlana screamed as she attempted to wrench herself from Scott.

Scott slammed her to the ground and wrestled himself atop her. "Svetlana, stop it!"

"We're coming down on your position," Travis said over the comm. "Look up."

Engines roared above them as the *Pariah* descended. Baranov and David knelt by the bay door, their arms outstretched to retrieve Svetlana and Scott.

Svetlana continued to struggle against him.

Scott held her firm. "Don't make me knock you out!"

"Lift her up!" David yelled from above.

Scott grabbed her from behind and hoisted her into the air. She kicked and screamed, but Baranov and David snatched her before she could writhe away.

Scott was next. He moaned as his burned shoulder flexed its muscles, but with the help of the others, he was pulled inside.

"Hold on," Travis said from the cockpit. "We're picking the rest up on the ridge!" As the bay door rose, Scott collapsed to the floor.

"What the hell where you thinking!" David asked.

Scott didn't respond. He didn't know what to say.

It took only another minute for the *Pariah* to arrive at the ridge, where Clarke and his crew were retrieved. Once that was done, the transport set its course for *Novosibirsk*. The outpost and the Noboats were left behind; there were too few Vindicators to mount an assault. Instead, the fighters looped back and escorted the transports home.

Almost half of the operatives in the Fourteenth bore some sort of wound. Of the initial ground team, only Baranov and Fox returned unscathed, the latter of whose armor was severely charred. Konstantin sat numbed on the floor with a cauterized hole in his thigh, and Scott's entire shoulder and arm cramped. David cautiously cradled his own arm, and Kevin scrutinized the small gash in his leg.

Max's chest wound was the most serious. Varvara monitored it constantly and made it clear that serious medical attention would be needed as soon as they landed. As she kept over him, Max kept watch over Svetlana, who remained huddled in the corner. Though her armor was charred and twisted, she was not seriously hurt.

A somber quiet permeated the transport as it cut through the Siberian sky. It was a quiet indicative of many emotions—fear, anger, sadness, and bewilderment. Even the Nightmen among them, Baranov and Dostoevsky, remained silent and still. The only sound in the rear bay, aside from the hum of the *Pariah*, was Svetlana's choked breathing as she cried. Her body, crumpled and weak, shivered as Baranov sat beside her, his arm supportive around her shoulder. There was little more that could be done. This was something no one had prepared for.

Everyone heard the click. It was impossible not to. It was a static noise, a subtle crackle, and it caused every one of the operatives to lift their heads and turn their attention to the wall. To the speaker.

Someone was on the channel.

None of them could have prepared for the voice they heard next. "Sveta?"

Nobody made a sound. The operatives all riveted their eyes on Svetlana. She trembled as the voice repeated itself through the speaker.

"Sveta?"

It was he. Deep within the walls of the Bakma outpost. It was Novikov.

Svetlana leapt to her feet and scrambled to the wall. She shot up her hand to press the button beneath the speaker, as tears steamed down her face. "Tolya?"

The voice moaned. "Sveta…"

She swallowed at the sound of her name. Pressing her forehead against the speaker, she held one hand firm on the button, while the other braced against the wall. Her body trembled and she broke down.

Scott watched as she lost her composure. He watched as her body surrendered, and she slid down the cold of the *Pariah*'s hull. The cursed ship. He watched as other eyes began to glisten, and he felt damp with sympathy. Behind the lifeless frame of the speaker mount, Novikov's rasping breaths heard her. His voice wavered and he began to whisper.

Svetlana choked sobs as her hand held up the wall. "Nyet, Tolya…nyet…" The words barely escaped her lips.

Novikov whispered back inaudibly as Svetlana whimpered and closed her eyes. She couldn't make a sound. Her lips parted in a frozen gasp. Her hand sunk down the surface of the wall.

Her sobbing was interrupted as Thoor's voice cut through the speaker. "Are all units cleared of the facility?"

"Twelfth clear."

"Third clear."

Travis covered his mouth with his fist as moisture trailed down his cheeks. He lifted his gaze to the sky. In the seat beside him, Boris wiped his eyes and turned to face him. Neither man spoke.

"Fourteenth, are you clear of the facility?"

Svetlana trembled as she attempted to stand. She pressed her face against the speaker and said softly through the waver in her voice, "Ya tebya lyublyu."

Novikov smiled. Everyone could hear it. "Ya budu vsegda lyubit' tebya, Svetlana."

"Fourteenth, you will respond."

Closing his eyes, Travis leaned his head back against the seat cushion, and raised his hand to rub his face. He reached out and placed his finger on the comm button. Beside him, Boris looked away.

Travis's finger lingered for several seconds before he gave the button a weak press. The channel was open. "Fourteenth clear."

"Detonate."

"Ya budu vsegda lyubit' tebya," Novikov said.

Static. The signal was gone.

Svetlana collapsed against the wall. The tear-stained faces of the Fourteenth followed her movements. Nothing else came from the speaker. Nothing else came from anyone. Svetlana froze in mid-sob, and she slid to the floor.

Only Baranov moved, rising to his feet and stepping behind her. He knelt on the floor and embraced her with a reddened stare. She crumbled into his arms.

There were no congratulations when they arrived at *Novosibirsk*. There were no handshakes. The *Pariah* was docked, and the Fourteenth retired in silence. No one needed to speak. The empty bunk in Room 14 said enough for all of them.

15

EVERYONE IN THE conference room focused on Judge Kentwood as he adjusted his bifocals and cleared his throat. "Detonation occurred at 0814 hours on Thursday, April 14th, Novosibirsk time. Scouts confirmed the detonation with a visual check just before 1100. There were no hostages taken, and as far as we can tell, no survivors. The access lift caved during the course of the explosion, so it's only right to assume that any Bakma who might have survived below ground will perish. As far as we're concerned, this chapter is closed."

There was a quiet in the room as Kentwood lowered himself into his chair. Pauling leaned forward. "Thank you, Darryl. I assume a full report will be ready within the next few days?"

Kentwood nodded. "Yes sir. We'll have a unit investigate the site on hand—hopefully we'll be able to get deep enough down there to get some kind of salvage. Unfortunately, we aren't sure how probable that is, considering the facility was destroyed internally."

Pauling nodded. "Our priority was to incapacitate the base, and that was done. Salvage was secondary."

Before he could comment further, another judge spoke up. It was Richard Lena, one of the youngest judges in the High Command at thirty-six years old. "I think it should be noted that General Thoor was once again present during this operation."

"Yes," Kentwood said. "I was going to mention that again as well. It's only a matter of time until he gets killed...perhaps we should consider a reprimand of some sort...we *have* mentioned this to him before."

The room became quiet. Pauling's expression was momentarily distant; then he turned to Kentwood. "No. That would only spark retaliation."

Kentwood sighed. "With all due respect, sir, it is *we* who are in control of EDEN, not General Thoor."

"Thoor is too valuable to lose," Pauling answered adamantly. "If he feels he's losing his authority in *Novosibirsk*, he may pull himself and everyone at that facility away from us."

Lena interrupted. "The backlash from such retaliation would be overwhelming, sir. Does he truly think that those soldiers would, if given a choice between EDEN and *Novosibirsk*, choose to side with him?"

"Yes. He does," said Pauling. "And he'd be right. Keep in mind, Mr. Lena, *Novosibirsk* is run more by the Nightmen than by us."

"Which is something *else* that needs to be addressed," Lena said. "It's high time we let the general know that *Novosibirsk* is, contrary to popular belief, an EDEN facility."

Several of the judges closed their eyes. "Thoor is a unique situation," Pauling answered. "This is a case where it's in the best interest of both EDEN and Thoor if he is allowed to do as he wishes, provided he doesn't get out of control. We've had this discussion before."

"I second that."

The vote of confidence came from Judge Rath, who sat several seats left of the president. "Thoor is too valuable to lose. The minute he feels we're threatening his authority, he'll pull himself and every Nightman away."

Lena sighed. "I still feel it would be best to at least send a note asking him to consider taking better care of himself. We don't have generals coming out of the woodwork...and he'd be a very hard one to replace."

"The hardest," Kentwood agreed.

"Noted," Pauling answered. "Mr. Lena, I'll have you tend to that notice. I do advise you, however, to be careful in how you choose your words." Lena nodded, and Pauling looked at his watch. "I'm sorry to have to call this meeting to an end early, but I have an important call coming through concerning the proposed facility in Sydney. Before we leave, are there any further comments? Questions?"

Silence presided over the table, until Kentwood cleared his throat. The rest of the High Command turned to face him. "Yes, sir…"

"Very well, Darryl. Go ahead."

"As you know, sir, I've been doing a lot of work with Intelligence lately." He reached down to the tabletop, where he produced a single sheet of paper. "There are some…"

The sentence trailed off, and his eyes lingered on the document in his hand. The rest of the room watched in silence.

"…there are a few things I've found that concern me, I'm not sure if this is the appropriate time to discuss this, but I've come across some interesting findings. I don't have a full report ready, but given time, I should be able to produce one. I was wondering if I could be allowed full access to the Intelligence Department. Supervised, of course."

Several of the judges raised their eyebrows.

"I don't want to report anything that I can't prove or at least back up to some degree," Kentwood said. "Given a few weeks, I should be able to have a full report of what I'm talking about on your desk."

Pauling looked thoughtfully for a few moments, then said, "I don't have issue with that. I'll notify Kang tomorrow."

"Thank you sir," Kentwood said.

"Is there anything else?" No one else spoke. "Very well, then. We'll convene again tomorrow at 1500. You're dismissed."

The members of the High Command rose and filed out of the room as Kentwood gathered his papers. Before he could step out, Judge Rath approached him. "What exactly did you find that's so intriguing?" Rath asked. "Is it something we should be aware of?"

Kentwood smiled and offered a half laugh. "It's probably nothing. It could just be errors in documentation for all I know. I rather not get into details until I've looked into it further…no use spreading news that may not be news at all."

Rath cocked his head. "So it's nothing we should be worrying about then?"

"No, not yet, anyway. It's probably nothing, just me looking at things too critically."

"Nothing wrong with that."

"No," Kentwood smiled, "I guess not."

"All right. Well, good luck with the report. I look forward to hearing about it."

Kentwood bowed his head in dismissal. He made his departure from the room, and Rath followed several steps behind.

Rath slowed to a stop just outside the conference room. As soon as Kentwood disappeared ahead of him, Rath scanned the hall until his gaze came to rest on the eyes of another judge—Malcolm Blake—who stood at the far end of the hallway. The two locked eyes for several seconds before the brown-skinned Blake nodded in acknowledgment and disappeared around the corner.

Rath remained in front of the conference room doors, where his gaze sunk to the floor. Several moments passed, before he too turned to walk away. The meeting area was left empty, and the doors to the conference room left closed in silence.

*   *   *

2032 HOURS

NOVOSIBIRSK, RUSSIA

JAYDEN STARED AT the bottom of the bunk above him. "That's twice in a row now," he mumbled. Over twelve hours had passed since the strike on the Bakma outpost, and the unit was divided. Scott, David, Kevin, Konstantin, Max, and Svetlana were among those injured enough to require medical housing. The others remained unharmed in Room 14. While most of those in the medical bay were expected to be released within the week, Max and Konstantin were in for considerably longer recoveries.

Becan, in his own bunk next to Jayden, said to the Texan, "Mmm?"

"Twice they left me out," Jayden repeated.

Silence fell around them. "Righ'."

"I'm serious. The bug-hunt and this one. The only mission I got to be a part of was Chicago." Jayden's hand reached down to drag his cowboy hat from the floor. He lifted it to his chest.

"Yeh didn't want to be at the bug-hunt," Becan said. "An' wha' are yeh talkin' abou'? Yeh saved Remmy's life. Saved Svetlana's, too. Yeh think they could've lived through tha' without yeh?"

"I did that on my own. They still never picked me to go on the team that got to do stuff."

"Righ'," Becan said as he rubbed his face. Though it was late, none of the operatives slept. Aside from Becan and Jayden, the only others present were Galina and Varvara, both of whom exchanged quiet conversation on the other side of the room. Curfew seemed not to matter, as none of the other non-injured operatives were there.

"Scott's the only reason I got to do somethin'," Jayden said. "I feel useless."

"You're not useless," Becan answered. "If yeh were useless, yeh wouldn't be here at all."

Jayden stretched back his neck. "I just want to be a part of the action, that's all. I want to be called out to fight, I want to be given responsibility, like everyone else is."

Becan hummed as he pursed his lips. "Righ', well yeh need to talk more."

"What?"

"Yeh need to talk more. Remmy talks to everyone. It's not tha' he sucks up, he doesn't, but he just…well, he talks. The more yeh talk, the more people get to know yeh, the more they get to know yeh, the more they trust yeh."

"So you're sayin' I don't talk?"

"Yeh don't. All yeh do is say 'yessir' an' snore."

The bunks fell quiet. Jayden slid his cowboy hat to cover his stomach. "I don't snore."

At that point, the door to Room 14 opened and Commander Baranov stepped inside. Becan and Jayden observed as he offered a subtle nod to Galina and Varvara, then closed the door behind him. The two women replied with somber smiles, and Baranov lumbered toward his bunk. As he sat, the frame of his bed sunk several inches.

"Start talkin'," Becan urged Jayden under his breath.

Jayden cleared his throat. "Hello, commander," he said nervously.

"Gentlemen," Baranov said as he leaned forward to untie his boots. He released a long breath as he stretched his neck to the side, where it popped out loud. Jayden cleared his throat again.

"How are you doing, sir?"

Baranov scrutinized the Texan suspiciously, then unzipped the top half of his jersey. "As good as one could be on a terrible day."

"Are they letting anyone into the med bay yet, sir?"

"Yes. I am just coming from there now." Baranov sighed.

"How is everyone? Sir."

"They are all resting now. Max is lucky to be alive, but he will pull through. Kostya is also full of luck."

Jayden hesitated. "How's Svetlana?"

Baranov shifted on his bunk until he sat sideways across it, at which point he leaned back and propped his hands behind his head. His eyes slid shut. "She is not hurt bad...her armor saved her from that, but...I do not know. I think her heart has died already."

Silence overtook them until Becan addressed Baranov for the first time. "Why did tha' happen this mornin'?"

Baranov sighed. "I cannot give you an answer for that. There are things that happen...that do not seem as if they are right." Becan listened intently. "There are many things that the general does that many people do not agree with, such as what you have seen today. I know I do not like it, I do not think I could ever order such a thing as he ordered. But...General Thoor is one of the greatest military leaders to ever live, in any time. If you look at his history, and look at the history of other EDEN generals, you will see that nobody else even compares. He does good work...he just does not do it in a...good way, if I may say that."

He sighed. "Tolya had no choice today. I cannot tell you why this is true...but Tolya did what needed to be done. We may not like it, but...we are not required to like everything. The general knew that there was no way the base was going to be captured, and so knew that it had to be destroyed. He had to make sure that it was destroyed the first time, and the only way to do that was to leave someone behind. If Tolya would have disobeyed…" His words trailed off. "He did what he had to do."

Jayden spoke up. "What would have happened?"

Baranov hesitated before he answered. "If the base would have needed a second attack, there would have been more loss of life. The general knew this. He did what had to be done for the situation to work the first time…and that is why he is such a great leader."

"A great leader?" Becan said skeptically. "Tha' 'great leader' killed one o' his own for no bloody reason. Doesn't tha' upset yeh at all?"

"It does, but what can I do? I have cried my tears already. Tolya was my friend. I had known him for very long time, but what can I do now? Nothing I can do will bring him back, what has been done has been done." He sighed. "I have lost comrades before, and it is not something I enjoy at all, but it is inevitable. There comes a point where death does not surprise one anymore—one comes to expect it. I will probably die here, the two of you will probably die here. It is something that has to be accepted."

Becan scoffed. "Accepted, yeah, but not in the way the lieutenant died today. He should be here, now. The bomb went off, there were no problems…he died a needless death." He paused, then added, "An' wha' abou' Svetlana? Wha' is she supposed to do, eh? Do yeh think everythin' you're sayin' now is goin' to make her feel better? She's still goin' to be alone, an' *tomorrow* she'll still be alone. She can't even fall back on the mindset tha' the lieutenant died a hero, 'cos he didn't. He died 'cos some bucket o' snots told him to die."

Baranov sighed. "Today a Bakma facility was destroyed. That is what was supposed to happen, and that is what happened. The general did what he felt needed to be done to guarantee victory."

"Yeh never answered me question. Wha's Svetlana supposed to do? How is she supposed to take all this?"

"She will grieve," Baranov answered. "That is her right, it is what is to be expected. She will hurt, as we all hurt when we lose someone we love. But she will move on. It will be hard for her, and it will take some time, but she will move on. She is a strong-hearted woman."

"If she had a right mind on her she'd take a gun an' blow tha' plonker's head off," Becan said.

"That is enough."

"Enough until when? Someone else is told to die?"

"I said that is enough." Baranov's tone became firm. "You are not expected to like everything that goes on here. But you will accept it. That is how things are done. Now, that is the end of this discussion."

"Yessir," Jayden quickly answered. He turned and glared at Becan. "Wha'?"

"You're gonna get us fired!" Jayden whispered.

"Aw, you gackawacka. Nobody's goin' to get fired."

"Well you'd better watch how you talk to the commander."

"Blarney. I could take tha' overgrown ape anny day."

"I can hear you, you know," Baranov said. "I am like, two meters away."

Becan and Jayden shifted their attention to the commander. His eyes were still closed, and his hands still rested behind his head. The rest of the room was silent.

Jayden flopped down on his pillow and turned away from Becan. "You need to talk less."

"Aw, dry up."

*   *   *

THE INFIRMARY SAT in quiet desolation. Two full rows of beds were occupied by those injured in the outpost assault. With the initial bustle of stabilization over, the aides exchanged whispered conversation as they prepared to clock out. The evening had set in.

There was a disinfected stench to the air. Wounds of various degrees—full burns, clean incisions, open holes—poured their peculiar odors into the atmosphere. Despite attempts by the medical staff to dampen them, the smells lingered—a reminder of the mortality that loomed over *Novosibirsk*.

It was past eleven when the last lights were turned off, and the last nurse made her designated nighttime round. For Scott, it couldn't have been more welcomed.

The room had been silent all day, and aside from the occasional cough or grunt, it remained that way. It was fitting that when it came time for Scott and David—who had been comrades from day one—to engage in conversation, their first words were not words at all.

Scott's lips parted, and he released a solitary sigh into the silence. The noise disturbed little, but it did garner David's attention. Silence prevailed, and then David finally spoke.

"What are you thinking?"

Scott remained fixated on the ceiling. What was he thinking? It was a question he was used to hearing all the time. Just not in this context. He feigned a smile. "That you just sounded like my fiancée." David made no response, and the smile faded from Scott's lips. "I'm thinking things were a lot better about a month ago."

David's head straightened, and his gaze too fell upon the emptiness of the ceiling. "I keep thinking about Sharon."

Scott's stomach twisted into a knot. David continued.

"I keep thinking...about the look on her face. When that EDEN officer comes knocking on the door and tells her that her husband is dead. I see Stevie and Timmy running to the door to see why their mom is crying...and she asks the man why..." Scott closed his eyes as he listened. "And he can't give her a reason."

Scott slid his arm across his stomach. That was every soldier with a family's greatest fear. The fear of death, not for themselves, but for those they would leave behind. For those who would suffer from it. "That's not going to happen," Scott said.

"I have two sons," David said. "They haven't seen me in two months. I want them to see me again."

"They will."

"You keep saying that, but how do you know? What if Thoor asks me to do what he asked Anatoly to? And I have no choice?"

"He's not going to say that."

David offered no response. Across the room, a soldier's cough disturbed the air. Scott's gaze remained on David, until the older man said, "I shouldn't be here."

Scott started. This from David? From Henry back at *Richmond*, yes, he would have expected that, but...David? He was everyone's pillar of strength. If *he* was having doubts...Scott could only stare with bewilderment. "What?"

"...I should be home," David said, "being a father. I should be doing something safe. Selling real estate, giving financial advice. Something else. Something that gives them something other than a knock on the door and a total stranger."

Scott frowned. He had never thought about it until then, but when he first met David, David told him that his family was moving to Richmond—to be closer to him. David never brought it up again. The transfer to Russia must have been killing them. And Scott never thought to ask him about it. For a moment, he hated himself. "Dave...back at *Richmond* you were helping me through this same thing with Nicole..."

David made eye contact with Scott. "This is different now. Now, we're being *told* to die. Tell me you haven't been thinking about this, too. Look me in the eye and tell me you haven't been thinking the same thing. After what just happened."

"Dave...I haven't stopped thinking about it since Chicago, but..."

David said nothing. His stare returned to the ceiling, and he slid his hands behind his head. Scott's eyes remained on him as he lay there, even as David's contact broke away. The infirmary was quiet.

He was supposed to say something. What was he supposed to say? Wisdom, realistic expectations...that was David's department. What did Scott have to offer? It didn't take long for him to find it.

It was the only thing he knew.

"None of us are promised tomorrow," Scott whispered. "Not me, not you...not Sharon or Nicole. We live in a world where things happen all of a sudden. But I know things happen for a reason. I know everything happens for a reason. I'd like to think they happen for an overall good that's just a little too far ahead for us to see." Why was it so effortless to say? Was it all that programmed in his head? "I know...that God has a plan for me. I know He has a plan for you. I know He'll never put me, or you, or any of us through something we can't handle."

David was listening intently.

"You know I think about it," Scott said. "I think about it all the time. That same scene you replay in your head...I see it too, with Nicole. I love her, Dave. I can't *not* be terrified at the thought that I may never see her again. I know it must be ten times as bad for you. I can't even imagine what runs through your head at night when you think about it. But I know that every night I pray and ask God to watch over us, me and Nicole, and you and Sharon. And your kids. Every night I pray for as many people as I can remember their names. Everyone in the unit here, everyone in Charlie back home, everyone. I don't do this to feel self-righteous or to feel good about myself. I do it because sometimes prayer's all we've got. I believe God listens."

David's gaze remained on Scott, but his eyes fell distant. Several seconds passed before he replied. "I wish I had your faith."

"No you don't," Scott said. "I don't have enough." It was true. All of his talk about spirituality, his reading of Scripture...and when night came, his fears were the same as the most faithless around him, like he was some spiritual hypocrite. His faith was there. It just wasn't as strong as it needed to be.

David cleared his throat and looked up. "You hear anything about Svetlana?"

Scott leaned back his head. He didn't want to think about Svetlana. It hurt too much. "No. I don't think she was injured too bad, just..."

"...yeah, I know," David answered. "I don't think I could take it. I don't know how she's taking it now."

"What makes you think she's taking it? She's across the room, but I still haven't heard her say a thing all day. I know she hasn't been sleeping this whole time."

"Poor thing."

"She wanted to die with him," Scott said. "Just run down the hill and get mowed down by the Bakma...she was ready to do it. If she'd have made it to him there's nothing she could have done. Just died with him."

David's head tilted to the side. "Would you have done it for Nicole?"

"In a heartbeat."

David nodded. "Me too." He adjusted his hands behind his head. "You saved her life, you know."

Scott frowned. He had saved her life. He and Jayden. He knew that. But it didn't make him feel any better.

"Why did you do it?" David asked. "You didn't have to, the transport would have been there in another minute, and she might have been fine."

Scott shook his head. "Might is too big of a risk, I couldn't accept that. She could have been killed."

"You could've, too."

Scott stared at the ceiling. "It just felt like the right thing to do."

David chuckled. "You'll always do the right thing even if it kills you, huh?"

Scott furrowed his brow. Even if it killed him? It had almost killed him. It had almost killed both of them, he and her. But who else would have done it? Nobody else had tried to save her. They just watched her run. They watched her almost die. Would they have left her body to be picked up later, too?

"I hope so," Scott answered. She was worth it. She was worth the jump, she was worth the risk. She was worth it to him. He looked narrowly at David. "You'd better not have just jinxed me with that."

David smirked. "What are you going to do if I did? You'll be dead."

"I'll haunt you." The two men chuckled. "What do you think Becan and Jay are doing?" Scott asked.

"I don't know. Whatever Jayden's doing, I'm sure he's doing it very quietly."

Scott stifled a laugh. "Poor guy."

"Jayden's great."

"Yeah," Scott said. "Awesome shot, too. That whole Chicago thing would have been ugly if he hadn't been there. Guy's brilliant with the S-27."

"That's his job."

Scott smiled. "I think the fact that he's a sniper makes him seem cool."

"Yeah. Want to hear my Jayden impression?"

"Sure."

David drew a breath. The room fell silent. "Well howdy pilgrim, reckon I'd better pull out my trusty ole' sniper rifle and rustle me up some extra-t'restrials." As soon as he finished, he broke into snickers.

Scott laughed. "That was the worst impression *ever*."

"Shut up."

"You actually did a really good job of *not* being him."

"Man, shut up!"

A voice from several cots down interrupted the conversation. "Do you two ever *stop talking*?"

"Yeah, you two quiet it down over there!" David called out.

Scott fought off a laugh. David was forty, but there was still some kid in him.

"Idiots," the man from several cots down murmured.

"We better be quiet," Scott said. "Some people need to sleep."

"All right," David answered. "We can be respectful just this once." Scott relaxed as they laid in silence, and the natural sounds of the night resumed. After a time, David whispered, "I'm going to try and get some sleep, but…I have to say this."

"Come on, man…we gotta be quiet."

"No. I really mean what I'm going to say." Scott furrowed his brow and turned to face him. "You're a good guy," David said solemnly.

Scott turned his head. It wasn't what he'd expected to hear. "What?"

"I mean that. You do a great job as a soldier, I mean, you won a Golden Lion on your first mission, but…what you did out there for Svetlana…that was something different. Nobody else was willing to do that. I respect you a lot for it." Scott began to speak, but David cut him off. "I know what you're going to say." He smiled. "It's okay. Just accept it."

Silence fell between them. Finally Scott nodded. "Thanks, man. Really. I appreciate it."

"Keep praying, man. Don't ever stop doing that."

"I won't."

"Good night."

"Night, Dave." Scott rolled back onto his back and stared upward. A good man. If that was all he accomplished in life…that was okay. If that was all Nicole thought him to be…that was even better. His eyes slid shut, and the sounds of the night once again took their place in the room. The rest of the infirmary was quiet.

Within minutes, they were both asleep.

16

FIVE DAYS LATER

RAIN POUNDED ON the city of Novosibirsk. It had done so for the last several days, as the weather in the city had turned into something strange. Novosibirsk never had been known for its hospitable climate, but now a different kind of thickness loomed in the air. The sky was supernaturally black, and the winds moaned like a chorus of banshees delivering their farewell. Some EDEN soldiers blamed Thoor for the heaviness, while others blamed the Nightmen. Some pinned it as something different—something new. It was as if God Himself was looking down on *Novosibirsk* through His darkened clouds, warning it of wrath that loomed over the horizon. But *Novosibirsk* was not afraid of God, or of banshees, or of anything.

Inside, the men and women of the Fourteenth slept, oblivious to the elemental onslaught that waged outside. Even amid the constant pound of rain, none of them stirred. None of them stirred until God struck the Earth with His giant hand, and a single crack of deafening thunder destroyed the steady thrum of rainfall.

Jayden's eyes flew open, like loaded guns cocked and ready to fire. He scanned the rest of the room quickly. Darkness shifted into reality. All bunks were still. All operatives slept. Only he was aware.

His brow furrowed and his senses perked. Something was wrong. Something in the room was different. Something was not supposed to be there. His ears adjusted as they tuned out the thunderstorm, and they began their silent interrogation of Room 14.

It was an accepted truth that snipers were in a class of their own. There was something distinct about the composure of their senses that few others possessed. It was their innate ability to tune in with the world around them, yet still be able to isolate and remove selective distractions. It was a natural ability, one that allowed them to pick apart their surroundings and to examine whatever inconsistencies they found. Snipers were born for one purpose—to be snipers. Jayden was no exception.

He filtered away the outside noise—the rain and the thunder. Then he removed the breathing of those who slept, followed by the creaks of bedsprings as operatives tossed and turned. Only then did his ears perk; his senses focused on the anomaly. There was definitely something else. There was another noise, one that was unnatural among the sounds of the night. Several noises. Voices. They were voices spoken in a way not meant to be heard.

There was only one place in Room 14 suitable for the nocturnal veil of secrecy. The lounge. A glance to the lounge door revealed sparse light beneath it. Jayden threw a glance around the room. Becan was in his bunk, as was Boris. Only Fox and Kevin had been released from the infirmary, and both were visible under their respective covers. Galina and Varvara were in plain sight, which left three people unaccounted for. Clarke, Baranov, and Dostoevsky. The officers.

Jayden slid from the covers of his upper cot and slipped down the ladder of his bunk, where his bare feet touched the floor with a jolt of iciness. The rain still slammed, and the thunder still boomed, though now they were little more than glorified distractions. Cautious to remain silent, he tip-toed across the room until he was beside the lounge door. He crouched to a knee, cocked his head, and placed his ear by the door frame. Despite their secrecy, the voices he heard were clear and recognizable.

"Well, we needn't someone to replace him in *that* aspect," Clarke said, eyeing Dostoevsky, whose face was lit by the portable lamp that illuminated the countertop. "His isn't exactly a necessary position." He shifted to Baranov. "But someone *will* need to take his rank."

"Yes, captain," Baranov answered. Dostoevsky nodded as well.

"In my opinion," Clarke said, "we've only got two choices, Travis or Max. Personally, I'm leaning toward Max. Travis never has struck me as a brilliant leader."

"He is not even a brilliant pilot…" Baranov said.

"He does what's expected of him," Clarke said severely.

"But only what's expected of him."

"That's why he's flying a Vulture and not a Vindicator," Dostoevsky said.

"That's enough," Clarke said. "We'll just consider that issue settled then, Max shall take over Tolya's position as lieutenant. Are we all in agreement on that?"

Baranov and Dostoevsky nodded.

"Very well. Tolya and Max were both technicians anyway, so we needn't adjust our orientation. So now that we've got that situation resolved, let's get back to our delta core. Who have we got?"

"I have always liked Fox," Dostoevsky said. "He's composed and he has a lot of common sense. Quiet, but…he's a sniper. He is supposed to be quiet."

"I agree," Baranov said.

Clarke nodded. "So we've got Powers. Who else?"

Dostoevsky sighed. "The only other gamma besides Galya is Remington."

"We've already discussed our medical situation," said Clarke. "So let's consider Powers and Remington. What have we got on Fox?"

Baranov looked bored. "Graduated almost two years ago, high scores. We all know this already, we do not need to discuss."

Dostoevsky folded his arms. "What I see is consistency. Fox has never done anything spectacular as far as I can remember. But he has always done his tasks well. He'll do the job right the first time. He is still young, yes, but he is dependable. He is a good role model."

"I agree," Baranov said. "Fox is a smart choice, he is a safe one. We do not have to worry about surprises."

Clarke propped his elbows on the table. "The question *now* is how would he be as a leader? Delta teeters on the edge of epsilon, and epsilon is a primer for lieutenant. Standing back and taking orders is fine and well, but when it comes time to pick up the reins and take command, will he have the initiative and the ability?"

Jayden shifted as he listened by the door.

"I believe so," Dostoevsky answered.

Clarke nodded. "As do I."

Clarke and Dostoevsky faced Baranov, who drew in a heavy breath. He hesitated before saying, "I am unsure. You cannot tell how a person will react until they are in a situation that requires it. Fox has never been in that situation before. He is not very vocal...but at times this is a good thing." He hesitated again. "I do not know. That is my answer."

Clarke nodded. "A perfectly legitimate one. Delta's no small task, and some people never get that high...but we'll have to see." He paused for a moment. "And then we have Remington, our little gift from *Richmond*. I'm very curious as to your thoughts on him."

"I like Remington," Baranov spoke without hesitation. "I had doubts at first, just as we all did, but after what I saw Thursday I was impressed. He has ability and initiative."

"Remington is overestimated by everyone," Dostoevsky grumbled.

"And where were you when Sveta was running away?" Baranov asked.

Dostoevsky's eyes narrowed.

"He performed well when he was with me," Baranov said. "He followed orders and engaged the Bakma. The only time he acted was when somebody *had* to act. He was not waiting for an opportunity to be hero—he watched Sveta run down the hill like the rest of us. Only when he saw that she was not going to make it did he jump, and then there was no hesitation.

"Many times I have seen new soldiers rush into battle and do something so stupid that it makes me want to shoot them myself to save the enemy the trouble. I am even embarrassed for some rookies who try so hard to be noticed. But I did not feel that way about Remington...this is how I know he was not acting like a hero. I was not embarrassed for him. I envied him."

Clarke listened carefully.

"I am a leader," Baranov said. "I am supposed to lead by example. When I watched him running across the snow, I remember thinking to myself...that should be me. We have all known Sveta for a long time, almost a year, and none of us," he glanced at Dostoevsky, "*none* of us did anything to save her. It took someone who had known her only for a few days to jump out of a ship and run after her, alone. My heart hurt after that. When I visited Sveta for the first time, it was hard for me to look her in the eye. If not for Remington, we would have all just watched her get shot to death."

"And we almost lost two operatives instead of one," Dostoevsky said.

"Do you *have* a heart?"

Clarke edged between the two. "Okay, gentlemen. This argument is a no-win situation. Personally I've never been fond of soldiers taking matters into their own hands, but at the same time there is an excellent chance that Svetlana would have died had he not interfered. That's undeniable."

Dostoevsky remained silent as Clarke continued.

"Mr. Remington's knack for heroics, whether intentional or not, is also undeniable. I looked over the report filed by his colonel at *Richmond* after Chicago, and I must confess, it was a very impressive read. It's definitely a difficult choice, between he and Mr. Powers, if not an interesting one." Baranov and Dostoevsky stared at Clarke, who smiled and leaned back in his chair. "Do I need to ask you for your verdicts?"

"Fox," Dostoevsky answered.

Baranov shook his head. "I say Remington."

Clarke chuckled. "Difficult call. And ultimately it's mine." The lounge fell quiet, as Clarke scrutinized the tabletop. Rain continued to drum outside. "Remington might be a good choice," he said, "...but I know what I'm getting with Fox."

Jayden muttered.

"Powers is a good choice. He will do well," said Baranov.

Clarke nodded. "They're both good choices. I would just rather go with someone I feel like I know and trust. Fox is one

of the most consistent operatives I've worked with. He'll do bril-
liantly." He looked between the two men, where his gaze held on
Dostoevsky.

Dostoevsky's eyes moved away from the table, and trained on
the crack at the bottom of the lounge door. Clarke opened his
mouth, but Dostoevsky snapped a signal of silence. Clarke held
his tongue, and he and Baranov stared at the bottom of the door.

Dostoevsky stood and stepped away from the table. Clarke
and Baranov watched as he edged to the far wall, then glided to
the door's edge. He placed his hand atop the doorknob, gripped
his fingers around it, and jolted the door open.

No one.

Dostoevsky padded into the bunk room and scanned it. Every
operative was accounted for beneath the covers of their bunks.
He hesitated for several seconds, then his gaze narrowed.

Beneath the covers of his bed, Jayden laid still. The only movement that came from his body was the subtle breathing that
caused his chest to rise and fall. Though the rain pounded outside, he could hear the quiet clump of the lounge door as it was
closed. He made no attempt to look. He simply laid there and
waited for true sleep to catch up with him. Almost thirty minutes
later, after he heard the three officers leave the lounge and retire
to their bunks, it did.

*   *   *

WEDNESDAY, APRIL 20TH, 0011 NE
0618 HOURS

By the next morning, the violent thunderstorm that had shaken
the city of Novosibirsk had evolved into an airy snowfall that blanketed the base, typical Russian weather for that time of the year.

The Fourteenth's morning routine came in its traditional
manner, as operatives donned their attire and set the coffee and

tea to brew. Soon after initial wakeup, the first breakfast crew ventured out of the living quarters—Becan, Jayden, Fox, and Travis. It was a new custom for them to meet with William and Joe at that time for breakfast. They met in the hallways of the barracks, and went to the cafeteria together. This time, only William was there to find them.

The days began to lengthen, as sunrise was at almost a quarter after five. It gave Novosibirsk the stark comfort of brightness to greet the base's earliest risers. The frigidity lasted throughout the day.

The snow-covered landscape in Novosibirsk was different than in America. Together with the faithfully overcast sky and the coldness of the base itself, the scenery was more bleak than beautiful.

As soon as they stepped outside, the still blast of arctic air bit them.

"Another scorcher," Travis said as he clutched his arms against his chest. Vapors from his mouth and nostrils hovered then vanished.

William smirked as his body tightened. "Weather Mike must be ticked."

"Who the bloody hell is Weather Mike already?" Becan asked irritably.

"Weather Mike is Dr. Michale Eckstein, our base meteorologist," Fox answered, "and the man to blame for any and all problems with the weather."

"It's his fault," William said. "He gives us this."

Becan's teeth rattled. "Well in tha' case it makes total sense then. I mean, weathermen are directly responsible for the weather."

"Exactly," Fox nodded.

"So how is this Weather Mike bucko?" Becan asked.

Fox glanced at him. "That's the other thing. Nobody's ever seen him."

William blew a frosty breath. "Sort of like Loch Ness or Bigfoot. People see him just rounding a corner and out of view or something...blurry photographs, footprints that lead to nowhere...that sort of thing."

Becan mm-ed. "I see. Are there Weather Mike hunters, too?"

"Nope," William answered. "He's responsible for the weather, and that's all we need to know."

The cafeteria bustled with activity—the drowsy conversation of comrades, the stifled yawns of the recently awakened, and the clank of metal utensils. It took a short while for the five-man entourage to claim their breakfast, at which point they wandered through the room until they discovered an unclaimed table.

Travis adjusted his tray as he sat down. "How long do you guys think everyone else will be in the med-bay?"

Becan sipped his tea. "Remmy and Dave shouldn't be in there too long. They're not as bad off as the others."

"They might be let out today," said Fox. "I know Sveta is supposed to be released tomorrow. As far as Max and Kostya…they might be a while. At least a month, easy."

Travis offered a sad chuckle. "Strange how that happens. One minute you're fine…next minute you've got bullet-holes…that's got to be a scary thing."

"Yeh never been shot?" asked Becan.

"Nope. Been lucky so far," Travis said, shaking his head.

"How long yeh been in EDEN?"

"Four years now. All of 'em here, all of 'em with Vultures."

Becan whistled. "I can't see how yeh can stand bein' here so long. I been here a week an' I already miss *Richmond*."

Fox took a sip of tea and nodded. "*Richmond* is one of the nicer facilities. I'd imagine *Novosibirsk* ranks among the worst, comfort-wise. Maybe with *Leningrad*."

"Russians don't exactly put luxury at the top of their list," said Travis, half-frowning. "But hey…it's the military. If we were supposed to be staying at a first-class resort then we'd have a right to complain."

"Yeah," Becan said, "guess you're righ'."

They were drawn into a lull of silence. As the collective chewing mixed with the conversation around the cafeteria, William shifted in his chair to face Jayden. The Texan's eyes surveyed his plate as he ate in quiet. William watched for several seconds before he pointed and spoke. "You're too quiet. You freak me out."

Jayden opened his mouth, but Becan cut him off. "He's a wee bit cheesed off at the moment. See, he never gets called into action, always has to sit back an' watch everythin' happen. That's 'cos he couldn't hit the broad side of an elephant."

Jayden shook his head and took another bite.

"Is that so?" Fox asked.

"It is," Becan answered. "He thinks his life's so difficult 'cos he's from Texas, they don't favor education very much over there. Long as yeh can rope a steer an' spit tobacco you're good to go in their eyes, tha's why the rest o' the world is such a challenge to them."

Jayden was unable to stifle a chuckle, and he set his fork down. The others grinned.

"So as yis can imagine, bein' the poor shot tha' he is an' withou' anny formal education, me boyo's kind o' had the odds against him from the get go."

Fox turned to Jayden and smiled. "You don't have it that bad. At least your parents didn't name you Fox."

The others laughed, and jovial conversation returned in full force. As the group talked, Travis's gaze shifted to the cafeteria door. "Fox, you said Svetlana was supposed to be let out tomorrow?"

Fox nodded. "That's what I heard."

"Well, for the first time in as long as I can remember…you're wrong."

Fox looked puzzled, then followed Travis's gaze around to the front of the cafeteria. The others at the table did the same. There, propped in the archway of the cafeteria door, was Svetlana. Galina and Varvara were at her sides, as they inched toward the food line one step at a time. All conversation at the soldiers' table stopped.

Galina and Varvara each held a hand on Svetlana's shoulders. Svetlana's look was non-cognizant; she cast a blank stare to the floor in front of her. The expression on her face was no expression at all.

They watched in silence as Galina and Varvara led her to the line, where they progressed until they reached the counter. There they took a small portion of food, then left to claim a solitary table in the far corner of the room. Neither Galina nor Varvara carried a tray for themselves.

The three women lowered themselves into their chairs, then they sat motionless. Svetlana's tray was placed square in front of her, though she made no effort to sample anything on it.

Becan watched in silence as Galina and Varvara's hands remained on Svetlana's shoulders. They made occasional gestures to the untouched tray of food, none of which prompted a response from her. Becan's own gaze fell to the tabletop, where his tray of half-eaten food sat.

Before any of his comrades could say anything, Becan pushed back in his chair and rose to his feet. They watched as he excused himself in silence and began to weave through the cafeteria toward the table with the three women.

Varvara caught sight of him as he neared. She offered him a sad smile as she massaged her hand on Svetlana's shoulder, then she leaned in to Galina to whisper. A moment later, Galina glanced Becan's way. Her expression mirrored Varvara's, and she slid from her chair to stand. She joined Becan as he drew close, then turned to regard the now-empty chair next to Svetlana. "Please sit," she whispered. "That would be good for her."

Becan hesitated. He looked at Galina, then Svetlana, who made no indication that she was aware of his arrival. Finally, after a slow approach, he lowered into the chair.

Svetlana was a mess. What was once a striking and elegant appearance was now ragged and unkempt, as the golden hair that flowed to her shoulders was now tucked behind her ears in an oily slickness. The blue eyes that entranced with dangerous allure were now dim, suppressed above dark bags that revealed a woman who had not slept in days.

She stared at her tray despite Becan's presence beside her. Silence surrounded them until Becan rested his hand against her back. "Yeh have to eat." She offered no response, nor made any indication that she was aware of him. Becan's eyes trailed to her tray, then returned to her. "Please…"

There was nothing. No response, no movement, no lift of the eyes. Svetlana sat beside him, thousands of miles away. Becan closed his eyes, then slid his arm around her shoulder and inched against her. As he gave her a hug, he leaned in to whisper in her ear. "We're here for yeh, girl." Her head turned a bit, though that was the extent of her reply. Stillness fell again.

Becan withdrew his arm, pushed away, and stood up. Galina joined him, placing her hand on his shoulder. "Thank you," she mouthed. Varvara offered the same expression from her seat before the two women resumed their aid.

Becan stepped away from the table and slid his hands in his pockets. He looked back to the table from which he had come, where his male counterparts watched him. He locked eyes with them for a moment, then back-stepped, turned around, and shuffled out of the cafeteria.

Jayden frowned as Becan exited, then looked at the Irishman's abandoned tray of food. "Man...that sucks."

"Yeah," Travis said as he sighed and looked at his own plate. "He tried, though. That's the best he could do. I feel for Svetlana, she really is a good girl."

Fox turned in his chair to face them. "Tolya was a good guy."

"What do you think's gonna happen with you guys now?" asked William.

"How do you mean?" Fox asked.

"Well you lost a lieutenant. I mean, someone's gotta replace him, right?"

Jayden stared deliberately at the table space in front of him.

"That is true," Fox nodded. "I'm actually surprised nobody's been moved up yet. They usually get to that kind of thing faster than this."

"Maybe Clarke's slacking." William harrumphed.

"I doubt that," Fox said. "Clarke's usually very good with that kind of thing. He's probably just been busy." He reached for the untouched apple on his tray and held it in hand. He raised it in front of his face, inspecting it thoroughly. "But I don't know who'll end up getting promoted over this."

Travis offered a half-smile. "I wonder if I'll get moved up."

Jayden looked at the pilot, saying nothing.

Fox smirked. "You've only been here what, four years? I think pilots have to be in for at least a decade before officer consideration."

"Yeah, that seems about right," Travis said, laughing.

"I wonder about Remington," Fox speculated. "I'm sure he won't be promoted to lieutenant, but...well, I'm positive they'll need someone to take an extra delta role."

"They certainly ain't gonna bump him based on his fighting skills," William laughed.

Fox chuckled under his breath. "He is an interesting individual though. Don't forget—he is the Golden Lion. It's not every day someone like that comes around...some people just have it."

"What's 'it'?" William asked.

Travis offered an absent nod. "I like him."

Fox pointed immediately. "That is 'it'. Why do you like him, Travis?"

"I don't know," Travis shrugged. "He just seems like a really good guy. And I mean...look at what he did in Siberia. He saved Svetlana's life."

Fox nodded in conclusion. "Travis doesn't know him, but he likes him. And that's what 'it' is. It's a combination of initiative and charisma that not everybody has."

"But he can't fight." William shook his head.

"Well I'm sure there's a lot he can't do," said Fox. "One thing he can't do is please everyone, as is obvious with Max. But you don't have to please everyone. You just have to please your superiors. If you can do that, there's no limit to how far you can go."

For the first time in the discussion, Jayden sparked to life. "Scott doesn't suck up. He's never sucked up."

"I never said he did."

"And what he did in Chicago was great."

Fox sighed. "I never said it wasn't. What he did in Siberia probably saved Sveta's life, too. I'm simply stating the facts."

"Yeah well," Jayden said, "Scott's a great leader. I'd rather follow him than anyone else."

"Come on," Fox said. "How can you say that? He's not even in a leadership position."

The Texan sat upright. "Because he's the only person who gives me a chance. I never get to do anything. I got left out of a bug-hunt back at *Richmond* and I got left out on the mission here. And it's all because I don't go around talking to every-one."

All eyes focused on Jayden as he continued. "I can't help it—I'm not all social like everyone else. I wish I was, but I'm not. Nobody even notices me around here, and I know it's me, but that's just me. That's who I am. But that shouldn't stop me from being given a chance. In Siberia they needed a sniper on the mis-sion, and you got to go but I didn't. That's not your fault—you're probably a great sniper, but if nobody gives me a chance how am I supposed to prove anything?"

Jayden was forced to take a breath before he went on. "When Scott was in control in Chicago, he gave me a chance. He told me to get high in the building and shoot at the aliens, and he put faith in me to do it right. It wasn't like he was there watching me to make sure I didn't screw up. He trusted me. He even said, 'go do your thing'. I was so proud to be a sniper that day, and I did a good job.

"He gave everyone a chance. He told Becan to take command if he went down, he told Sasha to set up a hospital, and he even let Donner drive the van. That was all our first mission, and he never even met Donner before. But he gave us all a chance to do what we spent years training to do. Nobody got left out."

He paused briefly. "That's why I say I'd rather follow him than anyone else, 'cause he gives everybody a chance. And that's why I don't appreciate you sayin' things behind his back, like that he sucks up and stuff. So please don't say stuff like that, 'cause he's a hell of a good guy who tries to get everyone involved."

For several moments, nobody said a word. Jayden's face was flushed red, but he eventually slid back and reassumed his silent persona.

Twenty seconds passed before Fox replied.

"Sorry."

From that point on, the conversation dulled. Though a few words were spoken about those in the infirmary, as well as specu-lation on the lack of recent alien activity, it all served more as end-of-discussion filler than relevant subject matter. Eventually, the four men stood up from the table, replaced their trays, and filed out of the cafeteria. William bid them farewell and departed to his unit's room. The rest of them journeyed back to Room 14.

When they returned, Clarke awaited them. He, along with Dostoevsky and Baranov, sat beyond the open doors of the lounge at the central table. Kevin and Boris were with them, as was Becan; it became apparent they were just in time for an impromptu meeting.

As soon as those present were settled in the lounge, Clarke eased the door shut and cleared his throat. "There's a small bit that I'd like to speak with you about this morning while it's just us. I don't mind going on without the girls this morning, as this is a rather touchy subject, and their time is best spent together right now. For us, however, I'd like to conduct some business as well as a small bit of personal reflection, and wisdom, if you'll see it as such."

He took a beat before he went on. "I know that the death of Anatoly was something hard to swallow, for all of us. In no way do I intend, however, to look back upon his life and claim that his death was a wasted one. I know…that this has been a cause of tension in the unit in several areas, understandably so…but the lieutenant died doing what he dedicated his life to doing—protecting Earth. He was given a direct order, and followed it to the fullest extend of his capabilities. The general expects no less from each and every one of you, and I expect no less from each and every one of you.

"Svetlana has my heartfelt condolences, I've told her that already and left it at that. I've given her permission to request a temporary leave of absence, if she so desires it. She's yet to respond to me on the matter."

The group was silent as he continued.

"I've been serving in EDEN since its inception. If there is one lesson I have learned, and one that I suggest you all learn, quickly, it's that no one is given the promise of a tomorrow. We live in a time when attacks come unexpectedly, from all directions. We're forced into situations that we simply cannot plan for, against an enemy that has a technological advantage. Deaths are inevitable.

I have lost many friends throughout my years serving this organization, as you have all lost friends. While this is something I hope is never treated with apathy, it is something that must be accepted. The only thing that we as operatives can do is move on and continue to do our jobs to the utmost capacity. That is precisely what we, the command staff, intend on doing."

At that moment, Clarke glanced to Commander Baranov and nodded. "Ivan."

Baranov cleared his throat. "The following changes have been made to the ranking structure of this unit. Delta Trooper Axen will be promoted to the rank of lieutenant and tertiary officer. Gamma Private Powers will be promoted to the rank of delta trooper. And last, Beta Private Jurgen will be promoted to gamma. Though Axen and Jurgen are not here at present, we could not wait any longer before implementing these changes. They will be notified today of their new roles."

Clarke spoke as soon as Baranov was finished. "These changes are effective immediately. Fox, you're the only one of those three present, so I'll tell you here. I expect from you the excellence that you've always given."

Fox bowed his head. "Yes sir."

Clarke offered a faint smile. "Very well. Now, everyone get prepared for our morning session. It has not been overlooked. Today we'll be running several courses, so dress for the cold. Dismissed."

The operatives filed out of the lounge to change, as Clarke, Baranov, and Dostoevsky remained behind in hushed discussion.

As Becan crouched down to open his duffle bag, he grumbled under his breath. "Tha' was nice an' motivational."

Travis cast a faint smile to Fox, as he too changed into workout clothes. "Congrats, man."

"Thanks," Fox answered, offering a grim smile of his own. "Hate to get it that way, but...that's how it goes, I guess."

"Well," Becan said, "I'm glad they moved Dave up a rank. Keepin' him at beta is a waste o' his experience. Who d'yeh think is goin' to tell him?"

Fox knelt to tie his boots. "I'd imagine they'll send a courier or something. Or maybe one of the officers will go tell them today."

"Righ'," the Irishman said. "Hopefully they'll be back on their feet in a little bit annyway."

It took several minutes for the operatives to get bundled, at which point they gathered together and made the trek outside. The cold tore at them throughout the workout session, though it mattered little. As the procession of laps and exercises carried on, conversation flowed freely among them. There was a sense of forced, but necessary return to normality.

By the time the workout was finished, almost two hours later, all of the operatives present were adequately exhausted. It did not take long for Room 14 to fill with the warm steam that gushed from the showerheads. It was justifiable compensation for the cold sting of the outside. As soon as the rush of showers was over, each of the operatives returned to their individual expenditures of time.

The routine of *Novosibirsk* once again set in.

17

THE NURSE SMILED as she placed a finger beneath Scott's chin. "You watch that shoulder," she said through her Russian accent, before she turned her attention to David and teased. "And you… why were you here again?"

David, whose left arm was almost completely healed over, grinned. "I came for the personal attention."

The nurse laughed. "Take care, you two," she said with a gentle wave, as she checked off their exit forms.

Scott and David waved in return, then made their way out of the infirmary.

They had spent eight days in the infirmary altogether, and it was decided that morning that they were both cleared enough to return to active duty. While David was without hindrance, Scott wore a protective cloth over the burnt area of his shoulder and arm. It was an area that, while limited, was functional. He would have to return to the infirmary in several days for a reexamination, though the advanced healing gels were expected to do their work well, as modern technology usually did.

They left the medical wing in lifted spirits. It was impossible not to. After so many days, the odor of the injured became too familiar for comfort. When that happened, they knew they had to get out soon. Their health agreed.

The morning was freezing as always, though they welcomed the change. Anything different was better by that point, even if it was the icy chill of Russian air. Nonetheless, they soon longed for the warmth of the inside as they trekked across the grounds.

Room 14 was abandoned, though they didn't mind. The reunion of their nostrils and the stale smell of the room was as wonderful as anticipated. The others didn't need to be there for it to feel like home. The beds were all made, and the scent of old tea hung in the air.

"They must be working out," Scott said as he stepped in through the doorway and made for his bunk.

"Must be," David answered. His course was different, as he veered past his bunk and straight to his closet. He flipped through his clothes until he came to his uniform. The gamma patch was embroidered on the front of its chest. "That's a beautiful thing," he said with a grin.

Scott smiled. "Welcome to the club."

"Do I get any benefits?"

"Two weeks of paid vacation and a free Russian lap dance."

"That'll work."

Scott knelt beside his duffle bag, where he rifled through its contents. When he pulled out his hand, his football was firm in its grasp. As his fingers squeezed the dirt-stained leather, he felt a welcome rush of familiarity.

David clapped his hands together and held out his open palms. "Hey." Scott saw the gesture and underhanded him the ball. It spiraled across the room, where it padded into David's hands. "Long time since I caught one of these."

Scott eased into an open area of the room and held his hands out. "You think they're running?"

"Probably," David said as he underhanded the ball back.

"They'll probably be back in about a half hour then."

"We'll find out soon enough," David said. "Want to get breakfast before they get back?"

Scott knelt down and rolled the football under his bunk. "Sure. I miss the cafeteria food."

David grinned. "Which is a very revealing sign of the times."

They checked over their personal belongings, then they made their way out of Room 14. As they ventured across the grounds toward the cafeteria, something out of place caught their eyes.

Off in the distance, away from the sidewalk but close enough to be seen, stood the form of a massive man. His backside faced *Novosibirsk*, as he stared off into the unending snowscape. Scott recognized him immediately.

"Is that *Will*?"

David's brow furrowed. "I think it is...what the hell's he doing out there in the snow?"

"He's not getting a tan," Scott laughed.

They stepped away from the sidewalk and trudged toward the demolitionist. The snow crunched under their feet with every step. Within seconds, William turned, indicating his awareness of their presence.

"Hey man. What's up?" said Scott.

William's expression caught Scott completely off guard. It was hardened. It was devoid of emotion. It was the most un-William-like expression Scott had ever seen.

"Hey," William rasped.

"You lookin' for Yeti out here?" David asked.

"No." William's cheeks were glossed over with a frozen red, and his hands were shoved in his pockets with little ambition. Several awkward seconds passed before he moved away from them and returned his gaze to the icy landscape.

"What's wrong, man?" Scott asked.

The wind whipped up with a gusty blast, and William said nothing. His stare remained dedicated to the nothingness that stretched out in the distance. It wasn't until David took a half step toward him that he answered. "Joe's dead."

Scott's jaw gaped. Joe's dead? Joe *Janson's* dead? He blinked. "What did you say?"

"He's dead," William answered dully. "You want me to spell it out for you?"

David's expression fell. "I didn't know anybody got called out..."

"Nobody got called out," William said, turning to face them. "He died in his sleep."

Every trace of conversation slammed shut. For thirty seconds, Scott and David stood speechless. Died in his sleep? How could Joe have died in his sleep? Old men in their nineties died in their sleep. The chronically ill died in their sleep. But healthy soldiers? Scott asked the unavoidable question. *"How?"*

"He went to bed early, said he had a headache. When we woke up this morning, he was dead." William looked away.

"He died of a *headache*?"

William shot him a glare. "That's what I said, isn't it?"

The conversation lingered in awkwardness, as neither Scott nor David spoke a word. William broke the tension. "I want to be alone right now."

David hesitated. "Sure thing, man. Whatever you want."

Scott was quick to affirm. "If there's anything we can do, let us know. Definitely."

"I appreciate it," William answered.

They turned back to the sidewalk and left William on his own. When they were out of earshot, Scott shook his head. "How does that happen? You think he had some kind of a problem?"

David looked at him. "If he did, you think he'd be here?"

Scott's gaze sunk. "They came in together from *Atlanta*."

"I know," David answered soberly, "I know."

They resumed their trek to the cafeteria, despite the news from William. Neither had known Joe beyond a handful of short conversations, though they nonetheless felt the inevitable emptiness of one less conversationalist at the table. The man had been good company.

They picked at their plates, finding themselves devoid of the desire to eat, at which point they rose from the table and once again journeyed across the grounds, back to the barracks.

The Room 14 they found when they returned was different from the one they had left. Laughter saturated the walls, and when they opened the door to step inside, they realized that the whole of the unhospitalized crew was back from their morning workout. David pushed the door open, and they stepped inside. They were welcomed immediately.

"Remmy! Dave!" Becan leapt from the foot of his bunk, skipping across the room to greet them. "It's abou' time they let yis ou'!"

A wide grin spread across Jayden's face. "Hey guys!"

The room bustled as a mist of warm steam rose from the occupied showers and shrouded half the room. Conversation flowed back and forth in Russian and English, as was the custom whenever operatives returned from the morning session.

David slapped a hand out to Becan. "You guys missed out," he said as he hit the Irishman with a fist-hug. "Med-bay is where the party's at."

"I bet it is, but I'm sure it's not as happenin' as the pool," Becan laughed.

Scott grinned. "Is that where you guys have been?"

"All mornin', nice an' warm!"

Scott scanned the room, looking at the rest of the operatives. Sure enough, their damp hair affirmed it. It made him jealous. Every time he went on a morning workout, it was a bitter-cold jog.

"You should see the pool, man," Jayden said. "It's awesome. I hope we go there all the time."

"Yeh just like seein' Varvara in a swimsuit," Becan smirked.

"Man," Jayden said, "she's *hot*." He glanced across the room to the showering medic.

Scott grinned. Saying *she's hot* wasn't exactly making a move, but for Jayden, anything was progress.

Travis joined them and slapped David on the arm. "Congrats on the promotion."

"Thanks," David answered. The two exchanged smiles for a moment before Galina scooted past from the direction of the showers.

"Welcome back," she said, whisking a pink towel through her hair.

Clarke and Dostoevsky emerged from the lounge a moment later. "How goes it, gentlemen?" Clarke said with a grin. "Glad to see you both back here in once piece! I trust your recovery went well?"

"Yes sir," they said.

Clarke drew nearer and motioned to the protective bandage wrapped around Scott's shoulder. "How long will you need that?"

"Doctors say just a few days, sir. It's precautionary. I have a checkup Sunday and if it looks good by then, I'm good to go without it."

Clarke smiled. "Brilliant! Well, I'll let the two of you go ahead and get reacquainted with your comrades. If you need me or the lieutenant we'll be in our office." He smiled and gestured to the lounge. "It's good to have you two back with us."

As Clarke and Dostoevsky returned to the lounge, David remarked, "This place has livened up since we were here last."

Becan smirked. "I wonder if tha's indicative o' annythin'."

David stifled a laugh. "Right."

At that moment, Scott realized that someone was absent, someone he knew had already been released. Svetlana. She was nowhere to be seen. "Hey," he said as he leaned toward Travis. "Where's Sveta?"

Travis's smile faded. "Svetlana?"

"Yeah."

Travis cast his eyes upon the floor and slid his hands into his pockets. "She's gone, man."

"She's *gone*?" said Scott incredulously.

The pilot nodded. "She left this morning. Well, she might be still here—there aren't any flights scheduled to leave for another hour and nothing else is scheduled to arrive. But yeah…she's leaving EDEN."

Scott felt his stomach bottom out. "You've got to be kidding me."

"I wish I were," Travis answered. "Supposedly she talked to Clarke about it last night—I don't know what she said exactly—but…she packed her things this morning, told everyone bye…"

Becan chimed in. "If yeh could even call it tellin' everyone bye."

"Yeah," Travis nodded. "A few hugs…she really didn't say much of anything, Clarke did all the talking, but…yeah, she left before we started our workout." Galina, who stood within earshot of the conversation, listened quietly.

Scott slumped against the wall. Gone? She *couldn't* be gone… he had just gotten to know her. "I can't believe it. I mean…I can believe it, it's just…"

"We know wha' yeh mean. We feel the same way…it wasn't righ' wha' happened, but…at the same time it's never good to see someone leave like tha'…it's a bloody mess."

"Everything's been all gloom and doom around here," said

Travis. "It wasn't exactly the best way to start the morning, but… what can you do? Who's to say any one of us wouldn't have done the same thing in her shoes?"

No one could say that. Scott knew for sure that he couldn't. But…gone? He couldn't believe it. Not Svetlana. Not the Svetlana he had known. He stopped at that thought. He hadn't even known Svetlana well. They'd had only one meaningful conversation, and prior to that they'd almost been enemies. She was an acquaintance. She was an acquaintance who had listened to him when he needed someone to listen. What if Galina had been in the lounge that night instead? She would have done the same thing. Wouldn't she?

Scott came out of his reverie. "You said she might still be here?"

Travis glanced at his watch. "It's almost 8:30…I'm pretty sure the first flight out of here is at 8:50. She'd likely be in the hangar if you want to catch her. To say goodbye, or whatever." He frowned. "I thought about going, but…what would I say? I don't see how anyone could even try to convince her to stay. I don't know how she would after what happened. I wasn't one of her closer friends, so it'd be awkward. That's kind of how everyone felt, I think."

Galina cleared her throat with a soft cough. She said to Scott, "I was going to stay with her until she left, after I finished this." She tilted her mug of tea. "I had morning workout, so I could not go until now. If you would like to come, you may do that."

Scott stared at her. What would he say to Svetlana if he did go see her? One conversation. That was all they'd had. One conversation that had lasted for only a short while. It would be just as awkward for him as it would have been for Travis. His being there would only make Svetlana more uncomfortable. It would be stupid to go.

"Yeah," Scott answered. "I'd like that. If you don't mind."

"Not at all." Galina smiled. "I'm sure she would love to know that you cared. In fact, I can finish this drink on the way over there. Do you want to go now?"

His words deceived his thoughts. He had to go see her. He didn't know why. But he had to. "Yes," he answered. "We can go now."

"Let me go get my boots on." Galina stepped away, leaving Scott with his thoughts.

It was right. It was the right thing to do. She was sitting in the hangar right now, by herself, waiting for a transport that was cold and lifeless. Everything around her was cold and lifeless. Someone else had to go, someone aside from just Galina. She had to know that someone else cared.

"Are you ready?" Galina asked as she returned.

"Ready."

As they stepped into the hall, Scott said to David. "Don't forget to tell them about Joe."

David nodded, and Scott and Galina departed. David's gaze lowered for a moment before Becan stepped to him and cocked his head.

"Wha' happened to Joe?"

As SCOTT AND Galina traversed the halls, Galina offered Scott a faint smile. "She will be happy that you're coming. She likes you."

Svetlana liked him. For some reason, that gave him a warm feeling. He remembered why. She was the first person he'd won over. When they first arrived at *Novosibirsk*, every reception had been so cold. But she turned warm. She proved that it could be done. But it was more than that. He felt warm because she wasn't simply an acquaintance. She was his friend.

And she was about to leave.

"I like you, too," smiled Galina.

"I just tried to be friendly. That was it."

"She noticed," said Galina. "Nobody else here gave her that when they first met her. Not even Tolya."

"I don't understand why not," Scott said. "She's a nice girl."

Galina hesitated a moment, then smiled. "Yes. She is."

Though snow no longer fell outside, the stark coldness of the wind still burned through the air. The scent of open oxygen brought the only aspect of life to the grounds of *Novosibirsk*. The

land itself was devoid of activity; Galina and Scott found themselves a rare couple in the outdoors.

The walk to the airstrip was bleak, as the whole of *Novosibirsk*
seemed on the verge of mechanical hibernation. A lull of extra-
terrestrial activity justified the recent stillness, and no one
complained.

Vultures and civilian transports were perched outside the
hangar doors, as mechanics tended to prepping and charging. It
didn't take Scott and Galina long to find Svetlana. She was the
only woman in sight, seated alone on a bench along the far wall
of the hangar. Her only company was a duffle bag. Scott saw her
for the first time since Siberia.

She sat with her head bowed and her hands clasped together.
A cascade of recently washed hair shone down the sides of her
face, and as she lifted her head to see them approaching, it fell
back behind her ears. She brushed several of the loose strands
from her forehead, and her blue eyes widened.

As she rose to greet them, Scott saw her body perk up. She
gazed from Galina to him, and then back to Galina again, and
she trembled for the first time. As she took her first step toward
them, Scott noticed the shimmer of tears beneath her lids. When
their paths finally met, Svetlana collided into Galina's embrace
just as her arms opened up to accept her.

Svetlana wrapped her arms around Galina's back and pressed
her face against her chest. A burst of sobs choked out as she
gripped the back of Galina's uniform. Galina's expression soft-
ened; she placed a hand on Svetlana's shoulder as Svetlana began
to whimper. She was saying something. Scott couldn't understand it, but she was saying something through her tears. The
Russian words were repeated over and over.

Galina slid her hand to massage Svetlana's back. "Shhh…it's
all right."

Svetlana sniffed and took in a deep breath. Her face remained
buried in Galina's chest as she continued to cry.

"It's going to be okay," Scott said as he placed a hand on her
shoulder. He didn't know what else to do. "You're going to be

okay." He looked past Galina to the technicians as they went about their business. He watched them for a moment as they traveled back and forth across the hangar. They were completely oblivious to the scene. Or completely uncaring.

His attention returned to Svetlana, as she lifted her eyes to regard him. "Thank you," she said shakily, "for saving my life." The words were sincere, but forced. Scott felt his heart break. Her grip tightened on Galina again, and her face fell back into her fellow medic's jersey.

"Let's go sit down, okay?" said Galina.

Svetlana looked up at her. "I am sorry," she said.

Galina smiled. "Sorry for what? You have nothing to be sorry for."

Svetlana stepped away from Galina and wrapped her arms around Scott. Scott had known that an embrace was coming. He just wasn't sure how he'd feel when it did. It felt good. Surprisingly so. Something felt right about holding her. They stood together for several moments until Scott pulled away and peered at Svetlana's face, where he reached up to brush away a strand of hair. Svetlana managed a small smile. "There we go," Scott said. "That's what we want to see."

Svetlana remained silent, her lips still curved faintly.

"Yes," Galina said, "it is. Now, let's go have a seat. I know you are tired."

They returned to Svetlana's bench, where the two women lowered themselves. Scott knelt on the concrete floor and propped his hand against the bench's frame.

"Did you eat today?" Galina asked as she rested her hand on Svetlana's leg.

Svetlana nodded.

"Good. What did you eat?"

Svetlana made no immediate response. Her feet moved restlessly and then crossed. "Just some bread…"

Galina raised a brow. "That is it? You know you need to eat more than that. When you get back home, tell your mother to cook you something nice. A warm homemade meal will be good for you."

Svetlana sat in silence, feet crossed and head bowed. Behind them, the footsteps of technicians tracked across the concrete floor. Svetlana slumped against Galina, and her eyes glazed over.

"Sveta..." Galina said as she angled her body to support her friend, "are you *sure* you want to do this?"

Svetlana was quiet for a moment, then she nodded her head and sniffed. "I cannot stay here," she answered. "I cannot work for *him*."

Galina closed her eyes, and her expression faded. "I understand." Her hand massaged the edge of Svetlana's back.

"I am sorry," Svetlana whispered.

Scott's own gaze sunk as she spoke, and he rested his hand on her knee. There was nothing he or Galina could do. Her decision was made. It was a decision nobody could hold against her. Her spirit was dead. It had been murdered by the most fearsome leader in the modern world.

"I am sorry."

Scott saw a single tear droplet trace down the side of her cheek, a small stain of water barely visible behind it. She lifted a hand to wipe it away.

Had he been in her shoes, Scott knew he might well have made the same decision. What if Thoor had killed Nicole? What if her life was tossed in the trash like a piece of debris, an unnecessary expense for an unnecessary assignment? Anatoly had spoken with Svetlana until the moment of his death. There had been no Bakma voices in the background, no pounding on the door of the room where he hid. The bomb stayed secure. Anatoly had stayed with it for nothing. He died for nothing, and there was nothing anyone could do to make it different.

"You Voronova?"

It was a new voice. Scott turned to face an oily technician observing them, wooden clipboard in hand.

Svetlana looked from Galina to Scott. Her transport. Her ticket out of *Novosibirsk*. Her escape. Scott watched as she offered the technician a nod. For a fleeting moment, Scott swore he saw hesitation.

The technician continued. "That bird over there's gonna fly in about five minutes." He pointed to one of the civilian airbuses. "Might wanna go ahead and board right now."

Svetlana rose, sliding her hand from beneath Scott's.

All Scott knew to do was be there and remain calm. "Do you need any help? With bags or anything?"

"No," she paused. "I will be okay."

Galina placed her hand on Svetlana's shoulder, and Svetlana pulled her in for a final hug. Galina whispered something into Svetlana's ear, to which the blond-haired medic nodded.

Galina smiled as they separated, then Svetlana turned to face Scott. "Be safe with yourself," she said as she stepped toward him and fell into an embrace. "There is a beautiful young woman in America waiting for her love to come home."

Scott fought to hold back tears of his own as he held her close. A week ago, he had known nothing of Svetlana Voronova. Now, the thought of her leaving knotted his stomach. "You too," he said. "You'd better come back and visit us, all right?"

Svetlana dipped her head, and she peered into his eyes. "Don't let them change you," she whispered. "Please."

It was the second time he had been told that, first from Clarke, now from Svetlana. It struck him as curious to hear. His mind returned to the present as she leaned in and pressed a kiss between his cheek and lips, then pulled away. She bent down to pick up the strap of her duffle bag.

She backed away from them, then turned toward the airbus. As she walked away, Galina fell back to Scott's side. Svetlana was in the doorway of the airbus, when she turned to offer a final wave.

Scott allowed his gaze to linger on her. She was such a beautiful girl, despite the wear and tear her emotions had taken on her. Her hair shined golden again. The sparkle in her eyes was subdued, but it was still there. Blue like the ocean. Just like he remembered them. He didn't want her to go.

He lifted his hand to bid her farewell, and for a faint moment, he thought he saw her smile.

The door to the airbus slid shut. She was gone.

The airbus sat for several more minutes, before its engines roared to life and it taxied down the runway. They watched as it rolled forward, picked up speed, and then rose from the ground. It rocketed skyward with an ionic burst.

Scott sighed, and he dropped his hands to his sides. "There she goes."

Galina wiped her eyes and nodded. "Yes…there she goes."

For almost a full minute, they stood by the entranceway to the airstrip and watched the airbus grow smaller and smaller in the distance, until it finally disappeared from view. Scott turned back to the hangar. The technicians still hustled back and forth, and the other aircraft still awaited their turns for flight. Everything continued on. It was as if nothing changed at all.

He sighed and glanced to Galina. "What time is it?"

She looked at her watch, then she shifted her gaze to the airstrip. "8:57."

8:57. A day of routine awaited them. Nothing had changed at all. Scott slid his hands into his pockets, and he faced the main building of *Novosibirsk*.

Galina's gaze lingered on the horizon, then she turned to join Scott.

They walked away from the hangar and began their journey back across the grounds to the barracks.

The technicians never noticed they were gone.

18

SCOTT ENTERED THE lounge, where he found Clarke leaning against the countertop, a cup of steaming tea resting on the marble surface next to him. Scott had been summoned to the room only moments earlier by the captain, a request that tugged Scott away from the company of his comrades in the bunk room. He didn't mind. Any business that Clarke had for him took immediate priority—that was in the job description.

The past week had consisted of a stark routine, one that became almost alarmingly normal to Scott. Every morning the unit worked out, and the remainder of each day was spent in personal training. The only new development was the final report on Joe Janson. According to the base coroner, the soldier died of the Silent Fever, an illness that had reportedly reared its head in *Novosibirsk* several times in the past. No further elaborations were offered.

The only other thing on Scott's mind was Svetlana. Though she was gone, inside his head she had yet to leave.

"You wanted to see me, sir?" Scott asked.

Clarke scrutinized him. "Yes, private, I did. Come in, and please close the door."

"Yes sir," Scott said as he turned to seal the room. It was an odd request, he thought, but not completely unwarranted. The crew in the bunk room was prone to ruckus.

"Ask the captain if he wants some cereal!" Jayden said as he lifted a bowl of dry oat puffs. The others around him laughed as they reveled in their juvenile banter.

The door was sealed shut, and Scott again faced Clarke. The captain's face was deadpanned. "How is your shoulder?" he asked.

Scott rotated his now castless shoulder several times, then he offered an uncertain smile. "It's all right, sir. Feels a little more like normal every day. Not completely there yet, but…it's coming."

Clarke nodded. "Good, that's very good." The lounge was silent. Clarke's eyes were fixed on Scott, who continued to stand in a semi-attentive pose. Scott knew it wasn't going to be a normal conversation the moment the captain resumed.

"Remington…you know that I expect a lot out you. I hope I've made that clear since your arrival."

There was a moment of hesitation before Scott answered. "Yes sir…"

Clarke continued in a calculated tone. "I'm going to be expecting more now." As Scott stood, puzzled, Clarke indicated the countertop, where he retrieved an opened envelope and letter. He appeared all too familiar with its contents. "Effective today… your new rank is epsilon."

Scott's eyes flew open. His jaw hung down. "I'm sorry sir…*what*?"

"Your new rank is epsilon."

Epsilon? How in the world had he become an epsilon? That was a rank designated for officer training, the neutral ground between delta and lieutenant. A quick promotion, that was fine. But a leap in rank like this threw red flags everywhere. "Sir, there has to be some kind of a mistake…"

Clarke almost cut him off. "It's no mistake. Believe me, I checked. I wish it were a mistake. In three missions, you've managed to move up four ranks. Some soldiers wait years to reach the delta core, and you've flown right up the chain of command like your daddy owns the Earth."

A chorus of laughter, unrelated to the lounge, could be heard from next door in the bunk room. "Why'd you do that!" Jayden's voice whined.

"I didn't do a *thing*! I didn't even touch yeh!"

But Scott heard none of it. His stare remained locked with Captain Clarke's. Something wasn't right. Clarke obviously wasn't thrilled with the thought of Scott being an epsilon, but it was Clarke's unit. If he didn't want Scott there, why had he promoted him? "Sir, I don't think I understand what's going on..." It was an understatement.

Clarke folded his arms across his chest. "This wasn't my decision."

"Whose decision was it?"

Clarke removed the letter from its envelope and jostled it open in his hand. His glare lingered on Scott for a moment, before it moved down to the letter. "'Advance Remington to the rank of epsilon. Signed, General Ignatius van Thoor'."

Scott blinked. Thoor? General *Thoor*, demanding his promotion to officer training? That didn't make sense at all. What did he have to do with Thoor? Aside from the same welcome that all new arrivals got, he hadn't spoken to the general. Not at all.

Placing the letter blindly on the countertop, Clarke slid his eyes back to Scott. "I discovered it in my mailbox this morning."

Scott offered no explanation. He didn't have one.

"I'm sorry," Clarke said. "You've done nothing to show me that you deserve this in the least. I see no reason to even consider moving you to epsilon right now. But the general does. My opinion has been overruled. I don't understand this, nor do I approve it, but I was never asked to do either." Tension saturated the lounge. "Apparently you've found favor with the general. Not many men can do that." Clarke leaned forward. "Please show me that you deserve this."

Scott was speechless. Only the standard military response could escape from his mouth. "Yes sir..."

The captain nodded. "That's all I wanted. Thank you."

"Yes sir."

There was a cordial exchange of salutes, and Scott turned to leave the lounge. As he stepped back into the bunk room and eased the door shut behind him, his comrades halted their levity to stare in his direction. All of them wore etched-in grins. Dry oat puffs were scattered across the floor, as a shirtless Jayden knelt on the ground to pick them up.

"Welcome back!" Becan said. He glanced to Jayden. "Show him tha' thing where yeh throw your cereal all over the room again."

Jayden laughed. "Shut up! It was your fault!"

"I didn't touch yeh!"

The group laughed, and Becan returned his attention to Scott. Scott's expression remained solemn. Becan sobered up. "Wha's the matter, Remmy?"

Scott stood in silence in the doorway for several moments, then sighed over the inevitable. This one was going to be fun.

*   *   *

"So then he comes up to us an' says, 'I just got promoted'," Becan said as William listened from the weight machine.

William huffed. "Man." He pushed the massive set of weights up from his chest. "Some people are born lucky."

"Righ'," Becan said. He watched in awe as the demolitionist lifted. "God, how much is tha'?"

"Six thirty," William grunted. He held the bar up for a moment then steadily lowered it down.

"But annyway, isn't tha' bloody grand? Someone up there must really like the lad."

William sat up and reached for his bottle of water. "Yeah well, he saved some chick's life, didn't he?"

"Yeah."

"Then I don't really have a problem with it. I mean…I'm a beta, and I've only been on one real mission…well, only one that I've been any big part of anyway. I got no problem with Scott, he's always been cool to me."

Becan lifted his hands in defense. "No, no, don't get me wrong now, I don't have anny problems with it at all. Hell…I'd rather be under him than annyone else in the unit."

"Well there ya go. Good deal all the way around."

"Yeah."

William ran a towel over his face. "I've been meanin' to ask you. Where the hell'd you learn to fight like that?"

"I'm sorry?"

"Like you did in that practice fight, way back when you first got here. Where'd you learn that junk?"

Becan fell silent as William stood up and moved to another

machine. "Oh...I guess I've just been in a few scuffles here an' there. Yeh pick up new stuff every time."

"You musta been in a hell of a lot of scuffles." William sat in front of some pull-down bars. "No...wait, hell no...you were kickin' and flippin' and junk. I never met nobody in no street fight who kicks and flips. I know you studied martial arts, had to."

"I didn't. I mean, how hard is it to kick, yeh know? Yeh lift your leg an' push."

William laughed. "Harder than you make it look."

"Jus' got lucky, I did. I didn't think I'd win when I went up there."

The demolitionist eyed Becan. "Okay...I don't believe you, but I'll let it go for now." He gripped the bars above his head, grunted, and heaved down the ridiculously massive set of weights.

"God! You're a bloody flickin' ox."

William only laughed.

*   *   *

THE FOLLOWING DAYS passed as normal. Max and Konstantin remained in the infirmary, visited on a daily basis by their comrades from the Fourteenth. Max stoically accepted the news of his promotion to lieutenant, as well as the promotions of Scott and Fox. On one occasion, Scott ventured to the infirmary to pay Max a visit, but spans of awkward silence discouraged him from a second attempt.

Scott remained emotionally detached from the unit for several days. His unexpected promotion sent a slew of questions his way, none of which he could answer. Though Nicole was noticeably detached, she still offered him her support. "God is putting you in the places you need to be," she said, though it didn't sound as if she believed it. All Scott could do was hope she was right.

None of the promotions were accepted as graciously as David's. It seemed a silent indicator of the respect his comrades held for him, and several times, much to his delight, he was granted the opportunity to lead the morning workouts. This went over well with the crew, who relished their chances to be led by the fourteen-year NYPD veteran. Scott did get a chance to ask David about the status of his family, and he was pleasantly surprised to find out that Sharon and the kids were handling David's transfer well. They had cancelled their move to Richmond to remain in New York, but anxiously awaited an opportunity to reunite with their father and husband. Scott admired their perseverance.

Becan's skills in hand-to-hand combat sparked a reputation surge among those who observed the Fourteenth's free-sparring sessions. He rarely lost, and when he won, he won convincingly. Only Dostoevsky and Baranov challenged his level. Becan's ability to consume alcohol bought favor among the Russians, as he became one of the regular late-night vodka drinkers.

Jayden was quickly learning the social skills of an extrovert, to the point where he ventured into a flirtatious relationship with Varvara. One evening, by way of a Becan-proposed dare, he pinched Varvara's side as she walked past, an action that garnered a shocked, though tantalized response from her, one that hinted of mutual enjoyment. The distance between joking and seriousness was unknown, though it did begin a fresh set of rumors around the coffee machine. When asked about the relationship, Jayden laughed and refused to comment.

The most noticeable transformation took place in Galina. After the departure of Svetlana, she scheduled a series of personal examinations with each of the operatives, for the purpose of getting acclimated with their individual levels of health. It was executed so professionally that it garnered praise from all three officers, and the debate on whether to recruit a new chief medic was promptly forgotten. She socialized more with the men than Svetlana had, as she often joined them in late-night rounds of vodka and poker, though she never drank herself.

On one occasion, she snapped at Baranov for his excessive alcoholism, and he laughingly mocked her by downing a bottle of vodka in front of everyone. She did not take offense to the gesture; rather, she calmly informed him that he was denied his alcoholic privileges for the remainder of the week. Baranov treated it as a joke until Clarke informed him that she indeed had the authority to impose such restrictions. Needless to say, Baranov was in a bad mood for the next three days.

Clarke, Baranov, and Dostoevsky grew more anxious with every passing night. When questioned about it by the operatives, they insisted that things in *Novosibirsk* were moving along as scheduled, and there was no cause for concern. The three officers still talked and joked with the unit, though when it came down to business, they spoke among themselves under a veil of secrecy that the older members of the unit had never seen before. There was concern on Scott's part that he was a cause of their apprehensiveness, though a brief discussion with Baranov absolved him of any involvement.

Such were the conditions of the Fourteenth when Saturday, May 7th arrived. Life phased into as much a routine as possible in a unit decimated by circumstance. The weather in Novosibirsk remained frigid, as the rain evolved into snow. Everything was cold. Everything was miserable.

Everything was normal.

19

THE ROOM WAS quiet. The operatives of the Fourteenth had been given permission to enjoy free time so long as they adhered to the nine o'clock curfew, and thus many were away. Only Scott, Kevin, Boris, and Varvara remained in the bed chamber, with Clarke and Baranov behind the closed doors of the lounge. Each of the operatives was sprawled across his or her bunk; Kevin and Boris exchanged hushed conversation, while Varvara flipped through the pages of a magazine.

Scott, like Varvara, kept his mind occupied through the pages of a book, though his was his Scripture. Lately he had felt distanced from it. More than just from it. From God. Nothing made sense anymore. Nothing added up. If everything that happened was part of a plan, he had no idea what it was. It seemed as if every time he relieved his doubts, something new was thrust his way.

The rest of the room showed signs of casual abandon. Boots were strewn in front of closets, and a concluded game of chess sat in strategic disarray in the corner. For those who chose to spend their time in the room, the organized mess was a welcomed sanctuary.

Stretching, Scott felt his neck pop. He reached beneath the bunk with his fingers until he found his cardboard bookmark, which he picked up and slid into the Scripture. He placed the book beneath his bunk.

A drink. That was what he needed. Nothing alcoholic—he never did that. Coffee. He could already smell its aroma in his mind. It was a walk to the lounge and a flick of the coffee machine away.

As he sat up, he made eye contact with Varvara. She offered him a smile, which he promptly returned along with the word, "kofey."

Her smile broadened, and she proceeded to speak in a flow of steady Russian.

Scott laughed. He didn't understand any of it. Not one single word. "I'm not that good yet."

She grinned. "I said, you muster to go get some."

Scott laughed at her failed English. "I *must* go get some?"

"Yes, sorry! You *must* go get some." She laughed and winked. "I am not that good yet, too."

Scott smiled as he stepped away into the lounge.

As soon as he entered, whatever conversation that was taking place between Captain Clarke and Commander Baranov slammed to a halt. Both officers stared at him as he stood in the doorway. Scott raised up a hand defensively. "Am I interrupting something?"

Clarke shook his head. "No...you may enter." Baranov remained quiet as Scott slid into the room and shut the door behind him. Clarke motioned to an empty chair. "Have a seat."

Scott offered a polite smile. "Thanks, sir. Just going to get a cup of coffee first."

Clarke pointed to the counter. "There's a pot brewed. We put it on, what...a half hour ago?"

"Close to that time," said Baranov.

Scott retrieved a coffee mug from the cabinets, which he promptly began to fill. As the black liquid steamed into the mug, he cast a look back to the captain. "You're sure I'm not interrupting anything, sir?"

Clarke shook his head. "No, not at all." As soon as Scott's coffee was poured, Clarke said, "How is your training going?"

Scott chuckled under his breath. That had been an unexpected aspect of the epsilon rank—personal sparring lessons from Lieutenant Dostoevsky. The purpose was to train Scott beyond his inferior, as Dostoevsky mocked it, education from the Academy. The lieutenant made it clear that imperfection was unacceptable, thus the personal lessons were born. They were daily and brutal. He had the bruises to prove it.

He slid the coffee pot back into its holder and dropped a spoon of sugar into the mug. "Painful," he answered. "But helpful. Lieutenant Dostoevsky is a good trainer."

Clarke nodded. "That he is. He says you're picking it up quickly."

"It's hard work," Scott said as he sat down. "But I enjoy it. I've always liked training."

Clarke nodded. "That's good. Effort will always pay off."

Scott drew the coffee to his lips and took a sip. It tasted every bit as good as he'd expected. A kettle of tea—undoubtedly Clarke's—sat beside the coffee pot.

As soon as Scott sat the mug down, Clarke cleared his throat. "Ivan and I were discussing the absence of activity lately. Since the attack in Siberia, there hasn't been a single registered Bakma intrusion anywhere on Earth."

Scott focused his attention to the captain. "What do you think that means, sir?"

Clarke sighed. "That's what we were discussing. We've got no idea what that means. That's over three weeks, coming on four, with nothing. Not so much as a reconnaissance craft, anywhere. It's as if we've won the war."

Scott knew it was a ridiculous claim. If destroying the outpost had defeated the Bakma once and for all, then EDEN had seriously overestimated one of its most stringent enemies. "What about the Ceratopians?"

"We're at a bit of a lull right now concerning them as well," Clarke answered, "but that's come to be expected. For some reason or another their attacks are more sporadic. But we've had two Ceratopian hits this week...one in America and one in India, nothing unusual there. It's the Bakma who've got us scratching our heads."

"What does EDEN Command think?" Scott asked.

Clarke sighed. "Command are like us—they don't know what to think. I, personally, believe they're gearing up for something big. I'm afraid it will only be a matter of time."

Something big? What did that mean? "Big like what, sir?"

"Of that I'm uncertain. An attack, a full fledged invasion. I've got no idea. I still don't understand why we're still here in the first place. Their technology is obviously superior, both the Bakma and Ceratopians. They can *get* here…why toy with us this long? Why not send an entire task force here to wipe out humanity once and for all, in a single sweep? Why send ships every now and then?" Scott didn't have any answers. "Granted, most of the strikes are tactically placed…but we've got two separate races, both attacking Earth for reasons that we're still unaware of, and neither bringing anything even resembling an armada of any sort to the table. Why shove when you can punch?"

Scott continued to listen attentively.

"We're not winning these little skirmishes because we're stronger. If anything we're just good enough to compete. We're winning because we can match them with numbers and because they give us the opportunity to beat them. I know they must have magnificent bombing capabilities, but we've yet to see them bomb anything. They always land and engage in ground warfare."

"The Ceratopians have bombed before," said Baranov.

Clarke eyed him. "Perhaps in one out of every ten incursions. But why not ten out of ten? Why land in a city when you could obliterate it from above? And as far as I can recall, we've never had a Bakma bombing."

Scott thought for a moment, then ran a hand through his hair. "And you think the Bakma are setting up for something bigger?"

"I don't know," Clarke answered. "But I'm afraid that may very well be the case. We've never had such a drop in activity before, at least not after any defining event, such as what happened in Siberia. From that day forward, we've had nothing…and that's making a lot of people nervous."

"Whatever plan they had, many think we threw a witch into it. What they do next is what we do not know," said Baranov.

"Wrench."

Baranov glanced to the captain. "What?"

"Threw a wrench. Not a witch."

Scott looked from one officer to the other. "But this may be nothing, right?"

Clarke nodded. "It's possible. But this *is* very odd behavior, even if on a large scale. It's not to the point where it's making headlines yet, but give it another week or so, and you'll start reading about the sudden decline in the newspapers."

That was the last thing the world needed. The rumor mill was already a driving force in media misinformation. "Have a lot of the operatives noticed yet?" Scott asked.

"I suspect those who pay attention have," Clarke answered. "A lot of operatives don't know what day of the week it is, let alone what's going on across the globe. But it's starting to draw some attention, even from standard operatives. People start noticing when none of the units get called out for Bakma attacks."

"What about the general? Has he said anything about it?"

Baranov spoke up. "Thoor knows it. He does not have to speak of it to let others know he is aware. You can look at him and tell that something is not right. He is a smart man."

Clarke nodded. "He's had Vindicators flying to and from Siberia since the attack, checking to see if anything has picked up there. The site hasn't been touched. It's as if the entire Bakma army have decided to leave Earth completely alone."

Scott sat up straight in his chair. Brain strike. "Maybe they can't afford to." Clarke and Baranov looked closely at the young epsilon. "Aliens have to have money too, right? Maybe every time they send a ship, it costs their government umpteen million dollars…or whatever it is for them. That outpost might have been the most expensive thing on their budget, and maybe they don't have the money to send anything else right now."

"It's possible," Clarke answered. "Anything is possible."

"They questioned one of the Bakma in Confinement," said Baranov. "One of their officers. We cannot understand much, but we've heard nothing of money up to this point. They don't talk much. But it is possible."

It was an idea, at least. It was better than nothing. The thought of his own theory at least gave Scott a sense of contribution, which was far more than anything he had felt since his promotion. Whether he was right or not, at least he was trying.

Taking his last sip of tea, Clarke set the cup down on the tabletop. "I'm sorry. I think I'm going to catch some zeds early tonight. I've been knackered all day."

Scott looked at the captain as Baranov nodded. "Stress," the commander said.

Clarke smiled ruefully. "May bloody well be it." He stood up and walked to the sink, where he deposited his empty cup. "I'm going to my quarters tonight, Ivan. Make sure everyone's in bed by nine."

"Yes sir," Baranov answered. "Good night, captain."

"Good night, sir."

"Good night Ivan, Remington. I'll see you both tomorrow morning."

Clarke straightened his uniform and stepped out of the lounge and into the bunk room. The door eased shut behind him.

As soon as he was gone, Scott asked Baranov, "His quarters?"

"Yes."

"I thought everyone slept in here."

Baranov shook his head. "That is usually the case, yes. But all officers have their own personal quarters. The captain has his, I have mine...Dostoevsky has his, and so will Max. They are just rarely used by us."

That made no sense at all. If Scott had his way, he'd sleep in his own private room every chance he got. "Why not?"

"It has more to do with the captain. In many units, all officers stay in their quarters...they are like small rooms, but they have beds, desks, and privacy. Clarke prefers for us to stay together as a unit, more so than many of the other leaders. If it were up to me," he laughed, "I would sleep in my quarters every night. But it is not up to me, and if the captain asks us to stay here, we will stay."

Since his first day at *Novosibirsk*, Scott couldn't remember a time when any of the officers had slept anywhere else. "Why is he going to his quarters tonight?"

"Probably because he is very tired," Baranov answered. "He does hard work, harder than most people think. He is responsible for this unit, and sometimes he simply needs to be on his own to sort things out. Tonight is one of those nights, I am sure."

"Must be nice," Scott said. "To have your own room."

"It is."

There was still so much for Scott to learn. Up until that point, he thought he had seen everything *Novosibirsk* had to offer. Now he knew otherwise.

It struck him just how much he didn't know, not only about *Novosibirsk*, but about everything. For one, aside from their reputation, he knew little about the Nightmen. Every rumor he had heard pinned them as monsters, but then here he was, in the middle of a pleasant conversation with Ivan Baranov, a Nightman himself.

A Nightman. Ivan Baranov was a Nightman. That meant, if the rumor was true, that he'd had to murder someone to become one. That was the Murder Rule. Scott thought about it for a moment.

No. That couldn't be true. Ivan was a brute, but he was a pleasant brute. Outside of combat, he rarely saw the man in anything other than an easygoing demeanor. But William and Joe had heard about the Murder Rule. They'd heard about it from someone who knew. And then they'd told Scott about it. Joe had told him about it. Joe was dead.

It hit him right then. Joe was dead. A chill broke out across Scott's skin. Had the Nightmen found out? Had they found out that Joe had unveiled their secret, and had they killed him for it? Scott had never heard of the Silent Fever before. But he had heard of covered-up homicide.

Wait. No. Joe hadn't told him. It had been William who'd told him, and William was still alive. William was in perfect health.

Before Scott could reflect further, the first sounds of life came from the bunk room. A brash laugh erupted, easily recognized as Becan's, and the once quiet room livened with activity.

Baranov smiled. "Time to settle everyone down."

Scott watched as the commander pushed from his chair and stood. Ivan was a Nightman. The Nightmen were murderers. Ivan was a murderer. He couldn't stop those thoughts from running through his head. "Good luck, sir," Scott said, offering a smile.

Baranov smiled wryly. "I can always just knock them out."

Scott chuckled as Baranov made his way out. He heard the commander shout a stream of Russian words, only to be rebutted by an Irish drinking song yelled from Becan at the top of his lungs. Scott chuckled further as the bunk room erupted with laughter.

Scott stayed by himself in the lounge for several minutes as he listened to chatter flow freely on the other side of the door. Eventually the showers were turned on one by one, and the volume level descended into sporadic waves of conversation. By the time Scott returned to the bunk room, the rowdy behavior had declined into pre-sleep whispers.

Baranov ordered the lights out soon after, and the operatives filed into their beds. Some found sleep quickly, while others struggled with the ever-familiar restlessness of a night in the barracks. Some laid still, while others tossed and turned on their mattresses. Ultimately, they all fell asleep, and Room 14 of *Novosibirsk* found itself once again surrounded by silence.

*   *   *

SUNDAY, MAY 8ᵀᴴ, 0011 NE
0134 HOURS

THAT NIGHT

IT WAS COLD and late. The main airstrip of *Novosibirsk* stretched out in front of the hangar's giant doors, and the fresh scent of arctic stillness hovered in the calm of the night. Aside from the faint dusting of snowfall that drifted onto the ground, the airstrip was a desolate span of frozen emptiness. It was almost pitch black, and if not for the dim illumination of the guard shack and the hollow glow of runway lights, only the moon and the stars would have cast their glow down upon Earth.

It was in that guard shack that the only signs of life outside of *Novosibirsk* were found—two Nightmen, outfitted in their black sentry armor, huddled in the warmth of the primitive building. One was complacent, his feet propped on a desk and his body eased back in a metal chair. He was listening to a radio at low volume—the rebroadcast of a soccer game; there was nothing else to listen to.

The other Nightman was taller and watchful. He was staring out through the window, his arms folded across his chest and his zombified helmet set aside on the desktop.

The man in the chair laughed quietly as he listened to the voice of the radio announcer. "They will not win this game," he said in Russian.

Beyond the static, the announcer's tone grew more intense. "Chernenko passes forward, it's a dangerous situation in front of Moscow's goal..."

The watchful soldier, arms still folded, turned to his companion. "You're going to be short another two hundred tomorrow."

"Be quiet," the Nightman at the desk answered as he focused on the radio. "I still haven't been paid for last week."

The radio announcer continued on. "Kamov dodges the defender, now it's just him and the goalie. He kicks the ball... goooal!" Shouts and applause erupted in the background.

The Nightman at the desk slammed down a pen. "Terrible!"

"Pavel is never going to let you forget this," said the other.

"Be quiet."

"That's why you shouldn't brag before the game is played."

Clunk.

Both Nightmen flinched. The sound was barely audible over the crackle of the radio, but it was there and their ears perked up. The Nightman by the window scrutinized the landscape, while the other turned off the radio. "Did you just hear that?"

For several seconds, both men fell quiet and listened.

There was no more sound. There was nothing at all. The Nightman by the window moved to the edge of the door.

The one behind the desk stood up. "You did hear that, right?"

"Yes." The watchful man twisted the knob and eased the guard shack door open. Coldness crept into the room, and he stepped to look out. "Where did it sound like it came from?" he whispered.

The Nightman from behind the desk inched over to the window. "It sounded like it came from right outside."

The airstrip was empty. The snow continued its steady downward drift, as the dim runway lights shone an evanescent hue over the ground. The silhouettes of wide hills loomed in the distance. There was nothing else.

Both Nightmen peered outside until the taller one finally stepped from the doorway to the desk, where he retrieved his assault rifle and slung it over his shoulder. "I'm going to take a look."

The other man glanced his way, then returned his gaze out the window. The watchful one slipped out of the door and onto the airstrip.

What little wind there was howled around the corners of the guard shack; aside from that and the sound of the Nightman's footsteps, there was nothing. The air burned with cold, and he winced as the frost bit at his eyes. Nonetheless, he continued forward as his comrade watched through the window.

The airstrip was empty. He swiveled his head in all directions as he marched on. There was nothing. There was nobody. His pace declined until he drew to a stop halfway down the strip, his attention drawn to the hills that loomed in the distance. Snowflakes floated down around him, barely swayed by the gentle breeze that hung in the night and disappearing as soon as they touched the ground. His gaze narrowed on the hills. He reaffirmed his grip on his assault rifle, and strode forward once again.

Clong!

The sound was simultaneous with the force that slammed into his face. His nose and mouth contorted; he stumbled backward and toppled onto the ground.

Back at the guard shack, the other Nightman raised a brow.

The fallen Nightman scrambled to his knees and reared his assault rifle. Then he froze.

There was nothing there.

He propped one hand on the ground and pushed himself up; his other hand hovered over his face. His fingers touched the end of his nose and he felt wetness. Withdrawing his hand, he focused his jostled gaze on his fingertips. Blood. His nose was busted open.

He shot up a sharp glance, his eyes flitting in every direction. But there was nothing there. Only hills loomed in the distance, and only the snowflakes drifted in the air. There was nothing there at all. All was quiet. He was alone.

Then he stopped.

In front of his face, splattered unceremoniously against the surface of the air, was his own blood. He blinked as it dripped down the surface of nothing whatsoever, and trickled into invisible indentations and unseen curves. He stared at it for several seconds, then he took a step back. His gaze widened the moment he did.

None of the snow that fell over the airstrip reached the ground. Something stopped it before it could.

He sucked a breath and spun around to the guard shack. "Noboats! We have Noboats!"

Before he could scream another word, an army of unseen doors opened across the airstrip, and he was riddled with plasma.

The other Nightman's jaw hung open as he reached out to sound the alarm. At that moment, a wave of plasma missiles screamed toward the guard shack.

20

A WAIL REVERBERATED from the walls of Room 14, and its occupants were brutally awakened. Half of the room lurched upright.

Travis groaned and slammed his head against his pillow. "Not this *tonight...*"

Under his breath, Fox muttered and wrapped up in his covers.

Boom!

The floor trembled, and the operatives' eyes flew open.

Boom!

Galina screamed and shot up from her bunk. "This is real!"

His heart pounding, Scott shot a glance at Galina, then to the wall. Shouts rang out from the neighboring room.

Baranov leapt to his feet. "Everyone up! This is not a drill!" The room burst to life as the operatives dove out of bed and scrambled to their closets.

Within seconds, Clarke's voice crackled over Room 14's loudspeaker. "Ivan, please get everyone up! We've got something serious!"

"Everyone is up!" Baranov answered. The operatives threw on their combat armor. Assault rifles and handguns were ripped from the weapons locker. Another explosion shook the earth.

Clarke burst into the room just as everyone was loading their weapons. "Ears, everyone!" They turned to face him. "Communications are haywire! All we know is that Bakma have landed on the airstrip! Numbers are *not* verified, though we have confirmed that Noboats are on the ground!"

Scott and David exchanged nervous looks as Clarke continued.

"The entire base is under attack! We *have* to defend this facility! Come please, time is critical!"

It took no second order. The Fourteenth rushed from the safety of Room 14 into the hallways.

Operatives from other units bumped past Scott as a throng of EDEN soldiers flooded from the barracks.

Noboats. On the ground. If they had landed undetected, there was no telling how many there were. As Scott was jostled toward the exit, his mind raced to speculate what the situation was.

When he and the others emerged outside, it became clear. Far from the barracks—in the direction of the airstrip—plasma fire lit the sky. Orange plumes exploded against the hangars as the sounds of total warfare ripped apart the night. Units and individual operatives stampeded ahead.

"This is not good," Travis said as he reached for his handgun. "This is *not* good!"

Before anyone else could comment, a platoon of Bakma emerged west of the barracks. As soon as the first wave of plasma seared by, Clarke swiveled around and dropped to a knee. "About!" The rest of the Fourteenth obeyed, and they returned fire.

"My God," Becan said, "they're this far in *already*?"

Fractured chatter burst through Clarke's comm, and he ducked out of the fight. Baranov and Dostoevsky took his place at the lead.

Scott fired a shot, and a Bakma fell. Two more alien platoons emerged from beyond the cafeteria. Another explosion rocked the hangar. Human screams filled the air.

As Scott trained down his E-35, he swung to Fox. "How many you think there are?"

"I don't know!" Fox answered. "And I don't like not knowing!"

Clarke returned to the unit. "Attention, everyone! Here is the situation! Approximately thirty Noboats have materialized on the airstrip! Four additional Bakma Carriers are en route!"

Four Carriers? Scott couldn't believe it. This wasn't an attack. This was an invasion.

Clarke continued. "We're to dispatch an away team to Confinement! They believe that the Bakma will attempt to free some of the prisoners!"

"We have some of their officers," Baranov said.

Clarke faced Dostoevsky. "Yuri, you shall lead the defense effort there! Take Travis and Becan! Two other teams are en route to that location as well, but right now we're the closest!"

Dostoevsky motioned to Becan and Travis. The three men pulled out of the fight.

"Jurgen!" Clarke said to David, "you and Boris make your way to the infirmary! They're attempting an evacuation! You're all I can spare!"

David looked at Boris, and the two men left immediately.

"Everyone else, avert to the airstrip!"

BAKMA SURGED DOWN the airstrip like a plague. As EDEN forces merged to intercept them, floods of plasma crashed their way. Grizzly APCs burned in their dens. Vindicator fighters were blasted to death before they could leave the ground. Charred pieces of armor and flesh fell amid the concrete.

Far in the night sky, the lights of four Bakma Carriers grew larger among the stars.

ALIEN CONFINEMENT WAS at the center of the Research Center, which was in the center of *Novosibirsk*. Becan had never seen Confinement before. Standard operatives weren't supposed to.

Dostoevsky yelled back to Becan and Travis, urging them to keep up. "Run faster!"

Bakma emerged as they ran, though the stronghold of EDEN operatives was enough to hold them at bay. The Research Center loomed ahead. As soon as they reached it, Dostoevsky propelled himself up the outer stairs of the building, where he jerked the door open. "Inside, go!"

"Where's Confinement?" Becan asked, dashing up the stairs.

Dostoevsky pointed down the hall as he passed through the door. "This way, follow!" Sirens pulsed throughout the Research Center, as clusters of scientists elbowed their way to the exit. The doors to Confinement were midway between the hall and the far corner.

Dostoevsky pointed. "Ahead! Watch f—"

Two Bakma emerged from the end of the hall. Dostoevsky flipped out his handgun and launched four shots—two for each chest. The Bakma were thrust against the wall and scraped to the floor.

"...for resistance."

They reached the doors a moment later. Becan and Travis prepped themselves at Dostoevsky's side. "Open on three," Dostoevsky said, positioning his handgun. Becan angled against the doors as Travis hung back. "One, two, three."

The doors whisked open, and Dostoevsky darted inside. Four scientists—two men and two women—were huddled behind a workstation. "Down," Dostoevsky said. The scientists ducked out of view.

Becan followed Dostoevsky into the room, gaping at what he saw there. Five cells ran along the back wall, and a cell was on each side. Transparent impact-glass covered them. Everything was stark white.

Four of the cells were inhabited. In the first was a Ceratopian warrior—the first Becan had ever seen. It was as large as rumor claimed, as it towered in the cell. Its golden, scale-covered skin led to its prehistoric head. A bone-plated frill, lined with spikes, crested over its skull and arched up. Twin horns protruded from its forehead as a third, smaller horn jetted from its nose. Its brown, penetrating eyes narrowed, and it bellowed.

"Bloody God..."

In the next cell, two Ithini were pressed against the shielding, their opaque eyes watchful of the new action.

Next, there crouched a necrilid. Though the creature was motionless, the glass was ravaged with claw marks.

Two cells down stood the three Bakma officers.

The Ceratopian rammed its horned frill into the glass and growled.

Dostoevsky took position outside the double doors. "Confinement isolated," he said through the comm.

CLARKE HEARD THE transmission as soon as he reached the airstrip. "Brilliant," he answered as he took position behind a dismantled Grizzly APC. "The other teams should be reaching you shortly!"

Scott followed behind Clarke, and the Noboat fleet came into view. The airstrip was an enemy fortress. Plasma bolts and plasma missiles soared from the invaders, as EDEN soldiers flooded the area around the hangar. The hangar itself was engulfed in fire. Bodies spilled across the ground. On the other end of the airstrip, behind the Noboats, the Bakma Carriers descended.

Scott stared in awestruck amazement. How had this happened? How could a whole fleet appear out of nowhere? Were the invaders really *that* superior? There was no time to think about answers, and less time to think about questions. Scott dropped to a knee at the corner of the Grizzly, propped up his assault rifle and opened fire.

Clarke swung around to Galina and Varvara. "Tend to the wounded!" Then to Fox and Jayden. "Find height and engage!"

The four Carriers touched down, and he looked at Scott.

"When those transports open, this is going to get considerably more difficult."

"You mean *this* isn't difficult?" said Scott sarcastically.

DAVID AND BORIS arrived at the infirmary just as the attack began. A squad of EDEN soldiers held off the Bakma forces that threatened, though they were outnumbered threefold.

The evacuation of the infirmary was in progress, as surgeons and nurses dodged past David and Boris, wheeling the bedded patients in their care. Some unattended patients crawled from their beds and hobbled away from the fight themselves. Explosions boomed behind the building, and the earth shook.

Grabbing the nearest surgeon, a heavyset man with a patient in a cart, David asked, "What do you need?"

The surgeon pointed to the patient. "I could use one more person for this one!" He motioned to the center of the infirmary. "But they need more help than I do!"

David said to Boris, "I'll help in the infirmary. You help him, then come back to me."

Boris nodded and grabbed the cart.

David weaved through the mass of nurses and patients until he found two aides. They struggled to lift an unconscious man into a wheelchair. David brushed past them, locked his arms around the man and lifted him into the chair.

One of the aides said, "Spasibo balshoye!"

"What else can I do?" David asked.

The aide's mouth hung open for a moment. "Here," she enunciated as she pointed to several more bedridden patients. "Help?"

"Absolutely," David answered, as he joined her in the effort.

BAKMA ATTACKERS GRUNTED down the halls of the Research Center. Dostoevsky readied his position in the hallway. "They're coming," he said to Becan and Travis.

Inside Confinement, the Ceratopian bashed its fists against the glass.

Becan took to Dostoevsky's side and propped himself into a ready position. "Travis," he said, "watch our backs."

Kneeling behind them, the pilot aimed his assault rifle at the Research Center's entrance.

The four scientists brandished handguns and took a defensive formation inside Confinement.

The Bakma grew louder down the hallway, as their footsteps clotted against the floor. Dostoevsky's glare focused on the corner. "Get ready."

A Bakma attacker burst into view. Dostoevsky triggered his handgun, and the alien fell. Two more Bakma leaned their plasma rifles around the corner and opened fire. Dostoevsky flinched as the shots careened against the walls.

"We got backup!" Travis yelled.

Becan looked back, where four EDEN soldiers charged into the Research Center.

The Bakma fired around the corner again. Dostoevsky, Becan, and Travis ducked in avoidance, then dashed into Confinement. The EDEN soldiers returned fire in the hallway, then followed inside behind them.

"What unit are you in?" Dostoevsky asked as he hung halfway out the door and engaged the aliens. Becan mirrored him from behind.

"The Twenty-first, commander."

A plasma bolt whizzed past Dostoevsky's head. He singled off a shot with his handgun and cut the attacker down. "How many more are coming?"

"We are it."

A team of Bakma broke through the Research Center's main entrance. "Other side!" Becan said. He and Dostoevsky ducked into Confinement to avoid the crossfire.

"We cannot hold the doorway!" Dostoevsky said as he leaned out and returned fire. "They will press here soon!"

Behind them, the necrilid came to life. Its claws and fangs collided into the glass shield as it lurched forward with primal aggression.

Dostoevsky sunk back into Confinement to reload. A scientist replaced him in the doorway. One of the EDEN soldiers fell dead. Dostoevsky panned to the computer console inside the room. He slid behind it, and his fingers worked the controls. "Hold them off a little longer!"

Baranov growled as a plasma bolt ripped through his shoulder. He took cover behind a chunk of debris and reloaded his assault rifle. His shoulder bled through the twist in his armor, though he moved unhindered.

Across the airstrip, the Bakma Carriers opened their doors.

Slamming a new clip into his assault rifle, Scott called out, "Here they come!"

Bakma poured from the Carriers.

"*Now* it's going to get difficult!" Clarke said.

The Bakma charged forth like hell-sent marauders. Flashes of orange and yellow reflected in their eyes, as their alien war cries filled the air. As they stormed the airstrip, the barrels of their plasma guns flared with fire.

Jayden and Fox were situated atop a guard tower, where they rained precision fire onto the impending throng. The tower was two stories tall, and the height of the rim around it provided them with duck-behind cover.

Jayden's eyes narrowed as he pulled the trigger. A Bakma dropped to the ground.

Fox slid his scope over the Carriers, where several canrassis lumbered down the ramps. Atop them, riders manned their mounted plasma cannons. "Canrassis," Fox said as he took aim for one of the riders' heads. He snapped off a shot, and the Bakma toppled to the ground. "I've got these, keep track below."

"I'm on 'em," Jayden answered.

FROM THE COVER of the dismantled Grizzly, Scott fired with abandon. He, Clarke, and Kevin unloaded their ammunition on the battlefield, though it made not a dent. There were too many Bakma. When one fell, two others took its place.

As Scott reached down to grab a fresh clip, a loud whiz reached his ears. He knew the sound immediately. A plasma missile. Before he could whip up his head to find it, the nose of the Grizzly exploded. It lurched upward. The three men scattered as it crashed upside down against the earth. Clarke and Scott dashed behind a barricade, while Kevin retreated toward the engulfed hangars.

Scott dove for cover, knelt down, and turned to the hangar. Kevin ran full speed toward it. There were flashes of white. Scott flinched. A barrage of plasma struck Kevin in his side. He fell to his knees. Scott jumped to his feet, but it was too late. A plasma bolt tore through Kevin's helmet, and his body flopped to the ground.

Scott stared in silence as Clarke reloaded behind him. "He's dead," Clarke said. "There's nothing we can do."

THE INFIRMARY WAS chaos. David assisted the aide as best he could, though with the constant flow of doctors, nurses, and patients, it was just as hard to keep up with her as it was to evacuate her patients.

In the midst of the bustle, David's eyes caught sight of a familiar face. Max. The newly christened lieutenant struggled to wrench free from a nurse, as he tried to push himself up from a wheelchair.

"Do not get up!" the nurse said. "You are not in right condition!"

"I are not stay!" Max snapped back in intentionally broken English. "I go to fighting! You go to hell!"

David abandoned the aide and rushed to Max's side. "Axen, what are you doing?"

Max gave him a withering look. "Not being a gutless wonder!"

He shoved to his feet against the nurse's demands. He swept his hand to David's belt, where he snatched David's handgun from its holster. "I need armor. And you. We're about to kill some purple monkeys."

David smirked. "Yes sir." He looked around until his eyes came to rest on a nearby soldier. "There. He looks about your size."

Max nodded. "Don't wait for me—you can go faster by yourself. I'll meet you at the entrance!" David turned to go as Max snagged the indicated soldier. "Hey, what size are you?"

The soldier hesitated. "But sir, I'm—"

"And I'm a lieutenant, half-wit, now get out of that armor!"

THE CANRASSIS' MOUNTED plasma cannons exploded with white, as the bear-sized war beasts tromped ahead. Their spider eyes darted around the battlefield as the Bakma atop them imprisoned their will.

The forces of EDEN wallowed in chaos. Platoons were split in half. Officers were separated from their squads. Pilots fell back from the hangar.

It was an onslaught.

THE BATTLE RAGED in the halls of the Research Center. Becan and Travis continually unloaded clips, as the EDEN soldiers and scientists fired around them. Dostoevsky remained inside behind the computers.

As a bolt struck the wall next to him, Travis recoiled. "We can't hold them back much longer!"

Dostoevsky shot up from the console. "Everyone clear the door, now! Come inside!" The operatives did as ordered. The doors to Confinement slid shut. Within seconds, Bakma stormed the hall outside.

Becan propped his hands against his knees. "A lot o' bloody good *this* does! Now we're trapped!"

Dostoevsky remained behind the console, and two of the empty cells whooshed open. He pointed to the scientists. "You four, get in that cell!" They complied and rushed into the nearest one. "Everyone else get in the other!" Dostoevsky worked the controls, and the scientists were sealed behind the glass barrier. Dostoevsky said to Becan, Travis, and the soldiers from EDEN, "Stay in the open cell! I will remain here behind the controls! I will open the door to Confinement and let the Bakma in. Then I will release the necrilid!"

Becan's eyes almost popped out. "You're goin' to do *what*?"

"That is why you will stay in your cell!" Dostoevsky answered. "Your cell will stay open, but you will be out of the necrilid's path!"

One of the soldiers stepped forward. "Commander, you will be right in the middle of it."

"Yes," Dostoevsky answered, "but the Bakma will be the ones moving. I feel lucky." Becan and the soldier looked doubtful. They back-stepped into the open cell, and soon Dostoevsky was alone by the console. "Is everyone ready?" Inside its cell, the necrilid rasped at the glass. "Opening the doors now!"

The doors slid open, first the main doors then the necrilid's. The Bakma charged inside. Dostoevsky ducked.

It took a half-second for the first Bakma to die. The necrilid leapt from its cell into the Bakma's chest, and the warrior's face was shredded off. The creature swerved to the next Bakma, and it pounced atop him. Its claws dug into the Bakma's chest as it screamed.

The aliens scrambled—some into Confinement and some into the hallway. They trained their plasma rifles on the necrilid as Dostoevsky rose from the console.

"Engage!"

Becan, Travis, and the soldiers dashed from their cell into the room. Gunfire shattered the air. The fight for Confinement was on.

ATOP THE GUARD tower, Fox and Jayden rained sniper fire. Jayden picked off individual Bakma on the airstrip, while Fox focused on the canrassis and their riders. Six riders and four canrassis had fallen to him thus far.

An explosion of white erupted against Fox's trigger hand and he howled. His gun flipped from his grasp and flew off the tower's edge. He crumbled to the floor.

Jayden spun around to face him. "Hey man, you all right?"

Fox clenched his teeth and rose to his knees. He clutched his right hand against his stomach.

Jayden drew to his side. "Let me see it."

Fox trembled as he allowed his hand to be viewed. As soon as Jayden saw it, he flinched backward and twisted his mouth. Fox's right thumb and index finger were blown off. The rest of his hand was a blackened char of blood and bone.

Jayden was on the comm immediately. "Medic!"

Clarke's voice crackled through. "What's wrong, Timmons?"

"Fox is down!"

"Can you move him?"

Jayden paused. "Yes sir, I can move him!"

Clarke was quick to answer. "I'm sending Remington to assist! Bring him to the ground level!"

"Yes sir," Jayden answered. "C'mon Fox, we're gonna get you downstairs."

Fox again placed his hand on his stomach and trembled to his feet. Jayden balanced him against his body, and they shuffled toward the stairwell.

DAVID WAS EN ROUTE to the infirmary's entrance when he bumped into Boris. The Russian tech was on his way back inside. He spoke before David could open his mouth. "Kostya is dead." David gaped. "He was killed in the explosion on other side of the medical bay. It was the first place to get hit."

Beyond the infirmary, gun and plasma fire flooded the air. The ground vibrated.

David breathed heavily. "Well let's make sure nobody else dies."

Boris agreed.

"I'm going out front," David said. "I think there are enough extra hands here to help now. You keep doing what you're doing."

"Right."

"You be careful back here," David said, shaking Boris's hand.

Before Boris could respond, a third voice interjected.

"Boris! What are you doing here, boy?"

David and Boris looked back to see Max limping toward them in full combat armor. David's handgun was firm in his grasp. "Didn't you get the memo? Techs are all supposed to die this month."

Boris offered a weak smile. "Bad news for me."

David stepped to Max's side. "Kostya didn't make it."

"Then we'll see him in hell," Max said as he readied his sidearm.

SCOTT WAS READY for Jayden and Fox when they arrived on the ground. "What happened?" Scott asked.

"Look at his hand."

Scott glanced at Fox's hand and recoiled. "Come on," he said as he slid his arm around Fox's shoulder. "Let's get him to Varvara."

THE NECRILID SCREAMED as its plasma-riddled body fell into Confinement. Bakma entrails lay splattered around it.

The fight raged in every direction. It wasn't even close combat. It was no-space combat. Every time Becan dropped a Bakma, another was there to challenge him from behind. If not for his knack for fighting, he'd have been massacred.

Confinement was overwhelmed.

WHEN SCOTT AND Jayden returned to Clarke's side, the airstrip battle was in full force. Plasma bolts seared past them as explosions rocked the sky.

"Fox is with Varvara!" Scott said. "He's going to be okay!"

Clarke flung a grenade toward a cluster of Bakma and ducked back as it detonated. "Good!"

Scott drew down as a plasma bolt ricocheted off the tower's corner. Everywhere he looked, plasma fired chased him. His body was covered in cuts and scorch marks, and he couldn't remember where any of them had come from.

Clarke screamed.

Scott spun around to see the captain collapse to the ground. A hole was torn through the hip of his armor. "Captain!"

Clarke's teeth grinded. *"I'm bloody all right!"*

Before Scott could respond, Clarke reached up and grabbed him by the collar. Scott was jerked to the ground. Behind him, a plasma bolt shattered the concrete where he had just stood.

Scott scrambled to his feet as Clarke pulled himself to cover. Jayden fell back to match them.

"Where *is* Varvara?" Clarke said as he tore off his helmet and pressed a hand to his hip.

Scott thrust himself back behind the barricade. His eyes darted between everything around him. Jayden's sniper fire. Clarke's hip. The hole in the concrete. Everything was happening too fast.

"Over there, sir!" Jayden answered. Varvara was still positioned behind the tower, where Fox lay in her care.

"Get her over here!" Clarke said.

Scott snapped into focus and adjusted his comm. "Varvara! We need you behind the barricade!"

"But what about Fox!" she answered.

Clarke slammed his comm to his lips. *"Fox will bloody live, drag yourself over here!"*

DAVID AND MAX reached the infirmary's entrance. EDEN soldiers were clustered around, as several dozen Bakma held the open area just beyond them. Dead and wounded were strewn in all directions. Assault rifles rattled the air.

Max groaned as he sunk to his knees and lifted his handgun. His finger assaulted the trigger.

The battle for the infirmary had begun.

BARANOV UNLOADED HIS assault rifle toward the airstrip. He had lost count of the Bakma he dropped long ago, though he knew it was well over thirty. An occasional plasma bolt streaked past him, though he remained protected behind the large chunk of debris. A bolt had caught the edge of his hip earlier, but the wound was easily ignored.

He was about to release another burst when his eyes caught something on the battlefield. It was Galina. She was far ahead of him, in front of the hangars, where she struggled to drag a wounded operative to cover. As soon as he saw her, a plasma bolt hit her shoulder. She toppled to the ground.

Baranov stood up. "Galya!" A second bolt clipped her side,

and she tumbled again. As she cried out on the ground, Baranov's eyes narrowed. "Forgive me, Sveta."

He switched his assault rifle to one hand and charged toward the airstrip. As soon as he was open, a wave of plasma tracked him. He stumbled as a bolt caught his thigh, though he maintained his balance. He swung his assault rifle forward and held down the trigger. Two Bakma fell.

Galina struggled to stand, then collapsed from her lack of strength.

"Galya, I am coming!"

Baranov plowed ahead until he reached her. He lowered his free arm to scoop her up, and pressed her body against his. Galina mumbled incoherently. He scanned for the nearest cover—a charred Vindicator that sat, unused, alongside the main hangar. He fired his assault rifle behind him as he charged toward the fighter.

Suddenly he felt the small of his back burst open as a spray of blood splattered against the side of his neck. He stumbled, but his legs moved on. A second plasma bolt opened his thigh, followed by a third against his shoulder. His teeth clattered together as he crumbled to his knees. The Vindicator was right in front of him. His knees pressed forward as his internal organs ruptured. When the final plasma bolt struck the center of his back, he lurched forward in one last surge.

Safety. They were behind the fighter. Galina was sheltered in his arms, and he toppled onto her. His gaze sunk to her as he coughed a spat of blood. His eyes glossed over, he lowered his head, and he breathed his final breath.

THE BASE WAS a war storm. Bakma pressed against the hangar and the surrounding structures. Mounted riders ripped holes through EDEN's defenses, as the blood-crazed canrassis tore apart everyone in their paths.

Chaos covered the ground. The hangar was destroyed. The infirmary was aflame. The main building was on the verge of invasion.

Novosibirsk was dying.

CLARKE'S TEAM STRUGGLED against the tidal wave of Bakma forces. Plasma burned their nostrils, as the bloody cries of death tortured their ears.

Though his clips ran low, Scott launched volleys from behind the barricade. Jayden abandoned the futility of his sniper rifle and claimed a more versatile E-35. Clarke fell under the care of Varvara, whose armor and skin were stained with blood.

Everything shook. Everything flashed. Everything screamed.

Then, the crisp static of *Novosibirsk*'s loudspeakers cut through the chaos. Someone was on the channel.

Becan focused on the metal wall mount.

Doctors and nurses looked up from their patients.

Clarke's team panned their gazes to the massive speaker towers.

The voice they heard was clear and firm.

"Attention all Novosibirsk operatives. This is General Ignatius van Thoor."

Becan's attention snapped back to the fight as a Bakma warrior swung a fist at his face. Becan ducked to the floor and bashed a kick into the alien's chest.

"Today, the enemy comes to our doorstep. They feast in our halls."

David growled as a burst of plasma whizzed by his face. He reloaded his assault rifle as Max returned fire.

"They dine on our blood."

On the airstrip, the army of Bakma plowed toward the barricades. Scott slammed a new clip into his assault rifle, and he flung his last grenade into the fray.

"For years, you have prepared for a day such as this. You have prepared for a day when they bring their battle to us."

"We're not gonna hold them!" David said. As he raced back to find Max, his eyes froze on the silhouettes in the distance.

Their shadowed horns gleamed in the darkness. Their crimson triangles shone with anger.

"That day has finally come."
Scott was about to raise from the barricade to fire, when Jayden clapped his hand onto his shoulder. Scott stopped and followed Jayden's rearward gaze.

Amassed in their wicked glory, a legion of Nightmen thundered onto the field.

The hair on the back of Scott's neck tingled.

"Fear is for the foolish."
Dostoevsky's scowl twisted as he snapped a Bakma's neck.

"Mercy is for the weak."
The Nightmen charged the strip. The Bakma forces hesitated.

"We will stand as death. We will fight as victors."
Scott regripped his assault rifle and steadied himself.

"And today, we will show the world…"
"Engage!" Clarke said. "Engage with the offensive!"

"…that The Machine has teeth."

SCOTT ROSE FROM the barricade, and his assault rifle unleashed fire onto the airstrip. Three Bakma fell before he rushed back to cover.

Around the hangar, the dark knights of the Nightman army charged into the Bakma stronghold. The Bakma advance ground to a halt as the Nightmen stormed through their midst.

IN CONFINEMENT, DOSTOEVSKY came to life. The Bakma continued to press in, but the close-range combat of the Nightman and his defenders matched their surges with renewed energy.

Down the halls of the Research Center, beyond the doors of Confinement, the shouts of Nightman warriors emerged from the plasma fire.

"They are coming!" Dostoevsky said as he crushed a Bakma's face with the butt of his rifle. "We will have victory soon!"

SCOTT'S TRIGGER FINGER paused as he stared at the battlefield. Nightmen surrounded the hangar area. Their vicious guns took to the Bakma like missiles to flies. They were outnumbered by the aliens five to one. But they refused to acknowledge it.

All because of him. All because of the god of *Novosibirsk*. All because of Thoor.

What monster had the general created?

"Remington! Timmons!"

Scott fell back as Clarke called his name.

"Remington," Clarke said, "we have our orders." As soon as Jayden had joined them, he continued. "*Novosibirsk* Command want us to free the airstrip's rear turret towers."

Turret towers? Scott looked at the airstrip, where the towers came into view. They loomed in the distance…behind the fleet of Noboats. His attention returned to Clarke.

"If we can activate *Novosibirsk*'s turret defense system," Clarke said, "we can rain hell on them." He glanced at his wound and moaned, then his eyes sought Scott. "I cannot do this. And the Fourteenth is scattered in every direction." He hesitated. "I don't have it in me to ask you…"

There was no hesitation from Scott. There was no doubt. "I can do it, sir."

"You realize that the Bakma stand between us and the towers. The canrassis, the Noboats…everything. Are you absolutely sure?"

He felt it. Exactly what he'd felt in Chicago, when Grammar told him about the failed strike on the Carrier. Exactly what he'd felt when he earned the Golden Lion. "Yes, sir."

Varvara looked at Scott, and Clarke nodded his head. "Show me why you deserve it, Remington."

Scott rose to his feet and scanned the battlefield. Clarke was right. The turrets were behind everything. This wasn't a task that a worn out old van would complete.

Scott thought for a moment. A worn out old van. His eyes flashed across the airstrip until he found them. The most beautiful things he had ever seen. Three Grizzlies. Their nose-mounted chain guns blazed as they plowed through the fray.

"Jayden," Scott said, "get ready to ride." His gaze darted to Clarke. "Sir, can you patch me through to one of those Grizzlies?"

The captain nodded. "I can."

"What's going on?" Jayden asked as he knelt beside Scott.

"You're about to see what you missed back in Chicago."

"You're set," Clarke motioned to Scott. "They're on your frequency."

Scott cupped his helmet mic. "This is Scott Remington of the Fourteenth! A comrade and I need to be picked up immediately on the southwest corner of the airstrip!"

A voice crackled through a second later. "Negative, Fourteenth, we are not in position to help you. There's another Grizzly much closer to you, we'll direct him there instead."

Scott nodded. "That'll work, thank you!" As the channel closed, Scott beckoned Jayden. "Come on," he said as he motioned to the corner of the strip. Jayden rose to follow.

"Wait!"

Scott turned. The shout came from Varvara. Her gaze was settled on Jayden.

"Be okay…" she said to him.

Jayden's eyes stayed on her for a moment, before his lips curved into a grin. "Yes, ma'am."

For a moment, Scott's mouth dropped in half-shocked wonder.

Jayden turned around and flashed him a smile. "What?"

Scott laughed as Jayden strode past him. "Nothing, Tex. Lead the way."

OUTSIDE CONFINEMENT, THE tat-tat of assault rifles grew closer. More Bakma fell. As victory was imminent, the final handful of aliens threw down their weapons, dropped to the floor, and raised their hands over their heads. Bloodstained Nightmen charged into Confinement from the hallway and trained their guns on the intruders.

The Research Center was secure.

THE GRIZZLY AWAITED Scott and Jayden at the corner. Scorch marks charred its hull, and its forward chain gun smelled of cinders. The top hatch swung open, and a giant of a man emerged. Harbinger.

"Son of a gun!" William said.

"Will!" Scott grinned. "You ready to make some fireworks, big man?"

William bellowed a laugh as Scott and Jayden climbed to the hatch. "Hell yes, we are, friend!" William ducked down in the Grizzly as Scott and Jayden slid behind him. Plasma slammed against the APC's hull. The Grizzly shuddered.

The entire Eighth was inside. Their faces glistened in the cabin's red glow. Jayden dropped behind Scott as the hatch slammed shut.

"Here's the plan, guys," Scott said. "We're taking one of the turret towers!"

"The ones on the other end of the strip?" asked William.

"Those."

Derrick Cole stared at Scott. "They're surrounded by Noboats. At least two deep on every side."

Scott didn't respond. He shifted his eyes to Derrick, and after a moment of pause, they both broke into smiles.

William thrust his fists into the air. *"Battering ram!"*

A cheer bellowed from the Eighth, and the Grizzly pulled away from the corner.

THE BATTLE AT the infirmary began to sway in *Novosibirsk*'s favor. For the first time, human soldiers outnumbered the Bakma. Max stood and signaled his hand. "Move! Move in on 'em!"

The operatives charged from their barricades, a wave of bullets before them.

The two forces collided, and a maelstrom of combat erupted. David swung the butt of his assault rifle against a Bakma's face. Bullets ricocheted at his feet. He unloaded a flurry of bullets. It was a free-for-all.

THE GRIZZLY'S RUSSIAN driver announced to Scott, "We are ready to go! The Noboats are ahead!" A two-deep row of Noboats stood between the Grizzly and the nearest turret tower. A throng of Bakma fired at the APC.

Scott knelt in the cabin. "Once we break through the Noboats, Jay and I are going to leave the Grizzly and take the tower! Cover us, then follow us! No one stays behind!" The Eighth erupted with a *yes sir*! "Let's do it!" Scott commanded.

The engine roared in mechanical fury as the Grizzly's giant wheels churned forward. William snagged a support rail. "*Battering ram*! It only works if you yell *battering ram*!" The men cheered. Scott and Jayden held on.

Their emotion was interrupted, as a white streak emerged from the Bakma. The driver turned to face them. "Hold on! Plasma missile!"

The cabin braced. William cackled. "We're all gonna die!"

The driver floored the accelerator and spun the wheel right. The rocket rammed against the Grizzly's side. It leapt on two wheels. The cabin roared as a hole blew through the hull of the vehicle. Flames blazed up, and the Grizzly skidded sideways as it crashed down to earth.

The Grizzly grabbed concrete and lurched forward. As the soldiers reoriented themselves, they scanned the cabin. Nobody was dead. A defiant cheer arose, and the driver plunged the accelerator down. "Do not shoot what you cannot stop, you purple monkeys!"

Scott stood and wiped the soot from his face. The battlefield was plainly visible through the newly blown hole in the hull. Two of the larger men knelt beside it and propped rocket launchers against their shoulders. Rockets whizzed out as the Grizzly surged ahead.

The Noboats were upon them and the driver white-knuckled the wheel. "Brace for collision!"

Scott turned to the cockpit window. His eyes bulged. William screamed.

"*Battering ram!*"

They hit.

The Grizzly's frame rocked as the forces of tonnage collided. Sparks and metal exploded as the men flew forward. Shouts bellowed; blood spattered everything. The Grizzly bucked as its wheels whined ahead. Its nose crashed to the ground.

They were through.

The pair of Noboats parted and the Grizzly cruised beyond them. One more pair stood between them and the tower. Moments before impact, someone in the back shouted.

"Hold on!"

The Grizzly slammed into metal again. Grips were jarred loose as operatives flew in all directions. The massive wheels churned. The engine screamed. The Noboats gave way. There was a burst of traction and the Grizzly lurched ahead.

"We are through!"

The vehicle skidded to a sideways halt.

"Tower's here, pop the top!"

The top hatch burst open. Plasma bolts soared toward them. The nose-mounted chain gun erupted. "Go!" the driver said. "Get out!"

Scott and Jayden scrambled out of the hatch; William followed. Scott bolted to the tower door, where a handprint pad secured the entrance. The security lockout. Scott placed his hand on it. The door swung in. "Tower's open!" Jayden and William hurried in as the rest of the Eighth engaged behind them. "Will, turret's yours! Go! Everyone, come on!"

ACROSS THE AIRFIELD, Clarke issued orders through his comm to an orphaned platoon. "The northeast end of the airstrip has become a stronghold! We've got to clear a path to it and reclaim some lost territory!" Varvara placed her hands on his chest to keep him still. He shoved them away and struggled to a stand.

"Captain!" she said. "You must not!"

"I can walk!" Clarke said as he groaned.

"Nyet, captain! You must not—"

"Are you in charge or am I?"

Varvara became quiet.

Above them, silver streaks tore across the sky. Clarke swung his gaze upward. Vindicators. "That's *Leningrad*!" he said. "That's *Leningrad*!" EDEN operatives cheered as the fighters strafed the airstrip. The Bakma scattered.

Clarke waved to the hangars. "Rally up, everybody! We're taking back our base!"

ATOP THE TURRET tower, William slid into the forty-barreled chain gun's seat. A protective shield sealed around him, and mechanical gears twisted to propel the turret up. The twin barrels discharged and a wave of orange poured into the Bakma from behind. The eruption from the turret was deafening.

The rest of the Eighth formed an offensive perimeter around the top of the tower. A barrage of heavy weapons fire rained down as the Bakma dashed for cover. Jayden's eyes squinted as he fired his E-35.

Scott held suppression fire as the last of the Eighth dove into the tower. He watched and attempted to count them as they bolted up the stairwell. Was that everyone? Yes. It was. He whacked his hand over the inner print sensor and it acknowledged him. Security lockout activated. He heaved the door shut.

It stopped within an inch of the frame.

Oh no.

The door swung back open; plasma streamed in. Scott dove for the floor. As he rolled over onto his back, a pair of Bakma rushed into the tower. Shut the door. He had to shut the door. His legs flexed and he kicked the metal door frame. It slammed closed and the security lockout chirped. The Bakma turned to face him.

Scott knew he was in trouble the moment he saw them. One was normal. But one was huge. Muscles flexed in its arms and legs. Even its neck bulged. The Bakma's opaque eyes shrunk to slits as he glared at Scott. They attacked.

Scott dove. Plasma jetted behind him. Scott rolled over his assault rifle and hit the trigger. Blood misted the air, and the smaller Bakma fell. Scott scrambled to his feet, and the muscled Bakma took aim.

There was nothing Scott could do. The Bakma's plasma rifle fired in front of him, and Scott stood petrified as the bolt flashed his way. Nicole. She was going to get a letter. Not an explanation, not a final chance to say goodbye. A letter. Her fiancé was dead.

No.

Scott braced up his rifle. The plasma bolt smashed into it. The gun shattered and he was thrown backward. The air fizzed as his vision whitened then returned. He clenched his teeth and looked down at his rifle. It was destroyed. A hole was charred through his armor. But that was it.

He was still alive.

He flickered his gaze up. The barrel of a plasma rifle hovered point-blank in front of his face. Scott crossed his eyes to focus on the weapon, before he looked beyond it. The lifeless, cold expression of the muscled Bakma awaited him. The Bakma's slit-eyes gleamed as he placed his finger on the trigger. "K'kanak t'ae, `Uman."

Click.

The Bakma blinked.

Scott blinked.

The Bakma looked at his gun.

Scott quirked a brow.

The Bakma hesitated, and his mouth dropped open. "Uhh…"

Dive! Scott lunged into the Bakma's chest, and the two fighters tumbled backward. Scott felt himself being thrust upward and the next thing he knew, he was flying through the air. His back hit the far wall upside down.

As he tried to regain his footing, a fist hooked across his face. His vision blackened and he stumbled sideways. Something pounded against his sternum. He buckled over. Before he could react, a foot crashed into his chest and knocked him backward.

When Scott landed, his mouth hung slack-jawed. His eyes watered. He could feel blood trickling down to his lips. Above him, the Bakma towered. This was not a fight the human was meant to win. Everything swung in the Bakma's favor. Except for one minor detail.

Scott's handgun.

It was still fastened at his side. Without a second of hesitation, he flicked it out of its holster and trained it up. The Bakma froze.

Scott staggered to his feet. The handgun stayed out. "Do you understand me?"

The Bakma looked puzzled.

"Do you understand me?" Scott repeated.

The Bakma hesitated. "Duthek horu `Uman lkaana?"

What was that word? Scott's mind raced as the gun-checked Bakma stared back at him in confusion. *Grrashna!* That was it. The Bakma word for self-surrender.

"Grrashna!" Scott said emphatically. He motioned his handgun to the ground.

The Bakma's eyes grew wide with understanding. "Grrashna," it nodded. It lifted its hands above its head and sunk to a knee.

Jayden's comm crackled as Scott spoke. "Jay, I've got a prisoner down here."

Jayden stopped firing. "You got a *what*?"

"Two Bakma slipped through. I don't know if you heard the gunshots or not," Scott answered.

Jayden shook his head. "I didn't even know you were still down there! I can't hear nothin' up here!" Above him, the turret's blasts deafened the tower. Jayden covered his helmet comm with a hand.

"Well I got a live one! He looks important!"

"How do you know?"

"I don't know—they all look important! Do they need me up there?"

"Nah man," Jayden answered, "we got it! We got too many people up here already!"

"All right," Scott answered. "I'll be down here then!"

"Okay! Be careful!"

"You too!"

Clarke's eyes peeled across the airstrip, where the twin-barreled turrets roared in anger. For the first time, the Bakma fell into disorganized chaos. Clarke stared at the turrets and smiled. Remington had done it. He'd freed the tower. "Brilliant, Remington. Brilliant." He peered skyward as a pair of Vindicators strafed the Noboats.

Near the hangars, Dostoevsky, Becan, and Travis rejoined the fight. Close behind them were David and Max. EDEN forces poured into the battlefield to join the Nightmen already there.

Captains and their platoons, amalgamations of broken units, and any others able to fight rallied together in full force.

Clarke swung up his assault rifle as a pair of riderless canrassis tromped down the strip. They chattered shrilly as their spider-eyes passed from one soldier to the next. Bullets pierced through their fur and their bodies stuttered in mid-gallop.

"Surround and concentrate!" Clarke said. He dropped awkwardly to one knee and opened fire. It took several seconds of yanking the trigger before the gun's bullets sunk into one of the beasts' heads. It roared, reared on its hind legs, and toppled over.

The second canrassi shook as bullets peppered it. It fell toward the nearest EDEN soldier, where its jaws—filled with three rows of teeth—clamped across the man's torso. The soldier screamed as his body was torn in half. Bullets poured into the beast's flesh until it lurched forward and landed neck-first onto the ground. Its pale blue tongue slipped from its mouth, and it fell still.

The Bakma were decimated. EDEN soldiers stormed the airstrip. Nightmen warriors fortified the hangar. Vindicator fighters assaulted the Noboats.

From the turret tower, Jayden smiled softly.

It was almost over.

As the last of the Bakma drew within close-combat range, gunfire from assault rifles rained at them in torrents. The turret towers held their fire. The Vindicators ceased their strafes. As human forces broke through the barrier of Noboats, the Bakma that remained threw down their weapons and lifted their hands. Full surrender.

The battle was won.

THE TWIN TURRETS whirled to a stop, and William relaxed. Beneath him, Jayden set down his weapon for the first time. The whole of the Eighth withdrew their guns and either sunk to their knees or sat back. Only Jayden rose to his feet to overlook the battlefield.

It was chaos. Buildings flamed. Bodies littered the ground. Screams shattered the air. The scope of the damage was surreal. It was too vast to be understood.

When Scott heard Russian voices outside, he knew it was safe to open the tower. His gun remained on the Bakma as he stepped back and placed a hand blindly on the security sensor. The door whisked open and a trio of Nightmen hustled in. They recoiled as they saw the Bakma, readied their assault rifles to fire, then paused. The alien was no threat.

Scott lowered his handgun and released an enormous breath. He looked at the Bakma, whose stare met his. For several seconds the Bakma did nothing, until it offered Scott a half-frown and a nod.

Scott didn't know how to respond. The gesture was unexpectedly human. He watched the Bakma for several moments, before he returned a solemn nod of his own, turned to the tower door, and stepped out.

CLARKE HOLSTERED HIS pistol and removed his helmet. It clunked to the ground as he brushed his hand through his sweat-streaked hair. Cinders popped as the hangars burned, and the smell of charred flesh hung over the airstrip.

DAVID AND MAX fell to the ground—one exhausted and the other injured. Both men lay silent. Dostoevsky, Becan, and Travis were not far, and soon joined their comrades. They stared at one another as the efforts of security began to take place around them.

AS CLARKE LIMPED past the hangar, he found Baranov. He lay slumped on the ground with holes gaping across his armor and back. His body was destroyed. For several seconds, Clarke simply stared. There was nothing else he could do. Then he blinked several times. Something else was there. Something was underneath him.

It was a body.

Clarke quickened his stumbling pace and knelt beside the

commander. He strained to lift Baranov's corpse to see who it was. Galina. She was curled into a ball on the concrete. She was alive.

Her breaths were small, but they were there. They were stable. Immediately Clarke called out, "I need a medic over here!" He drew his focus back to Galina, rolling Baranov over to set her free.

As SCOTT AND Jayden returned to the hangars, Scott allowed himself a careful sweep of the airstrip. Debris and bodies were scattered. Blood was everywhere. In the aftermath of the gruesome battle, he realized the reality of the situation. Despite the victory, *Novosibirsk* had been hit hard. Harder than any base had been hit before.

He saw David immediately. His former roommate was bloodstained and bruised, but he was still alive. He looked so tired. Everyone did.

Scott knelt on the ground, and covered his eyes with his hands. He ran his fingers back through his hair and looked around again. Every operative was dirty and most had some degree of injury. Few had made it through unscathed. Scott closed his eyes and thought a prayer. It was the only appropriate one that he knew.

Thank You for keeping me alive.

He opened his eyes and, with great effort, forced himself up. "I tell you what, Jay..." He looked pointedly at the Texan.

Jayden stood meters from him, his arms wrapped around the small of Varvara's back, as the two stood locked in embrace. Varvara's lips caressed Jayden's mouth, as her arms slid around the back of his neck.

Taken aback, Scott returned his attention to the airstrip. *Go get her, cowboy.* He laughed to himself and returned to his teammates.

The task of collection now faced them. Little was spoken as word of the dead circulated, at which point they sought out the corpses. Once the bodies were claimed, there was nothing else to do. Those who could retire did so to the relative quiet of Room 14, where the remainder of the night was spent in restless slumber.

21

PRESIDENT PAULING STOOD with his back turned to the High Command. His arms were folded across his chest and his stern countenance scrutinized the EDEN logo on the wall monitor. Silence prevailed throughout the conference room. No whispered chatter. No Council addressor. No presentation.

Nothing.

Eleven of the twelve judges sat behind him, their quiet stares split between the president's back and the black lifelessness of the round table. No papers waited on its glossy surface. There were only the hollow reflections of the High Command.

Judge Rath broke the silence as he looked from the table to the president. As he began to speak, the judges around him edged their eyes in his direction. "Sir, there was nothing anybody could have d—"

"I'll tell you what could and could not have been done!" Pauling answered harshly.

Rath sighed and resumed his quiet observance.

"Complacency!" Pauling said. "This organization has grown complacent, and now we see the results!"

"Sir," Rath said, "if I may…"

"What?"

"*Novosibirsk* was defended, sir. The attack was repelled. If anything, this is a testament to our ability to react without warning."

Pauling drew a sharp breath. "This is a testament to the training of the Nightmen. The attack never should have happened in the first place."

"And who is to blame for that, sir?" Rath asked. "Who is to blame for inferior technology?"

"We're to blame for not finding a way around it." Pauling's glare targeted Judge Iwayama, a smaller man, and one of two Japanese judges on the High Command. "What's the progress of the Noboat Detection System?"

Iwayama stuttered through a reply. "We...we...are still trying to d—"

Pauling pounded his hand against the table. Several judges flinched. "Trying is not acceptable! We've been trying for years! We need to be *doing*! I refuse to believe that with all the scientists and with all the engineers we have working for this organization, we still have nothing!" Iwayama was speechless as Pauling continued. "For two years, you've been trying! That's *not* good enough!"

Judge Malcolm Blake cleared his throat. The eyes of the Council swiveled to face the African Englishman. "With all due respect, sir, Mamoru has had his hands full heading R&D." Iwayama looked at Blake. "And he's done a superb job. Perhaps some delegation would speed up our progress."

"We have more scientists than sand on a beach," Pauling answered. "How much more delegation do you want?"

"But only one judge to oversee it," Blake said. "That's far too much to rest on one man's shoulders. With your permission, sir, I'll assist in the workload. I'll pick up detection and whatever else Mamoru feels I can handle. With two of us overseeing, surely things will come to speed."

Pauling eyed Blake then diverted his attention to Iwayama. "Do you object to this?"

"No sir," Iwayama answered. "The extra help would be very good." He looked distant for a moment. "Perhaps detection needs a new approach."

Pauling nodded to Blake. "You have detection and whatever else Mamoru gives you."

Blake smiled. "Thank you, sir."

Pauling addressed Iwayama without looking. "Get together with Malcolm after we close, and get yourselves organized."

"Yes sir."

"We're protecting a planet, people," Pauling said. "We can't settle for anything less than perfection. It's a miracle we've arrived this far, and we're barely holding on as it is."

A distinct pause fell over the room as Pauling stood before them, severe and overbearing. His features were different—hardened and aged. He allowed his gaze to slide down to the table, where it lingered. Almost twenty full seconds passed before he lifted it again to regard Judge Rath. "As much as I hate to bring it up again, the mourning period is over. Have you been able to locate any of Kentwood's Intelligence documents?"

Rath frowned and lowered his eyes. "No sir. I even spoke with Kang. He too, was unaware of any documents. We can only hope that whatever concerns Darryl found, we can find, also."

"And the investigation?"

"There was no foul play," Rath answered. "It was as natural a heart attack as one can have. It just came at a bad time."

"I have yet to hear of one that comes at a good time," Pauling said. Rath nodded.

"I've spoken with Archer," said Pauling, "your suggestion as a replacement. You were right. He's an intelligent candidate. He's young, but he may have promise."

"Thank you, sir," Rath said. "I'm glad he was a worthy recommendation."

Pauling sank into his chair and stared at the opaque table. His older reflection stared back at him. After several moments he waved his hand in dismissal. "That's all this morning."

Nods of acknowledgment were offered to him, as the judges rose from their chairs and filtered out the room. Their exodus was quicker than usual, and the typical cloud of post-meeting chatter was absent. It was only a matter of seconds until Pauling was alone.

"Judge Archer," he said to himself as he pondered the empty seat where Darryl Kentwood used to sit. His eyes remained there for a moment, before he pivoted in his chair and turned his back to the conference room, losing his gaze on the EDEN logo in front of the room. "Welcome to the High Command."

*   *   *

NOVOSIBIRSK, RUSSIA

IT WAS DAWN, 0446 hours Russian time, when the sun broke over *Novosibirsk*'s horizon. The temperature was bitter cold, and a subtle breeze drifted over the freshly fallen snow. Despite the sparse cloud patches, it was a beautiful morning—at least from nature's point of view.

The scope of the damage could be seen for the first time as the overcast sky was illuminated just enough to dissipate the darkness of the night. The fires that raged only a few hours earlier were now extinguished, though the destruction was irreversible.

Novosibirsk's gargantuan hangar had been destroyed. Holes camouflaged its concrete walls, and one whole corner of the building was caved in beyond recognition. Rubble was piled around the hangar; cleanup crews hustled to make the way clear for repair vehicles. While several aircraft inside the hangar were salvageable, a majority were battered beyond repair.

The airstrip was in poor condition, more from clutter than physical damage. Of the Noboats that remained, few were in proper condition to be dissected and evaluated. The combination of heavy gunfire from the *Novosibirsk* defenders and attack strafes by *Leningrad*'s air force mangled all but a handful of the alien craft. The only other salvaged ships were the four Carriers, which were taken into custody along with the captured Bakma.

The infirmary, though defended, was in no condition to remain. An on-the-spot evaluation revealed massive structural damage that rendered the building more of a hazard to the wounded than a shelter. It would have to be torn down and rebuilt, a process that EDEN claimed would be more inconvenient than costly. All the recoverable medical supplies were transported to the gymnasium, which became *Novosibirsk*'s temporary hospital. As the medical staff settled in, the full scope of the wounded came into view. Undermanned medically, crews of surgeons and nurses from *Leningrad* and *London* were called in to assist the staff on hand.

Many of the damaged buildings, throughout the base, were also beyond repair. There were very few buildings that had survived the fight unscathed. Nonetheless, the battle was dubbed a victory. *Novosibirsk*—The Machine—would live on.

The human body count reached over three thousand, eighty of which were Nightmen. Some units were leaderless, while others were decimated from one end to the other. It had been the most deadly assault against an EDEN facility in the organization's history.

The Fourteenth shared in the casualties. Ivan Baranov, Kevin Carpenter, and Konstantin Makarovich were dead. An equal amount were wounded.

Fox's career with EDEN was finished. Though the doctors were confident in his ability to return to a normal life, they were certain it would not be one with the Earth Defense Network. He was due to be shipped to a United States hospital as soon as the next series of transports arrived. The rest was up to him.

Max's mishandling of his previous injuries prolonged his expected date of release. Several doctors paused by his cot to reprimand him for his foolhardy actions, as they ordered him to remain bedridden until given precise permission to leave. He made no promises nor offered apologies.

Galina was stabilized soon after the battle was finished, and she was given a special location in the new hospital, set aside specifically for the injured among the medical crew. Once was she calmed and aware, she was told of Ivan's sacrifice. She met the news, expectedly, with tears.

Then it was morning. Late Sunday morning on May the 8th, in the eleventh year of the New Era. It was not even the morning after the battle. It was the morning of the battle.

Scott remembered every hour that passed on the clock that night, if it could be called a night at all. 0400, then 0500, all the way to 0900. He knew that he slept, but it was anything but restful. It was more like periodic glimpses of the unconscious world. When true morning arrived, he found himself as exhaustingly awake as he had been in the aftermath of the attack. He was not alone. No operative in the Fourteenth remained still beneath the woolen covers of their bunks.

There was a quiet stagnation to Room 14. Amid the creaking of bedsprings and hourly face washes in the lounge sink, it was the empty bunks that mourned the loudest. By the time late morning came, the silence was unbearable. Scott rose from bed, donned his uniform, and ventured into the hallway. David offered him company, and Scott accepted gratefully. Together, they abandoned the emotional atmosphere of the barracks and ventured back into the outside world.

For the first time in daylight, they saw the aftermath of the assault. They saw the battle-scorched airstrip and the demolished hangar. They saw the unsalvageable Vindicators and the overturned Grizzlies. They saw it all without the need to explore. The damage was in every direction.

Nothing came full circle. Though Scott and David talked little, Scott knew that David's questions must have been as deep and uncertain as his own. What happened now? How would they rebuild *Novosibirsk*? How would they rebuild the Fourteenth? Yet above those hung the darkest question of all. Why was Earth still alive?

Baranov had said it before he died. The advantage clearly weighed in favor of the attackers. This latest attack furthered that. The Bakma could assault *Novosibirsk* without a single human aware of it. The base was defended...but for how long? When would the invaders decide that enough was enough? When would they send their full force?

Why hadn't they already?

Scott was in the midst of those thoughts when he noticed Clarke. The captain stood alongside the covered sidewalk between the barracks and the cafeteria, walking cane in his grasp as he stared at the remnants of the assault. He looked tired. His shoulders sagged like Scott hadn't seen before, and even from a distance, his anguished expression was unable to hide itself. Scott knew why. The Fourteenth was a decimated unit, and Clarke was the one it fell on. It took only a slight shift for Scott to alter his path to meet the captain, and he did for no particular reason other than the feeling that it needed to be done. David followed in silence.

As Clarke took notice of the two, he hobbled his body in their direction and waited. A metal brace was attached to his hip, which was stamped with healing cloth. The smile they were met with was a false one, but the attempt was there.

"How goes it, gentlemen?"

"Sir," Scott and David answered.

In the seconds that followed, no words were spoken. The three men exchanged glances until their gazes abandoned one another to observe the devastation around them. When Clarke spoke again, it seemed as though it was for the first time.

"I just got back from the gymnasium. Everyone is in stable condition. For now."

A gentle breeze brushed past them then disappeared. Scott shifted his gaze to the unblemished snowfields.

"That's good to hear, sir," David answered.

"Yes. Yes, it is." Clarke massaged the back of his neck as he continued. "None of this should have happened. We're too careful to allow this to happen." Scott canted his head down as he listened. "Changes need to be made."

Changes. That was all Scott knew. When he had joined EDEN, it was a change. When he fought in Chicago, it was a change. When he was brought to *Novosibirsk*…that part was still changing. The thought of change didn't scare him anymore. Change was home. "What are we going to do, sir?"

Clarke's answer was automatic. "We rebuild." He returned his gaze to them. "We count our losses and we evaluate where we stand. Then we rebuild." Spoken like a captain. All compasses read forward. "Yuri shall assume the role of commander, and when Max recovers he'll be good to resume his duties." Clarke looked between them before his eyes settled on Scott. "Which leaves us short one lieutenant."

Scott knew it was him without Clarke saying a word. God had put him in the place he needed to be, and he knew there was a reason. It was destiny.

All compasses read forward.

Clarke cleared his throat and returned his gaze to *Novosibirsk*. "Remember everything you've learned, Remington. Remember the things I've warned you about."

Scott nodded. "Yes sir."

"There are things none of us yet understand. Look around here...and we're seeing that now. Your beginning is over. What you give now is what is to be expected."

"Yes sir."

Clarke stared into the distance as Scott stood deep in thought. Everything had led to where he was now. Everything pointed to that moment. In the midst of the losses, Scott's heart mourned. But in anticipation of the future...it was ready.

"Gentlemen," Clarke said, "more is going to be asked of you than I expected by this point. But I know you both will serve us well." He straightened out his uniform, and when he saluted, Scott and David were crisp in response. "If either of you need me, I shall be in my quarters. Prepare yourselves, and prepare the rest of the unit, for new focus."

"Yes sir," they answered in unison.

Clarke lowered his salute. "Cheerio, gentlemen," he said before turning and hobbling away.

Neither Scott nor David spoke as they watched the captain leave. Their gazes lingered on him for a moment, then shifted to the pristine snowfields. They were beautiful. They were pure enough to be God's own artwork. Scott took several steps off of the sidewalk, where his feet crunched in the hardened snow.

"You know he meant you, right?" David asked.

Scott heard the question. He knew. In a decimated unit, people were destined to rise up. And destiny had taken him there. "Yeah," he answered as he looked into the horizon. "I know." The air was fresh as winter. It frosted as it escaped from his mouth and nostrils. He feigned a smile and turned around. "He meant you, too."

David watched Scott for a moment, before a smile crept from his lips. "Whatever you say, sir." Scott chuckled, and David stepped off the sidewalk to his side. "It's beautiful when you take the time to look at it, isn't it?" David asked.

"Yeah, it is."

It was beautiful. The longer he stayed in *Novosibirsk*, the more he noticed it. He was determined to notice it more than ever.

David smiled and stepped back. "Now if you'll excuse me… there's a woman a few thousand miles away who just heard about an attack on *Novosibirsk*. I think she's gonna want to know if her man is okay. And I don't think she's the only one."

"Go make your call," Scott grinned back. "I'll be right behind you."

David turned and walked toward the barracks. Scott continued to smile to himself. There *was* a woman a few thousand miles away who needed to hear her man. And there was a man in the middle of Russia who needed her just as much.

Scott's gaze returned to the snowfields. They were indeed so beautiful. As if they were God's own artwork.

He stepped back and returned to the sidewalk that led to the barracks. There was a very important phone call that he needed to make, and he could not wait any longer.

Inside, he had never felt so warm.

EPIC · BOOK 2

OUTLAW TRIGGER

—coming soon—

ACKNOWLEDGMENTS

To Mom and Dad: Thank you from the bottom of my heart. Your love and support has been steadfast from the moment I came into this world. I am who I am because you were there to guide me, and for that I will always be grateful.

To my family: You have always stood behind me and believed in me. Thank you so much for being there, as you've been since day one.

To Lindsey: Words can't express how much you've been a blessing to me. Thank you for believing in me through the ups and downs of this project. I love you.

To Barbara Colley: Only God could have put you in my path like He did. You are an amazing author and friend. Thank for you showing me how to endeavor to persevere.

To my editor, Arlene Prunkl: You brought my book to life. Thank you for sharing your world of words with me, and for letting me borrow a few.

To my book designer, Fiona Raven: You took the most stressful part of the book publication process, and made it feel effortless. Thank you for not once giving me a reason to doubt that you were the right one for the job.

To my cover artist, Francois Cannels: Your talent is truly sensational. Thank you for giving this project a face that stands out in the crowd.

To my web designer, Justin Durban: Thank you for giving this series a home to rival the best. Your work is almost beyond belief.

To my photographer, Tammy Mars: It's always a joy working with you, and this time was no exception. Thanks for waiting those few extra minutes for the rain to slack off!

To Marina Bovtenko: Thank you for teaching me so much about Russian life. You are an amazing person and friend, and I truly hope to meet you someday.

To Mike Eckert and Jon Kahl: Your meteorological data was invaluable. Between the two of you, I was able to bring the world to life the way it should be. Thank you both for being incredible helping hands. Thank you Mike, for being a friend.

To Gerry Coughlan: If not for you, Becan McCrae would not be the character he is. Thank you for giving me an Irish voice.

To James Hartley: You took time out of your busy schedule to answer my questions. Thank you for your willingness to help out a novice.

To Earl Matherne: Seeing your excitement gave me the confidence to keep this engine running. You helped me believe in this book so much, and I can't thank you enough for that.

To Denise Matherne: I still have no idea how you do it. You know exactly what I'm talking about. Thank you for finding things that no normal human being should have found!

To everyone at the BCC: What a terrific church family! I didn't know what Christian fellowship was until I found you. Thank you for being a light unto the world.

To Luke: You have no idea how much I appreciate you, man. Thanks for always being willing to help. We all owe you one.

To Stevie: Dude, you know how awesome you've been. Thanks for being an incredible friend for all these years. Thanks for almost letting me beat you in Halo, that one time.

To James, JP, and Bob: thanks for being such a special part of this story. It wouldn't be what it is without you three.

To all the Snow Pirates: Mediocrity at its best doesn't even begin to cover it! Thanks to each and every one of you, for your inspiration, your openness, and your friendship.

To D-200: Thanks for putting that recliner in my parking space, jerks...and for being the best roommates / brothers / friends that an R.A. could ask for. I miss you guys the most. Y'all too, J&J.

To everyone at SR (especially Andrus): You encouraged me to flex my creative muscles, and you always made me feel like it was worth it. Never stop bleeding black and gold. Geaux Saints!

To everyone at the TBBBB: Thanks for keeping the fish biting, and for laughing in the process. You're my home away from home.

To my friends from IRC: You guys have been such an amazing influence. You gave me the confidence to create, and I thank each and every one of you for that. And to my compadres from XCS/XSD/OLS/TDF...you will *always* be truly special to me. God blessed me when he put you all into my life.

To the guys at FYE: I told you I'd do it. Only took me six years!

To Pooky: Thanks for being fun to watch. Thanks for eating all my fish flakes.

Additional thanks to Paul Ruderham, Malcolm Dickinson, Julia Leddy, and Dottie Norkus for volunteering their wisdom and expertise, and for Natalija Nogulich for taking time from her busy schedule to share a word with a fellow writer.

And last, but not least…thank you, reader, for giving this effort a reason. I can't wait to show you what else I have in store.

Photograph by Tammy Mars

ABOUT THE AUTHOR

Prior to his career in professional writing, Lee has worked in real estate, education, and the movie industry. Lee has also worked for the Department of Emergency Preparedness in St. Charles Parish, Louisiana, where he experienced the force of Hurricane Katrina firsthand in 2005. Though he has been to the other side of the world and back, he has always called Louisiana home.

He is a graduate of Louisiana College in Pineville, where he earned a degree in Communication.

To read Lee's Christian testimony, please visit his website at http://www.epicuniverse.com/testimony/, or request a copy by writing to:

Lee Stephen
P.O. Box 1470
Paradis, LA 70080-1470